City of Masks

Also by S D Sykes

The Butcher Bird
Plague Land

City of Masks

S D Sykes

HODDER &
STOUGHTON

First published in Great Britain in 2017 by Hodder & Stoughton
An Hachette UK company

1

A CIP catalogue record for this title is available from the British Library

Hardback ISBN 978 1 444 78584 5
eBook ISBN 978 1 444 78583 8

Typeset in Perpetua Std by Hewer Text UK Ltd, Edinburgh
Printed and bound by CPI Group (UK) Ltd, Croydon, CR0 4YY

Hodder & Stoughton policy is to use papers that are natural, renewable
and recyclable products and made from wood grown in sustainable forests.
The logging and manufacturing processes are expected to conform
to the environmental regulations of the country of origin.

Hodder & Stoughton Ltd
Carmelite House
50 Victoria Embankment
London EC4Y 0DZ

www.hodder.co.uk

The great galleys of Venice and Florence
Be well laden with things of complacence,
All spicery and of grocer's ware,
With sweet wines, all manner of chaffer,
Apes, and japes, and marmosettes tailed,
Nifles, trifles, that little have availed,
And things with which they cleverly blear our eye,
With things not enduring that we buy,
For much of this chaffer that is wastable,
Might be forborne for dear and deceivable.

The Libelle of Englyshe Polycye
Medieval poem

For Dad

Prologue

It was the carnival of *Giovedi Grasso*, the last Thursday before the Lent of 1358, and I had spent the afternoon in the Piazza San Marco, watching the many spectacles of the day. A group of young men chased a herd of bewildered pigs about one corner, whilst, in another corner, a different group of young men balanced acrobatically upon one another's shoulders to make a swaying tower of humanity. And then there was no missing the third group – those fops who simply strode about the square in order that everybody else might admire their fine brocade cloaks, feathered hats, and coloured hose. Oh yes, it was no wonder that I soon lost interest in these sights, and wandered away to seek the less innocent pleasures of Venice.

By the time I returned to the Piazza it was early evening, and the sun was shedding its last rays upon the arches and domes of the Basilica. Now that the night was drawing in, the carnival no longer wore the good-humoured, smiling face of earlier. Instead a sea of masks leered at me at every turn. Sewn from polished leather, and decorated with long noses, beaded edges, and feathered brows, each mask was more grotesque than the last.

I dropped my eyes to the beaten earth and tried to leave, but soon I was caught up in a band of men playing lutes and bladder pipes – their droning, repetitive tune cutting through my head like a long saw. I forced my way into a side street, but my progress became no easier. Horses might be banned in the Piazza itself, but there were plenty of the beasts here, tied to posts whilst their owners drank away their last few coins in the nearby taverns.

And it wasn't just horses that impeded my progress. Soon I was ducking my head to avoid a shower of perfumed eggs that had been thrown from an upper window. Lanterns were shone in my face, and a terrified pig ran over my foot – no doubt an escapee from the earlier game. I kept moving, as I was drawing the attention of people around me. They were surprised, even suspicious that I wasn't wearing a mask, so I raised my hood and then kept to the thinnest, darkest alleys of Venice in an attempt to go unnoticed and find my way back.

But this city is a labyrinth. Away from the vast, regimented quadrangle of the great Piazza, it is a bewildering maze of winding alleys and silent canals. A wide street promises to lead to another wide street, but instead it tapers away to nothing more important than a courtyard of washing, or an unannounced drop into stagnant water. To the untutored eye, each path looks exactly like the next.

So it was that I spent an hour or more, walking these dimly lit paths, and crossing the low bridges of San Marco, until I finally pushed my way into the deserted courtyard of my lodgings to hear the bell of a nearby convent ring for Nocturnes. The distant screams and screeches from the carnival still reached my ears, and the repetitive drone of the band still cut through my head. When I looked down at my clothes, I saw that my boots were covered in mud, and my cloak was peppered with the fragments of broken eggshells. Such were my mementos of the carnival!

I closed my eyes in an attempt to shut out the world, but now my ears fixed themselves upon the sounds of the house. The bang of an unfastened shutter. The lapping of the canal against the courtyard wall. The sudden rush of a bat that had woken early from its winter torpor. And then a different sound caught my attention. It was a faint, muffled dragging, and at first I dismissed it as another ordinary noise in this busy household until it came again, from the direction of the water gate and I could ignore it no longer. There was something too stealthy and furtive in its quality – as if somebody were deliberately leaving a gap between each sound to see if they attracted attention.

Creeping from the courtyard, I was still expecting to find a simple explanation for my noise. A servant working late. A delivery of goods from the canal, or even my mother's dog looking for scraps of meat. I had not imagined that I would find somebody lying face down across the marble steps of the water gate, with the cold and dirty water of the canal lapping across their boots.

There was no response when I addressed them, so I prodded their back, thinking this might be somebody who had stumbled home from the carnival, before falling asleep on this very spot in a drunken stupor. But this person was not drunk, they were dead, and my fingers had touched a body that was stiff and heavy.

I took a deep breath, pushed both hands beneath the chest and then forced the body to roll over, expecting to see a face. Instead I was confronted by the ugliest carnival mask I had ever seen – sewn from red leather and scored with a knife. I had to look a second time before I realised that the light had tricked me, and this was no mask. It was a person's face, with skin as raw and shredded as a butchered carcass. Their lips were swollen, and their hair was matted and blackened with blood. And then, as I looked closer again, somebody familiar looked back at me. Their eyes were dead. Their skin was torn and battered. But this was the face of somebody I knew.

It was somebody I knew very well.

Chapter One

The Venetians call their city *La Serenissima* – the 'most serene' republic, and so she had seemed as we sailed towards her from the port of Fusina in the June of 1357. From a distance she appeared to float upon the water of the lagoon, a thin line of dark green between the blue of the sea and the sky. But with each stroke of the oar, Venice came more and more into focus, her campaniles pointing up towards the heavens like the ascenders of letters; her houses and palaces the colour of crab shells or blanched almonds; her boats gathered about her jetties in a joyous, bobbing profusion.

Then, as we drew even nearer, the sounds of the city reached our ears – the loud, feverish roar of the place. We were no longer adrift in the silence of the lagoon, where lonely fishermen stood in the shallow waters and sifted for clams, or where the egrets poked about on uninhabited outcrops of mud and sand. Now we could see and hear the crowds as they thronged along the wide quay of the Molo, making their way to and from the many ships that were moored here. They were people of all races, many dressed in the finest clothes I had ever seen. The fur collars and sweeping capes of the men; the extravagant headdresses and embroidered gowns of the women. Even the lowliest manservants wore tailored tunics and coloured hose.

Venice might have started her life as a marshy refuge from invading barbarians, but now she was the largest and richest city in Europe. The hinge of two continents. The funnel of trade from the East to the West. She had once been a haven from the outside world, but now she found herself at the very heart of it.

I was dawdling in the Piazza San Marco on a warm September morning, three months after our arrival, whilst Mother pushed her way through the crowds to witness an execution. Today a tall pyre had been stacked at the water's edge between the two Columns of Justice, upon which a man was to be burnt to death. His crime, I learnt from an old woman in the crowd, was to have been caught in bed with another man by the Signori di Notte – the Lords of the Night – a group of odious noblemen who sent their spies about the city in their fight against anything they deemed to be immoral.

I was alone in my corner, for unlike most Venetians it seemed, I disliked executions. In fact, I would never have agreed to come here in the first place, had I known the true reason for our outing, but Mother had fooled me with some story about wanting to visit a merchant who sold lapis lazuli. Upon realising the truth I had quickly made my way to the other side of the Piazza, hoping to avoid all contact with this atrocity, but, as luck would have it, I passed the Signori di Notte's latest victim as I beat my retreat. He was a pitiful, quaking man who knew what torture awaited him before death. The poor fellow screamed for mercy, though there was no chance for his redemption, since the doge had now appeared onto the raised loggia of his palace to watch the execution, and the man's fate was sealed.

While the crowds roared in the distance, I leant against the stone pillar of a portico and pretended to read my small psalter in the hope of some distraction from the pyre. I had seen a person burn to death once before, and I had no wish to witness such inhumanity again; but as I studied the text, trying to distract myself by wondering what had inspired the scribe to draw such an array of strange beasts in the margins, I felt a nudge at my elbow. At first I ignored this, for the burning had attracted an army of beggars into the Piazza – gangs of men, women, and children who were now working their way methodically through the crowds, pulling at the onlookers' cloaks and pleading for alms. When the nudge turned into a prod however, I could ignore my pest no longer.

I looked up from my psalter to find that it was not a beggar at my elbow, instead it was a man in a polished helmet. He was flanked by two more men, dressed in the same uniform, so I stood aside, thinking that I might be blocking their path. Unfortunately, this gesture only appeared to rile them. They wanted to know my name, so I gave a shrug and told them in my loudest English that I didn't understand a word of what they were saying. This wasn't true, of course. In fact, after three months in this city I could converse quite adequately in their tongue, for Venetian is a soup whose main ingredients are Latin and Greek – two languages that I had studied in great detail at the monastery where I had been sent as a child.

They asked my name again, and now I realised that these men were wearing the helmets and tabards of the doge's guard. The winged lion of St Mark looked out at me from their breastplates, its mane flowing and its feathers splayed. As the people about me withdrew fearfully, I knew that I should be polite and deferential to these men – but somehow I was not in the mood. The Piazza was filling with the fumes of the pyre, as the man they were burning shrieked with pain – his prayers no longer able to douse down his agony. These soldiers were part of this barbaric justice, so they did not deserve my politeness, nor my deference.

In retrospect, this was a mistake.

I had wanted to see inside the doge's palace ever since we had arrived in Venice, but not in this way. Not as a prisoner. As the guards pushed me around the portico of the central courtyard, we passed scribes, monks, magistrates, soldiers, serving women, even finely dressed child-slaves from Africa in this city within a city.

Our journey ended in a chamber with a heavy door, but thankfully this was not the dungeon I had feared. Instead, this room reminded me more of the scriptorium at my old monastery, where the monks of the abbey had copied and illuminated their manuscripts. As the door opened, I saw a grey-faced man of middle age sitting alone at a long table and hunched over a large roll of parchment. He looked up at my entrance, squinted to see my face, and then indicated roughly for me to sit down opposite him. Once I had settled myself into the chair, he dismissed the guards and then offered me a bowl of wine.

'I demand to know why I'm here,' I said in Venetian. 'I'm an Englishman. Known to the King of England himself.' This lie had proved useful on our long journey south to Venice, when my declaration of a connection to the king was enough to rattle an awkward innkeeper, or silence a quarrelsome pilgrim. On this occasion, however, the lie had little effect, other than to cause the man to scribble on the parchment that lay in front of him. 'Who do you represent?' I asked. He didn't answer. 'The Consiglio dei Dieci?' I suggested, thinking of the Council of Ten, who were the true rulers of this city. The man did not react. 'Then is it the Signori di Notte?' I asked, unable to prevent a short gulp when I said their name.

My interrogator curled his lips in a wry smile, but said nothing and returned to his writing. As he leant over his parchment, I studied the great pile of wrinkled black velvet that was balanced on his head, and the chain of silver and gold that hung over his collar of weasel-fur – but there was something unconvincing about all this ostentation, as if this man were not as important as he liked others to believe.

He looked up at me at length, sighed, and then reclined against the carved spindles of his chair. 'What are you doing here, Oswald de Lacy, Lord Somershill?'

'I thought you might tell me,' I said. 'I was reading a prayer book in the Piazza, and your soldiers arrested me. And might I ask how you know my name?' I said, with exaggerated affront.

He ignored this comment and began to write again, his quill scratching and squeaking as he applied pressure to the parchment. 'My question is this,' he said at length, without looking up, 'what are you doing in Venice?'

'If you know my name already. Then you must know my purpose.'

He raised an eyebrow, before taking up the quill again. I have keen eyesight and have always been able to read upside down, so I could see that he was transcribing my words verbatim. 'Do you need some time in the Pozzi to consider my question?' he asked. 'You seem a little unsure.'

'I'm on a pilgrimage from England,' I said quickly, for the Pozzi were reputedly the worst dungeons in the whole of Europe. 'I'm waiting for a galley to Jerusalem.'

He continued to write, and didn't look up. 'But you're an unusual pilgrim,' he said at length. 'Most pilgrims have avoided Venice in the last few months. You have noticed perhaps that we are at war?'

I ignored his sarcasm. 'Of course.' I said, thinking of the Jaffa galleys that were moored, one against the other in the Molo, like pigs squeezed into a pen – whilst their crews loitered in gangs about the city like children who would not go to bed. The pilgrims' hospices were empty, and the holy shrines of Venice were selling off their relics and indulgences at vastly reduced prices. So yes, I had noticed the war.

My interrogator lay his quill down upon the table. 'Where is the rest of your party?' he asked. 'Pilgrims always travel in large groups.' He ran his finger along a line of text. 'Yet I see you arrived in Venice with your mother. And nobody else. Not even a servant.'

'Have you been following me?' I asked in reply.

'Please answer my question.'

How could I tell the truth? That we had set off in an adequately cordial mood with a party from England, formed mainly from members of my mother's family, only to quarrel with them until we could not bear each other's company for another day. These arguments, caused mainly by my black moods or Mother's ancient and odorous dog Hector, had meant that we parted on such bad terms that they would not even provide a servant to accompany us on the last leg of our journey to Venice.

'Our party split in Bergamo,' I said. 'The others continued to Bari.'

The man gave a short, disgruntled snort. Since the Hungarians had blockaded the lagoon, the Venetians had lost most of their lucrative pilgrimage trade to the port of Bari in the far south of Italy. 'Why didn't you join them?' he asked. 'You must have heard that Venice was under attack.'

'My mother was too ill to continue by road,' I said. 'We hoped that Venice would quickly make peace.'

His eyes flashed. 'You think Venice should surrender her ports in Dalmatia?' he said, as a bubble of foam formed on his lips. 'To such savages as the Hungarians?'

'No, not at all,' I said quickly – though it seemed to me that Venice had no particular claim to Dalmatian land on the other side of the Adriatic. These ports might have been vital to the transport of goods from Constantinople, but Venice had hardly made herself popular with her Dalmatian subjects, having stripped their forests of timber, and refused to pay dockage at their ports. I didn't find it difficult to understand why the Dalmatians had turned to King Louis of Hungary, in hope of a deliverance from Venice – but this was not an opinion I decided to share.

My interrogator wiped his lips with a square of white linen, which he then folded neatly and placed beside the parchment on the table. He dipped the nib of his quill into the well of ink, tapped it against the side of the glass pot, and then began to scratch his way once again across the page. When he had finished his long sentence, he blew on the writing and watched the ink dry. 'Why don't you wear the cloak and red cross of a pilgrim?' he said at length.

'I'm a nobleman. I've no need to rely upon charity to pay for my passage to Jerusalem.'

My boast only elicited a short huff. 'You're staying at the house of an Englishman, John Bearpark? Is that correct?' he said. 'A house that Bearpark calls Casa Bearpark?' He followed this comment with a further, scornful snort. It was usually only the palaces of Venice that carried such a name, and though Ca' Bearpark was grand, it was certainly not a *palazzo*.

'I am.'

'Why?' he asked. 'There are many inns and hospices in Venice. Even ones suitable for a *nobleman* such as yourself.'

'John Bearpark is an old friend of the de Lacy family,' I said, choosing not to mention that this so-called friend was also charging us to stay at his home.

'Bearpark has a beautiful young wife, doesn't he?' he said suddenly, taking me by surprise. I looked up to see that, for the first time in this interview, the man had smiled, cracking the skin at the corners of his mouth and revealing a set of irregular, pointed teeth.

'Is she beautiful?' I said. 'I hadn't noticed.'

I made the mistake of adding a shrug to this comment, which caused him to sit up straighter in his chair and fix me with a glare. 'Do you like women, Lord Somershill?' he demanded.

'Of course I do,' I said quickly, thinking back to the man who was probably still burning to death in the Piazzetta, 'but I keep away from the wives of other men.'

He raised an eyebrow at my comment, as if this was a curious principle, just as we were disturbed by a scratching noise from a side wall. My interrogator stood up with some reluctance, struggled over to this wall, and then lifted a small flap to reveal a tiny round hole. He put his ear to this hole and listened, whilst somebody on the other side whispered a string of mumbled instructions. Throughout this conversation, my inquisitor frowned and pursed his lips, before finally nodding with a sigh and replacing the flap.

'How long have you known John Bearpark?' he asked me, as he returned to his table, sitting down with such a heavy thud that it caused his enormous velvet hat to wobble.

'Who's on the other side of the wall?' I asked.

He shrugged. 'Nobody.'

'You had a long conversation with this nobody.'

His stare was humourless. 'Answer my question please, Lord Somershill. How long have you known John Bearpark?'

'I met him for the first time when we arrived in Venice,' I said.

He put his quill to the parchment in readiness for my answer. 'But you say Bearpark is an old family friend?'

'Yes. My father fought with Bearpark at the battle of Bannockburn, in 1314. They met again, years later, in Southampton.'

'Southampton?'

'It's a port in the south of England,' I said fractiously.

'I know where Southampton is, Lord Somershill. Why did your father meet him there?'

I could not curb a sigh. 'As far as I understand, Bearpark followed the Venetian merchant fleet to Southampton every summer. My father travelled from our estate in Kent to meet him there. Bearpark sold us Malmsy wine, silks and spices, and my father sold him fleeces. Does that answer your question?'

'And you sought John Bearpark out deliberately when you came to Venice?'

'It was my mother's idea. There's nothing to be suspicious about.'

How I regretted using this word, as he took great pains to write down my sentence, verbatim, before repeating it aloud. 'There is nothing to be suspicious about.'

'I just can't see why you're so interested in me?' I said, allowing the first trickle of despair to taint my voice. 'I'm just a pilgrim.'

He continued to study me for a few moments, and then pushed the bottle of wine across the table. 'Have something to drink.'

I folded my arms childishly. 'No thank you.'

We sat in silence as light streamed in through the opaque window behind him — a large casement glazed with a honeycomb of small circular panes, each pane as thick and warped as the end of an ale bottle. There was something absorbing about the pattern of sunlight that forced its way through these prisms and then cast such strange shapes upon the smooth terrazzo floor. For a moment I watched tiny particles of dust dance in the rays of light that now striped the air, but then a shadow loomed behind the window and the spell was broken.

The shape was blurred at first, but soon I knew its hunched, creeping outline as it paced back and forth before pressing its face against the opaque glass to peer in at me. I kept perfectly still and looked at my hands, just as I always did, and waited for it to disappear.

My inquisitor pushed the wine towards me again. 'I think you should have something to drink. You look pale.'

'I'm perfectly well,' I said defensively.

He tapped his quill upon the parchment, and sucked his teeth. 'Very well then,' he said, after a long pause. 'Have you visited the bones of St Nicholas?' When I hesitated to answer, he carried on. 'Or what about the crystal ampoule that contains the miraculous blood of Christ?' I managed to raise a smile at this, which caused him to frown. 'Every pilgrim who stays in Venice visits these relics. You say you are a pilgrim, and yet I see here that you haven't visited a single shrine.'

What was I to say? That I would rather drink the water from my own bathtub than waste an afternoon staring at bones, or viscous potions claiming to be a thimble of Christ's blood. The Venetians were devoted to their relics, having plundered most of them from Greece, Egypt, or Constantinople, but I could not muster any of the same enthusiasm.

'I do intend to visit these shrines,' I said. 'Of course I do. But I have had a fever, and it seemed unholy to present myself to the relics when I was suffering an illness.'

He barely suppressed a laugh in response to my obvious lie. 'There are two other English pilgrims staying at Ca' Bearpark. Is that right?' He cocked his head to one side, causing the top-heavy chaperon to sway again.

'Yes, yes. Bernard and Margery Jagger,' I said wearily, thinking of the odd pair who shared our supper table and slept in nearby rooms. Mother complained that this brother and sister were as ill-mannered as pedlars – which, after all, was the true meaning of their family name – but these jaggers had enough money to sit at the same table and eat the same food as us, so who were we to look down upon them? Not that they were the easiest of company, however. Bernard constantly wore a distant smile, as if he were laughing at some undisclosed joke, and his sister Margery had sworn a vow of silence since leaving England, not intending to speak again until she cast her eyes upon the Holy House of Nazareth. Her strangeness was only amplified by her insistence upon wearing the hooded white habit of a Dominican brother, and the wimple of a nun.

'The Jaggers have been seen at many shrines,' my inquisitor told me. He traced his finger across the roll of parchment. 'Now. Let's see. They have visited the arms of Saint George and Saint Lucy; the feet of Mary the Egyptian, the ear of Saint Paul the Apostle, and the molar of Goliath.' He looked up at me, as if he expected an answer to this.

'They've enjoyed better health than I have.'

'But you have been well enough to visit the Rialto market?' He rolled back the parchment and pointed to a word. 'Yes. I also see here that you have been to the taverns of Castello. Many times.'

'Enrico Bearpark has been showing me around Venice,' I said quickly. 'He is John Bearpark's grandson. We are roughly the same age, and he thought—'

He interrupted me. 'We know who Enrico Bearpark is, thank you.' He leant forward again. 'I'm more interested in you, Lord Somershill. So, tell me this. Why is a devoted pilgrim spending so much time in the inns of Venice, when he says that he's too ill to visit the shrines?'

'It was Enrico's idea,' I said weakly. 'He thought it would lift my spirits.'

'Is there something wrong with your spirits?'

I looked away. Another question that was difficult to answer truthfully. 'Does Venice always spy on her visitors?' I said instead. 'As if we were common criminals.'

He gave a disdainful smile. 'We are only watching out for our enemies.'

The tapping came again from the wall, causing the man to sigh and then make his way, once again, from the table to the flap. This time the whispering was low and measured, as my interrogator nodded repeatedly and muttered the occasional *yes* or *I agree*.

When this conversation ceased, he returned to his chair. Finding his place at the end of the writing, he once again pressed the nib of his quill against the parchment – this time with more force, as if he wanted to hurry things along. 'Which way did you travel here?' he asked me sharply.

'The same way that any pilgrim comes to Venice.'

He lifted his eyes to meet mine. Without breaking his gaze, he then dipped his quill into the ink pot, tapped it, and let it rest upon the parchment.

'We came through Germany,' I told him.

'Your exact route please.' He coughed. 'From England.'

'We joined my mother's family in Ipswich in late February,' I said. 'Then we sailed from Felixstowe.'

The quill once again began to scratch its way across the page. 'What was your destination?' he said.

'The port of Zierikzee in the Low Countries. We wanted to avoid France.'

He nodded at the good sense in this decision. 'And then?'

'And then we sailed south on riverboats to Constance, where we continued by land towards the mountains.'

'You had a guide?'

'Of course we had a guide! Who would cross the Alps without one?' I said.

He continued to write, noting down that this comment had made me angry.

I took a deep breath, and tried to calm my temper. 'There were late snows, so we were stuck in an Alpine village for two weeks. As soon as the weather improved, we travelled over the Splügen Pass to Bergamo, which is where, as I told you before, our company parted ways. The others travelled to Bari. We travelled to Venice.'

'Did you go through Padua?'

'Yes.'

'Did you stop there?'

I knew why he was asking such questions. The Lord of Padua was another enemy of Venice – jealous of his neighbour's wealth and power. He might have signed a recent peace treaty with the Republic, but now he was said to be amassing German mercenaries, ready to take advantage of Venice's vulnerability, should the Hungarians invade. If I admitted to staying in Padua for any length of time, then this man would, no doubt, accuse me of being a spy. 'We travelled straight through Padua,' I said. 'We did not even stop to eat.'

He wrote to the end of the page and stopped. He then perused the manuscript and struck out some of the words, whilst adding others. 'Very well, Lord Somershill,' he suddenly announced, 'you are free to go.' He stood up and indicated that I should do the same.

'No more questions?' I said, getting to my feet. 'I thought you might want to know my favourite colour, or the name of my first puppy?'

'No, no,' he said, as he ushered me hastily towards the door. 'Welcome to Venice. Please enjoy your stay.'

It was my intention to stride out of the chamber with something of a dramatic exit, but he blocked my path with his arm, allowing his long sleeves to drag across the floor.

'One last thing, Lord Somershill,' he said, before a long and deliberate pause. 'Please don't forget. Venice is watching.'

Chapter Two

To look at John Bearpark, it was hard to believe that he had ever been a young man, for he was wizened and whiskery, and possibly in his eighth decade – though it is sometimes difficult to age a person who has spent most of his life in the strong sun of France and Italy. I'm sure that once he had owned the pale complexion of a man with red hair, but now his skin was a patchwork of brown and orange, where his freckles had unified to form great blotches of pigment. A pair of scabs marked the top of his head, though he was quick to replace his cap if he thought anybody was looking, and if you were unfortunate enough to stand too close to him, he smelt as if he was already beginning to decay. I should say that these signs of decrepitude were mainly superficial however, for Bearpark's mind was quick, his step was sprightly, and he still possessed a surprising strength. I had often witnessed him move the long oak table single-handedly, or lift his heavy coffer up the stairs towards his bedchamber.

Nevertheless, the old man's appearance had still shocked Mother when we had first arrived in Venice. I believe she had expected Bearpark to look as he had done thirty years previously, when she had accompanied Father on their annual visits to Southampton – but time is cruel, even to the most resilient of bodies. It was the apparatus that Bearpark now wore, almost perpetually, upon the bridge of his nose that had most disturbed

her. Bearpark called this strange device his 'spectacles' and
claimed that these two circles of glass held together by a frame
of horn had saved his eyesight. Once or twice, for a little entertainment in the long evenings, Bearpark had even suggested that
I wear the things and then tell the assembled company what I
could see. The world only looked more warped and out of focus
through these strange circles however, so I quickly passed them
back to the old man before they induced a headache.

Bearpark might have suffered from the unavoidable deteriora-
tion of age, but this had not prevented him from marrying a
young Venetian woman named Filomena and getting her with
child. She was Bearpark's third Venetian wife by all accounts –
the first having died many years ago in childbirth, and the second
having perished in the Great Plague of 1348. In fact, the only
member of Bearpark's whole family to have survived the devastation of this Pestilence was his grandson, Enrico – a young man
of my own age who was determined to introduce me to every
tavern in Venice. The more I declined his invitations, the more
often they were made, resulting in my having to hide or invent a
sickness in order to avoid yet another of his 'lively nights of
entertainment'.

Not that I always shunned Enrico's company. In fact, in my
first months in Venice I often sought him out, particularly in
the long afternoons when there was little else to do. His
command of English was good, since his grandfather had been
sure to teach him a tongue that was so useful for trade. In other
circumstances, we might have become more solid friends, but
Enrico's fondness for spending his nights with loud and raucous
company and drinking until he was sick was at odds with my
own mood. Nevertheless, a companionship of sorts had begun
to flower, and in the afternoons we often discussed those topics
on which I held opinions, such as the trajectory of Venus, and
the writings of Pope Pius. Enrico was polite enough to feign an
interest in these subjects, but he soon turned the conversation

to the poetry of Petrarch and Dante, or the Travels of Marco Polo.

Such times with Enrico were pleasant diversions, but when his friends began to amass in the *piano nobile*, I made sure to disappear, especially if a man named Vittore was part of their company. I could tolerate most of Enrico's friends, though they were pampered young men with too much money, too many fine clothes, and too little to do. Some were just foolish, such as the peacock Michele, who always sported a long-feathered cap and had the unpleasant habit of delving around in his striped hose to rearrange himself in public. I could ignore such bad manners and boorishness, but Vittore was different. He unnerved me.

He was tall, with striking blond hair, and features that seemed too big for his face. His nose was wide and upturned, with large nostrils that reminded me of a pig's snout. I was not the only person to have noticed this porcine resemblance. In fact, everybody had remarked upon it at one time or other, though not, of course, to Vittore's face. I was not the only person to be unnerved by Vittore either, for he used his size to dominate and subdue a room, and the other men, including Enrico, showed him the respect they might pay to a prince. When Vittore spoke, they listened. When Vittore made a joke, they laughed. When Vittore said it was time to leave, they followed.

The man ignored me for the most part when we met at Ca' Bearpark, for I kept to my own corner and kept my own counsel, but whenever Enrico attempted to include me in a conversation, it seemed to irritate Vittore. Why should he listen to me? To his mind, I was just another pilgrim, an Englishman with no influence or importance in Venice, so why should he care what I had to say? When Vittore did take the time to notice me, it was only to sneer at some comment I'd made, or to make some joke at my expense. In fact, he soon coined a silly name for me that became adopted by the whole group – 'The Silent Englishman', and though Enrico advised me to laugh at this, as it was only a piece of innocent foolishness, I refused to comply. It was a veiled insult, so why should I have pretended to find it amusing?

One night, soon after my interview at the doge's palace, Mother came to find me in my bedchamber, whilst a noisy party were gathering in the *piano nobile* directly beneath my room.

'Why don't you join Enrico and his friends, Oswald?' she said, folding her arms and looking about my room with disdain. 'They've been asking for you.'

'No thank you,' I said firmly.

'Indeed?' she said. 'And why not?'

'Because I don't feel like it.'

She sighed with frustration. 'If you stay in your shell any longer, then you'll turn into a snail.' She then strode across the room to open the shutters as if a cold draught of air might bring me to my senses. 'You're not making any efforts to get better, Oswald!' she scolded. 'And let us not forget that a recovery of your spirits was the whole point of coming on this pilgrimage.'

I groaned, for I had heard this speech so many times before. 'Just leave me alone, Mother.'

'But I cannot leave you alone, can I? What would become of you?' She then placed a hand firmly on my shoulder. 'It's been more than a year and this cannot go on for much longer. You have a life to lead. You have responsibilities.'

'You think I can just forget what happened?'

'No. I don't expect you to forget about it, Oswald. But you need to make an effort to recover.'

Our conversation was interrupted by a sudden burst of laughter from below. This house may have been grand, but the walls of the upper storeys leaked like the cloth of a tent. I looked to Mother with a sudden entreaty. 'Please. Don't give me away.'

She drew back from me and returned to the window, closing

the shutters now that her cold air treatment had failed to work. 'Very well,' she said crossly. 'But what will you do instead? Sit with John Bearpark and that dull little wife of his?'

'I don't find Monna Filomena dull,' I said. Though, in truth, it was difficult to engage the young woman in conversation, or indeed communicate in any way with her. Bearpark's wife faced the world with the blank, unknowable mask of the Madonna, and hardly spoke to anybody, including her own husband. She often seemed so sad that it provoked my pity, so I sometimes tried to cheer her up with a little conversation – finding an opportunity to ask her opinion on a piece of news, or even to make a platitude regarding the weather or the taste of a meal – but my attempts at discussion were always immediately stamped upon by her aged husband or his officious clerk, a man named Giovanni. This pair of bullies either answered my questions on Filomena's behalf, or, in Bearpark's case, sent her from the room, as if to punish her for being noticed. If I did manage to speak to Filomena alone, then she met my smiles and politeness with an indifference equal to the reaction she meted out to her husband's slights and lack of respect. Cold and stoic dispassion. Her true feelings lived somewhere behind her face, and we were not invited to share them.

Mother puffed her lips. 'Well, Monna Filomena should learn to speak English. The girl cannot follow one word of the conversation.'

'Perhaps you should learn to speak Venetian?'

Mother dismissed this comment with a shake of her head, just as another great cheer reached our ears from below. I tensed up, fearing that Enrico was en route to gouge me out of my bedchamber and force me to join his crowd for another night of entertainment.

There seemed to be some sort of revelry in the city that night, though I had no idea what the Venetians were celebrating this time. I had looked out of my window earlier to see groups of young men sailing past in their small flat-bottomed boats; drinking wine from the bottle, and throwing perfumed eggs at the houses of a favoured lady. Mother had remarked that many of these eggs had been lobbed at our own residence. Their white shells were now floating upon the canal, as their sweet rose water stained the walls. She had even expressed her surprise at being noticed by the young men of Venice, assigning this compliment to her delicate English beauty. Was it for me to tell her that the eggs were thrown for Filomena's sake? I thought not.

As Mother left the room in obvious disappointment, I heard Enrico and his friends rowdily descend into the bowels of the house and then board the *sàndolo* that was moored at the water gate. They had not come to find me, and perversely I felt annoyed. Their songs and jeering echoed about the canal as they rowed away, and suddenly I had the desire to run after them, and beg to join their revelries. I was a young man of twenty-six years old, not some crusted old invalid.

I lay on the bed, feeling sorry for myself, but my bedchamber was no longer a sanctuary now that my mood had invited something else into the room. I could feel it lurking in the corners just to the periphery of my vision, so I stood up quickly and walked over to the small basin, splashing my face with cold water and then rubbing my eyes until they stung. Even so, I could still sense the thing behind me, both cringing and discontented, so I quickly descended to the *piano nobile*, knowing that it would not dare to follow.

I found Bearpark, his wife, and other house guests sitting at the table at the opposite end of this long chamber, and suddenly I wished we were staying in a warm and modest inn – somewhere that I might sit in front of a fire and stare silently into the flames. But this was Venice, and anybody with any money and good taste owned a house with a *piano nobile* – a vast room that stretched from the windows upon the thin street to the balcony over the canal, and was about as congenial and intimate as the nave of a cathedral.

I joined the others at the table, and, after moving a supper of grey liver and sodden onions about the plate for a respectable period of time, I then allowed a servant to clear my place. It was the third night in a row that we'd been served this same dish, and it was becoming more and more unpalatable at each outing. I noticed that Mother fed most of it to her dog Hector when she thought nobody was looking. The servants were watching however, with disappointed eyes. After months of the Hungarian blockade, meat was becoming increasingly scarce, and they had been hoping for the leftovers.

After dinner I was punished again for not joining Enrico's party, for tonight Bearpark was subjecting us to another one of his stories – tales that hailed from a surprisingly small collection of anecdotes. Tonight's account had received its last outing the previous night, but we would hear it anyway – even though I politely tried to indicate my familiarity by making such comments as, 'ah yes. I think I remember you mentioning this before.' Or, even the explicit, 'you told us this yesterday' Bearpark did not take the hint, and soon I came to the conclusion that he had not forgotten its recent performance. This story would be told because he wanted to tell it, and we would have to listen, whether it bored us or not. Such is the privilege of a host. Even one who is charging you to stay at his house.

Tonight's tale concerned Bearpark's rise to riches, and I resigned myself to hearing it yet again, in the hope that there might be some new detail to ease the experience. Bearpark had grown up as the son of a poor tailor, somewhere in the county of Essex. Far from being embarrassed by his lowly beginnings, Bearpark was keen to stress the poverty of his early life, so that it might emphasise his later achievements – his large house in the most fashionable district of Venice, his army of servants, and his young and beautiful wife. Becoming a tailor had not appealed to Bearpark, so he had joined the king's army instead, and was soon assisting Edward the Second's flight from Robert the Bruce, which is where Bearpark had first met my father. After this debacle, he had left England to find his fortune in Europe, arriving in Venice around 1320. Bearpark was vague about the intervening years, and how he had amassed enough money to set himself up as a merchant in this city. It was my suspicion that he had travelled through Spain and France as a mercenary, fighting for whomever would pay the highest fee – though when I made such intimations, Bearpark was suddenly keen to bring his story to an end. He might have been a respectable merchant now, but he had built his fortune on war. I was sure of it.

Mother had listened to Bearpark's story with rapt attention as if she had never heard it before, meeting every turn with a gasp or even a clap, even though Bearpark peppered his anecdotes with enough platitudes and pompous declarations to render the account painfully tedious. At least the story had ended. I might have made my excuses, but was still not ready to confront the darkness of my bedchamber again, so, when Bearpark's clerk, a man named Giovanni, joined our party and challenged me to a game of chess, I quickly accepted.

Giovanni spoke English, and could be tolerable company when he wasn't inventing words in the English language – words that he then insisted were genuine. I had often corrected such terms as 'childling' or 'unfortune', only for Giovanni to swear that he had frequently heard them spoken by other Englishmen, as if there might be something wrong with my intellect.

Giovanni was also apt to become another of the household bores if allowed to express his opinion on the sin of pride. His unsolicited sermons on this topic always caused me to roll my eyes, since Giovanni was possibly the vainest man I had ever met. His clothes were fashionable, his shoes were clean, despite the mud of Venice, and his hair was assiduously curled at its ends, as if he had slept with dampened rags twisted through it. I should also say that he never stinted from admiring himself in one of the many looking glasses that were hung from every wall in the house.

The only ugly addition to his appearance was the large ring of keys that were suspended from his leather belt. These dirty, heavy keys looked out of place against the fine wool of his hose and the embroidered velvet of his doublet, but Giovanni clearly didn't feel that they ruined the look of his outfit – in fact he seemed excessively proud of having been given such responsibility, and made sure that these keys were always on display. In any other household, the mistress might have been expected to hold this ring, but Monna Filomena had been denied this privilege, either because of her youth or, more likely, because neither her husband nor Giovanni trusted her with the task.

Sometimes, when Giovanni was boasting about how many doors he could open, I noticed that Filomena allowed the tiniest drop of animosity to slip through her mask. This was not only prompted by the snub regarding the keys however, it was also a response to Giovanni's behaviour, which was often disrespectful and even contemptuous towards her. Whether Giovanni was following his master's lead in this behaviour, or whether he had developed his own personal grudge against the young woman I could not say, but it was obvious to me that they heartily disliked one another.

As our game of chess proceeded towards my inevitable defeat, we were joined by Bernard and Margery Jagger. This pair had previously been sitting next to John Bearpark and his young wife, but the old man had fallen asleep and was now snoring in crescendos that peaked with violent, shuddering grunts. For a while, they had endured this noise by sorting through their piles of pilgrim's badges, those small pewter souvenirs of the many shrines they had visited over the years – Canterbury, St Albans, Bury St Edmunds – but seemingly this activity had not proved an adequate distraction to the cacophony of Bearpark's snoring, and eventually they had given in and migrated to our end of the room.

Our game of chess could hardly have entertained the new arrivals however, since Giovanni was easily outwitting me. Each time he took one of my pieces, he gave a short growl of victory that was starting to become irritating. As we played, Bernard spoke to his silent sister, whilst staring absentmindedly at the ceiling. 'Did you see those little silvery fish at the Rialto market today, Margery?' he said. 'They looked just like herrings.' Or, 'I think they should reorganise the streets of Venice, don't you, Margery? It would be far more efficient if a person was only allowed to walk in one direction.' To each of these comments, Margery simply nodded, her face almost completely hidden beneath a thick and messily arranged wimple.

Giovanni took an age between moves, giving me the chance to let my eyes wander about the room, and allowing them to settle on Filomena. Tonight she was sitting silently in a high-backed chair next to her snoring husband, stitching a gown for her child – a child that I had been told was due the following spring. Filomena didn't seem aware of my interest – or if she was, then she didn't look up. As I watched her work, I was reminded of my sister Clemence, back in England, and how she had stabbed and pulled at her embroidery, often unpicking great swathes of work in frustration. Filomena, by contrast, worked slowly and purposefully. Her small hands were industrious and light across the cloth, and I would say she found something satisfying and restful in this work. Sometimes she even smiled to herself, though only for the most fleeting of moments, before she once again withdrew behind her impassive mask.

As I looked upon her young face, I found myself wondering again why Filomena had agreed to marry such an old man as John Bearpark? If I had entered the room without knowing this family, then I might have supposed that she was Bearpark's granddaughter, and certainly not his expectant wife. I turned away with a sigh, for I had only to look around this elegant house to understand the old man's appeal. And then I found myself wondering what it feels like to buy a young wife. Does the man fool himself into thinking that the woman loves him for himself, or does he simply not care? If this arrangement pleases both parties, then I suppose it cannot be criticised, but it would not have pleased me, and I had the impression that it did not really please Filomena.

I put the thought to one side, for Filomena's troubles were none of my business, and turned my attentions instead to Mother, as she paced the room with her elderly, flea-bitten dog Hector in her arms, stopping a couple of times to ask Filomena questions about her needlework. Mother spoke loudly in English, as if this might assist Filomena to understand her words, but the Venetian's shrugs and half-hearted smiles of non-comprehension eventually caused Mother to give up and sit down with a huff, before making an observation about the young woman that was impolite. As Mother passed this comment I noted a flicker in Filomena's eye, and suddenly I had the feeling that the young woman understood more English than she admitted.

After losing my second match of chess to Giovanni, I decided, in a fit of irritation, that it was time to retire. My bedchamber seemed empty enough when I crept in, so I dropped down onto my bed and spent a while watching the moonlight seep through the shutters and cast her silver lines across the floor. When this no longer distracted me, I closed my eyes, and tried to think of happier times, at my family estate in Kent. But Kent seemed so distant and alien, and I found it hard to conjure her green, fertile fields and her wide, languorous rivers. Instead, it was the years of the Great Plague that played out in my mind. My escape from the monastery at the age of eighteen, as the other monks were dying about me. My unexpected advancement to the position of Lord Somershill after the death of my older brothers. The desolation of the years following the Plague, as I fought to save Somershill from neglect and ruin. I should have been proud of my efforts, for my tenants and villeins were contented enough, and the estate was prospering. But instead my mistakes and failings kept whirling about my head like a game of carousel at a tournament.

I jumped from the bed and threw a light cloak over my night-shirt, before returning to the *piano nobile*. The room was now deserted, so I opened the shutters onto the balcony and wandered out to stare into the canal below. The air was still, and the moon washed the waters with its silver glow. The scene was distracting, and I felt more composed, when somebody tapped me upon the shoulder.

'What are you doing, de Lacy?' I turned sharply to see Enrico. His English was slurred and his clothes dishevelled.

'You surprised me, Enrico,' I said. 'You shouldn't creep up on people.'

Now Enrico laughed and poked me in the chest. 'Well, you should have come out with us for the night.'

I walked inside to join him, and closed the shutters of the balcony behind me. 'Did you enjoy yourself?' I said, a little churlishly.

He shrugged. 'Yes. Enough.'

'But you've returned early?'

He waved my question away. 'The others have different tastes.'

I didn't ask for an explanation, for taste in Venice stretched far beyond the narrow spectrum that I had encountered in my own life.

Enrico tried to pass me a bottle of wine, indicating that I should take a drink.

'No, thank you,' I said. 'I'm going back to bed.'

He thrust the bottle at me again. 'Come on, de Lacy. Have a drink with me.' He was struggling to focus his eyes, and his legs were swaying.

I stepped away. 'Thank you, Enrico. But I'm tired.'

He smirked. 'Tired of what?'

'Just tired.'

I had reached the wooden staircase to my bedchamber, when he hissed at me from across the room. 'What exactly is wrong with you, de Lacy? Is it life that tires you?'

I froze. 'I have a problem sleeping, that's all.'

He laughed. 'I know about your sleeping. I hear you wandering the house at night.'

'Goodnight, Enrico.'

He followed me up the stairs, and caught up with me by the door to my bedchamber. 'Are you enjoying your suffering?' he said, as he pressed a fist into my shoulder. 'Your own little dark carnival?'

'No. Of course not.'

'On the contrary. I think you are.' Now he leant forward and whispered into my ear. His breath smelt of brandy and garlic. 'I think you revel in it.'

'That's not true.' I moved aside, and he fell forward against the wall. 'You're drunk,' I said. 'You don't know what you're saying.'

'And you're miserable.'

'I have reason to be,' I told him. Then I opened the door. 'Now leave me alone.'

He heaved a great sigh, and then staggered back down the stairs, waving the bottle in the air. 'I know about you,' he said, as he nearly tripped on his descent. 'I know all about you!'

For a week after this unpleasant encounter, I succeeded in avoiding Enrico. I came to dinner late, or to breakfast early. If Enrico entered the room, I childishly left immediately, or if there was no possibility of escape, I made an effort to laugh as loudly as was appropriate. I thought to convince Enrico that I was not wallowing in self-pity. Not in the least. But Enrico seemed troubled, rather than impressed, by my displays of jollity, often trying to catch my eye, or to take me to one side. It is to my shame that I rebuffed every one of his approaches.

One morning, before I had risen from bed, a square of folded parchment was pushed beneath my door. I picked it up with some trepidation, for I knew the seal – it was Enrico's, and I suspected the letter to be full of criticism and rebukes for my unfriendly behaviour. I put the thing to one side for a while, but then it sat upon my bed and looked at me reproachfully, until I broke the seal and unfolded the letter.

De Lacy. I apologise if my words to you were hurtful. Your mother has explained your troubles to me, and I am sorry indeed for your woes.

I was tempted to screw the letter into a ball and throw the thing from my second-floor window into the canal. Mother had no business in discussing my private life with strangers. No wonder Enrico had taken to regarding me with sad eyes and exaggerated concern. I would write back immediately and tell him to keep his sympathy to himself, as I did not need it . . . and yet I carried on reading.

You have every reason to be sad, but I ask only this. Please, take care with your disposition. I have suffered such spasms and moods in my own life, and I know that an ill-tempered mind may commit treason against its own body. Be kinder to yourself. The past is done, and you cannot change what has happened, especially as it was not your fault. So, why not come out sometimes with men of your own age? You spend too long with your mother. I mean her no disrespect, but her company will not lift your humours. You need to laugh and be merry. You need to spend your nights with beautiful women and handsome young men. It is time to put your sadness aside and live again. Please de Lacy, let me help you.
Enrico Bearpark, Your Friend

I folded the parchment and fell back upon the bed – both furious and shamed. How dare Enrico write such a letter to me? I did not need his help. What condescension! But lying in bed made me feel no better, so I stalked over to the window and opened the shutters and looked into the canal, where a solitary boat cut through the water, its hull loaded with lumpy sacks of cloth and great casks of wine.

This was not enough of a distraction, for then I heard something behind me. It sounded like the scampering of feet – and yet I dared not look, for I knew what it was. I need only have turned around to see its face.

I stared at my hands and waited until it was gone, then I looked up and opened the letter again. As I read along the lines, I knew that Enrico was right. I did need to take care with my disposition, for my mind was ill. It was, indeed, committing treason against my body.

So I re-folded the letter and placed it safely away in my chest. I wanted to trust Enrico. I wanted to believe that he could save me.

Chapter Three

'So, de Lacy. You've never spent the night with a nun? Is that what you're saying?' Enrico turned to Vittore, and the two of them laughed.

'No,' I said, urging my stomach to be still. 'And I don't want to.' I looked up from my feet and saw that our boat was approaching a small island somewhere out on the lagoon. 'Tell the oarsman to turn the boat around,' I said, but instead we carried on in the very same direction. Cutting silently through the water, under the light of a full moon. The boat was long and thin, with seats draped in fine silks and cushions of fur, and the air about us was cool and salted, but it was not cold. Not truly cold. As I leant over the side of the boat and was sick into the glossy water, the oarsman cursed me, so it was lucky that he didn't notice that some of my vomit had dripped onto the silk of the seating.

Enrico took my hand and whispered. 'Come on, de Lacy. A night with some women will cheer your mood.'

'Is this your idea of helping me?' I said. 'Plying me with wine and then throwing me into bed with a nun?'

'The sisters of Santa Lucia are very generous, de Lacy.' He laughed. 'Why not give their charity a try?'

'I'm not going to a brothel that masquerades as a convent.'

Enrico drew even closer and whispered into my ear. 'What could be the harm? The sisters are charming. And if you don't like the look of what's on offer, then just imagine that she's Filomena.'

I flinched at this. 'What are you talking about?'

He laughed. 'Don't be shy. I've seen how you look at my grandfather's wife.'

'That's not true!'

'But Monna Filomena is a beautiful woman. Plenty of men like to look at her.'

'That's an outrageous suggestion,' I said. 'I'm not the least bit interested in Monna Filomena, or some nun, or any other woman for that matter.'

He gave a small, mischievous laugh. 'Would you like me to introduce you to some men then?'

I called to the oarsman. 'Turn this boat around!'

As I leant over the side of the boat to be sick again, Vittore gestured to Enrico. His yellow hair appeared silver in this moonlight, and his large nostrils cut into his face like caverns. 'Just give the fool some more wine and tell him to stop shouting,' he said. 'I prefer it when this Englishman is silent.'

At Vittore's command, Enrico lifted the bottle to my lips and attempted to pour another mouthful down my throat, only causing me to throw up again as soon as the wine met my stomach.

'You're not my friend,' I said pathetically.

Enrico nudged me playfully, before he wrapped his cloak about my shoulders. 'Of course I'm your friend, de Lacy. Perhaps the best one you ever had. Who else would take you to the finest taverns in Venice, and then entertain you in a convent?' He nudged me again. 'Not your friends in England, that's for sure.'

I cursed Enrico, and called him some obscenity or other. It was no matter, for my insult only amused him.

'Ask for Sister Donata,' he told me. 'They say she's the best.'

'Ask for her yourself. I want nothing to do with this.' I heaved again, this time causing the oarsman to shout at me, and to throw his hands briefly from the oar. Enrico shouted a rebuke, and we carried on, as I left a trail of spittle in the water. The world revolved, and I could have dropped overboard so easily. Part of me wanted to.

Eventually the boat slowed as we reached the landing stage of the island, where we stopped beside a decaying platform. Two figures waited for us in the dark. The smaller of the two held a lantern aloft.

Vittore grabbed hold of the first stake and hauled himself onto this platform, before offering his hand to Enrico. As they both embraced our welcoming party I sat resolutely in the boat. The oarsman flicked his head to indicate that I should also leave, but I refused to move.

Enrico pushed his two companions forward to speak to me, and now I could see their faces in the light of the lantern. The first was an older woman in the belted tunic of an abbess, with a white wimple covering her head and shoulders. She smiled at me, but I saw little of her face except a set of teeth. Her companion was a young man, of maybe twenty-five. His face was handsome, and his hair was as golden and curled as the angels in the stained-glass windows of my family chapel.

Enrico leant down into the boat and held out his hand to me. 'Come on, de Lacy. Just get out.'

'No.'

His good humour soured a little. 'Come on. Don't be rude.' Then he thrust his hand at me a second time. 'You'll have a good time.' He smiled sweetly. I liked Enrico's smile. 'What could be the harm?'

Vittore's tone was harsher. 'Just get off the boat you fool!' he shouted.

Enrico ignored the pig-faced oaf, allowing his voice to remain kind and soft. 'Come on, de Lacy. You don't have to do anything,' he said. 'You can sit in the cloister and remain silent. In fact, I will ensure that every beautiful young woman in the place ignores you. How does that sound?'

'I don't know,' I said, feeling the first twinges of surrender.

Enrico offered me his hand again, and this time I took it. 'Well done,' he said. 'You won't regret this.'

I was getting to my feet when I noticed Vittore exchange a look with the abbess – a devious, knowing smile, and suddenly I knew that they were all lying to me. No doubt I would be fed more wine and then thrown into the bed of a sister, whether I was capable of making love to her or not.

'Take me back to Venice,' I said, pulling my hand away from Enrico and sitting back down with a thud. 'Take me back now!'

My tone must have been convincing, as Enrico looked to Vittore and then gave a shrug of defeat, signifying that he would not force this any further. The boat then turned back for the city, and Enrico put his hand on my shoulder and tried to make me laugh, whereas Vittore folded his arms and could not bring himself to look at me. As we glided away from the island, I looked up to see the abbess and her young companion watching our departure from their jetty. The lantern cast a soft light upon the man's angelic features, and picked out his halo of golden curls. I had rarely seen such a handsome face, and yet there was a taint to his beauty. A drop of bitterness, perhaps even spite.

I hoped to return to Ca' Bearpark immediately – but it seemed my torment was not to end so quickly. If I could not be persuaded to get out of this boat at a brothel, then I would be dragged to yet another drinking hole. This time the establishment was located at the dead end of a dirty canal somewhere in a distant part of Venice. I didn't recognise this *sestiere*, though I could tell immediately that it was an impoverished neighbourhood, for the houses at each side of the canal seemed abandoned, with boarded windows and crumbling, mouldering walls. I found it hard to believe that anybody lived in such a place, but when we reached the head of the canal, and had manoeuvred ourselves past the floating debris that always accumulates in such places, a small

door opened and a large man squeezed himself out onto the
wooden jetty. When he pulled me from the boat with a hand that
was the size of a plate, I had no choice but to follow the others
inside.

A sea of faces looked up briefly to observe our party enter, but
these drinkers soon turned back to mind their own business.
They were huddled around candles, deep in conversation; or
they were staring into the bottoms of their empty bowls as if
they might have missed a final drop of wine. After my experience
at the convent, I have to say that it came as a relief to see that
there were no women in the place.

We were served sour wine and some stale bread, which
seemed to poison Vittore's mood further. In fact, he seemed to
be spoiling for a fight after our aborted visit to the convent, and
boomed sporadically, berating the assembled drinkers for being
such a boring and ill-favoured crowd. When this failed to elicit
any particular response, he shouted, 'death to Hungary!' adding
his opinion that Venice should sail every ship in her Arsenale out
to sea and obliterate her enemy. When this assertion was once
again met with only the most perfunctory of enthusiasm, Vittore
demanded to know why the assembled throng did not agree with
him? Were they not true Venetians? Were they traitors to the
Republic?

An old man, with drooping eyelids and long hair straggling on
either side of his bald pate was the only person bold enough to
answer Vittore's call. 'The Consiglio dei Dieci should negotiate a
peace with Hungary,' he said calmly. 'We need to be trading
again. *That* is the only reason to sail our ships from the Arsenale.'
A few souls about him nodded their assent, which served to
embolden the old man. 'I only get paid when I sail,' he said. 'So,
what good is a war to me? I need to reach Flanders by the spring.'

Now a chorus of approval spread through the tavern, with
more calls for a negotiated peace, and more complaints that a
continued war would only further harm trade. A drunkard raised

his mug and announced that Hungary was welcome to Dalmatia, for the Dalmatians were no better than filthy dogs and he'd had nothing but trouble from them when docking at their second-rate ports.

Vittore banged his fist upon the table. 'Cowards!' he shouted. 'All of you. I'll report you to the Consiglio.' The room became instantly silent. Then, as he scanned their faces, he noticed what I had seen immediately upon entering the tavern. 'Or maybe I should bring the Signori di Notte here?' he said menacingly. 'For I see no women.'

Fear spread through the room instantly. The drunkard stood slowly to his feet. 'Death to Hungary,' he called, with little feeling. The men about him murmured the words and raised their bowls of wine to show their support.

Vittore smiled, for victory was his – but there was still a little more entertainment to be extracted from this episode. 'Is that the best you can do?' he shouted.

The call came again. 'Death to Hungary!' Now the words were delivered with more enthusiasm and vigour, apart from the old man with the drooping eyelids, for the change of heart in the room had not spread to his own chest. He folded his arms and turned his back to Vittore, making a surly comment that I did not catch.

Vittore had heard exactly what the man had said, however. Grabbing the fellow by the back of his tunic, he then ejected him with great force from the tavern, before slamming the door in his wake. When Vittore turned to ask if there were any other cowards in the house, his question was met with universal denial. Vittore then surveyed the room with all the menace of a hawk searching for prey, before the murmur of conversation finally returned and the incident was forgotten.

Now I wanted nothing more than to return to Ca' Bearpark, and I might have taken my chances and walked home, had I known the way. But I could not tell if I was in San Polo, Dorsoduro or even Cannaregio. And anyway, it was not easy to pass from one *sestiere* of Venice to another. Each of these districts had started life as a separate island – until wooden poles had been driven into the mud of the lagoon to form new land and the islands had merged together to form the city of Venice. Even so, each *sestiere* still felt like a separate parish. Each was a close, watchful community that knew its own people and distrusted strangers. All in all, it was better to stay where I was.

I sank against the wall and began to watch the three men at the next table, for no other reason than boredom. They were playing a game of dice – a game that I recognised as Hazard from the inns of England – with determination and concentration, as if nothing else in the world mattered to them, starting each game with their call, 'Roll the bones! Roll the bones!' These 'bones' were large, yellowing dice, carved from ivory.

The more they played, the more interested I became in their game, until they asked me to join them. At first I declined, but when I noticed that Enrico and Vittore were involved in a game of their own – a drinking challenge with a pair of sailors – I realised that there was little prospect of an imminent departure. I had a few spare coins in my pouch that I could afford to lose, so I accepted.

At first I was unlucky. I hadn't properly understood the probabilities of winning, when predicting the throws of the caster's dice. But I am a man with a fast mind, particularly when it comes to arithmetic. Soon I understood the best way to improve my chances, and which numbers to bet upon, and which numbers to avoid. Also, when it was my turn to throw the dice, I employed a little showmanship to disrupt my opponents' concentration. Such behaviour is out of character, but I was bored, I was drunk, and I would never come to this inn again in my life. So what did I have to lose?

Each time I threw the dice, I held the warm cubes of ivory to my mouth and whispered into their stained grooves. At first my fellow gamblers were amused by my antics, but as the dice increasingly began to obey my commands, they no longer found me quite so entertaining. Soon my winning streak had drawn a crowd, and my few *soldini* had grown into a mound of shining coins. As my behaviour became increasingly flamboyant, I felt something that I hadn't felt for many, many months. It was the warm, intoxicating glow of joy, and its return was more welcome than I can say.

But joy is as ephemeral as luck, and soon it was time for both to run out. My fellow gamblers had become irritated by my success. At first it showed itself as some grumbling and peevish complaints behind a hand. As my pile of coins grew taller however, and the applause for my good fortune became louder from the crowd about us, my fellow players began to accuse me of cheating – of using tricks, or even sorcery to bend the dice to my will. Enrico came over and tapped me on the shoulder, telling me it was time to leave, but I was having such a good time that I told him to wait. That I wasn't finished yet with this dark, smoke-filled tavern in the back end of Venice. I wanted to stay longer.

When I had rolled my last pair of winning dice, the man opposite me could contain himself no longer. He reached over and grasped me by the neck. The move had taken me by surprise, but, before I was able to fight back, Enrico and Vittore had pulled him away and thrown him to the floor, where he scuttled quickly away on all fours and hid beneath a table.

Enrico then looked about the room. The candlelight was dim and highlighted the wearied lines in the faces that looked back at us. 'Is there anybody else who wants to call Lord Somershill a cheat?' Enrico asked.

They shook their heads and quickly returned to their drinking and their quietly grumbled conversations. Nobody wanted a fight.

Enrico put his hand on my shoulder. 'Come on, de Lacy,' he said. 'Time to go home.' So I gathered up my winnings and filled my leather pouch, until the small bag was loaded with coins and I could hardly tie the drawstring.

As we left the tavern and stepped out into our boat, Vittore crept up behind me and whispered into my ear. 'You were lucky tonight, Silent Englishman,' he said slyly, 'but luck never lasts.'

I ignored his words, for I was exhilarated after my wins, and his menace would not press its finger into my skin and leave a mark – but, just as I was about to tell him as much, we heard a man shouting to us from the canal. Looking into the darkness, I could just about make out that the man was clinging onto the slimy pole of a landing stage a few yards away – unable to drag himself out of the water.

'Are you going to get me out then?' he called, with some desperation. As my eyes adjusted, I realised that it was the old man whom Vittore had thrown out of the tavern. He must have been launched straight into the canal.

Vittore laughed. 'No. You can stay there,' he shouted.

Enrico nudged his friend. 'Come on, Vittore. He might drown.'

'I don't care if he does,' said Vittore. 'Venice doesn't need cowards like him.'

Enrico sighed, and it seemed he would give up on the fellow, but I could not leave an old man to die in this polluted canal – so I jumped from the boat and climbed back onto the landing stage, telling the oarsman to wait for my return. Vittore shouted after me as I clambered across the rotten boards, but I ignored his calls and offered my hand to this stranded stranger. The old man clasped it with relief and thanked me profusely, but his gratitude was premature, for he was heavier than I had expected, and I was unable to lift him and his sodden clothes from the water by myself.

I was about to call for some assistance when I felt another person at my side. It was Enrico. I smiled at my friend, and together we pulled the old man to safety, but as I noticed the look upon Vittore's face, the joy of the evening dissipated. Once he had disliked me. Now he hated me.

Chapter Four

It was four months later — the last Thursday before Lent of 1358, *Giovedi Grasso* — and the carnival would go ahead, no matter that the war with Hungary continued to rage. There were still no ships either leaving or entering the lagoon, and now the Venetian stronghold of Treviso had fallen. With Treviso being less than twenty miles from Venice, rumours were circulating that King Louis's army would soon be at the very shores of *La Serenissima*.

There was much despondency and talk of invasion over breakfast that morning. Bernard, flushed with a panic, informed us that he and Margery had sewn every one of their pilgrim's badges to their nightgowns the previous evening, in the event they needed to flee Venice at a moment's notice; whilst Mother asked for a pike to be placed beneath my bed, should I need to defend the two of us against the reported monstrousness of the Hungarian soldiers.

The conversation was becoming hysterical, when Bearpark announced, with something of a flourish, that we must not give in to despair — for Venice would find a practical solution to her problems, just as she always did. He then went off into a story we had not heard before. It concerned the Plague, and how he had donated his cog ship to the Republic, so that she might bury a great many of the dead at sea. The story seemed unlikely, but then again, I had often heard it said that Venice had quickly run out of places to bury her dead during those terrible years, so perhaps the story was true. And it would explain why Bearpark no longer seemed to own the cog ship that he had once used for his annual trips to Southampton.

As soon as this tale finished I quickly excused myself from the table, in the hope of getting away before Mother asked where I was going. It had been two days since I'd last played at dice, and the coins in my purse were hopping against the strings. I wanted to get into the city and find a tavern, but my escape was not to be so easy.

Mother placed her hand upon my arm. 'Oswald. I thought you might accompany me to the carnival today. It would be pleasant to spend some time together, before the city is overrun with Hungarians.'

My heart began to beat quickly. 'I have to meet with somebody, Mother.' I gave a quick, apologetic smile. 'I'm sorry.'

'Whom are you meeting?' she said sharply, causing all other conversation about the table to stop.

I tried to pull a name from thin air, but as I hesitated, Bearpark came to my rescue. 'I expect Lord Somershill is visiting a young lady,' he said. 'The carnival heats the blood, you know. Especially in such times as these.' He then laughed coarsely. 'The threat of death is a great arouser, my lady. A great arouser!'

Mother grimaced at his comment, before turning to me with a look of disapproval. 'Is this right, Oswald? Have you befriended a young woman?' I shook my head, but clearly she didn't believe me. 'Then why don't you invite her to Ca' Bearpark,' she said. 'I would certainly like to meet her.'

I could feel the blood rushing to my cheeks. 'There is no young woman.'

'Is she married? Is that it?' Mother raised her eyebrows in rebuke, as if this indeed was the answer to the mystery. 'Then you should be very careful. Venetian husbands can be violent when provoked.'

'I am *not* visiting a married woman,' I said.

'Then you can take me to the carnival,' she said, patting my hand. 'An English noblewoman cannot wander about Venice unaccompanied.'

'No, Mother,' I said very firmly. 'I'm sorry, but you will have to find another companion.'

Mother turned, wide-eyed to Bearpark. 'John. Why don't you take me instead?' She clapped her hands together. 'Indeed, I would enjoy your company a great deal more than my son's.' She threw me a reproachful glance. 'He's become so dull recently.'

I had to admire Bearpark's speed of thought, for he shook his head despondently and feigned a great sorrowful frown. 'My dear Lady Somershill, how I would love to accompany you to the carnival. But you know how painful my knees have become in recent days. The bone grates like blades against my flesh.' Mother went to object, but the old fox was too quick for her. 'But I have the answer,' he boomed, before Mother had the chance to speak. 'I'm sure that Bernard here and his sister Margery would love to see the carnival.'

I could never be sure that Bernard was following a conversation, but, in this instance, it seemed he had understood every word. 'But, Master Bearpark,' he said with a low bow of his head, 'I'm afraid that Margery has committed herself to prayer today, as otherwise we would be most delighted to join Lady Somershill.' He gave a short cough. 'Margery is always at her most devout in the days before Lent, and therefore cannot leave the house.'

Having appeared initially horrified by the suggestion of attending the carnival with Bernard and Margery, Mother was suddenly peeved by the pilgrim's excuses. 'Margery seems to have left the house often enough in recent days,' she said. 'In fact the two of you are barely here.'

Bernard smiled. 'We have been visiting the many venerable shrines and holy places of Venice, my lady. Before Margery enters her period of reflection.'

Mother pursed her lips. 'I see. And can your sister not begin her reflection tomorrow? There are still five days until Lent begins.'

Bearpark jogged the pilgrim's elbow. 'Of course she can. Can't she, Bernard?'

Bernard drew his arm back, as if it were scalded. He was cornered, and he knew it. 'But, Master Bearpark. If only you—'

Before the excuse could land, Bearpark heaved himself to his feet, and then pointed to Mother. 'Would you allow this poor noblewoman of England to roam the streets of Venice alone? Is that what you're saying?' He spoke fiercely. 'What sort of pilgrim are you, Bernard Jagger? Where is your charity?'

Bernard regarded Bearpark with a strange, sullen stare, as if making one last silent entreaty to be excused from this ordeal – but it was an entreaty that Bearpark ignored, giving the pilgrim no choice but to get to his feet and bow to Mother with a flourish.

'My dear Lady Somershill. It would be an honour to attend the carnival with you,' he said. 'I thank you for requesting the company of this humble pilgrim and his poor sister.' I looked to Mother, and could tell that she suddenly regretted this victory – but she had forced the invitation, so now she would have to endure its consequences.

I left the house soon after, following some of Bearpark's servants along the Calle Nuova, as they noisily made their way towards the city. Their master had given many of them the rest of the day off, so that they might also attend the carnival. They were rowdy and full of laughter, ready to forget the war with Hungary and enjoy themselves before the long and arduous privations of Lent.

I kept my distance, but as I turned the corner into the Campo Santo Stefano – I happened to bump into Giovanni Bearpark. He looked tired and unkempt, and the creases in his tunic betrayed that he had not returned home the previous night.

He embraced me, and I could smell the clammy, smoky scent of Venice upon his clothes. 'De Lacy! You're out early,' he said to me in his perfect English.

'I'm going to the Piazza San Marco,' I said quickly, hoping that he wouldn't want to join me. 'I've heard there's some entertainment worth watching?'

Enrico wrinkled his nose. 'It's tolerable, I suppose. But let's meet later,' he said with a sudden grasp of my arm. 'The evening of the *Giovedi Grasso* is much more exciting. Do you have a mask?'

I should have lied and pretended to have one of the leather creations hidden somewhere in my cloak, but instead I gave an embarrassed shrug and admitted the truth. 'No.'

Enrico regarded me for a moment. 'You do intend to go to the carnival?'

'Of course.'

He hesitated again and dropped his hand. 'I haven't seen so much of you lately, de Lacy,' he said gently. 'Too many games of dice, I think?'

I feigned a laugh to hide my irritation at this comment. 'It is just a way to pass the time,' I said quickly. 'But I'll see you tonight, Enrico. You can show me the delights of *Giovedi Grasso*.'

He studied me for a moment, not convinced by my sudden act of enthusiasm. He looked tired, and he needed to shave. 'Take care of yourself, Oswald,' he said, before we embraced again.

'Oh de Lacy!' he shouted, as I scurried away.

I considered pretending that I hadn't heard him, but my friend didn't deserve such rudeness. 'Yes, Enrico,' I said, turning around.

'Take care of your money,' he shouted to me with one of his mischievous smiles. 'Remember that Venice is full of thieves and murderers!' This was enough to stop some passers-by in their tracks, but whether they were offended by his words, or merely surprised at his English, I could not say.

I raised my arm and shouted back. 'Until later, my friend.'

*　　*　　*

I was soon at the great Piazza San Marco, pushing my way past the many Venetians who had gathered to watch the spectacles of the day. The human pyramids, the pig-chase, and the display of fine clothes did not hold any interest for me, so I continued through the Piazzetta, towards the *sestiere* of Castello with single-minded strides, heading for a tavern where I could find a game of dice.

I had visited my money changer the previous day in the Rialto to draw down against my Letter of Credit, and now my purse clinked with the sweet jingle of coins. Since my first introduction to dice games the previous September, on the night of my abortive visit to the convent of Santa Lucia, I had become an enthusiastic player at Hazard, finding every opportunity I could to slip away from Ca' Bearpark and find a table at which to gamble.

It had started well enough, though I should admit that my early winnings had been cancelled out by recent losses. In fact, I had been rather surprised to learn from my money changer, the day before, that my Letter of Credit was now exhausted. We had argued, until he showed me his ledger, and it seemed the old crook was telling the truth.

This lack of funds should have caused me a great deal of concern, but it didn't. For I knew that I was going to be fortunate again that night – winning back everything that I'd lost in the previous weeks and more – much more. This was a certainty. I only needed luck. And luck would not continue to desert me. Why would she? I was not a lord. I was a king. King of the dice!

I had been a prudent, cautious boy, and I had grown into a prudent, cautious man. So you might wonder how I became a gambler? How the thrill of taking a risk had suddenly become so appealing to me? The answer was this – that playing dice had reawakened something within me. It had reminded me of what it felt like to be joyful. And this was an emotion that had been absent from my life for too long.

Mother had dragged me on this pilgrimage in the hope that a holy expedition would heal my sorrows – so she would have been disappointed to discover that it was gambling instead that had been my salvation. She would not have understood that throwing the dice threw light upon my shadow. That it helped me to forget my creeping, watchful follower, and blot out its misery with the thrill of excitement and anticipation. Gambling seemed to have no downsides, for even when I lost my stake, there was always the promise of the next game, and the next win. To sit and play at dice was more than a distraction, it was a liberation, so I was blinded to the harm in it. Not even when I had gambled down to our last few ducats, and further losses would mean that we were stranded, without funds, in a city that was a thousand miles from our home in Kent. I didn't see this as a problem, because I was convinced that my luck would turn at the next throw. I was convinced I would win again.

Today I was returning to an inn on a narrow lane that ran along the border of San Marco and Castello. I had been to this establishment before on a few occasions and it had been a lucky place for me. In fact, the last time I'd played here, I had won a whole ducat in a single game. In the main chamber, at the street level, the inn served the sourest, second-pressed wine, and a cloudy ale that tasted as if it had been brewed from oats and canal water. But at the back of the establishment was a dusty staircase that led to a further, airless chamber where the dice games took place. Not everybody knew about this room, as there was sporadic suppression of gambling by the Signori di Notte, though they were apt to ignore the practice during the carnival season, especially if the innkeeper was minded to pay them to stay away.

I nodded to the man sitting on the foot of the stairs, and, after looking me up and down, he indicated that I could pass with a flick of his hand. I then took my place at a table, in a room that was lit by tallow candles, and filled with silent, sweating men — each of whom looked as if they might pull a dagger upon a fellow player at any moment. There was something about the degradation of this place that also thrilled me. As a younger man, I would never have entered such a den, and yet here I was, sitting among them, brave enough to take a chair at their table.

At first I was lucky. The dice obeyed my commands, and my opponents were both poor in their calculations and wearied by a day of drinking. It was easy to take their money, and soon, one by one, they had exhausted their meagre funds and dropped out of the game.

When left without an opponent I turned to the other men in the room. 'Who will play me now?' I asked. My question was met with wariness. They had seen my luck was in, and none of them was willing to take their chances.

I had decided to leave, when somebody called to me from the far corner of the room.

'I'll play you, de Lacy,' he said. As I focussed my eyes, I could see that the voice belonged to my old adversary Vittore, his ugly, porcine features just discernible through the gloom.

I should have turned and run at that point, but I didn't. Instead I welcomed him and his two friends to my table. I had never seen this pair before, and they were rougher, dirtier men than the usual spoilt young followers who flocked to Ca' Bearpark.

'Roll the bones,' said Vittore.

I hesitated. There was a menace to this man that always caused me to catch my breath, no matter how hard I tried to keep my composure. At least it was dark and he could not see the blood rush to my face. He banged his hands upon the table and leant towards me. 'I said, roll the bones, de Lacy. Time to play.'

I began well enough. The dice were falling in my favour. But this promising start was my downfall, for it only encouraged me to take greater risks. To throw my restraint into the fire and watch it burn. And how it burnt! Soon I had lost all of my early winnings, and had to reach into my pouch to retrieve yet more and more coins. Whenever Vittore threw the dice now, they fell in his favour, but when I threw these same cubes of ivory, they rarely showed me any kindness. I began to suspect the man was cheating, perhaps even swapping the dice at each throw for a pair that were loaded – but I could not prove this accusation. The presence of Vittore's two dirty, menacing friends watered down my willingness to make such a claim. Instead, I relied upon luck to save the day, so I gambled more. And then some more, to win back my losses. At each throw I hoped to save my situation, but only succeeded in digging myself deeper into the mire. Over and over I made the same mistake, until there was nothing left. Nothing at all from the great sum I had deposited with the money changer in London, to draw upon as we travelled.

Vittore laughed. 'No more money, de Lacy?'

I scratched my ear to stop myself from throwing a punch. 'I have plenty more at home,' I lied.

'Shall I accompany you back to Ca' Bearpark? And then you can fetch this money?'

I coughed. 'It's not actually there,' I mumbled. 'I just need to raise more from my Letter of Credit. And, of course, the money changers won't be working today.' I stood up to leave, but Vittore put his hand upon my arm. His grip was firm and unwavering.

'Your credit is good with me,' he said, as he forced me to sit down – his two friends grinning at me like demons. 'Stay here,' he said. 'I trust you.'

'I would rather play with real coins,' I said weakly.

'Come on, de Lacy. Don't leave now.' Then he leant forward and leered at me, and I couldn't help but hate him. His pig-like snout. His protruding, rabbit-like teeth. 'You could win all your money back,' he told me with a menacing grin.

'But—'

'Don't worry about it,' he said. 'I know you'd honour your debts. You're an Englishman, after all.' He looked about the room and caught the eye of our fellow drinkers. Until this point I had not realised how much interest the other men in the tavern had been taking in our game – but now I could see that we had been playing something of a spectator sport, and Vittore's comments about my nationality were the comedic interlude.

It was their laughter that persuaded me to carry on. Another weakness: to be provoked by the ridicule of others. I should have left the tavern there and then. I should have cut my losses and run, but instead, I became determined to win all my money back from Vittore. To watch the men of this tavern laugh at his misfortune instead of mine.

It was Vittore who stopped the game in the end. I would tell you that he felt sorry for me – but, in hindsight, I believe he was just protecting his winnings. He knew that a victor should not obliterate his opponent, for fear of never receiving his money. He didn't want to find my body, and his debt, washed up in a canal the next day. I owed a lot to Vittore, but not so much that I would give up hope completely. He wasn't to know the truth. That I could not draw down another *soldino* from my Letter of Credit. That I had thrown away a fortune on dice.

I left the inn in a daze. In my pouch was a square of parchment that I had signed under the menacing eyes of Vittore's two rough-looking friends. Vittore had an identical copy. On both these documents I had written the words: 'I, Oswald de Lacy, Lord Somershill of Kent, owe forty ducats to my friend, Vittore Grimani. Payable within a week and one day.'

I had no idea how I would find this sum. No idea at all. At first, Vittore had asked me to pay the following morning, but I had managed to negotiate a little more time to settle my debt, claiming that my money changer would need longer to come up with such a sum. But one week and one day was hardly long enough to conjure up forty ducats that I didn't own. And yet I knew what would happen to me if I couldn't pay. Vittore's companions had made this very clear.

I left Castello, needing to get away from the crowds of the *Giovedi Grasso* and to find a silent place where I could think. How could I extricate myself from this predicament? As I sped through the streets in a panic, ideas spun through my head and were dismissed as soon as they appeared. Perhaps Mother had some jewellery that I could sell, though she had left most of her best pieces at home, for fear of being robbed by bandits. Or perhaps I could borrow the money? I had heard rumours that a Jew was secretly practising usury on the island of Giudecca. It was a good enough idea in principle, but this man would require security against any advance. And what security did I have to offer? My clothes were old-fashioned, and my sword was blunt. I might raise a ducat or two if I were lucky.

And then, as I fought my way through the crooked and unpredictable streets of San Marco, I felt something following me, scampering along in the dimness, always on the periphery of my vision. I moved faster, so that it could not catch up with me, for I knew what it was. After many weeks of freedom from its unwelcome company, it had found me again.

When I reached the courtyard of Ca' Bearpark I threw myself down upon the bench beneath the budding fig tree, and dared not look up from my hands. I felt that it was near to me now, creeping towards me across the stones, wanting to touch me with its fingers, so I closed my eyes and concentrated. At first I just wanted it to leave, but as I pushed it from my mind an idea began to form in its place – and it was a good idea. It was a solution to my problem. There was somebody who might lend me money to pay off Vittore's debt without security. The sum I needed was extremely large, but this person was my friend, and would understand my predicament. He would not lose out from this arrangement, as I would promise to repay my debt with a generous excess, as soon as I got back to England . . . whenever that might be.

I smiled at the cleverness of this idea, because I knew he would help me. He was my friend. But the next time I saw Enrico Bearpark, he was dead.

Chapter Five

All thoughts of Vittore and my debt receded, as I raised the alarm – calling for the servants of Ca' Bearpark to come quickly as their master had been murdered. Somehow I had recognised my friend Enrico, as he lay on the steps to the water gate, even though his poor, mutilated face had resembled the most grotesque of carnival masks. As the men and women of the household answered my call, I realised that the doors to the water gate were open, when they should have been closed and locked for the night. Leaning out to look up and down the canal, I could just see a hooded man clinging to the outside wall of the house. The light was poor and his hood remained pulled over his head, but I caught a brief glimpse of his profile before he sidled along the ledge to make his escape.

I clung onto the metal curls of the water gate, swung myself onto the same ledge, and then gave chase until he reached a bridge at the turn of the canal, after which he disappeared into an alley. I hauled myself up onto this same bridge and then pursued him along the pinched streets, thin bridges, and covered passageways of this *sestiere* – but my efforts were in vain, for he knew these paths, and I did not. It was not long before I had both lost my quarry, and my way.

I sank down against a damp wall to catch my breath, and it was then that the reality of Enrico's murder truly struck me. My first reaction was a blow of sadness – but I'm ashamed to say that another ignoble thought quickly intruded into my mind – that I could no longer ask my friend to lend me money. As I tried to shake this dishonourable idea from my head, I noticed a group of ragged children staring at me from the shelter of a nearby door- way. It was time to leave, for whilst I didn't dress with the usual flamboyancy and excess of the typical Venetian, the quality and style of my clothes still marked me out as a wealthy man. A person who should not have been hanging around in this dirty alley at this time of night.

I stood up, but the children had crept towards me and were now blocking my exit. As the tallest boy advanced, I grabbed him by the ear without warning. For a slight, undernourished child, he was surprisingly strong – squirming like a piglet to be rid of me. His ragged friends held back, not knowing whether to run away or come to their companion's aid. It would not be long before these same children roused some older ruffians who would pose a much greater risk, so I whis- pered to the boy in Venetian – telling him that he must lead me to Ca' Bearpark, where I would reward him with a *soldino*. Lead me into danger, I warned him, and I would pull the ear from his head.

At this proposal, he ceased wriggling and then looked me in the face, as if sizing up the true weight behind my threat. Despite the fact that I still held him by the ear, he guessed rightly that he held the advantage, for he asked for two *soldini*, and I had no choice but to agree. Once the deal was struck, he then led me at a great pace through the back alleys of San Marco until we finally reached the street entrance to Ca' Bearpark – just a plain door in a plain facade, without the opulence and ostentation of the house's water gate. When the boy demanded his fee, I told him to stay where he was, promising to return immediately. He was suspicious, of course, but what else could I do? I had no money to my name, not even the smallest coin.

The house was in uproar as I entered. Servants were running up and down the stairs with lanterns, and I could hear a wailing from the depths of the building. Mother stopped me in the hall, dressed in her white linen bed chemise – her hair was wild and loose. 'Enrico Bearpark has been murdered,' she told me.

'Yes, I know. I found his body by the water gate.'

I tried to sidestep Mother, but she succeeded in blocking my path by swiftly placing her hand against the wall. 'What happened to him?'

'I don't know,' I said, as I gently removed her arm and then pushed past, only stopping when I remembered that the boy outside was still waiting for his money. 'I need you to do me a favour, Mother.'

She folded her arms suspiciously. 'Oh yes?'

'There is a group of children outside. I need you to give them two *soldini*.'

She gave me a strange, bewildered look. 'Why?'

'Please, Mother. Just do it. I'll tell you why later.'

'Where are you going?' she called after me.

I chose not to answer.

I experienced some difficulty in getting past the guard at the door from the courtyard to the water gate. Beyond him was a noisy confusion of shouting and rushing feet, and it was only when I called for Bearpark's clerk, Giovanni, that I was allowed entry to this part of the house. I had guessed that Giovanni would be at the centre of this melee, given that his sleeping quarters were near to the gate, but I had not expected to see John Bearpark there as well. I thought the old man might have been spared the sight of his grandson, but instead Enrico's dead body had been pulled up the steps, and was now laid out upon the marble floor, his face turned up to the ceiling. Thankfully somebody had thought to place a length of silk over his battered head, hiding the cruelty of his death from the eyes of those about.

Bearpark squatted on a barrel near the body, with his wrinkled hands dug into the loose skin of his cheeks.

'I'm sorry,' I volunteered, not knowing what else to say.

Bearpark tried to press his tears away with his fingers, before clearing his throat with some determination. 'The servants told me that it was you who found Enrico. Is that true?' he said, his words a rasping whisper.

'I heard a noise at the water gate. But, when I got here, I—' I wasn't sure how to continue, so I bowed my head, in what felt like an apology. 'I found Enrico. He was dead.'

Bearpark wiped another tear away. 'I understand you chased somebody along the canal?'

'Yes, that's right.'

'Did you catch the fellow?'

I shook my head. 'No. He escaped.'

Bearpark covered his face again with his hands, and I had to draw close to hear his words. 'Did you recognise him?' he asked.

Once again I shook my head.

An awkward silence followed, punctuated only by Bearpark's heavy, laboured breathing. I wanted to comfort the old man, though I doubted my sympathy would be welcome, so I remained at his side until Mother appeared.

'You poor man,' she said, before placing her hand upon Bearpark's shoulder. I could see that her attentions were neither welcome nor comforting, but Bearpark couldn't muster the energy to rebuff her.

Mother then clicked her fingers in the air, as if a servant might appear. 'This man needs some brandy,' she shouted to nobody in particular. 'And a bone broth. Look at the pallor in your master's face. He's as white as a corpse.'

In truth, Bearpark was a good deal pinker on hearing this word, so before Mother could make any further unfortunate remarks, I encouraged her to leave.

'Perhaps you should go to the kitchen, Mother?' I said. 'You could instruct the cook to prepare a suitable dish.'

She shook her head. 'No, no. I'm needed here, Oswald.' Now she whispered. 'And where to goodness is Monna Filomena? You'd think she'd be at her husband's side after such a terrible disaster, wouldn't you?'

I manoeuvred her away from Bearpark. 'Why don't you go and find Monna Filomena?' I said tactfully. 'Perhaps nobody has told her what's happened.'

Mother shrugged me away. 'How could the woman be ignorant of this murder? The whole household is awake.'

'She might be concerned for her child. It is due soon and such a shock can send a woman into labour.'

Mother hesitated and drummed her fingers together as if giving my suggestion great thought. 'No,' she said at length. 'I shall go to the kitchens instead and have them prepare a dish. In times like this, an Englishman needs English food.'

With Mother's departure, I turned back to John Bearpark. Tears now streamed down his cheeks, making forked channels across his freckled skin. Once again I guessed that my sympathy would not be welcome, so I took a lantern and then stooped next to Enrico's body, shooing away a couple of the servants. Pulling back the silk, I looked again upon my friend's face – though this time without the shock that had accompanied my first examination.

From the condition of his face, it was clear that Enrico had been involved in a fight, but when I looked at his hands, I found no scratching or bruising upon his fists. His skin was cold to the touch, and, though there was some stiffness to his face and shoulders, the rest of his body remained slack – suggesting that he must have died a few hours ago, rather than being killed in the moments before I found his body.

I wanted to study the injuries to his chest, for this assault had not been confined to his face and head. When I lifted the silk back further, I could see great patches of blood staining his linen shirt. I pulled down at his collar in order to look further, when a hand pressed itself into my shoulder.

'God's bones, de Lacy! What are you doing?' It was Bearpark. 'Leave my grandson alone.'

'I only wanted to look at his injuries,' I protested.

'Enrico's dead! Is that not enough for you?' Bearpark's nostrils flared. 'Have some respect!'

I replaced the silk gently and stood up. 'I apologise. I didn't intend to upset you.'

Bearpark's anger subsided as abruptly as it had erupted. Now he placed his hands over his face and openly wept. The sobs echoed about the chamber, springing back at us from the stone walls, and then settling on the water. Outside, a thin light indicated that it was nearly dawn, and the early morning boats were beginning to make their way along the canal. When I noticed a passing oarsman straining to look inside the house, I quickly called the servants to move Enrico's body out of view, and then to shut and lock the gates.

When I turned back to look into the room, Filomena had joined us, passing Enrico's body with a short gasp, before she clutched her husband's head to her breast and let him sob into her chest. I had never seen any tenderness between this pair previously, and the sight of their embrace shocked me.

I left the room in haste, and tried to cast the image from my mind, but it continued to trouble me as I climbed the stairs to my bedchamber. I couldn't say why exactly, but their intimacy had upset me.

Chapter Six

A strange, exhausted sleep found me, leaving me to dream that I was trapped inside my own coffin, whilst somebody hammered nails into the lid. I woke to discover Mother knocking insistently at the door.

'Come quickly please, Oswald,' she called. 'It's urgent.'

'All right, all right. I'm coming,' I said, placing my tired feet to the cold terrazzo, and then opening the door a crack.

'You must come to speak with Master Bearpark,' she told me, trying to push her way in. 'He's calling for you.'

I closed the door before Mother could make another attempt to barge past, quickly threw on some clothes and then descended the narrow staircase to the *piano nobile*, where Bearpark sat stiffly in his carved chair – waiting for my arrival with his hands clasped around the curled arms of the seat, as if he somehow feared falling forward. Despite my hope that Mother might decline to join this conversation, she had followed me into the room, with no indication that she might leave. Filomena still attended her husband, but as I approached, Bearpark dismissed her so rudely with a flick of his hand that I could not help but give a loud puff of disapproval.

As Filomena passed me, she took the trouble to catch my eye with a fleeting nod of thanks. I felt a short surge of pleasure at this, for the young woman usually ignored me, scorning all my attempts to communicate, but unfortunately Bearpark had also noticed her gesture, despite not wearing his spectacles. 'Go on, get out of here,' he shouted at his wife. 'Be quick about it!'

At this order, Filomena cast her eyes to the floor and then scurried from the room, whilst I made the mistake of turning to watch her leave.

'She carries my child, Lord Somershill,' said Bearpark, when I looked back. This sounded decidedly like a threat, but given that the old man had lost his grandson only the night before, I decided not to respond.

I shook Filomena from my thoughts and cleared my throat. 'You asked to speak with me,' I said.

He wiped his brow. The tears from the previous night might have ceased, but his eyes were still red-rimmed and watery. 'I apologise for my sharpness when we last met, Lord Somershill. I was overwhelmed with grief.'

I bowed. 'No apology is needed.'

He reached out to a side table, felt about for his spectacles and then balanced the device carefully onto the bridge of his nose. The thick glass magnified each of his eyeballs, giving him the curious, bulging gaze of a frog.

A long silence then followed, which I felt obliged to end. 'So. Have you informed the local constable of Enrico's death?' I said, at length.

Bearpark responded to my question with a scathing huff. 'This is not England, Lord Somershill. There are no constables in Venice.'

'But you must report the murder to somebody?'

He only shrugged by way of an answer.

'I'm sure Master Bearpark will inform the relevant parties, Oswald,' said Mother. 'You've no need to worry in that regard.'

Bearpark turned his head with a sudden twist, so violent that it dislodged the spectacles from his nose, and caused them to fall onto the floor. 'Indeed I will not!'

'Oh yes?' said Mother, somewhat surprised by his reaction. 'Do murders not matter in this city then?'

Bearpark paused, regaining his composure before he wiped a wrinkled hand about his face, carefully mopping the sweat from his skin. 'Venice is not like England, my lady.'

Mother exchanged a glance with me. 'But surely somebody will care about your grandson's murder, John?' she said, reaching down to pick up the spectacles from the floor, and then passing them back to Bearpark with great caution, as if she might provoke his anger again.

Bearpark did not restore the spectacles to his nose. Instead, he let them rest in his lap, as he heaved a great sigh. 'There is a war against Hungary, my lady, so who will care about poor Enrico's murder? You must understand that.'

Mother would not admit defeat so easily, however. 'Surely not? The Bearparks are a good family. Citizens of Venice.'

'My family is above the mob, that's true. But we're not named in the Golden Book.' His hands tightened over the carved knuckles of the seat, causing his veins to stand out in long, crooked channels.

'What Golden Book?' said Mother. 'I've never heard of such a thing.'

'It's a list of the oldest and most noble families in Venice,' said Bearpark. 'You may only sit on the Great Council of Venice if your family is named in this book.'

Mother regarded the old man quizzically, as if he might have invented this fact. 'Then you should have your name added, John. After all, you donated your best ship to this city, didn't you? How else would they have disposed of the Plague dead? That must count in your favour?'

'You cannot just have your name added,' snapped Bearpark. 'The membership has been closed to new families for seventy years.'

Mother gave a long shake of her head. 'What an inequitable system,' she said, as if she had never supported the concept of an elite. 'But even so. A murder is a murder, John. No matter if you are named in some foolish book or not.'

'How many times must I repeat myself? Nobody will care,' said Bearpark in a thunderous voice, before rising unsteadily to his feet, and knocking his spectacles once again to the floor. 'My grandson's murderer will be brought to justice, have no fear. But I will do it myself.' He then wagged his finger at the two of us. 'You must not speak to anybody about Enrico's death. Do you understand?'

'If that's what you want, Bearpark,' I said, not managing to hide my affront at his tone.

'I would like to keep this tragedy quiet, that's all,' he said quickly, realising that he had caused offence. 'Until I've started my investigation.'

These words caused Mother to clap her hands. 'Well now, John, if you're conducting an investigation, then you must use our great investigator.'

I felt a tightening in my shoulders, and my heart began to thump. I tried to indicate that I didn't want her to say another word, but Mother was staring fixedly at Bearpark.

'Investigator?' said Bearpark, looking at Mother disbelievingly. 'What investigator?'

'Why, he stands in front of you,' said Mother, pointing to me with something of a dramatic flourish. 'It is my son Oswald, of course.'

Bearpark turned to me, wide-eyed. 'Lord Somershill is an investigator?'

Mother nodded enthusiastically. 'Indeed, he is famed for it. He has even come to the attention of the king himself.'

I picked up Bearpark's spectacles from the floor, so that neither of them would see my face redden. 'Please don't exaggerate Mother,' I said, passing the glass contraption back into Bearpark's limp hand.

'You see how modest he is,' said Mother. 'Yet he has solved the mystery of many, many murders about the Somershill estate.

Not to mention the killing of his own sister's husband, Walter de Caburn. But I expect you have heard of that particular case, John?' She poked a stray hair under her veil. 'Yes, indeed. The murder of Lord Versey is very well known in England.' She cleared her throat, in order to underline her next statement. 'Amongst our circle, at least.'

Bearpark lifted the spectacles to his nose, peering at me curiously through the disconcerting circles of glass. 'Is that why you were examining Enrico's body?' he said. 'Because of your interest in mysteries?'

I coughed. This room was stuffy for once, as a fire had been burning in the hearth since dawn. 'I only wanted to understand how Enrico died,' I said quickly. 'I thought you could convey my thoughts to—' Once again, I wanted to say *to the constable*. 'To whomever might be interested,' I said instead.

Bearpark held my gaze. 'Tell me. I'm interested.'

I coughed a second time. 'If you're sure.'

He grunted. 'I just said I was, didn't I?'

'Very well then,' I said with some hesitation. 'Enrico was badly beaten before death. Perhaps even tortured.'

The old man's face fell. 'Tortured?' He paused to catch his breath. 'Are you sure about that?'

I nodded awkwardly, regretting having used the word.

'We didn't hear anything?' he said. 'This house is large, but I have many servants. Surely someone would have heard such an assault?'

'But it was *Giovedi Grasso*,' I answered. 'So perhaps the noise of the carnival drowned out the sounds of an attack?' I said. 'And don't forget that most of your servants were allowed to attend the carnival, so there were fewer people than usual in the house.'

Bearpark sank back into his chair, scratching at his forehead with his twisted hands. 'I still can't believe it,' he blustered. 'Not in my own house. I was here all day with Monna Filomena, and we heard nothing.'

'Did you fall asleep at any point?' I asked.

'No! Of course not,' he roared. 'I never fall asleep in the daytime.' I didn't dare to disagree.

''Tis a shame that I was not here then,' said Mother, with her usual talent for poor timing. 'For there is little that misses my ears.' Then she folded her arms petulantly. 'But I was forced to spend all day at the carnival with that pair of clot-poles, Bernard and Margery.'

'You wanted to go,' I said with some frustration. 'You made quite a fuss about it, if you remember?'

Bearpark ignored Mother's interjection and held his head and groaned. 'I can't believe that my own grandson was tortured and murdered here. In my own house.'

'There is another possibility,' I said quickly. 'The attack happened elsewhere, and Enrico's body was returned to Ca' Bearpark. Probably by the man I chased away from the water gate.'

Bearpark looked up at me. 'Why would anybody do that?' he said. 'Surely a murderer would try to hide his victim?'

'Perhaps this man wasn't the murderer then?' I suggested. 'It's possible that he only found Enrico's body, and thought it should be returned? Perhaps he is even a friend of Enrico's.'

'Then why did he run away when you called to him?' said Bearpark, shaking his head. 'It doesn't make sense.'

'People often flee in such circumstances,' I said. 'Even if they are completely innocent.'

'Then it's a pity you did not catch him, Lord Somershill. He could have answered these questions.' The old man reclined in his chair and looked upward, in an attempt to hide more tears. 'So. Will you help me to find Enrico's murderer?' he said, once he had wiped his face clean again with his hand.

I had problems of my own, without the distraction of an investigation. 'I can't,' I said 'I'm sorry.'

Bearpark fixed me with a glare. 'I see,' he said, his voice now spiked with affront. 'My grandson was not known to the King of England. Is that it?'

'No,' I said quickly. 'I'm just concerned that we may have to leave for Jerusalem at any moment, and I wouldn't wish to start something that I couldn't finish.'

Mother interrupted. 'What nonsense, Oswald. You know, full well, that there's no settlement between Venice and Hungary.' I went to reply, but she didn't give me the opportunity. 'Even if the war were to end tomorrow, the galley masters will not sail the pilgrim ships until all of their boats are full. Which may not happen until April at the earliest.' She stopped briefly for breath. 'You know what these captains are like. They keep everybody waiting, and will only set off for Jaffa in one of their convoys.'

She cast me a bewildered glance as I attempted to pull her to one side. 'It's been a long time since I've investigated a murder, Mother,' I whispered. 'I'm not sure that I possess the skills any longer.'

Mother had no intention of keeping this conversation private. 'Nonsense again, Oswald,' she said loudly. 'You haven't lost the ability to find a killer. Look at you.' She poked a finger into my chest. 'Racing to be the first to look upon the dead body. Chasing a man from the murder scene. Drawing conclusions from a few scratches and a tiny spot of blood.'

'Anybody could look upon Enrico's body and conclude that he had been tortured, Mother. It does not take the skills of a genius.'

Mother folded her arms. 'Don't be so sure, Oswald. Your mind is quite unlike anybody's I have ever known. Sharp as the blade of a falchion.' Then she gave a despairing sigh. 'Even though you deny yourself enough food and sleep. A man cannot survive on watery broth and a few shavings of hard cheese, you know.'

Bearpark interrupted. 'So, will you help me, or not, Lord Somershill?'

'Of course he will.' Mother glared at me. 'Won't you, Oswald?' Mother took my hand, and this time she did succeed in whispering. 'For the sake of Christ. Say that you'll do it. The poor man is desperate.'

'I can't,' I said weakly, before turning my back and heading for the stairs to my bedchamber. How could I undertake a murder investigation at such a time as this, even if the victim had been a friend of mine? I felt guilty for refusing to help, but I needed to concentrate on finding the funds to repay my colossal debt to a man who would not listen to excuses. It was Vittore's face that came to mind, as I placed my foot upon the bottom tread of the staircase. How well I remembered the smug flush upon his ruddy, porcine cheeks as I had signed my foolish letter, declaring that I owed him forty ducats. Forty! At the thought of this sum, my legs felt weak and my bowels began to loosen. How, in the name of Christ and all the angels and archangels of Heaven, was I to find such an amount? And if I couldn't conjure up this money, then I had a clear enough idea of the consequences. It was then, as I began to climb the stairs, that a thought occurred to me. I would never have asked under usual circumstances, but desperation is a piercing spur.

I cleared my throat, turned around and made my way back across the room to Bearpark. 'Of course, I could undertake the investigation for a fee,' I said, aware that Mother was glaring at me in stupefied shock. Nevertheless, I would not be deterred from continuing. This was a good idea. Or, at least, it was the only idea I had. 'I always charge for my services as an investigator,' I added, at which point Mother's jaw nearly dropped onto her chin.

Bearpark was not shocked, however. Instead he regarded me with something of a wry smile. He had been a merchant for long enough to know an opportunist when he saw one. 'Is that so, Lord Somershill?'

I struggled to hold my nerve. 'My mother was correct,' I said. 'I am an experienced investigator, but this would be a difficult case.' I coughed to disguise a sudden urge to laugh, such was the absurdity of my lie. 'There has to be some compensation for such danger,' I added.

Bearpark's smile faded. His tongue moved about inside his cheeks while he studied my face. I expected him to demand an apology for my impertinence, or to ask me to get out of his sight. Instead he laid his hands in his lap. 'Ah yes. Danger.' He paused for a while, and sucked at his lips. 'Very well,' he said, drumming his fingers against his legs. 'I'm not averse to your proposal. In principle.' Mother tried to interrupt, but Bearpark silenced her with a raised hand. 'I could use the skills of a young man.' He leant forward and fixed me with a stare, his eyes rheumy and bloodshot. 'It will take a young man to find Enrico's murderer.'

I had to stop myself from cheering, for, against all of my expectations, this foolish gamble had paid off. 'We would have to discuss the fee, of course,' I said quickly. 'I can guarantee a successful outcome, but my charges are not insignificant.'

'Oh, you will be paid well enough,' said Bearpark with a sniff. 'Have no fear on that account.' He hesitated, before straightening his tunic and putting his hand to his chest. His voice was now a low croak. 'Draw nearer,' he said, 'there is something you should know, before you agree.'

'Oh yes?' I said, now feeling a little apprehensive.

Bearpark cast a glance towards Mother, and then pulled me to within inches of his mouth, allowing me no escape from the sourness of his breath. 'Come back later alone,' he said, 'we'll discuss it then.'

As Mother and I left the room, Filomena hurried past us, only risking another stolen glimpse when her husband wasn't looking. This time I read something different in her eyes – not thanks this time, but apprehension, and suddenly I had the feeling that she had listened to our conversation from wherever she had been hiding. And, though she claimed to speak no English, she had understood every word.

While I waited for this next audience and the agreement of my fee with Bearpark, I started my investigation – there was no time to sit around and be idle, for I had seven days left to repay my debt, and no more. I began by interviewing members of the Bearpark household, in the hope of speaking to the last person to have seen Enrico alive. It seemed the obvious place to start, so I interviewed every valet, lady's maid, scullion, groom, and cook in the house, though they each told me the same tale. Enrico had returned to Ca' Bearpark directly after I had seen him in the Calle Nuova the previous morning. He had eaten a late breakfast of stale bread and olive oil, before retiring to his bedchamber in order to catch up on the sleep he had clearly missed the night before. Because it had been the day of *Giovedi Grasso*, nobody had checked his room, nor offered him a meal later that day. The servants were embarrassed, even sheepish about this admission, as somebody in the household should have looked in upon their master, but it seemed that the carnival had taken precedence over their duties, and they had completely forgotten about him. So, after his sighting at breakfast, Enrico's day was somewhat shrouded in mystery.

My next step was to search Enrico's bedchamber, finding nothing of interest except his collection of fine clothes. It was upsetting to handle these garments. Tunics, capes, and fitted cotehardies of silk, velvet, and leather, each decorated with golden threads, brocades, and embroidery – clothes that I had often seen my friend wear. Once I put such gloomy thoughts aside, I remembered instead that Enrico had been dressed in only a simple linen chemise and a pair of hose when I found him at the water gate, leaving me to wonder if he could have left the house at all between his last sighting by the servants and my discovery of his body. If Enrico had left Ca' Bearpark, then his clothing must have been removed, or even stolen from his body before it was returned.

I called for Enrico's valet, asking the man to look through his master's wardrobe to see if anything was missing, but this man had only recently been appointed, and seemed to know so little that our conversation was pointless. Having dismissed the fellow, I remained in the room in the hope that some obvious clue would present itself. The chamber was fresh with the smell and spirit of Enrico – as if he might appear at any moment, in one of his fine outfits, and laugh at me for having been gulled by an elaborate hoax. Just the sort of joke to amuse his friend on a carnival night. I smiled at this thought, before the reality of his murder stung sharply at my breast. This was no trick, and all that was left of Enrico's young and vibrant life was an empty, melancholic room. I left immediately, for this was the type of place where my shadow could easily be found.

I then concentrated my search in the warren of chambers that were located on the ground floor of Ca' Bearpark, beyond the water gate. My own feeling was that Enrico had been murdered somewhere in this house, despite Bearpark's assertion that this could not have happened. I believed that the man I had chased from the water gate was Enrico's killer, not a kind Samaritan who was returning a dead friend to his family. If nothing else, then how could he have transported the body to Ca' Bearpark, other than by the canal? And yet he had fled on foot, leaving no abandoned boat. And yet, on the other hand, if this man was the murderer, then why had he been lurking by the water gate so long after the murder? By the temperature and stiffness of the corpse, Enrico had been dead for at least two hours when I found him.

I decided to put these thoughts to one side and concentrate upon finding a secluded spot where Enrico could have been tortured and killed, hoping to find bloodstains or some other obvious signs of violence on a floor or wall. At this lowest level, Ca' Bearpark was a sprawling and incomprehensible building, and it was easy to become disorientated in the dark passageways that lay beneath the house like a network of burrows. The servants' quarters lay beyond the water gate, and beyond this cramped accommodation was a network of storerooms designed to hold Bearpark's stock. There was a lingering scent of cloves and cinnamon in these rooms, but otherwise the shelves themselves were empty.

As I made my way into the furthest chambers, I had the impression of walking gradually downwards, as the floor sloped and the ceilings became lower. I held my lantern aloft, and made my way into the very last room at the end of a passageway, where Enrico's body was laid out upon a table, awaiting his burial. He was attended by one of the oldest servants in the house – a woman who sat in near darkness with only a small smoking candle as company. A long black veil nearly obscured her face, and her hands held a rosary.

I was a guest in this house and known to this woman, and yet she was still reluctant to allow me to examine Enrico's body. When I ignored her objections and lifted the silk veil from his face, she babbled some rebuke at me before grasping the length of cloth from my hands and returning it to its previous position. I tried politeness and my clearest Venetian to reassure her of my good intentions, but when this approach had repeatedly failed, I spoke harshly and told her to let me continue, or leave the room. She chose the latter option, shuffling away angrily, whilst declaiming the ungodliness of the English and their allegiance to the Devil.

Now I found myself alone with Enrico's body, and suddenly my resolve to continue this investigation waned, for the thing that lay before me had once been my friend, and now what was it? Nothing but a slab of skin, hair, fat, and bone. I took a deep

breath and told myself to be stronger. I had the chance to examine Giovanni's body a second time, before it was taken away for
burial, and I needed to take full advantage of this opportunity.
Where they would bury his body, I could not say – given
Bearpark's insistence upon keeping Enrico's murder quiet, so
they could hardly dig up the floor of the nearest church and place
him alongside the other dead of this *sestiere*.

I put this thought to one side, for a good death was not a
preoccupation that I shared. I had seen enough bodies thrown
into pits during the years of the Great Plague, to know that, if
there is a God, then He will accept you, no matter where or how
you are buried. For my own part, I hoped only to nourish the
roots of a tree, or the flowers of a meadow with my earthly
remains. I came from the earth and would return to it. As food
for the worms.

Now alone with the body, I lifted the silk veil again to find that
Enrico was still dressed in the same chemise and hose that he had
been wearing at his death, and I guessed that the women of the
household had been unable to undress him before his body had
become too stiff to handle. They had made an attempt to clean
away the blood from his clothing at least, but the white linen of
his chemise remained stained with red. His corpse was not yet
stinking, but the fishy, fermenting odour of death still reached
my nostrils with its unique perfume. This was a scent that I had
not smelt for many years, but I recognised it from my days at the
monastery, when I had prepared the dead of our brotherhood for
burial. Because of this work, I understood each stage of death
intimately – from the first flaccid heaviness of the body before
the rigid constrictions of rigor mortis sets in, through to the
final bloated distortion as the flesh begins to slip from the bone.
Death held no fear or disgust for me. In fact, I might say I found
it comforting. For each of us will end this way, no matter who we
are and how we live.

I worked quickly now, in case the old woman returned, noting the placing of Enrico's bruises and cuts. The injuries were mainly to his chest and face, suggesting that he had been punched repeatedly. Some of his teeth were missing, and there was matted blood in his hair – though once again the women had also made an effort to wash this viscous mess away from his scalp. And then I noticed something that was so obvious that I should have seen it before. When I had discovered Enrico's body on the steps to the water gate, it had only been his boots that were trailing into the water of the canal, but now I could see that his hose was wet too, right to the top of his legs. My next task was not pleasant, but had to be undertaken. I pressed my nose against the weave of the wool, needing to be certain that Enrico had not simply wet himself upon death, as I knew, from experience, that the body will release its fluids as soon as the spirit flees. But this was definitely water and nothing else.

I was replacing the silk veil upon Enrico's face when I heard footsteps echoing along the stone floor of the passageway outside, and I expected to be confronted at any moment by the truculent old woman – but it was Bernard, the English pilgrim, who appeared through the gloom. For once he was alone, and more unusually still, he began our conversation by saying something that made sense.

'I was so sorry to hear of young Master Bearpark's death,' he said, as he strained to look over my shoulder. 'Is that his body?'

'It is.'

'May I see it?' he asked. When I hesitated at this request, he added. 'I came to pray for his soul, and to pin our most precious pilgrim's badge to his chest.' Bernard waved a small pewter circle under my nose – a badge that carried the image of two bent-backed pilgrims leaning against their staffs as they trudged towards a distant shrine. 'I chose this one, as I imagined that it looks a little like Margery and myself,' he said, before looking back over his shoulder. 'Margery will be here soon. She's bringing her miraculous water of Saint Thomas to douse upon Enrico's face.'

'Enrico is beyond a miracle,' I said tersely. 'Unless this water has the powers of resurrection?'

Bernard smiled in some confusion at my answer. 'But Margery purchased this water in Canterbury, my lord. It contains a drop of blood from poor Saint Thomas's wound.' He sighed. 'Such an appalling crime. To be murdered in the house of God.'

'I'll leave you to your prayers,' I said, feeling irritated that Bernard was lamenting the murder of Thomas Becket nearly two centuries previously, when a young man lay dead in front of him in the present day.

At my attempt to depart, Bernard's face suddenly stiffened, and his eyes focussed. 'I understand that you're investigating the murder, Lord Somershill?'

'That's correct,' I said, a little surprised that this information had already reached Bernard's ears.

'Have you discovered the identity of the murderer yet?' he asked.

'No,' I said, almost wanting to laugh. 'I've only just begun the investigation.'

'Of course not. How foolish of me to ask.' He looked to the ceiling and began to bite his fingernails. 'I'm just so concerned for my sister's safety, Lord Somershill. As you must be for your own mother's. To think that there might be a murderer in our midst.'

'You need not worry. I'm sure that nobody else in the household is in danger.'

He frowned. 'I do hope so, my lord.' He then held his pilgrim's badge aloft. 'May I?'

I decided to wait as Bernard lifted the silk from Enrico's face and studied my friend's mutilated features at length before placing his badge gently upon his chest. 'When did you last see Enrico?' I asked, remembering that I had not yet interviewed Bernard.

'Now let me see,' he said, scratching his head. 'It must have been the day or so before *Giovedi Grasso*.' He smiled absentmindedly. 'My sister and I kept very different hours to young Master Bearpark, my lord. Our paths rarely crossed.'

'What time did you return with my mother from the carnival?'

Once again he scratched his head, more vigorously this time, as if friction would spark a memory. 'It was later than I would have liked, but there was so much that your mother wanted to see. Poor Margery was exhausted, and could barely lift her feet up the stairs.'

'What time, Bernard?'

He stared at the ceiling pensively. 'I believe it was after supper and before the bells struck for Compline, but perhaps you should ask your mother?' He gave a defeated sigh. 'She was a good deal more lively than we, after a day at the carnival.'

I smiled at this thought, for my mother was years older than these two. 'Did you hear anything upon your return? Any disturbances in the house?'

'Indeed not,' said Bernard. 'Ca' Bearpark was a peaceful sanctuary after all the commotion of the carnival. Margery and I went straight to our beds and didn't hear a thing.'

This was a fruitless conversation, so I bade Bernard good day and turned to leave – but as I walked into the passageway an unexpected draught of air tickled my skin and caused me to stop. Holding my hand aloft to trace its source, I found that it was seeping from the edges of a thick rug that was hung upon the wall to my side. I patted this rug, expecting to feel a hard surface beneath its woollen weave, but instead it gave way, and I realised that the rug was covering a void. I pulled back one of the edges and held my lantern aloft to see a short, dark passageway before me that ended in a door. A dank and fetid smell filled the air, and explained why this passageway had been screened.

I was curious, so I stepped through, making my way towards the small door at the other end, soon discovering that I was standing in a shallow puddle. I cursed out loud and was about to retrace my steps, but the door at the end of the passage had intrigued me. It was reduced in scale, as if it had been designed for a child. I looked for a latch, but found only the nails of an escutcheon plate and a large keyhole, into which I was able to squeeze my little finger. A push at the door only confirmed that it was locked. And then, somewhere in the distance, somewhere far behind this door, I heard a noise. It was a prolonged creak, like furniture being scraped across a wooden floor, followed by a slam. I pressed my ear to the surface, and tried to listen for more. Could I hear voices? The sounds were muted and warped, like listening to a conversation from behind a pillow. Was somebody locked in the chamber beyond? Or did these noises originate from upstairs in Ca' Bearpark? I strained to hear more, but nothing came to me, only the thud of my heart drumming in my ears.

It was time to leave, but as I turned, I came face to face with a pair of eyes that peered sharply at me through the darkness. I nearly yelled out, thinking that my shadow had tricked me at last – but these were human eyes.

'Giovanni?' I said.

He held up a candle to his face. 'Lord Somershill?' He looked at me with a disapproving stare. 'You mustn't come down here. The air is foulish.' He faked a cough, in order to emphasise his point.

'I was interested in this door,' I said, ignoring his linguistic error. 'Do you have the key?'

He shook his head. 'No. And my master says you must come.'

His brusqueness annoyed me. 'Is that so?' I said, holding my lantern to the small door and surveying its construction with greater scrutiny. The door was made of oiled oak, and it fitted tightly into its frame, with no gaps about the rails.

'Do you know what's behind here?' I thumped the door, making a hollow thud.

Giovanni frowned. 'It's a cesspit, my lord.' He then pointed to his feet. 'See. The water sometimes creeps through into this passage. That's why we don't come here.' He turned to leave, as if expecting me to join him, but I wasn't yet finished with this conversation.

'You definitely don't have the key?' I said, refusing to move.

'Please. You must come. My—'

'But you have the keys to every other room in the house?'

'Yes. I have every key.' He then jangled the ring. 'But this room belongs to the house next door. It is not the pit for Ca' Bearpark.'

'So why is there a door on this side?'

Giovanni shrugged. 'I don't know. Perhaps it was once part of this house?'

'So, you've never been in there?'

Giovanni was becoming increasingly frustrated. 'Why would I go in there, my lord? It's a cesspit that fills with filth, until the high tides flood the chamber and take everything away.' He shuddered, as if imagining the contents of the room. 'Now please. You must come to my master's chamber.'

I folded my arms. 'Oh yes? And why is that?'

Giovanni took a deep breath. 'My master has a . . .' He put his fingers to his lips, as if this might help him to find the correct word. 'An attack in his body. A compulsion.'

'Do you mean a convulsion?'

Giovanni flared his nostrils. 'Yes. That's what I said. A compulsion. A terrible attack.'

I shouldered past him. 'Just take me to him, Giovanni.'

Chapter Seven

Bearpark's bedchamber was situated at the top of its own staircase, reached via a concealed door from the *piano nobile* — a door through which the old man liked to make a sudden and dramatic entrance, particularly if there was company in the house. As I climbed the meandering steps behind Giovanni, I had the sense that we were leaving the confines of Ca' Bearpark. My suspicions were soon proved correct — for when I looked out of a small window at a turn in the staircase, I realised that we were now standing above the first floor of the adjoining house. As ever, the crooked, jumbled architecture of Venice continued to surprise and confuse me. Bearpark must have purchased the floor from his neighbours and then built an access from his own home. Ahead of me, Giovanni waited impatiently at an elaborately carved door, as he fiddled with his ring of keys.

After we had knocked three times at this door, a servant admitted us with the hushed reverence of a monk leading an Easter procession. We stepped inside to find an airless room, even though its proportions were nearly as large as Bearpark's *piano nobile* on the floor below. The shutters were closed, and the curtains about the bedstead were half drawn. Sombre candle-light illuminated the gold-leaf motifs that were embossed into the dark red leather of the walls. And there, in the middle of this dark and strange theatre was Filomena, propped up beside her husband like an iron firedog in a hearth — straight-backed, forward-facing, and perfectly still.

I nearly gasped at seeing her face, for it was almost beatific in this low, shimmering light — the luminous, unmoving mask of the Virgin, staring at me through the dim, candlelit gloom. Behind her, the intertwining bowers and leaves of gold crawled across the walls and made this room feel like a mysterious, warped Eden. It was so strange and dreamlike that I felt like turning to leave, but suddenly my mother was at my shoulder, and there was no escape. Then a servant pulled back the curtain of the bedstead and I was called to Bearpark's side. The old man held out an aged hand, and I could not refuse to take it — though it felt like the cold, hard claw of a corpse.

'So, Lord Somershill,' he said. 'Are you still willing to undertake the investigation?' He was weak, and his voice was difficult to hear, but I saw nothing of the convulsion I had been warned to expect. Bearpark's face was animated on both sides, and did not appear to be suffering from any form of palsy. The candlelight about the bed was thin, and flickered from the faces of the gathered company. Filomena didn't join the others in looking down upon her ailing husband, however. Instead, she scrutinised me with dark eyes that never seemed to blink, in a gaze that made me feel both uncomfortable and strangely flattered.

'Of course I want to continue the investigation,' I said to Bearpark, before hesitating, for my next statement would sound avaricious, even contemptible, in the circumstances. 'Though we've yet to agree my fee, of course.'

Bearpark pulled me closer, putting his hand onto mine with a grip that was surprisingly strong. 'You'll get your fee, Lord Somershill. Don't you worry about that!' He then let go of my hand. 'But first you must know the true nature of this investigation. In case you change your mind.'

'I won't change my mind,' I said. 'I can guarantee it.'

He gave a dry laugh. 'Oh you might do, when you hear what I've got to say.' Bearpark then squinted at the crowd that had gathered about his bed. 'Get rid of them,' he said. 'All of them.' Following his instructions, I encouraged Filomena and the various servants to move to the other end of the chamber, though Giovanni and my mother were harder to remove from the bedside – and it was only when Bearpark gathered the strength to bellow at them, that they complied with the request.

I then pulled up a stool and sat beside the old man, trying to remain upwind from his breath. 'So, Bearpark. What is it that you want to tell me?' I said, feeling like a priest at confession.

He motioned to the side table. 'Pass me my spectacles.'

I did as he asked and helped to settle them upon his nose – waiting as he blinked until he was able to focus. 'Enrico was a good boy,' he told me, his voice still shaking. 'I loved him dearly.'

'Of course,' I said.

He dropped his voice, and looked about to make a final check that this conversation was private. 'But he also had secrets,' he said. 'Dangerous ones.'

'Oh yes?' I said, feeling a prickle of unease. 'What manner of secrets?'

Bearpark cleared his throat. 'I will tell you, Lord Somershill. But only because it matters to your investigation, and not because it is any business of yours otherwise.' He paused. 'But it might help you to understand why I cannot inform the authorities of Venice about Enrico's murder.' He peered at me through the spectacles. 'I know my refusal to alert them troubles you.'

'I just thought it was unusual,' I said. 'That's all.'

He made a dismissive gesture with his hand. 'You will understand my reasons well enough, when I tell you this secret.' He continued to hold my gaze. 'But first, you must promise not to tell a soul.'

I nodded.

He ran his tongue between his lips and gums before speaking. 'Very well then,' he said at length. 'I can tell you this. Enrico did not like women. He was a   ' He sighed. 'No. I will not use that word. Enrico loved men. Do you understand me?'

I thought back to my many nights out with Enrico, and was certain that I had seen him dancing and laughing with women. Then again, I had never seen him hold a woman, nor kiss her. 'Are you sure about this, Bearpark?' I said.

The old man screwed up his nose at me. 'You think I would lie to you about such a thing? It is dangerous to have Enrico's tastes in this city. You've seen the fires that the Signori di Notte light in the Piazzetta. You know what they do to such men!' His anger at my question had induced a fit of coughing that took a few moments to subside. 'Now are you quite so keen to investigate? Still willing to put yourself in peril?'

What choice did I have? I still had a debt to repay, regardless of this new complication. 'Yes. I'm not deterred,' I said.

Mother called to me from the other end of the room. 'Is everything all right over there, Oswald? Do you need some help?'

'Stay where you are please, Mother,' I said. 'There's nothing to be concerned about.' Giovanni then repeated my words loudly and self-importantly to the others in the group, as if this command had been his own.

Bearpark pointed weakly to the bowl of wine that rested on the table beside the bed. I lifted the thing to his lips, as if it were a silver chalice and I were offering him the blood of Christ. The wine dripped onto his chin and then pooled in the wrinkles of his neck, but when I tried to wipe the spill, he pushed my hand away. 'Does my story shock you, de Lacy? Do you call Enrico a sinner?'

I shook my head. 'No, Bearpark. I do not.'

'Will you run to the Signori now and tell them our secret? Causing trouble and shame for the name of Bearpark?'

'No, I will not.'

His face broke into a weak smile. 'Then you are the perfect man for this investigation. I would struggle to find Enrico's killer, but you are young, just like my grandson was. You can infiltrate his group of friends and bring me his murderer.'

'You think Enrico was murdered by a friend?'

'Not a friend, Lord Somershill. His lover.'

'Do you have evidence against this man?'

Bearpark hesitated. 'I know that he and Enrico frequently argued. And their quarrels often turned into fights.' He gave a shrug. 'You know what young lovers can be like. Their passions are easily inflamed.'

'What's this man's name?'

Bearpark shook his head. 'That's my problem, Lord Somershill. I don't know.'

'Yet you know that he frequently argued with your grandson?'

Some colour crept into Bearpark's face. 'Enrico could be very secretive, but there were times when he confided in me. He told me how this man could be jealous and vengeful.' Bearpark heaved a great sigh of regret and tightened his fists as if preparing for a fight. 'I should have forced Enrico to tell me his name. Then this mystery would be solved.' He suddenly relaxed his hands and appeared almost tearful again. 'I would search for the fellow myself, but I'm an old man and well known in this city. My investigation would only succeed in attracting the attention of the Signori di Notte.' He pointed his finger at me – its tip as rounded and flat as a wooden spoon. 'Those brutes would not care about finding Enrico's murderer. They would only be grateful that I had provided them with another victim to persecute. And I will not feed their filthy bloodlust. I will not assist their vile campaign against their fellow man!'

I bowed my head. 'That is to your credit, Bearpark,' I said, surprised and heartened by his outburst. 'But what happens when I find the murderer?' I asked.

'We will inform the courts, of course. Just as you wanted in the first place.' He coughed. 'Though we will not mention the other thing.' I went to answer, but he cut across me, anticipating my question. 'Oh, don't worry. The man will not mention it either. A murderer will hang in this city. But a sodomite is always burnt.'

I scratched the back of my neck. 'And you can tell me nothing more about him?'

He shook his head solemnly. 'Nothing, I am afraid.' The old man pulled me closer, and I was unable to avoid the pungent eddy of decay that always laced the puffs of his breath. 'Giovanni will help you with the investigation. He knows Enrico's secret, so you need not worry about betraying confidences.'

The prospect of working with Giovanni did not appeal to me in the slightest. 'No, no. I'll work faster on my own,' I said quickly.

'Nonsense. Giovanni can help you. Especially with the language.'

'But I speak good Venetian,' I said.

Bearpark laughed and then made an effort to peer at me through his spectacles in disbelief. 'Your Venetian is terrible, de Lacy.'

'I wouldn't say that.'

He raised his aged hand in an attempt to wave away my opinion. 'You take the wrong meaning. You cause offence all the time. And most importantly, you miss the detail. No, no. It will not do. This investigation needs a native Venetian speaker.'

I was insulted, and, under different circumstances, I might have insisted upon working alone, but there was still my fee to agree, so I was forced to keep Bearpark sweet.

The old man seemed to read my mind. 'So, we come to your payment,' he said. 'I propose ten ducats.'

Ten ducats. What use were ten ducats to a man who needed forty? I shook my head. 'No no. I would need at least fifty,' I said.

Bearpark's mouth hung open in genuine shock. 'Fifty? God's bones, de Lacy. I only want you to find one murderer. Not a whole gang of them!'

'I guarantee that I will find the man responsible for Enrico's murder,' I said with bravado. 'But my price is fifty ducats.'

Bearpark rubbed the wrinkled skin of his cheeks. 'Twenty.'

I needed forty ducats to cover my debts to Vittore, and a surplus to finance our journey home. 'Fifty,' I insisted.

The old man bristled with indignation. 'How can you justify such an extraordinary fee? It's outrageous.'

'That's my price, Bearpark.' I paused. 'But, of course, if you don't think that your grandson is worth such a fee, then I will bow out.'

'Now wait a minute,' said the old man, 'that's not what I mean.'

'And let's not forget that the investigation will be dangerous, Bearpark. You said so yourself. I might even come to the attention of the Signori di Notte.'

He looked me up and down. He was a trader after all, and this was just another negotiation. 'Thirty-five.' I tried to object, but he spoke over me. 'I will not pay more.'

'Forty-five.'

He heaved a great sigh. 'Very well then. Forty-five. It is absolutely my last offer.'

A spare five ducats might suffice, as long as I was careful. 'Forty-five it is.'

'Payable when you bring me the name of the murderer,' added Bearpark.

'Well, perhaps you—'

Bearpark clenched his fists and fixed me with a glare. 'The name of the murderer, de Lacy. Then you get your money.'

The group at the other end of the room was now edging closer, like a gang of nervous dogs creeping up upon a carcass, so I decided not to argue. I looked back to Bearpark, but it seemed our negotiation had exhausted the old man and he had closed his eyes, allowing his spectacles to slip down from his nose and fall onto the bed. When I went to lift them away however, he woke up and grasped my hand. 'Report to me, Lord Somershill. And me alone,' he urged, as the others came nearer. 'When you find the man, you must tell me first. Do you understand?'

I must have hesitated, for now Bearpark squeezed. His grip was firm, and I was unable to pull my hand away. 'Find Enrico's murderer,' he told me. 'Then I can die in peace.'

I looked down upon his ancient face and it was impossible to stop the thought that now intruded into my mind. Would Bearpark last long enough to pay my fee?

It had been a number of years since I had turned my mind to solving the puzzle of a murder investigation, and I will admit to being momentarily invigorated by this new challenge – but when I cast my mind back to my previous cases, my enthusiasm waned. My first investigation had involved finding the killer of two young women, and my second, the murderer of two newborn babes. Neither memory could be described as fond. Instead they invoked an old, familiar gloom, and when I retired to my room, I knew what was waiting for me – skulking in the corner and watching me with its vigilant, unblinking eyes.

I walked to my window, and tried to ignore its presence by looking out upon Venice – even though my view was restricted to the canal below and the houses on every side. On a rooftop terrace opposite, a servant was hanging wet tunics onto a long pole that she then pivoted out to lean over the canal. On the floor below, her mistress sat at a tall, arched window, reading a book while a servant combed and plaited her long hair. A finely woven Persian carpet had been hung over the low sill of this window, announcing the woman's status and the wealth to every passer-by.

When she turned to look at me, I shifted my eyes back to the canal. The dark buildings and blue sky reflected in the glassy green surface of the water. There was a tranquillity to this view, a peacefulness that was only interrupted when a small *piatta* glided past causing a series of ripples and eddies. Seated upon the crude bench of this small boat were Bernard and his sister Margery, no doubt on their way to visit yet another holy shrine of Venice. The pair had not wasted their time in this city, and were always out somewhere buying yet more relics, badges and indulgences to add to their already enormous collection. Even from my vantage point on the second floor, I could see that Bernard was staring into space, while Margery was picking at her fingernails. She looked quite relaxed, in contrast to her usual demeanour at Ca' Bearpark, when she sat stiffly at the supper table with her head bowed and her hands clasped. Now she leant against the back of the bench and let her legs spread out into the hull of the boat.

As I watched the pair drift away into the distance, I stopped daydreaming and made an effort to concentrate upon the investigation. Would I follow Bearpark's advice and start by looking for Enrico's lover? The idea made some sense, but then again, it sniffed of being too simple an explanation – relying upon hearsay and Bearpark's own conjecture, whereas I knew that murders are solved by the examination of facts. I left the window and strode about the room with purpose, deciding that I should start by writing down everything that I knew this far. What I needed was a blank manuscript – a small booklet in which to catalogue the facts I already had in my possession. A wax tablet and stylus would not suffice, for it was too small and temporary for my purposes.

Having made this decision, I walked down to the courtyard, where I found a servant and bid him go to the Rialto market on my behalf and purchase something for me to write upon. With Bearpark's criticism of my Venetian still ringing in my ears, I thought I might use this instruction as a test of my skills in this language. So I told the man specifically to buy me a pamphlet that was small and easy to hold, no larger than the average psalter. It should have at least ten leaves and be without a fancy binding or cover, so that it would not appeal to a thief. I would even accept a palimpsest, where the previous writing had been washed from the parchment with oats and milk. The man seemed to understand me well enough, and when he returned with the exact object I had described, I felt vindicated. I then sat in a corner of the *piano nobile* and thought through the events.

Enrico had been assaulted and tortured before his death. I didn't know why, and I didn't know where. I only knew two things for certain — that I had found his dead body at the water gate, and that I had chased a man from the scene. I wrote these points down in my pamphlet and stared at them for a while — thinking, at first, that they were formless and faint. But soon I realised that they raised another question. A question that should have occurred to me before all others. I tucked the pamphlet under my belt and went to seek out the man who could give me an answer.

I found Giovanni on the lower floor of the house, where he had his own small and musty chamber amongst the storerooms. This room, or 'bureau' as he liked us to call it, was lined with wooden shelves for the many records and ledgers that pertained to Bearpark's trading. At first, Giovanni seemed flustered, even annoyed by my presence in his cramped domain, but since he could hardly ask me to leave, he offered me a stool at one side of the room, as if trying to tidy me away.

'Lord Somershill. Please,' he said, 'sit down.'

I complied with some reluctance, as the stool was low, and once I was seated, my legs were nearly bent to my chest. 'I need to ask you a question, Giovanni,' I told him.

He flushed a little, and began to touch the keys at his belt. 'Yes, of course, my lord. What is it?'

'Firstly, you may call me Oswald.'

His face fell at this suggestion. 'As you like, my lord,' he said tensely. 'I mean, Oswald.'

'You know that you are to assist me in my investigation?'

He nodded. 'Indeed, yes. My master has informed me.'

'Good. So we should not be slowed down by unnecessary epithets.' I chose the word deliberately, hoping that he would have to ask me what it meant. He didn't.

'Yes. Very well . . . Oswald,' he said, touching the keys again, as if this ring of iron shanks and bows were a sacred talisman. 'What do you want?'

I bristled at his choice of words. 'Please say it this way, Giovanni. What would you like to discuss?'

He bowed his head. 'I'm sorry, my lord.'

I rolled my eyes. 'You must call me Oswald.'

Giovanni took a deep breath and paused before enunciating each word. 'What would you like to discuss, Oswald?'

We could begin at last. 'There is something that's troubling me about Enrico's murder.'

'Yes?'

'Where was the guard to the water gate? He should have found the body, not me.'

Giovanni looked away awkwardly. 'Ah, yes. The man has disappeared.'

'Since when?'

'Nobody has seen him since yesterday.'

'What's his name?'

'Adolpho Bredani,' said Giovanni softly.

'And you're not suspicious that he's disappeared?'

Giovanni jumped to his feet. His face had flushed. 'It was not my idea!' he blurted, waving his hands about in the air. 'I did not want Bredani as a guard. The man is . . .' then he stopped himself.

'The man is what?'

Enrico sat down again, in an attempt to control his temper. 'He is bad and untrustful.'

'The word is untrustworthy,' I said quickly, not giving him the time to argue otherwise. 'Why did you employ this man, if he's of such poor character?' Giovanni frowned. He had not under stood me, so I rephrased the question. 'Why did you give him a position as guard?'

His anger flared again. 'I did not! I warned my master against him. Adolpho Bredani might be the brother of Monna Filomena, but he is a bad man.'

'He's Monna Filomena's brother? Are you sure about that?'

'Of course.'

This revelation had taken me by surprise. 'That seems a strange arrangement, Giovanni. A member of Monna Filomena's family employed as a servant in her own household.'

Giovanni shrugged. 'The family is poor, Oswald. She is always looking for . . .' Yet again he seemed to be struggling for the right word. Usually his English was more fluent than this. 'My master tries to help her family. You understand me? There was a cousin who worked in the kitchens. And now Monna Filomena's brother works as a guard.' He huffed. 'Even when I spoke against it.'

So this was the arrangement behind John Bearpark's marriage to Filomena – her beauty and youth in return for the old man's patronage of her extended family. It was a common enough contract, usually brokered by the bride's father, though I still found it unpalatable, especially in cases such as this, where there was such a vast disparity in their ages.

I put aside such thoughts, and returned to my questioning. 'What does Bredani look like?' I asked, hoping that I might remember the man.

Giovanni frowned, as if this was a difficult question. 'He is tall, with black hair and brown eyes.' He pursed his lips and could not hide a short snort. 'The women say he is handsome, I believe.'

'I see. And is it only the women who like him? He didn't catch Enrico's eye for example?'

Giovanni regarded me for a moment. 'So, my master has told you of Enrico's shame?'

'He's told me the truth, yes,' I said.

'Well Adolpho was not one of his lovers,' said Giovanni. 'I am sure of that.'

I tried to recall an attractive young man of good height, but I'm ashamed to say that I had become like so many noblemen in recent years. I had allowed myself to adopt the failings of my rank and had stopped noticing what servants looked like. They moved about in the background, facilitating and enabling my life, and yet I took no more notice of them than I took of a stranger in the street.

'Very well. I need to speak to this Adolpho Bredani,' I said with purpose. 'Somebody must know where he is.'

Giovanni gave a short shrug. 'I expect he's hiding. Ashamed that he left the water gate.'

I raised myself from the low stool and rubbed a cramp from my legs, before wandering across the small chamber to the corner, where Giovanni had erected a shrine to the Virgin. The diptych was a crudely painted trinket, but clearly a prized possession. The light of a small candle flickered beneath the Christ child, and a rosary was hung upon one corner of the frame.

'You say Monna Filomena's family is poor?' I said, turning back to Giovanni.

Giovanni kept his eyes from mine. 'Yes. But her marriage has richened them.'

'Enriched.'

Giovanni frowned at my correction, before launching into a new invective. 'Bredani was nothing before my master helped him.' He threw up his hands. 'Nothing! Just a fisherman, digging clams from the mud of the lagoon. Master Bearpark brought him to the heart of the city, and gave him money and new clothes. He wants the boy to learn his letters and numbers, so that he can assist me with the ledgers.' He puffed his lips. 'He gets everything that he wants.'

'Are you jealous of him, Giovanni?'

Now he sprang to his feet in dismay. 'Of course not! The man is lazy and refuses to learn. I can work better without him.' Giovanni took a deep breath, smoothed his hair, and sat back down rather heavily upon his chair. 'Bredani was forced upon me,' he said.

'And you have no idea where he might be hiding?' I asked.

'No, no.' Giovanni reached over to the shrine and picked up his rosary. 'I do not go where his type go.' He sneered. 'Whorehouses. Taverns. Gambling pits. The most sinful places of this city.'

I smelt a sermon brewing. 'I'm not suggesting that you do,' I said. 'But Adolpho must have gone somewhere?' Giovanni only shrugged by way of answer. 'You say he comes from a small island?' I said. 'Which island is that?'

'Burano.'

'Is his family still there?'

Giovanni sucked his teeth. 'I don't know. I don't speak to such people.'

'Then I will ask Monna Filomena,' I said. 'She might know where her brother is hiding.'

Giovanni stood up in a panic. 'No, no, Oswald. Please. Don't speak to Monna Filomena about this.'

'Why not?'

'Because you are saying things against her brother, and she will cause trouble for us.' He looked to the door, as if his mistress might be hiding in the corridor.

I frowned. 'What sort of trouble?'

'She doesn't like me. She whispers lies about me to my master.'

'Are you sure about that? Monna Filomena hardly seems to talk to her husband at all. Let alone about you.'

He waved away my opinion with some vexation. 'She will warn her brother that we are looking for him. Then we will never find the man.'

'So what do you suggest then?' I said.

As Giovanni thought how to answer me, I scrutinised his face. He was young and cleanly shaven, and the candlelight sat well upon his oiled and glossy locks, but he disliked my examination and pulled his cloak about his shoulders. 'I don't think Adolpho Bredani is important to this investigation,' he said at length. 'My master said we must look for Enrico's . . .' He hesitated. 'His *special* friends.' At the utterance of this word, he kissed his rosary.

'We will do,' I said. 'But first I want to speak to this Adolpho.'

Giovanni shook his head. 'No, no. We must follow my master's instructions.'

'An investigator never follows instructions, Giovanni. He follows clues.' The clerk opened his mouth, but then closed it again. 'Questioning Adolpho is the obvious place to start,' I said. 'The man should have been guarding the water gate, but he wasn't there. So we need to find out why.'

'He was just in a tavern somewhere, Oswald. Celebrating *Giovedi Grasso* and drinking too much wine.'

I ignored his scepticism. 'That's possible, of course. But perhaps he witnessed something, and now he is too afraid to speak? Or perhaps it's even worse than that?'

Giovanni's eyes narrowed. 'I don't understand.'

'Perhaps he was involved in the murder himself?'

At this Giovanni gasped and then kissed his rosary again. 'No, no. Adolpho Bredani is a sinner, but I cannot believe such a story.'

I yielded, as it was too early to come to such conclusions. 'You're probably right, Giovanni, but nevertheless I need to speak to him.' I paused. 'Let's go to Burano. I expect he's hiding there with his family.'

Giovanni frowned. 'It's a long journey, Oswald, and it's too late now.'

I paused, knowing that he was telling the truth, for we wouldn't be able to cross the lagoon to Burano and return to

Venice in daylight. 'Very well then,' I said. 'We will sail tomorrow, at dawn.' Before Giovanni could object, I added, 'And keep
our plan a secret. We don't want word of our visit reaching the
island before we do.'

Supper was another stew of liver and onions – a meal that had
filled the whole house with its evil perfume for most of the afternoon, though we were lucky to be eating meat at all. Mother
made this remark, and we all heartily agreed. Not only was it
true, but it broke the awkward silence that had dominated the
meal, for as surprising as it was to admit, we had all rather missed
John Bearpark and his library of anecdotes. Our only distraction
was Filomena's constant wriggling, as she tried to find a comfortable position in her chair. She was wearing a lighter gown this
evening – a dress that revealed the true advancement of her
pregnancy. It seemed that her child might be born any day.

I caught her eye and smiled, as I could see she was ill at ease,
but Filomena's discomfort did not meet with universal sympathy. Each time she readjusted her posture, Mother gave a short
snort of annoyance accompanied by a comment that the girl
should really be staying in her bedchamber at this point in her
confinement. In the end I asked Filomena, in Venetian, if she
would like me to fetch one of the small feather bolsters from my
bed, and given that neither her husband nor Giovanni was
present, she was able to answer my question herself. When I
returned with the bolster, she seemed genuinely grateful, and
rewarded me with one of her sweet and seldom-seen smiles.

After this short episode we returned to an awkward silence,
only punctuated by Bernard's odd and nonsensical observations,
to which nobody bothered to respond. It was only when Margery
emitted a sudden and unexpected belch from beneath her
wimple that the atmosphere was once again lifted. It was a
resounding and rather odorous burp that prompted the rest of us
to break out in laughter, but this moment of light-heartedness

did not last, for a servant entered the room and handed me a letter.

'Who's it from?' Mother asked, leaning over my shoulder, as I tried to open it. I pivoted, so that she could not read the thing, then pulled at the seal, opening the spool of parchment. 'What does it say?' demanded Mother.

I cleared my throat. 'It's from the galley master. That's all. He says that we will have to carry on waiting for a berth for Jaffa.' I quickly crushed the letter in my hands.

'Let me see that,' she said, trying to snatch it from me. 'Of course we cannot leave yet for Jerusalem. Venice is still at war.'

I threw the letter in the fire before Mother could make a second attempt to grapple it from me. 'He just likes to keep me informed of the situation. That's all.'

She cocked her head. 'Indeed?'

'Indeed.'

How could I tell her what the letter really said, and who it was really from? That it had been written by Vittore, saying that he had heard the sad news of Enrico's death, but also warning me not to use this as any sort of excuse. I still had one week to repay my debt.

Chapter Eight

We set out at first light the next morning for Burano, after Giovanni had decided that we would hire a boat from the oarsmen who plied their trade on a jetty near to the Rialto Bridge, rather than use the family's *sàndolo*. This way, he argued, we would not have to answer any questions from the household regarding our destination.

However, it was impossible to leave Ca' Bearpark without drawing the attention of my mother. 'Where are you going, Oswald?' she asked, as we were about to close the main door of the house. She held Hector in her arms, though the small dog had spotted a rat in the street and was trying to free himself urgently from Mother's grip.

I had to think quickly. 'Giovanni is taking me to one of Enrico's haunts. It was his favourite tavern.'

'At this time of day?'

'Yes,' I said. 'So we'd better hurry.'

I tried to close the door once again, but Mother put her foot across the threshold. 'Oh do let me come with you, Oswald. I feel so cooped up in this place.' She whispered so that Giovanni would not hear her words, though, as usual, her whispers were perfectly audible to anybody with even the poorest hearing. 'They are cooking up that terrible food again,' she said. 'The whole house reeks of it, and I can hardly breathe.' To demonstrate her point, she gave an astonishingly loud cough. 'And the company is appalling, now that poor Enrico has been murdered, and John has taken to his bed. My only companions are that foolish wife of his and that pair of dim-witted pilgrims.' She turned back into the hall. 'Just wait a moment for me. I'll fetch my cape.'

I went to respond, but Giovanni did so on my behalf. 'My lady,' he said with a patronising bend of his head, 'you cannot join us. It's not possible.' I had already formed the impression that Giovanni preferred women to keep their opinions to themselves, and this latest episode only confirmed my suspicion.

Mother clasped Hector to her breast. 'Why ever not?' The dog let out a low growl. 'That's right, Hector,' she said. 'We can join them, if we care to.'

I touched Mother's arm. 'The tavern might be too dangerous for you, Mother.'

'Nonsense. I'm not afraid of drunkards,' she said.

'But you know how there are robbers and cutpurses at every corner of this city.' It was one of her favourite phrases.

'I go out most days, Oswald,' she said indignantly. 'And I have not been set upon by criminals.'

'But we will be walking,' I lied, before pushing the door to the street ajar, so that she might look out along the muddy alley that ran from the house towards the Canal Grande.

She only shrugged. 'It is no matter to me. I shall wear over-shoes.' I thought about the strange, stilt-like pattens that the rich women of Venice fastened to their shoes, so that they could walk about the city without their gowns dragging along the mud of the paths. Sometimes these pattens were so tall that the women could only walk with the assistance of a servant holding a hand at each side.

'But you will not be able to balance.'

'Of course I will. If Monna Filomena can walk in the things, then I'm sure I can manage.'

The conversation was interrupted by a gaggle of children, who ran up to the house, and were soon baying for our attention like a litter of starving puppies. I noticed immediately that their leader was the boy who had led me back to Ca' Bearpark on the night of Enrico's murder. He, and his noisy gang of skeletal friends must have been hanging around ever since, in hope of some further charity.

'Goodness me,' said Mother. 'Not this lot again. I gave them some money, as you requested, Oswald, and now they won't leave.'

Giovanni shooed the children away in the harshest terms, whilst at the same time threatening to send out the house guards and have them arrested. The children dragged their feet back into their various nooks and crannies, but not without making a selection of rude gestures and cursing at us in their shrill voices.

They had pricked my conscience, so I forced Mother to part with a coin that I then threw to the boy, telling him to buy some bread for the others. This pathetic gesture caused a cheer of joy that resounded about the street like the chorus of a crowd at a jousting match. The children soon disappeared in the direction of the nearest baker, but their appearance had been enough to change Mother's mind about leaving the house. She could not possibly join us on an excursion into Venice, so we should stop trying to persuade her otherwise. Giovanni glanced at me with confusion, not understanding Mother's proclivity for changing her mind, but I did not acknowledge his look of disdain. For my part, I was pleased that Mother had confounded him.

By chance, we had only to wander to the end of our street Calle Nuova, where the alley ended abruptly at the Canal Grande, to find a boat willing to take us to Burano. The journey would be long – given the two hours or so it would take for the oarsmen to row across the lagoon to this far island – but they were not discouraged from taking the fare as trade was slow at this time of the day. If the wind was in the right direction, they might even raise their small, square sail, and be back in Venice by the early afternoon.

I sat next to Giovanni on the middle bench of this long *sàndolo*, while one oarsman stood in front of us and the other behind, each balancing nimbly upon a raised platform. They faced forwards to row, each moving a single oar through the water with two hands, so that we were soon gliding silently along the Canal Grande with only the slightest sensation of being on the water. We moved at a good speed, but I still had the opportunity to study the many grand houses that lined this stretch of water. Whereas Ca' Bearpark faced an almost identical house across a narrow and dark canal, the *palazzi* that adorned each flank of this wide waterway were like two rows of jealous courtesans, each trying to surpass the other with the most lavish dress and extravagant jewels.

With their pointed windows, balconies, raised loggias, quoins, and even marble-encrusted *oculi*, the *palazzi* of the Canal Grande were nothing like the castles of England. Our grandest residences are surrounded by land. And yet more land. But in Venice, wealth has nothing to do with the ownership of fields, forests, or lakes. It has nothing to do with the wheat yield an estate can grow, or the number of sheep it can shear. Wealth comes from finding a trusted supply of goods from the East, and selling these goods at a profit in the West. The wealthiest men of Venice are not earls and barons. Instead they are merchants, with a reputation to uphold. And what more visible way is there to announce your wealth to the world than by heaping more and more ornamentation upon your home, particularly if it is situated in the best location in Venice. And so most *palazzi* of the Canal Grande reach upwards to the sky, perhaps three or even four storeys high. They are decorated with statues and mosaics, twisted columns and great, ostentatious water gates that lead out onto the canal for all to admire. They are filled with beautiful furniture, beautiful carpets, tapestries, and art. And let us not forget – beautiful women.

Giovanni spoke constantly as we sailed, pointing out the many churches or monasteries that could be seen in the distance. His commentary was repetitive and dull however, and I soon found myself paying little attention to his words, other than to make the occasional, empty response. Instead, I let the wind brush my face – a fleeting freedom from the constriction of the city, with its thin, stifling streets and tall, overbearing buildings. Out here on the water, there were no dark corners or hidden crannies. There was nowhere for my shadow to hide.

As we left the bustle of the Canal Grande, the oarsmen raised their small sail, and we ventured out into the vastness of the lagoon itself. The air now smelt of the sea, and the waters were harder to navigate. In the far distance, the mountains of the Dolomites rose into the sky – their jagged, angry peaks coated in snow. The wind was in our favour, and we soon passed the island of Murano, where the great glassmakers' furnaces belched their smoke into a sullen sky. Heading east towards Burano, we then encountered an archipelago of lonely, unpopulated islands – hillocks of sand, tamarisk, and grassy reeds. Islands that might dissolve away into the marsh at any moment, and then be forgotten for ever.

Now that Venice had receded into the distance, I could let my hand fall into the water without fearing what I might touch. This was not something I would risk nearer to the city, where the water was infested with worse debris than rubbish – especially when the tides flooded the cesspits and pulled their effluent into the canals. Out here, on the lagoon, the water was clean, and the air was free of the eggy stink of humanity.

As we travelled further and further away from the city, we passed fishermen hauling their long nets into the hulls of their small *piatte*. Sometimes their catch was so large, I thought the weight of fish might sink the boat itself, but there was little danger of anybody drowning in this lagoon. In those areas where the channels are not dredged for larger ships, the water is only a few feet deep. I leant forward and let a thin sun warm my skin, whilst a cormorant flew over my head, so close that I could almost feel the flap of its wings in my face. A distant bell tolled, and a seagull mewed. I felt content. I might even say hopeful. So much so, that I forgot about my debt to Vittore. I forgot about Enrico's murder. I even forgot about my shadow, and for a moment, the world seemed at peace with itself.

And then a cold wind of winter stung my face, and I turned away to see that Giovanni was praying.

'What's wrong?' I asked.

'The wind.' He pointed somewhere at the horizon. 'It's blowing from the island.'

'What island?'

He pointed again at an outcrop of land on the horizon. From this distance it seemed little more than a dismal, marshy bank, topped with a few ramshackle buildings that appeared to be falling down. 'It's the Lazaretto,' he whispered. 'The lepers' island.'

'What are you scared of, Giovanni?' I said. 'You cannot catch leprosy from the wind.'

Giovanni closed his eyes again and returned to his prayers, so I looked back at the island. Now it was little more than a smudge on the skyline, disappearing beneath a low, billowing cloud that had rolled in from the sea. This cloud was dark and formless at first, but then it gathered into a familiar shape, with a lolling head, long arms, and fingers that reached out towards me across the lagoon. I closed my eyes and turned my back on it, for it was not real. I would not believe in it.

The oarsmen agreed to wait for us at the jetty in Burano, but only if we paid them another five *soldini* for their troubles. Giovanni made a great fuss about this expense, since he had made it clear to me on several occasions that he considered this whole journey to be a waste of time. In his opinion we should be following his master's instructions and looking for Enrico's lover. It

was only when I convinced him that I would take full responsibility for this visit to Burano, that Giovanni reluctantly untied the
leather bindings of his money pouch and grudgingly passed over
the coins to the oarsmen.

As we disembarked onto the quayside, I stretched out my
arms, and took a deep breath to fend off a wave of nausea. The
cloud above the lepers' island had unnerved me, though I
pretended to be suffering from seasickness when Giovanni asked
me if I was unwell. We then set off towards the house of the
Bredani family, followed by the gangs of children who gathered
about us like noisy disciples, and watched by the men and women
of the island, who conspicuously ended their conversations and
turned to look as we passed.

Giovanni was aware of this scrutiny, but strode forward with
the determination of a hound that has picked up the scent of a
hind. When I asked him to slow down, he refused, pointing to
the clouds that were gathering in the sky, before warning me that
we should not delay, as we risked sailing back to Venice through
a fog. At this resolute speed, we soon reached a small house in a
backstreet, which, Giovanni claimed, was the right building –
though I must say it seemed unlikely at first sight. This was an
impoverished place, squeezed into a tight corner between two
taller homes – its walls bulging into the street like the swelling
in the fork of a tree. Much of the stucco had fallen from the
walls, revealing weathered bricks that gave support to a spindly
vine.

'Are you sure that Monna Filomena lived here?' I said, finding
it hard to disguise my surprise.

My companion straightened his tunic and smoothed his hair.
'Yes, Oswald. This is the exacting house.'

'You mean exact.' He tried to argue, but I held up my hand to
prevent a reply. 'How do you know?' I asked.

'Because I once lived on this island.' Giovanni delivered these
words as if this were a confession. An admission of shame.

This was another surprise. With his fashionable, elegant clothes and his soft, manicured hands, there was not the slightest trace of Burano about Giovanni. 'Did you know Monna Filomena before she married?' I asked.

He lifted his eyes to the sky. 'I knew of her. Yes.' He grunted a laugh. 'Which man didn't?'

'Does your family still live here?' I said, ignoring his barbed jibe.

At this question, he reached instinctively for the ring of keys that still hung at his belt. 'No. They died in the Plague. All of them. So I left this island soon after.'

'To work at Ca' Bearpark?' I asked.

Giovanni nodded. 'Yes. I can read, and I learnt arithmetic,' he said. 'I offered my services to many families in Venice, but Master Bearpark gave me the best opportunity.' He licked his finger and held it up in the air. 'Now, we should be quick,' he said, deftly changing the subject. 'The wind is turning.'

Giovanni then thumped at the door to the dilapidated house, causing some interest from passers-by, but eliciting no response whatsoever from within. He tried again, and this time an ancient woman pushed open a shutter and then peered out at us, squinting to see Giovanni's face. It was clear that she recognised my companion, but there was no affection in their reunion, and it was only with a great reluctance that she admitted us into the house. We stepped through a low door into a small and dark chamber, where the cries of a child in the neighbouring house could be heard through the thin walls. Through the smoky gloom, I saw another individual crouched near the fire. I guessed this old man was Filomena's father, for, though his face was as gnarled and twisted as a staff of waxed blackthorn, I could see something of her features in his profile.

The old woman offered me a bowl of wine in a dialect that I could not understand, but Giovanni refused it on my behalf, causing her to slam down the bowl with some affront.

'Don't upset them,' I said. 'We need their help.'

Giovanni inhaled, puffing up his chest. 'They offered you bad wine, Oswald. It's an insult.'

'I don't care about the wine. Just ask them where Adolpho is?' I took his arm. 'And do it politely.'

Giovanni bowed his head, though I noted that my question was still delivered in the tone of a man attempting to train a dog. It was therefore not surprising that Adolpho's parents gave short, hostile mumbles in response to his questions.

'They say that they don't know anything,' said Giovanni in the end. 'They think Adolpho is at Ca' Bearpark, working for my master.' He added a sigh, as if to emphasise his opinion that this whole journey had been a complete waste of time.

'Very well then,' I said, refusing to be riled. 'Ask them when they last saw Adolpho.'

After a further mumbled conversation, some of which sounded argumentative, Giovanni translated their answer. 'They say they haven't seen Adolpho since he left for Venice. Months ago.' This time the sigh became a more effusive Venetian shrug. 'You see, Oswald. I knew it was foolish to come here.'

I would not be so easily defeated. 'Ask them if they know where Adolpho might be hiding. Does he have friends on this island, for example? Or, where does he like to drink?'

The old couple shook their head in response to each question, and shrugged repeatedly in earnest. It appeared that they knew absolutely nothing about anything.

I pulled Giovanni to one side. 'Do you think they're telling the truth?' There was something about their fulsome sincerity that troubled me.

Giovanni placed his finger on his parting and carefully rearranged his fringe. 'Yes, Oswald. I do.' He looked about the small chamber with some distaste. 'Adolpho Bredani left this island as soon as he could. And I do not blame him.' He gave a short shudder. 'May we go please? It smells rotting in here.'

'You mean rotten.'

It seemed we had indeed wasted our time, and this irritated me, though not as much as having to admit that Giovanni was right. I bid the old couple good day and then strode out of the house in something of a temper, with Giovanni scurrying along behind me with a self-righteous skip to his step. My instincts about coming to Burano had not been completely misplaced however, for we had barely reached the end of the street, when a man caught up with us and begged to speak with me. He wore the loose, leather tunic of a fisherman, causing Giovanni to call him a beggar and attempt to chase him away, but when this man shouted the name of Adolpho Bredani, I told Giovanni to let him speak.

This time I conducted the conversation myself. If I spoke slowly enough, the man would understand my Venetian, no matter that I had not been raised in Burano. 'Why do you ask about Adolpho Bredani?' I said.

His voice was hoarse and strange to my ears, but his words were comprehensible, as long as I concentrated. 'I have information about the man,' he said. 'I think you will be interested.' The fisherman then uncurled a hand that was blackened by the oily stain of pine pitch.

Giovanni huffed and folded his arms. 'You see, Oswald,' he said to me in English. 'This man is a beggar. Don't speak to him.'

I turned to my companion and whispered, though it was highly doubtful that this so-called beggar could understand any English. 'He might know something. It's worth a *soldino*, isn't it?'

Giovanni stiffened. 'If you say so.'

I held out my hand and waited for Giovanni to delve reluctantly into his purse in order to retrieve a single coin. When I presented this same coin to the fisherman, the man shook his head, indicating that he expected more. 'This is it,' I told him. 'And you were lucky to get this much.'

He took the coin from me with a sigh and then slipped it into his sleeve. 'Bredani was here two nights ago,' he told me. 'I heard him banging on the door.'

I looked to Giovanni, but my companion merely raised his eyebrows to indicate that he thought the man was a liar. I ignored him and turned back to the fisherman. 'Where is Bredani now?' I asked. 'Do you know?'

He shook his head. 'He was only at home for a short time,' he said. 'I heard some shouting, and then his mother was crying.'

'What were they arguing about?'

The man shrugged. 'The walls are thin, but not *that* thin.' He hesitated, and then the curled, dirty hand appeared again. 'But there is something else.'

'There's no more money,' I said, but as he turned to leave, I persuaded Giovanni grudgingly to part with another *soldino*. 'Come on then,' I said, waving the coin in the air. 'What is it?'

The man grasped the coin greedily from my hand. 'Bredani's father bought a pig yesterday.'

I turned to Giovanni, thinking I had misunderstood. 'What does he mean?' I asked, in English. 'Did he mention a pig?'

Giovanni responded with a puff of exasperation, 'Yes. He did.'

I turned back to the fisherman. 'Why are you telling me about a pig?'

'Because the Bredanis are a poor family,' the man said, 'yet they can suddenly buy a pig. The day after their son comes to visit.' I must have seemed especially stupid, as he now spoke very slowly. 'Pigs are expensive, and we are at war. Who has the money to buy such a beast?'

We returned to the house immediately, but Adolpho's elderly mother was no keener to admit us a second time, and we were left with no option but to push our way inside.

'Where is Adolpho?' I demanded in Venetian. The fisherman in the street had understood me well enough, so there was no reason why I should not communicate with this elderly pair. Nevertheless, they pretended to be confused, so I had to admit defeat and allow Giovanni to conduct the interrogation.

'Tell them that we know Adolpho was here two nights ago. Ask them why they are lying to us?' Giovanni repeated my question, prompting the old man to stumble to his feet and wave a fist at me.

I ignored this outburst and continued. 'Ask them where Adolpho is now?' I said. Once again, the pair claimed to have no knowledge of Adolpho's whereabouts, until the old man finally admitted, after a long bombardment of questions, that Adolpho had, indeed, returned briefly two nights earlier. After this confession, he returned to his stool, wiped the sweat from his forehead, and then wearily revealed that he hadn't told us any of this before, because Adolpho had been frightened about something. Something that his son had refused to reveal.

We were reaching the truth at last. 'Ask him about the pig?' I told Giovanni. The old man only stiffened at this question. 'Did Adolpho give them some money?' I asked. 'If so, where did the money come from? Had Adolpho stolen it from somebody? Was that the cause of his fear?' In response to this string of questions, the old man and his wife simply refused to speak, so what was I to do? I could hardly torture the pair into making further confessions.

I decided, instead, to search the house. Adolpho's elderly parents might not be willing to speak to me, but there might be some clue in this hovel that would give us more information.

As I made my way towards a door at the back of the house, Giovanni joined me. 'What are you looking for, Oswald?' he asked. 'Adolpho isn't here.'

'I know that. I'm just looking for clues.'

Giovanni frowned. 'What sort of clues?'

'I won't know until I've found them.'

Leaving Giovanni to watch over the elderly couple, I pushed at an internal door and found myself in a room that served as a primitive kitchen. In reality it was little more than a porch with a steeply slanted roof, a single table, and another door leading out into a small courtyard. This courtyard was surrounded on three sides by a high wall, and was a brighter place than the rest of the house. I could tell that the old couple spent as much time out here as the weather allowed, for a couple of chairs were placed beneath the naked branches of a fig tree. In the other corner was a collection of crab cages, stacked like barrels to make a rudimentary pen. And in this pen was the pig – this great object of mystery. I must say that it was a sickly-looking creature, with a freckled snout and flopping, ragged ears – but it was still a living pig, and must have cost the pair a great deal of money.

Giovanni followed me into the courtyard, but showed little interest in my observations regarding the animal. Instead he pointed to the overcast sky. 'Please, Oswald. We must go now. The fog is coming.'

I ignored this entreaty and returned to the main chamber, where I climbed the ladder to the rooms in the eaves of the house. As my feet ascended each rung of the ladder, the old couple seemed increasingly anxious, and I wondered what I might find up there. Perhaps they were hiding Adolpho after all? What I discovered instead was a cold, windowless space perfumed by the smoke from the fire below. I felt into every nook and cranny of this loft, but found nothing.

Then I sat down on one of the simple bedsteads and looked up through the beams at the underside of the tiled roof, as Giovanni shouted up to me from below.

'Please, Oswald. The wind is turning. I fear we will be stranded here.'

'Very well,' I said, casting my eyes about the room for the last time. There was nothing out of the ordinary here, nothing that might constitute a clue. To be truthful, there was hardly anything in this room at all. I had rarely seen such a bare home – without even a crucifix attached to the bedstead, or a holy niche carved into the wall. I was about to climb back down the ladder, when it occurred to me to check one last place. I lifted both straw mattresses from their frames, discovering a small slit in the canvas on the underside of one of them, and, feeling inside, I found a small leather purse. When I pulled the thing out of the mattress, I quickly looked inside to count eight golden ducats. More wealth than such an impoverished couple could ever save.

The coins could only have come from their son, but where had Adolpho acquired them? My guess was that this money was stolen, perhaps even from Enrico himself – which further suggested Adolpho's involvement in the murder.

I quickly dropped this leather purse inside my own, before descending the ladder, whilst making sure to keep my hand on the purse so that the coins did not chink against one another. I should have asked the old couple about this money, but I didn't. And when Giovanni asked me if I had found any clues, I lied.

Chapter Nine

The fog descended on our return from Burano, just as Giovanni had predicted. As we sailed into the lagoon it seemed we were navigating the river Styx on our last journey to the underworld. For long stretches it felt as if we might have been the only vessel on the water, but then, every so often, another solitary boat loomed out of the mist, before evaporating again into the haze. When we caught sight of these boats, our oarsmen shouted across to their crews, asking them the direction of Venice, only for their calls to be lost in the thick air.

Giovanni played alternately with his rosary and then his set of keys, while I clutched tightly at my purse, as if the coins I had found on Burano might give me away by scattering across the floor of the boat. The further we sailed from the island, the more a tantalising thought began to creep into my mind. Why not use these same coins to play at dice? What could be the harm? With this money I could win back my losses and more. Who would ever know?

I had almost planned which taverns to visit, when I came to my senses. The dice had betrayed me before, and they would do so again. I was a fool to even be having such thoughts. I decided instead to take the honourable course of action and reveal this evidence to Bearpark, asking if he knew whether they had been stolen from Enrico. And yet the thought of making this disclosure was not appealing. In fact, it made me feel a little sick.

I tightened the strings of the purse and tried to cast the coins from my mind for a while, when Giovanni jogged my elbow. 'I knew we shouldn't have travelled to Burano,' he said, with a note of despair in his voice. The fog was now so dense that we could barely see the oarsman at the other end of our boat.

'It was worth going, Giovanni,' I said. 'At least we know that Adolpho was involved in the murder.'

'Do we?'

'Of course we do,' I said. 'He fled from his post, and appeared on Burano in a panic. He was guilty of something.'

'He was guilty of abandoning his duties, while his young master was killed,' said Giovanni. 'There's no evidence that he was involved in any other way.'

I had evidence of Adolpho's involvement in something. It was sitting in my purse, and yet I said nothing. Instead I went back to staring at the still, syrupy water, whilst Giovanni bombarded the oarsmen with questions about our proximity to Venice. At first they gave noncommittal answers to his questions, but soon their responses turned to annoyance and then rudeness. Of course they were steering in the right direction. Of course they wanted to get back to the city as quickly as we did. Of course they would keep to the agreed fee, no matter that this journey had taken so much longer than they had anticipated.

When we came within feet of a great galley, Giovanni crossed himself and prayed out loud to the Virgin, which only caused the oarsmen to curse his existence. This ship was an unexpected sight, looming out of the mists like a great sea monster. There had been no such merchant shipping on the lagoon for months – as these vessels were either harboured in Venice, or they were elsewhere in the Adriatic, waiting for the hostilities with Hungary to end. The sail was lowered, and its many oars drove through the water in perfect unison. As it passed our bow, the galley created such a strong wave that we were rocked violently from side to side, whilst a great spray of water smacked against the wool of Giovanni's hose, causing him to cry out loudly with rage. Some of the crewmen looked down from their deck at this, and then jeered before their ship was gone, vanishing into the fog as quickly as it had appeared.

After this, the fog only continued to thicken, causing the worst of my moods to descend. With no horizon to offer distraction, my spirit drew back upon itself, scratching and plucking at the very worst recollections. Now I sensed that my shadow was close, waiting to creep up on me, so I concentrated on my hands, just as I always did, in the ardent hope that it would leave me alone.

When I sensed that it had finally given up, I felt able to raise my eyes as the oarsmen began to shout. The fog had lifted a little, revealing that we had floated close to land. Behind the sandy banks of the shore I could see grass, a row of stunted trees, and even a collection of crumbling, derelict buildings. And then, as the fog lifted a little more, a group of people materialised from the gloom – watching us silently from a low mound. They wore thick, unsightly tunics, and their heads were covered with hoods – but these garments did not fully obscure their ruined, leprous faces. At their fore was an old man whose eyeballs might have been two orbs of Carrara marble.

Behind me, Giovanni was panicking – demanding that the oarsmen row away from this place, warning that our boat must not touch the mud of the island, or we might be infected with their malaise. But I could not take my eyes from the faces of the lepers, for, in the midst of their ragged, dismal shapes, there was a figure I knew well.

It had found me, and for those few moments it was real – exactly as I had always imagined. Hunched and skeletal. Its coat black and matted. Its face circled by a fringe of dirty white fur. It looked straight into my eyes with a pleading, nauseating sadness that almost turned my stomach, and when it held out its bony hands to me in supplication, I could face it no longer.

I had been right to sense its presence through the fog, for this wretched, miserable island was its perfect haunt. I should have anticipated that it would be here and kept my eyes upon my hands. Instead, I had let it catch me out and now I would never be rid of it. The blood rushed from my head and I leant over the side of the boat in case I vomited. When Giovanni came to my aid, I pretended to be suffering from seasickness. But this was not nausea. It was much worse.

I do not remember the rest of the journey, but when we finally disembarked at Ca' Bearpark, I ran up the two sets of stairs to my chamber and closed the door firmly. Mother tried repeatedly to speak to me, but when I told her to go away in the strongest terms, she had the sense to leave me alone. I wanted to erase what I had seen from my memory, but a mind will not obey such a command. It cannot unsee something that it has seen. When I closed my eyes, I found the creature's face had been etched into my eyelids.

And so my melancholy returned with a vengeance, until the pain finally lost its passion, and in its place came something worse. A low, grinding inertia that sat in my stomach, reaching out through my chest and into my limbs, until my hands felt like lead weights. As I lay in this stupor, there was a rattle at the window. The Bora wind had blown straight from the Adriatic Sea, and was now banging the shutters against the frame, making a repetitive, harrying sound that I could not get out of my head, no matter that I stuffed my fingers into my ears. It thumped and thumped its fists against the wood until I could stand it no longer.

I stumbled to the window and opened the shutters, fastening them against the outside wall. Then I heard a whispering. At first I looked around, thinking that somebody had crept into the room without my noticing, but soon I realised that the voice was inside my head. I needn't stay in this ugly world, it told me. I could escape so easily.

It all made sense.

I climbed up onto the windowsill. I felt liberated and purposeful. This was the answer. I had only to launch myself from this window, and everything would go away. The lies. The guilt. The shadow. Why had I not thought of this before? The drop was high enough to kill me, or so I hoped. My heart was beating at speed. My body felt joyous and determined. I would have taken that leap, when somebody shouted my name.

I spun around to see Filomena looking at me from the door. 'What are you doing?' she said, as she ran over. 'Please come down.'

I turned away from her, but she grasped my hand and pulled me away from the sill with surprising strength. As I fell back to the floor she knelt down next to me, and all of a sudden I felt so hopelessly pleased that she was here. 'So. You do speak English?' was unfortunately all I could think of to say.

'Yes. I am married to an Englishman, after all,' she said with a smile, as she helped me to sit on the bed, and then placed her fingers lightly upon my trembling hands. 'I saw you from the balcony below. What were you doing?' She paused. 'I feared for you.'

'There's nothing to fear,' I said unconvincingly.

'Please, Oswald. Don't lie to me,' she whispered. 'I know that you watch me, but sometimes I watch you as well, and I have seen sadness at your heart.' She drew her face closer, and I was able to gaze into her gentle, solemn eyes. 'What is this sadness? Tell me,' she said. 'I will not speak of it to anybody.'

I didn't want to say anything, and yet the idea of unburdening myself suddenly became so appealing that the words tumbled out before I could stop them. 'I saw something today,' I said. 'On the lagoon.'

'What was it?' she asked.

I tried to laugh, but the sound was hollow and dishonest. 'You'll think I've lost my senses,' I said.

Filomena shook her head. 'No, I won't. I promise.'

'It wasn't real.'

She frowned at my words, though she quickly changed her expression to a sympathetic smile. 'Was it a ghost?' she asked.

'No. Not a ghost.' I paused. 'I think of it as a . . . shadow.'

'Do you see it often?'

'Yes. Though I've never looked into its face before.' I hesitated. 'Not until today.'

She drew closer to me. 'Did it frighten you?'

'No,' I admitted, 'it disgusted me.'

She bristled at this word, but did not pull her hand away. 'Why?' she asked. 'Why did it disgust you?'

Now I froze, for how could I tell this young woman that I'd seen a miserable, emaciated monkey amongst the wretched lepers on the island of the Lazaretto? How could I tell her that this imaginary creature had been pursuing me ever since I had left the shores of England; that it hid in the nooks and crannies of my life, judging me, condemning me, ready to leap out upon me when I least expected it? How could I tell her that I would rather die than have to face it again? 'It's something from my past that haunts me,' I said instead.

She put her hand on my shoulder and whispered into my ear. 'And this shadow. This ghost. Is that why you want to die?'

The frankness of this question took me by surprise, because now that she was sitting here beside me, I was relieved to be alive. I might even say that I was pleased of it. 'I thought I could ignore it. Drown it out,' I told her. 'But now it's found me, and it's stronger than ever.' I felt tears clawing at my throat. 'And I hate it, Filomena. I really hate it.'

'The Devil sends ghosts, Oswald.' We sat back to find that Giovanni had silently entered the room. 'They bring his disorder and malice to this world. You must not look upon their faces.'

Filomena sprang to her feet despite the size of her belly, picked up her skirts, and then marched out of the room without even acknowledging Giovanni. Her face was red with anger, or perhaps it was embarrassment, for she should not have been alone with a man in his bedchamber. The warmth and intimacy of our conversation departed along with her trailing gown, and instead a cold chill invaded the room.

'What do you want Giovanni?' I said, turning away.

Giovanni placed his hand upon my shoulder. 'You saw this ghost on the Lazaretto, didn't you?' He pressed his hand into my skin. 'I knew there was something wrong.'

'It was just a delusion,' I said. 'A figment of my imagination. I haven't slept well for many days, and my mind is exhausted.' I cleared my throat. 'But, you mustn't worry. I'm recovered now.'

He rubbed his fingers across my tunic, and more than anything I wanted him to stop touching me. 'It was a demonite,' he said. 'A spirit sent by Beelzebub to draw your soul into Hell.'

Suddenly I felt the urge to laugh. 'You mean a demon.'

Giovanni shook his head. 'No, no. It is a demonite.'

'There is no such word, Giovanni,' I said, feeling adequately revitalised to dislodge his hand from my shoulder.

'Your mind is unwell, Oswald,' he told me. 'This demonite is trying to possess you.' I looked away, but he cocked his head to look into my eyes. 'You must not be ashamed of this. Your mother has told me of your troubles.'

Now I felt my anger rising. 'Has she indeed?'

'I understand your sadness,' said Giovanni.

'I doubt it.'

He smiled oddly. 'But I do, Oswald. I've felt this sadness, as well. So you are not alone. But death will not ease your pain.' He placed his hand back upon my shoulder, before I had the chance to dodge away. 'To kill yourself is a mortal sin. You will spend an eternity in Hell.'

Now I could not suppress a laugh.

'Don't laugh at this, Oswald. Please.' He waited a few moments, and then reached inside his purse to retrieve a rosary that he then pressed into my hand. 'Please. Take this.' The rosary felt cold – its beads like tiny, sharp teeth against my skin, but Giovanni closed my fingers about his gift and pushed it to my chest. 'I do understand your sadness,' he said. 'I lost somebody once. The person that I loved more than anything in the world.'

I regarded him suspiciously. Was he telling the truth? 'Did you lose them in the Plague?'

He flushed and dropped his gaze. 'At first the pain was very strong,' he told me. 'At times I could not stand it.' He stared at the floor and whispered. 'I was like you, Oswald.' He hesitated. 'I wanted death. I even sought it.'

'You tried to kill yourself?' I could hardly believe this story, and yet Giovanni's confession seemed completely genuine.

He nodded awkwardly. 'Yes, I did. I thought it was the answer. But it was not.' He looked me in the eye again, trying to regain his composure. 'So you see. You are not alone.'

'What stopped you?' I asked.

'It was Mother Maria. She saved me from the sin.' He pressed the rosary again into my chest. 'Let her in, Oswald. Give her your soul.'

I hesitated to answer.

'Speak to Mother Maria, and she will listen.'

I looked at the rosary. Though it was only a simple string of wooden beads, it must have been a sacrifice for Giovanni to part with such a treasured possession. His lecture had annoyed me, but his kindness was touching and I almost felt some affection for him – though, predictably, this did not last for long.

Giovanni straightened his clothes and searched about the room for my looking glass. I had hung the thing behind the door, since I had barely bothered looking in a mirror in the last few months, and when I did need to for some reason, then I took care to be quick about it, lest I caught something of the shadow in my reflection. Seeing that the surface of the looking glass was covered in a thin layer of dust, Giovanni puffed and then carefully removed a small square of linen from his sleeve. 'Shall I tell my master that you will not continue with the investigation?' he said, as he cleaned away a swathe of grime to reveal the mottled silver finish beneath.

'No. Why would you do that?' I said sharply.

He stopped wiping. 'You are unwell, Oswald. Is it wise to carry on?'

I was unwell, that much was true, but I could hardly afford the luxury of giving up on my investigation – especially when I had only six days to earn my fee. 'I'm perfectly healthy, Giovanni,' I said. 'Have no fears on that front.'

For some reason I felt that my answer disappointed him.

Chapter Ten

I had not intended to buy a monkey. It was the summer of 1355, and I was in London to meet a wool merchant who had been causing me some trouble with payments for Somershill fleeces. I would not usually have undertaken such negotiations, as they were the remit of my reeve, but since I suspected my reeve of conspiring with this same merchant, I thought it worthwhile to supervise all transactions.

It was a warm June morning, and while I was waiting for the obstinate merchant to answer my latest entreaty for payment, I decided to kill some time by taking a walk along Cheapside market. My intention was to purchase some saffron and mace for the Somershill kitchen – for good quality spices were sometimes difficult to find in Kent. I was also in search of a gift, however. A souvenir from my visit to London. Some trinket or bauble to warm the tepid heart of a particular young woman. A young woman who had thus far remained immune to my advances.

Cheapside was noisy and overcrowded that morning – the air warm with the rotting stench of the nearby meat market at the Shambles. In the busy streets of West Cheap, the stallholders appeared to be as wilted as their vegetables; their customers as bad-tempered as bears in chains – quick to pick fights and slow to apologise. I kept away from the stalls, but the flies attracted by the sweating food still swarmed about my face, so I was forced to hold a hand over my mouth. When the miasma of insects, rotten food, and rude behaviour became too much to bear, I took a diversion into a side alley, hoping to find fresher air and a sanctuary from the crowds.

I was certainly able to remove my hand from my mouth now that I was away from the main thoroughfare, but this was still a dark and meandering passageway, located between two rows of houses that reached for the sun like closely planted trees. As a gang of shoeless children rushed past, I held tightly upon the leather pouch that hung from my belt. Such ragged children were always cutpurses, or so I had been warned by every servant, family member, and general busybody since I had declared my intention to visit London. And yet, thus far, I had managed to keep my purse safe from their villainous little fingers. As the children disappeared around the far corner, a mule strayed across my path, pulling at its tether as it tried to reach a pile of discarded cabbage leaves on the other side of the alley.

I pushed the stubborn beast aside, and it was then that I saw it – a creature crouching behind the iron bands of a crate that was no larger than a pillory cage. An unpleasant fug of droppings and rotten fruit hung about the crate, like the fumes of a steaming midden heap, and, as I approached the beast, it lifted its hands over its head, as if protecting itself from falling masonry. Even in this squalor, I could see that it had once been a magnificent animal. Beneath its dusted, matted topcoat was a pelt of glossy black fur with two flamboyant, fringed manes of white hair, which ran from its shoulders down to the base of its long back. Its small, leathery face was encircled by this same white fringe, as if it were poking it through the tasselled trim of a robe. It was unlike any beast I had ever seen, but, in truth, it was the creature's pathos that really appealed to me – for, more than anything, it needed to be nursed back to health. I thought about the young woman in question, knowing that this decrepit monkey would make a perfect a gift.

I pushed the door of the adjacent shop open to find a further menagerie of animals for sale. Goldfinches, jackdaws, spaniel puppies, kittens, and a pair of smaller monkeys, chained by their necks and crouching together on a perch as they picked at one another's fleas. Even by the standards of London, this was a repulsive-smelling den – though the shopkeeper seemed immune to the reek of his establishment, since he was whistling a merry tune as he fed peas to a rabbit.

I cleared my throat to get his attention. 'How much for the monkey outside?'

The shopkeeper stood back with some shock, as he had not noticed my entrance. 'Good day to you, my lord. How kind of you to visit.' He held out his hand. 'Please. Allow me to present you my collection of exotic marvels and curiosities.'

By now the smell had forced me to return my hand to my nose. 'It's just the monkey outside that interests me,' I said.

He dropped his smile. 'Ah, yes.' He paused, scratching his chin a little awkwardly. 'I'm afraid that beast is not for sale.'

So, this was his tactic. Well, I could play this game as well. 'Never mind,' I said, swinging my cloak with a flourish. 'Then I bid you good day.'

I turned to leave, but the man darted to the door with the speed of a jack hare. 'Sire. Why don't you take one of these lovely Barbary apes instead?' He pointed at the monkeys on the perch. 'They've just come in from the land of Granada. And they're such tender creatures. Very gentle with children. And look at their endearing little faces. They would keep your family amused for hours.' I looked across at the macaques, who were now baring their formidable fangs to me. In truth, it was hard to imagine a more unsuitable companion for a child.

'How much is the monkey outside?' I said again.

The shopkeeper bit his lip. 'You don't want that animal, my lord. It's inferior. As miserable as a leper.'

'Maybe that's because you keep it so miserably? Could you not clean out its cage occasionally?'

The man went to say something, but stopped. He could not be insolent to me, and he knew it. Instead he rolled his tongue about his gums and then gave a sigh. 'It likes the cage, sire.'

'I doubt that's true.'

He smiled awkwardly. 'No, no. It is. I've let the creature out before. With a chain on its foot, of course,' he added quickly. 'But it always crawls back into the cage of its own volition.' He tried the smile again. 'You really would be better with one of the Barbarys.' He rolled his hands together. 'I do have a fine and noble lady interested in one of them, but I could give you a very good price for the pair.'

I folded my arms. 'How much for the monkey outside?'

'I cannot sell it to you,' he insisted.

'Why not? Did you steal it from somebody?'

'No, my lord. Of course not.'

'Then name your price.'

The man regarded me for a while, before heaving a great sigh. 'Very well then,' he said. 'You may have it for half a mark.'

The price he named was surprisingly low, and I was unable to disguise my surprise.

'Oh, don't congratulate yourself, my lord,' he said with something of a smirk. 'I've sold that creature many times before. But it's always returned to me.'

'Oh yes?' I suddenly felt suspicious. 'Is it aggressive then?' I thought back to the fangs of the macaques. No doubt the monkey outside had a similar set of teeth – even if it was without the heart to bare them. I didn't have children myself, but there were children who visited Somershill regularly. Namely my nephew, Henry – a boy who was always accompanied by his over-protective and fussing mother, my sister Clemence. I was sure that she would have something to say about such a house guest.

The shopkeeper shook his head. 'No, no. It never bites or scratches. It just causes . . .' He hesitated. 'Well. Let me put it this way, my lord. It seems to cause melancholia. Even bad luck.'

'I don't believe in such things,' I said. 'So, you need not concern yourself on that front.'

The man merely raised an eyebrow.

I felt the sudden need to elaborate. 'It's a gift,' I said. 'For a person who is talented with such injured and abused animals. I can guarantee that she will not be disturbed by its melancholia. In fact, she will be moved by it.'

He disguised a snort, and then bowed to me. 'In that case, sire. The monkey is yours.'

My purchase was delivered to my inn later that same day. The monkey was free of its filthy cage, but the shopkeeper had made sure to fasten one metal ring to its leg and another to its neck. These two rings were then attached to a chain in order to create a double leash. Anybody would think the man had been supplying a lion from the king's enclosure at the Tower, rather than this reticent, cringing creature. The chains were heavy, so I chose to remove the ring from the monkey's leg immediately, so that it could enjoy a little more freedom of movement. But it refused steadfastly to take advantage of this new privilege, and instead chose to crouch in the corner with its face against the wall.

When the news of my purchase reached the innkeeper, he thumped at the door and entered the room without waiting for my command. The fool was full of bluster, claiming that the monkey was causing a great inconvenience to my fellow guests. The scent of the monkey had set off the dogs in the yard, and, in turn this had caused complaints amongst his other 'very respectable' customers. Neither of these claims bore any scrutiny, but the man demanded another shilling for a night's stay. I was due to return to Somershill the next day, so I offered to pay the greedy crook half what he was demanding and eventually we settled on a price, as long as I agreed to have all of the monkey's droppings removed before I left.

That evening, I tried to coax the creature into turning its face from the wall with a crust of bread, but my efforts were in vain. In fact, the harder I tried to gain its confidence, the more it shuffled into the corner, until its nose touched the damp wattle and daub of the wall, and it could shuffle forward no further. As I looked upon the patchy fur of its hunched back and the two knotted manes of white hair that flanked each side of its spine, I will admit that a wave of melancholia washed over me. I had purchased this creature with all the best intentions, but it seemed immune to my care. To be honest, its presence was starting to depress me.

However, I was determined not to be as fickle as those other people who had purchased the monkey, only to return it the next day. I was better than them. I would try harder, and where they had failed, I would succeed. So, when I heard the strawberry seller calling from the street below, I sent my valet to buy a punnet of the fruit. They were the sweetest, most delicious of strawberries, fresh from the fields, and guaranteed to tempt even this miserable simian from its solitude in the corner.

I offered the largest strawberry to the monkey, slowly provoking a reaction from the stubborn creature, as it turned its head and then picked the berry from my hand, before placing the fruit very gently into its mouth. It seemed to want more, so I continued to offer strawberries until we had exhausted the whole punnet. The monkey neither grabbed nor bolted the fruit. Instead it delicately ate each piece with the manners of a noblewoman.

With the strawberries exhausted, I would say that the monkey seemed a little revived. At last it turned from the corner, paying particular attention to the window from where the evening sun filled the room with shafts of golden light. Closing its eyes, the monkey allowed this burst of sunshine to warm its skin, blissfully soaking up the light after years in the dark confines of a London alley. Now its face no longer seemed sunken and skeletal, with its ragged corona of dirty fur. Instead the monkey seemed at peace. Joyful even. I looked to my valet, and we shared a smile. Our munificence had been justly rewarded.

The monkey opened its eyes sharply as a cock pigeon landed on the sill of our window and began to cluck and coo to a nearby hen. It was startled and then fascinated, as the pigeon strutted up and down the sill, puffing out its chest and bobbing its head. It stretched out its arms, as if it wanted to touch the other creature in an instinctive movement of delight, and suddenly I was reminded of my nephew Henry – flexing and clenching his fists in a passion to stroke Mother's small dog.

I don't know why I did it. Only that I should not have. But my pleasure in the monkey's change of heart was so great that it warped my judgement. I could save this creature. I could cure its melancholia. These things were within my power.

What foolishness. What vanity!

I unlocked the ring at the monkey's neck and I carried it to the open window. For a few minutes, the creature clung to my side and looked with unabated wonder at the world outside. The pale blue of the sky. The flock of pigeons on the opposite roof. The tendrils of smoke from the bread ovens of the inn. It cocked its small and expressive face and sucked in these sights, and when it seemed satisfied, I held it onto the sill, so that it might see more. This was my mistake. Now that the creature was away from the security of the room, it tensed. I tried to pull it back, but my reactions were too slow – for suddenly it leapt from my arms, jumping across the short gap between the inn and the building opposite. I called for it to return, but to no avail, and soon it was scampering away on all fours, across the roofs of London, as if it were fleeing a crowned eagle.

We looked for the monkey until the bells of St Bride's pealed their curfew, and we were forced to return to our inn. The next morning, I had an early meeting with the wool merchant, so I told my servants to renew their search. I even sanctioned a reward for the return of the creature. In truth, I felt as guilty as it is possible to feel. My foolishness in placing the monkey upon the windowsill had caused it to run away. It was my fault, and it could not survive long in the streets of London. It would either be set upon by dogs, starve in some corner, or be captured by a pack of mindless apprentices and teased to death. Its fate lay heavy on my conscience.

Nothing was found from our searches. No traces of the monkey, so I delayed my departure for one more night. Already the story of the escaping beast was making me something of a laughing stock. The next day, we packed our bags, mounted our palfreys, and departed for Somershill. As my small party progressed along West Cheap, I decided to call again at the shop in the dark alley. I would eat my pride, and buy one, or even both of the Barbary apes as the gift. But, as I turned the corner of the alley, past the mule and the mound of cabbage leaves, I saw it again. Its back hunched. Its fur matted. Its eyes cast to the floor.

I burst through the door of the shop, causing the shopkeeper to jump. 'Where did you find the monkey?' I demanded to know. The two Barbary apes shrieked and danced upon their perch, excited by my dramatic entrance.

The man took a deep breath. 'It came back here, my lord. Of its own accord.' He clasped his hands together. 'I found it in the cage this morning.' He looked genuinely ashamed. 'I thought about sending a message to your inn. But I thought you had abandoned the creature.'

'That's nonsense. Why would I do such a thing?'

'I told you before, my lord. The monkey causes melancholia. People cannot stand its company for long.' He cleared his throat. 'To be honest, it has the same effect on me. That's why I keep it outside the shop.'

'I don't believe you,' I said. 'No animal would willingly return to such a foul coop. I think you caught it and had no intention of letting me know.'

The shopkeeper was reddening, and his fists were tightening. 'I did no such thing, my lord! It returned of its own volition.'

'Nonsense!'

'Go outside then,' he said. 'Go on. Look at the cage yourself. You will see that the door is unlocked. The creature can leave at any time, but it chooses not to.'

I strode out of the shop, but knew already that he was telling the truth. The cage was, indeed, unlocked. The creature could leave, but didn't. The monkey recognised me, but I did not receive the warm welcome I had envisaged. It flung its hands over its head and cringed in the furthest corner of the cage. It truly was the most dismal, melancholic and pitiful of sights; and, for a moment, a great weight of despair bore down upon me.

The shopkeeper was at my shoulder. His indignation gone, replaced by a little of the resignation I felt myself. 'You mustn't blame yourself, my lord. You tried to save it.'

My chest tightened. 'What's the matter with it? What have you done to it?'

He puffed his lips. 'Please don't blame me, my lord. It was just as morose when I bought it five years ago.'

'Have you tried to restore its spirits?'

'Of course I have.' He threw up his hands. 'A monkey like this would sell for a very good sum indeed, if it were in better humours.' He then heaved another of his long sighs. 'But it will always be like this, no matter what we do. It cannot be cured.'

'I don't agree.'

The shopkeeper shook his head. 'No. I'm afraid you're wrong, my lord. I've tried and tried, but it never responds.' He paused. 'So, do you know what I think?'

'No.'

'I think it prefers to be miserable.'

'That can't be true.'

'Being miserable is all that it knows.'

I left London that same day, but for many nights after my return to Somershill, the monkey haunted my dreams. At first I felt all of the pity and compassion that I had experienced when first seeing the creature – alongside a certain amount of guilt that I had not tried again to save it. However, as the monkey continued to interrupt my sleep, turning up each night with a depressing and irksome monotony, I began to dread going to bed. I only had to close my eyes to see its matted fur, its hunched back, and its creeping, skulking gait as it moved across the room with its hands dragging to the floor. I could see its small, leathery face, and its dark, reproachful eyes, and I could feel all of its seething hopelessness and despair. I tried to retain my pity and compassion for the creature. I didn't want to believe the shop-keeper's assertion that it preferred to be miserable, but soon even the thought of the monkey made me feel sick. My sympathy had turned to dread, and then, in turn, my dread had turned to disgust.

Chapter Eleven

I might have convinced Giovanni that I didn't believe in demo-
nites, but I still had a hard job to persuade the man to leave my
bedchamber. After promising, for at least the fifth time, that I
was perfectly sanguine and had no intention of climbing back
onto the windowsill, he departed – but not before promising to
make visits at frequent intervals in order to check upon my well-
being. When I could be sure that he had finally descended the
stairs and was not likely to make a sudden reappearance, I
decided to change my clothes and wash my face. The whole
episode had exhausted me, though exhaustion was preferable to
the agitated madness that had gripped me earlier.

It was as I untied my belt and my purse fell to the floor with a
heavy thud, that I was suddenly reminded of the coins within. I
picked the purse up cautiously and then opened the strings a
little, but only enough to see that the coins were still there,
settled together like a clutch of golden eggs in a nest. Seeing
their glinting perfection did not cause any excitement this time,
instead I was struck by a short rush of guilt, so I quickly retied
the strings and then hid the purse in the bottom of my oak chest
– placing it firstly inside one of my old socks, and then adding a
second, before making sure to turn the key. I had no energy left
to consider what I would do with them, other than to know that
they were safe inside my locked chest.

After this I lay upon my bed, and must have drifted off into some much-needed sleep until being woken by a commotion from outside. This was more than the shouting and cheering of a carnival, so I quickly went down the stairs to the *piano nobile*, bumping into Bernard as he flew across the room with a bowl of water in his hands, and some lengths of linen draped over his sleeve.

'What's happening?' I said. 'I can hear crowds outside.'

Bernard was panting and took a moment to compose himself. 'There is peace with Hungary, my lord! Venice has signed the treaty.'

'Has Venice surrendered her Dalmatian ports to Hungary?'

Bernard continued to puff. 'Yes. I believe they are lost. But at least the ships can leave now.' So, this explained why we had seen a merchant galley in the lagoon earlier that day. It must have been sailing for the Adriatic the moment that peace was announced.

'How has this been received?' I asked, but my question appeared to confuse Bernard. 'Are the Venetians happy with the treaty?' I asked. When he continued to frown, I said, 'I could hear a commotion outside. Is there some trouble in the city?'

Bernard gulped, as if my three questions had arrived in his head in a single delivery. 'No, no, my lord. The Venetians are relieved, I believe. They can trade again, and there will be food for the poorest.' He let out a long and expressive sigh. 'It is mine and Margery's deepest wish that the suffering of the poor should be alleviated.'

I had yet to see evidence of this allegiance to the poor, as Bernard and his sister seemed more interested in visiting shrines and buying indulgences — whilst the destitute of Venice had to make do with their prayers. 'Are you unwell?' I asked, pointing at the bowl of water and the lengths of clean linen.

'Oh no, my lord,' said Bernard quickly. 'There's nothing wrong with me.'

I pulled at one of the linen strips and gave a short laugh. 'Are you helping to deliver a child?'

Now Bernard's brow puckered again with confusion. 'A child, my lord? Goodness me. I . . . um—'

'I'm just teasing you,' I said.

His face relaxed into an awkward smile. 'Ah! I see.' He moved back almost imperceptibly – just far enough that my hand could no longer touch his arm. 'Then, let me bid you good day.' He bowed quickly to me and then retreated towards his own bedchamber, continuing to bob his head until he assumed that I was no longer watching him. When he reached the centre of the room, he broke into a run towards the door of the bedchamber that he shared with his sister.

'Oh Bernard,' I said, deciding to give chase, as there was something questionable, even suspicious about his behaviour.

As I reached him, he quickly stood in front of the door to block my entry. 'Please, Lord Somershill,' he whispered. 'I can't stop. I must see to my sister.'

'What's going on, Bernard?' I asked, trying to look over his shoulder.

He wiped some perspiration from his brow. 'Please, my lord. Don't ask me to explain.'

I pushed the man aside and opened the door, to find Margery lying in near darkness. At my entrance, she hurriedly pulled her blanket to her chin, but even so, I could still see that her face was wounded and bloody.

Now Bernard behaved with some aggression. 'Please Lord Somershill. You must respect Margery's modesty. You are a man, and this is her private chamber, so I must demand that you leave!'

I stood my ground. 'What has happened to your sister, Bernard?' The man remained stubbornly mute. 'I'm not going to leave this room until you tell me.'

He heaved a long sigh, and then dropped the linen to the bed. 'She was set upon by two men. They threw her to the ground and beat her.'

'Where did this happen?'

'We were in an alley, making our way home from mass at the church of San Giacomo di Rialto.'

'Why didn't you walk along the Merceria?'

'Margery is afraid of the crowds, my lord.'

'So you walked down a dark alley?' I looked at him reproachfully. 'You know how dangerous that is.'

He wrung his hands. 'I know, my lord. I know. But Margery has a dread of being crushed. Cities do not suit her constitution.'

'Then I might ask why you chose to visit the largest city in Europe.' He looked at me blankly. 'Did you see your attackers?' I asked.

He shook his head. 'I'm afraid not. It was . . .' His voice trailed away.

'Dark?'

He nodded. 'Yes.' Then he fixed me with a sudden gaze, losing all former meekness. 'We were followed, Lord Somershill.'

'Followed? From where?'

He looked about the room. 'This house,' he whispered, drawing closer to me. 'Somebody is trying to murder us all, my lord. Every single one of us in Ca' Bearpark. First it was Enrico. Then it was to be my sister. If I hadn't roused some passers-by, then poor Margery would be dead.'

'Are you sure it was not just a robbery?' I said, causing Bernard to squint a little, as if unable to understand my train of thought. 'Did they steal anything from Margery?' I asked more plainly.

'Well yes,' he admitted. 'Her purse was stolen. But even so—'

'Then I think their motive was theft, not murder.' Before Bernard could argue with me, I tried to walk around him and approach the bed. 'I need to see Margery's injuries,' I said.

Bernard stepped in front of me with deftness, and nearly had the gall to push me away. 'I'm afraid I cannot allow that, my lord.'

I cleared my throat and straightened my cloak. 'I was trained under the infirmarer in a monastery, Bernard. I know how to wash wounds.'

'But Margery is the most pious of women,' he said. 'She would not want be touched by any man but her brother. It would only add to her misery.'

I looked over Bernard's shoulder to see that Margery had covered her head with the blanket, and was now curled up into a ball on the bed. 'Very well then,' I sighed. 'I wouldn't want to cause your sister any further distress, Bernard. Though it's important that the injuries are properly cleaned.'

He bowed his head. 'Thank you, my lord. I will make sure of it.'

'Do you have some salt?' I asked, as he directed me towards the door. 'It will help to clear any corruption.'

'I do.'

'If her wounds become infected, then you should apply some lard to draw the pus.'

'I will,' he promised, nodding his head profusely. 'I am most honoured at your concern for Margery,' he said. Then, as he opened the door, he whispered, 'But will you find the murderer, my lord? Poor Margery is so nervous.'

I tried to give a confident smile. 'Of course I will.'

There was a meal in celebration of the peace that evening, though it was hardly a festive affair, given the attack on Margery and the state of Bearpark's health. It was far too early for any imported food to have reached the markets, so the meal itself did nothing to lift our spirits, as the cook served a heavily spiced stew of fish from the lagoon. The heads of these silver fish bobbed about as if they were coming up for air, and the empty shells of the clams floated about the water like butterflies. Looking at this stew, I thanked the Fates that I had lost my appetite.

Mother complained about the seasoning and smell of the dish. Filomena once again seemed too uncomfortable to sit in one position for long, and soon took her leave of the table to sit upon a more padded chair in the corner. When Mother gave her usual refrain that Filomena should be confined to her bedchamber in readiness for childbirth, Filomena pretended not to understand a word that Mother had said. I caught Filomena's eye, and a spark of understanding, even amusement passed between us.

This thrill did not last for long, however, as Giovanni joined us towards the end of the meal with news that John Bearpark's condition continued to deteriorate. The old man was now refusing food, and had spent most of the day sleeping. There were now only two desires that were keeping him alive – to see his new son born, and to see his grandson's murderer brought to justice. For the second time that evening I shared a secret glance with Filomena, but this time it did not induce a surge of amusement. Instead we shared an unease, for the weight of expectation lay heavily upon both our shoulders.

Before I slept that night, I tried to write down my findings in my small notebook. The candlelight spread its orange glow across the parchment and picked up the indentation of the writing that had previously covered the page. For a while, I found myself trying to decipher what these old words said – but this was not the mystery I needed to solve. I washed my face in the basin, noting that the water had not been changed since the morning, and then I forced myself to concentrate my thoughts upon Enrico's murder. My efforts only resulted in two words. Two words that I circled three times – Adolpho Bredani.

Chapter Twelve

I rose at first light and sought out Giovanni, giving him instructions to assemble as many men as could be spared from among the servants, and then to meet me in the kitchen. When I joined him shortly after, I was disappointed to find that Giovanni had only managed to muster three men – a trio who could hardly be described as the most able from the household. One stooped like an aged hunchback, one squinted as if he could barely see, and the last one held his head at an angle, as if he were trying to rid his ear of water.

'Is there nobody else?' I asked Giovanni, in English.

'My master is near death, Oswald. No other servants can be spared.'

'I need you to find me some more men. Three will not be enough.'

Giovanni bowed his head, before giving me a sidelong glance. 'There is nobody to spare.' He reddened. 'With my master ill, the servants are already moving to new houses. Or even the palaces along the Canal Grande.'

It was an undeniable truth that the household of Ca' Bearpark was shrinking. I had noticed that there were fewer and fewer servants about the place, and I had even been obliged to air and then straighten my own bed the previous day.

'Very well,' I said, with something of a sigh. 'They will have to do. Please tell them that I need them to look for Adolpho Bredani.'

A look of surprise, or possibly disbelief, crossed Giovanni's face. 'You want these men to search for Bredani?'

'Yes. That's what I said, didn't I?' Giovanni attempted to answer, but I spoke over him. 'It's not a difficult task,' I said. 'Please ask them to visit the taverns and inns of the city, or anywhere else where Bredani might be hiding.' Giovanni tried, once again, to interrupt, so I spoke even more loudly. 'If they see Bredani, they must not approach him. Do you understand? I simply want to know where the man is.'

Giovanni remained silent for a few moments, toying with the keys at his belt. 'Is this wise, Oswald?' he said, after a long pause. 'I think we should follow my master's instructions today and search for Enrico's . . . friends.' This word dropped from his lips as if it pained him.

'Adolpho is still my main suspect,' I said. 'I've told you that before.'

He frowned. 'But I fear we are wasting our time again. As we did in Burano.' He bowed to soften the impertinence of this remark, but it still irritated me.

'Did Master Bearpark instruct *you* to conduct this investigation?' I said.

He bowed again. 'No.'

'Then, do as I ask.' I pointed to the three men who stood before us. 'Tell them to search for Bredani.'

I was staring out of the window from the *piano nobile*, watching my three unlikely scouts set forth upon their quest, when somebody tapped me on the shoulder.

'Venice is a wonder, isn't it, my lord?' said Bernard, looking down into the street. 'Every sight is a spectacle.'

'How is your sister?' I asked quickly, not wanting to be drawn into a conversation with Bernard about the delights of this city.

Bernard stared at me for a moment, as if he had forgotten about Margery's attack, before the memory alighted with a jolt.

'Ah yes, thank you, my lord. Margery is making a good recovery. God willing, her wounds have healed with miraculous speed, though I'm afraid that her spirits are less responsive.' His voice was suddenly full of regret. 'I'm afraid she will not leave Ca' Bearpark, for fear of being followed and attacked again.'

'She need not worry on that front, Bernard. I'm sure the robbery Margery endured has no link whatsoever to Enrico's murder.'

Bernard didn't answer, choosing instead to look at my face for a few moments, before speaking in a whisper. 'I wish that were true. Margery has something to tell you, my lord. About the murder.'

'Has she broken her vow of silence then?'

He gasped. 'Indeed not! She hasn't said a word since we sailed from Felixstowe.' He looked about to check that we were truly alone. 'She has written it down, you see. As a testament.' He then felt about in his scrip, disturbing his collection of pewter badges before producing a roll of parchment. 'I'm afraid it is written in English, as women do seem to struggle so with Latin. But I hope it is of some assistance to your investigation.'

I tried to take the roll from him, but he held onto the parchment with an unexpected determination. 'Will you promise to return the testament to me as soon as you have read its contents?' I tried again to pull the parchment from his hands, but Bernard would not give up this prize so easily. 'I beg you, my lord. The writing of this epistle has caused poor Margery a great deal of anguish, especially after her recent attack.'

'Then you must let me read it, Bernard.'

He released it with some reluctance. 'Very well, my lord.'

I waited for Bernard to wander away to the other end of the *piano nobile*, before I unrolled the letter. I must say, I had few expectations that anything of note would be revealed, but these were her words:

*Here begins the true and sincere testament of Margery Jagger, by
the mercy of Jesus. The knowledge of this sin has filled this creature's heart with sorrow and heaviness, and she has been disturbed
and tormented by demons and spirits ever since its occasion. In
response, this creature has desired to pitilessly tear at her skin in
penance, and to weep and sob with misery, but that such sounds
would break her holy vows of silence.*

This creature? Why was Margery calling herself such a name?
I nearly summoned Bernard to return this diatribe there and
then, but the next lines caught my attention:

*Two months ago, on the feast day of Saint Stephen in the last
year, this creature was seeking sanctuary for silent prayer and
reflection in a storeroom of Ca' Bearpark. It was here, Lord
forgive this said creature, that she witnessed Enrico Bearpark
engaged in a wicked and unnatural act with another man. She
did not see this other man's face, but she knew him to be a man
from the roughness of his voice and the shape of his body. This
creature has sworn a vow of silence, so she could not call out to
condemn their sin. Instead she hid herself and prayed for their
souls. While she closed her eyes and called upon the Virgin and all
the saints of Heaven, the two men began to fight like Devils. This
creature does not know the Venetian tongue, but she knows that
their dispute was cruel and vicious, for when they had departed
the room, she found blood on the floor. This is her true and
honest testament. Lord forgive this creature and preserve her soul
from sin.*

I quickly rolled the parchment up and walked across the room
to find Bernard skulking by the door, his vacant smile wiped
from his face. 'Margery regrets not telling you about this incident before,' he said. 'I do hope that you can forgive her.'
'Is this all she knows?' I said.

He nodded vigorously. 'Oh yes, my lord. Please don't press her further, particularly not in her current condition. There is nothing more that she can tell you.' He held out his hand for the letter, but I kept hold of it.

'I just need to borrow this a little longer,' I said.

'But you promised, my lord,' he called after me as I strode away.

'You can have it back later.'

I found Giovanni in his office, writing up figures in an account entitled 'investigation costs', with a column named 'items sanctioned by Oswald de Lacy, Lord Somershill'. I tried not to let this annoy me.

'Can you remember which of Enrico's friends were here on the Feast of Saint Stephen?' I asked Giovanni.

He gave a shrug. 'No, Oswald. I can't. That was nearly two months ago.' He paused. 'Why are you asking?' I passed him Margery's testament and let him read the document twice. His face fell. 'Such wickedness,' was all he could say, with frequent repetition, before he looked up at me accusingly. 'You see, Oswald. We should have followed my master's advice before. This murder has nothing to do with Adolpho Bredani.'

I would not accept defeat quite so quickly. 'Could the man that Margery describes here have been Adolpho Bredani?' I asked. 'He would have been in the house at the Feast of Saint Stephen.'

'Bredani loved women,' said Giovanni. 'I told you that before.'

'But—'

'Bredani returned to Burano for Christmas, Oswald. I gave him permission myself.' He waved the letter at me. 'Now we can be sure.'

I sat down on the small stool and let my head rest in my hands, making sure not to catch Giovanni's eye, for I needed to think, without the distraction of looking into his self-satisfied face. Perhaps I had made a mistake. Perhaps Bearpark was right?

I unhooked Giovanni's cloak from the wall and passed it to him. 'Come on then.'

'Where are we going?' he asked.

'Following your master's advice.'

It had rained overnight, so rather than walk to Castello, we took the family's *sàndolo* as far as the Piazza San Marco, weaving along the maze of narrow canals, until we disembarked on the north side of the square. Now that there was peace with Hungary, Venice was going about its business with energy and spirit, despite the fact that this was a Sunday. As they say in this city, you are Venetian first, and Christian second. Everywhere about us men were organising crews for ships; boys were running about with handcarts full of heavy sacks; merchants were locked in loud and argumentative debates with one another.

We were skirting the Piazza when we passed a gang of slaves, newly disembarked from a ship in the Molo. They were a dirty, hopeless-looking group of men, women, and children who had been captured in the lands to the north of the Black Sea by the Tartars and then sold to Venetian merchants. I could not look into their faces, but Giovanni made a point of crossing himself and calling them heathens and savages – condemned to slavery by the Curse of Ham. I walked away quickly, feeling saddened by their plight, but what use was my pity to these people? It would not free them of their chains, nor send them back to their own lands. I could only hope that they found kind masters and did not end up in the sugar plantations of Cyprus and Candia.

As we crossed the Piazza, the oblique light of the morning sun trained its weak rays upon the four latticed domes and golden mosaics of the Basilica. I had always admired this church, but after seeing the slaves, my mood was bleak and I found myself wondering if there might be a more ostentatious building in the whole of Europe? Clad in all the treasures that the Venetians had stripped from the cathedrals and palaces of Constantinople, it was as over-decorated as the king's latest mistress.

We walked on apace towards the Molo, with the doge's palace to our left, and the two Columns of Justice to our right. In the lagoon before us, men were already removing the poles of wood that had been designed to form a stockade against any Hungarian invasion. It was in this place, months earlier, that I had seen a man being burnt to death. Today's scene was little better, for now a cage had been suspended between the two columns, and within this cage was a man who was being starved to death. His legs and arms dangled hopelessly through the bars, and his head flopped to one side. As we stopped to look, a man pushed past us and then winched a bottle of water into the cage.

'Why are they giving him something to drink?' I asked Giovanni.

'So that he doesn't die too quickly.' When I recoiled at this explanation, Giovanni threw me a look of disapproval. 'He killed a child, Oswald. He deserves to die.'

'But this is a cruel way to execute a criminal. Don't you think?'

He raised his eyebrows. 'You don't do such things in England?'

I thought back to the executions I had witnessed in London and Rochester, and knew that I should not complain at the quality of Venetian justice? 'Not this particular form of torture,' I said. 'But I suppose we have our own versions.'

'At least this man had a trial,' he said pointedly. 'Not like some.'

'What do you mean?'

Giovanni looked over his shoulder, and then whispered into my ear. 'Some criminals are strangled. Silently.'

'Why?'

He rested a hand upon my arm. 'Because they are the enemies of Venice. They are spies or traitors, and nobody knows that they are dead until they wash up in the Assassin's canal. Their bodies are . . .' He struggled for the correct word. 'They are cut up. Do you understand?'

'You mean mutilated?'

He smiled. 'Yes. I do. Mutilated.' He said it again. 'Mutilated. That's a good word.'

'Is it?'

Giovanni dropped his smile and crossed himself, before dusting down his cloak and quickly changing the subject. 'So, Oswald, will you tell me where we are going now?'

'Just follow me,' I said. 'You'll know soon enough.'

We pushed against the crowd of people who were disembarking along the quay and making their way to the many stalls that lined the Piazza San Marco. Small children darted amongst us, and for a moment I thought that I glimpsed a familiar face – it was the boy who had led me back to Ca' Bearpark for two *soldini* on the night of Enrico's murder. He was still hanging around the house with his troupe of ragged friends, so was it possible that he had followed us here? Or was his just another dirty face in a crowd of dirty faces? I put the thought from my mind as the great campanile of the Piazza sounded the *nona* for midday, reminding me that time was passing quickly – too quickly.

Leaving the Piazzetta, we soon reached the small bridge over the Rio Palazzo, and it was here that Giovanni stopped in his tracks and refused to move. 'Are we going into Castello?' he asked.

'Yes.'

He appeared to stamp his foot. 'No, no. I cannot go into this *sestiere*. It is a place for the coarse and the dirty.'

'I don't care.'

His face froze with indignation. 'Why? Why must we go into Castello?'

I couldn't refrain from smiling. 'To visit one of Enrico's friends, of course,' before adding, 'just as your master wanted.'

He gave a huff. 'You think these friends are here?'

'I know they are,' I said. 'Enrico often drank at a particular tavern in Castello, and sometimes I accompanied him.'

Giovanni faltered. 'But, but we need to find . . .' he began to whisper '. . . a different type of friend. You know that.'

'One of Enrico's circle of friends was his lover. Margery confirmed that in her testimony.' Giovanni wrinkled his nose and shrugged at my assertion. 'You read the letter yourself, Giovanni,' I said, with some annoyance. 'Margery saw Enrico with this violent man on the feast of Saint Stephen. It must have been somebody from his circle, as otherwise what were they doing in the house?'

Giovanni shook his head vigorously. 'No, no. Enrico's friends were from good families. They were all noblemen.'

'So was Enrico.'

'It could have been a secret visitor?' said Giovanni. 'Or even a servant?'

'A servant?' I raised an eyebrow. 'So, you think that Enrico was murdered by somebody that you had employed?'

Giovanni's face froze in horror. 'Of course not. I'm very careful about the servants that I choose.'

'Then come on. Let's speak to one of his friends.'

As we walked along the Riva degli Schiavoni towards the Molo, we passed many galleys at anchor – their masts like a great forest of standing oaks. Across the lagoon the island of Giudecca and the monastery of San Giorgio were outlined against a pale blue sky. I stopped for a moment, for Venice could be so disarmingly beautiful, but then I thought back to the slave gang, and the rotting man who was hanging in his cage above the Piazzetta, and I remembered that there was poison beneath this perfection.

We soon turned from the Molo into the narrow lanes of Castello, where the water in the canal changed from a pale blue into the green lustre of a bluebottle's breastplate. We had lost the open vistas and cheering sunlight, and now found ourselves inside a cluttered cupboard of people who existed in some of the darkest and most overcrowded conditions in this city.

As we made our way along the streets, we stood out immediately as strangers – just as we had done on our visit to Burano. The eyes of Venice were upon us from every angle. Men stopped their carts to observe us, whilst women pushed their washing aside to look down on us from their first-storey windows. A group of girls, gathered about the solitary well head in the middle of their *campo*, broke away from their scheming huddle to watch us pass. Their leader had a striking face – beautiful, but severe – and I let my eyes rest upon her for a moment longer than was polite.

Giovanni shoved me in the back. 'Don't look at them,' he said. 'Keep walking.'

'They're just girls,' I said.

He scowled. 'Don't be fooled, Oswald.' Then he muttered something under his breath that I think was, 'she-devils'.

After dodging a group of boys who were throwing a leather ball against a wall, we came, at last, to our destination – a tavern that only advertised itself as a hostelry by the group of men laid about its door in various stages of inebriation.

Giovanni stepped back with revulsion. 'You came here?' he said, as I forced him to step inside a stuffy, poorly lit chamber with benches spread about the floor.

'Yes,' I said. 'What of it?'

He dusted down his cloak and took a deep breath of air, as if to brace himself for a fight. 'Who are we looking for, Oswald?'

'One of Enrico's friends,' I said. 'I know that he drinks here. His name is Michele.' I paused. 'But I'm sure that you know him too. He was a regular visitor to Ca' Bearpark.'

Giovanni nodded lightly and then flicked his fringe from his eye. He knew Michele well enough. Who could forget the man with the striped hose, long feathered cap, and habit of rearranging his bollocks in public? 'And why are we starting with Michele?'

I felt uncomfortable at this question. For how could I admit the truth? That I had decided to start with Michele, since he was the most effeminate of Enrico's circle. A man who wore the brightest, tightest clothes, and seemed the most interested in fashion and the curl of his hair. 'I think Michele is hiding something,' I said loosely. Then I tapped the purse that hung from Giovanni's belt. 'Have you brought any money with you?'

Giovanni tensed at this question. 'Why?'

'We may need to pay for this information.'

When Giovanni tried to object, I walked on, swiping away the smoke until I found Michele, elegantly lounging in a corner with one hand on a bottle of wine and the other, predictably, down his braies. As we approached, I gave a loud cough, in the hope of rousing the man; but when this approach had failed for a second and even a third time, I pressed my foot against his leg and gave the fellow a quick shove. At this, Michele jumped to his feet with the instinct of a startled dog, and drew a knife on us.

When he recognised me, he returned the blade to his sleeve and laughed. 'Oh, it's you. Silent Englishman. What are you doing here?'

'I wanted to speak to you, Michele,' I said.

His smile waned. 'What about?'

'Enrico Bearpark.'

Michele looked at me for a moment with suspicion, before sitting down again on the bench. 'I hear that my friend is dead.'

Giovanni and I shared a glance. 'Yes,' I said. 'Enrico died three nights ago.'

Michele gave a short, derisive laugh. 'Don't tell me he *died*. I know he was beaten to death by robbers at the *Giovedi Grasso*.'

I exchanged a second glance with Giovanni. So this was the story that was circulating? 'It might have been robbery,' I said.

'What else could it have been?'

'That's what I'm investigating.'

Michele let another smirk cross his lips. 'You? The Silent Englishman. Why would *you* be investigating anything?'

I tried not to be provoked by this. 'Enrico's grandfather has asked me to look into his death,' I said.

'Why?'

'Because I have experience with such investigations.'

Michele took a gulp from the bottle and then wiped the red residue from his lips. 'I don't know why you want to talk to me? I had nothing to do with Enrico's death.'

I took a seat beside Michele, leaving Giovanni to stand awkwardly behind us, with his eyes fastened to the floor. Even in this light, I could see that my companion had coloured, and when I looked across the smoky chamber, I could see the cause of his embarrassment. A figure in a far corner was waving to him – it was a woman with a very low neckline to her gown.

I extinguished a quick smile and turned back to Michele. 'I need to find out a little more about Enrico,' I said, causing Michele once again to regard me with suspicion. His eyes narrowed. 'I need to know about those parts of his life that he kept secret.' I hesitated, wondering how to phrase my next question. 'I understand that Enrico had lovers.'

Michele puffed. 'We all have lovers.' He then looked at me disparagingly. 'Apart from you, I expect.' He waved his hand over my outfit. 'I doubt you have any luck dressed in those clothes.'

I ignored the insult. 'Yes. But Enrico was different, wasn't he?' I dropped my words to a whisper. 'His lovers were men.'

Michele froze. 'Says who?'

'That doesn't matter.'

He sat up straight and focussed his eyes upon me. 'Who sent you here? Was it the Signori di Notte?' He reached inside his sleeve again for his knife. 'Are you one of their spies?'

'No,' I said. 'I'm nothing to do with the Signori. But even so I need to know the truth.'

'Get out of here,' he said, now pointing the knife at my face. 'Get out of here with your accusations.'

The knife glinted in the candlelight, but I didn't move. 'Was it you, Michele?' I said. 'Were you Enrico's lover?'

'Keep your mouth shut!'

'Did you argue with Enrico, and then kill him?' I pointed to his knife, which was now so close to my cheek that I could almost feel the blade. 'You seem very ready to attack.'

Suddenly he had grabbed me, holding my neck in an arm-lock with the tip of his knife biting into the skin of my throat. 'You think you can come in here and say such things to me?' he said. 'Such insults?'

I remained perfectly still, whilst Giovanni unhelpfully flapped his arms and made a great fluster behind me. 'Put your knife away, Michele,' I said evenly. 'I just want the truth.'

The knife bit harder. He hissed in my ear. 'I'll tell you the truth, Silent Englishman. I have never taken a man as a lover, and I never will. Do you understand? And if you ever come here and make such an accusation again, then I will cut your throat.' With this, he twisted the knife until it pierced my skin, before he released me with a thrust, sending me flying across the room. 'Go on!' he said, trying to chase me from the tavern. 'Go back to John Bearpark. Tell him that there are no stains on *my* conscience. Tell the old fool to look at himself in the mirror.'

I put my hand to my throat and found that he had drawn blood. 'What do you mean by that?' I said, standing my ground and refusing to be chased any further.

Michele folded his arms. 'Ask Bearpark about the letter of denunciation.'

I looked to Giovanni for an explanation, but my companion only re-fastened his eyes to the floor.

'Oh I see. You didn't know about that, did you?' said Michele, with a laugh. 'The Bearparks have been denounced. A letter was sent to the Consiglio.'

'I don't understand?' I said, looking again to Giovanni. 'What letter?'

Michele slipped the knife into his sleeve, and reseated himself upon the bench. 'Not so pleased to be John Bearpark's investigator now then, are you?' he said with a smirk. 'Not when the Bearpark family has enemies who will denounce them to the Consiglio dei Dieci. Enemies who will stick their nasty little accusations into the mouth of the lion.'

I turned to Giovanni. 'What mouth? What lion?' He shrugged, pretending once again not to hear me, so I grasped him by the fur of his cloak. 'What is this man talking about?'

Giovanni cringed away from me. 'There are special boxes,' he said nervously. 'Carved with the faces of the lion of St Mark.'

'And?'

'A person may post a letter into these mouths. It is read by the Consiglio dei Dieci.'

'What sort of letters?'

Giovanni tried to shake me off, but I would not release him. 'They are accusations of immoral behaviour,' he said, pretending to choke.

Michele interrupted. 'Don't tell lies, clerk. The Consiglio don't care about immorality. They care about corruption and treason.'

I squeezed my hand tighter, no matter that Giovanni's choking act was becoming more dramatic. 'So, what did this letter say?'

'I don't know.'

'Come on Giovanni. Don't lie to me.'

His coughing reached a new crescendo, and I was forced to release my hold, as we had attracted an audience. When he had finally cleared his throat, straightened his hair, and then felt for his keys, Giovanni looked up at me. 'I don't know what the letter said, Oswald. You must believe me.' He then gave a mournful sigh. 'My master wouldn't tell me.'

'But you knew there was a letter?'

Giovanni went to answer, but we were interrupted by Michele's laughter.

'What's so amusing?' I said, turning to the man who once again had a hand down his braies.

'What a skilful investigator you are, Silent Englishman,' said Michele, nearly choking on his own hilarity. 'Everybody knows about this letter, but you!'

Chapter Thirteen

I strode through Castello in a rage, whilst Giovanni trotted at my heels, only summoning the courage to speak to me when I had taken a wrong turn, or was about to be drenched by a bucket of slops from an upper window. He tried repeatedly to apologise for not telling me about the letter of denunciation, but I refused to listen to his litany of regrets and excuses. Giovanni should have told me, and that was the end of it. My mood only worsened when I happened to notice the face of the ragged boy again in the crowds. There was no doubt now, this child was following me.

When we finally arrived back at Ca' Bearpark, I strode through the courtyard and went up the exterior staircase three steps at a time, whilst the servants stood aside and let me pass. Giovanni still scampered in my wake like a dog, and it was only when I reached the bottom of the stairs to Bearpark's bedchamber, that he gathered the courage to stop me. I looked down to see his fingers grasping my cloak.

'Please, Oswald. My master may be sleeping.' He was panting, in an attempt to regain his breath after our brisk march across the city. 'You should ask if he is well enough to talk before you go in.'

I pulled my cloak away. 'Just leave me alone, Giovanni.'

As he attempted to hold on, I experienced the sudden desire to kick him away. My foot almost throbbed with enthusiasm. But thankfully the moment passed, for, as I looked across the *piano nobile*, I saw that Filomena was watching me with solemn intent.

I quickly bowed to her, and Giovanni did the same, though his acknowledgement was delivered with the usual contempt he showed to his master's young wife. I then asked Filomena if Bearpark was well enough to receive guests, and she nodded, giving me permission to proceed. I did not wait around to hear her answers to Giovanni's further questions to her on this matter. He wondered if she was sure of this fact, and did not Master Bearpark like to sleep in the afternoon? I only heard the tone of her response as I climbed the stairs, and it was not polite.

I pushed at the door of Bearpark's chamber to find Mother at the end of his bed, rubbing a pungent balm into the old man's bony feet. 'What are you doing here, Mother?' I asked, as Giovanni edged into the room behind me, only to remain by the wall.

Mother raised her hands into the air, splaying her fingers as if they were covered in dough. 'I'm rubbing some Treacle of Venice into John's feet,' she said. 'The poor man is losing the feeling in his toes.' She then pointed at a small glass jar beside the bed. 'I bought this remedy for you, Oswald. Do you remember? From that apothecary at the Rialto market.' She gave a sigh. 'Not that it did any good.' I did remember the man, and I did remember his remedy – the so-called *Teriaca* or 'Treacle of Venice' as it is known in England. It is a foul-smelling mixture of pulverised roots, leaves, and spices, with the addition, so the apothecary claimed, of crushed viper's skin and powdered scorpion. Mother had rubbed this balm onto my forehead repeatedly to cure my melancholia, but it will come as no surprise to hear that it had no effect upon my mood, other than to annoy me.

'Can you leave us please, Mother. I need to speak to Bearpark.'

She looked aghast at this request, as if I had announced that I wanted to take the man out for a gallop on his most hot-blooded stallion. 'But John is sleeping, Oswald. Come back later, when he's taking his broth.'

'No. I want to speak to him now.'

She directed me into a corner of the room, indicating that she wanted a private conversation. 'We've already had quite a disturbance this morning, Oswald,' she whispered. 'Those two foolish pilgrims burst in and caused an argument.'

'I thought Margery was staying in her room, after her attack?' I said.

Mother shook her head in irritation. 'Well she was here as well, Oswald. With her great shining black eye. Anybody would think the woman had contested a wrestling match on Lammas Eve.'

'The black eye is hardly Margery's fault, Mother. She was attacked.'

'Yes, I know all about that Oswald.' She crossed the room to the basin of water and washed her hands free of the *Teriaca*. 'It is her brother I blame, and his foolish desire for taking shortcuts. The very same calamity might have befallen me on *Giovedi Grasso*, you know. Even though I begged that fool to take the main streets.' She shook the water from her hands. 'The pair are very odd. Imagine the impertinence – striding in here and demanding that I leave the room.'

'Did you comply?'

She fanned her face with her hand. 'I had no choice, Oswald. Bernard might be little more than a pedlar, but he was very insistent.'

'And you didn't listen at the door?'

She folded her arms and looked back at Giovanni, to make sure that he was out of earshot. 'I only stayed on the landing in case John needed me,' she said defensively. 'I wasn't cavesdropping.'

'Of course not,' I whispered. 'But nevertheless, did you hear anything?'

Now that we'd established that her snooping was merely acci-
dental, she softened. 'From what I could hear, Bernard was upset
about Enrico's murder. There was a good deal of shouting until I
rushed in and put a stop to it.' She leant a little closer. 'I think the
foolish man was afraid that the murderer would return and
attack Margery. Or so he said, as I chased him out of the room.'

I turned to see that Giovanni had edged towards us and wanted
my attention. 'We should come back later, Oswald,' he said nervously. 'My master is sleeping.'

I now had two opponents, which only served to harden my
resolve to speak to the old man. So, instead of taking their advice,
I made a point of crossing the room and tapping vigorously on
Bearpark's arm until he woke with a start.

'What's the matter?' he shouted. 'What is it?'

Mother ran to his side. 'I'm so sorry, John, but my son seems
desperate to speak with you.' She then threw me a hostile glance,
before stooping to speak very slowly and deliberately into his
ear. 'I expect Oswald has made some important progress with
the investigation, so you must forgive his enthusiasm. He just
wants to tell you his news.' She then made a great display of
tucking the sheets under his chin, only for Bearpark to pull them
back immediately and wave her away. He would not play the
meek invalid to Mother's overbearing nurse. Mother brushed
over this offence by fiddling around with a bottle at the side of
his bed, and then upending the hourglass, so that the sand might
once again trickle from the higher bulb to the lower.

While Mother was carrying out this performance, Bearpark
motioned for me to sit next to him. 'So, tell me, Lord Somershill.
What is this news? Have you found Enrico's killer? Is that why
you've woken me?'

I remained standing. 'Why didn't you tell me about the letter
of denunciation, Bearpark?'

He coughed. 'The what?'

'The letter that was sent to the Consiglio dei Dieci.'

Bearpark's complexion suddenly matched the white of his sheets. More alarmingly, he appeared to be gulping, and I wondered if he were struggling to breathe. Mother rushed to tend to him, but Bearpark pushed her away. He coughed again, and found his voice. 'Who told you about that?' he said, squinting into the corner of the room, where Giovanni continued to lurk. 'Was it you?' Bearpark said, pointing at the young Venetian. 'You? With your loose tongue?'

Giovanni crept forward into the light. 'No, master. I swear it.' He glared at me ferociously. 'Please, Oswald. Tell my master. It wasn't me.'

'But you should have told me, Giovanni,' was my reply. I turned back to Bearpark. 'Instead I had to learn about this letter from one of Enrico's friends.'

The old man snorted.

'Why did you only give me half the information?' I said. 'Who am I? Uriah the Hittite. Sent into battle in ignorance of the facts?'

Mother bustled forward and tried to touch Bearpark's forehead. 'Do keep your voice down, Oswald. John is not deaf.'

She went to smooth down his hair, but Bearpark gripped her hand, and pushed it away. 'Please, woman. Stop touching me!'

'I think you should leave,' I said.

Mother looked at me, and then at Bearpark. Sensing defeat, she gave a great huff of dissatisfaction and gathered up her skirts. 'I can't stay here, Oswald.' She sniffed at the air. 'The broth needs attending to. I can smell it burning. Those fools in the kitchen can't be trusted.' She then strode out of the chamber with admirable haughtiness, before slamming the door in her wake.

When Mother had left, I returned to my questioning. 'Why didn't you mention this letter of denunciation to me?'

Bearpark had regained enough of his composure and colour in the intervening moments to demand that Giovanni pass his spectacles. Once the things were resting on his nose, he addressed me again. 'I don't want you to worry about this letter, Lord Somershill,' he told me. 'It's not relevant to your investigation.'

'Oh yes?' I said. 'And how can you be so sure of that?'

He waved my words away. 'I don't know why you're so upset. The letter was just a piece of mischief. It wasn't even signed.' He screwed up his nose and shook his finger to emphasise his point. 'If a person cannot put his name to an accusation, then the Consiglio do not take it seriously.'

'But you knew about the letter?'

'Yes, yes,' he said with some irritation. 'I was invited to the palace for a discussion, of course. But we just had a glass of wine and laughed about it.'

'But you weren't told what the letter said?'

'They read it out to me once, Lord Somershill. It was some tittle-tattle about the Bearpark family not being honourable Venetians. I can't remember the exact wording, I'm afraid. As I said before, it was just foolish mischief.'

'But who would send such a letter?'

Bearpark sniffed. 'I have some rivals in Venice. That's all. I may be a citizen, but I'm still a foreigner.' Bearpark paused. 'There are things about this city that you must understand,' he said at length. 'I've been a successful man, Lord Somershill. I've over-come all of my disadvantages, and prospered.' He cleared his dry throat and then motioned for Giovanni to hand him the bowl of wine that was resting on the table, next to Mother's pot of Venetian Treacle. The wine seemed to restore his spirits.

'But it's not easy for those of us who are not named in the Golden Book,' he said, passing the bowl back to Giovanni. 'For example I was never allowed to hire one of the great galleys from the Venetian merchant fleet. Yet I was not defeated, I still managed to follow their flotilla to Southampton each year. My cog ship might have been a little old and a little slow, but I still persisted through the storms of the Bay of Biscay, fighting off many Barbary pirates. Once I reached England, I often did better business than the Venetians.' He gave a short laugh. 'Some of them didn't like that, you see.'

'But you sacrificed your cog ship for the dead of the Plague.'

'That's right. And really this foolish rivalry should have stopped then, but Venetians have long memories, and every so often they still like to cause a little trouble for me.' He smiled. 'But I'm used to it, my lord. Really. It's only jealousy.' He clenched his fist with bravado. 'Oh yes. It takes more than an anonymous letter to dampen the spirits of a Bearpark.'

It was a rousing defence, but I was not entirely convinced. 'The timing seems odd,' I said. 'Don't you think? There is a denunciation of your family, and then your grandson is murdered.'

Bearpark shook his head so violently that his spectacles fell forward. 'It's just a coincidence,' he said, before pushing them back up his nose. 'These people only want to make my life diffi- cult, but they would not commit murder.' He was becoming angry, the frown lines deepening between his eyebrows. 'Believe me. If they were in possession of any genuine secrets to reveal, then they would have signed the letter.'

'So, why did you keep the letter a secret from me? If it means nothing?'

The old man settled down beneath the sheets again. 'Because I knew it would be a distraction. Something to set your investi- gation off on the wrong course.'

'How can you be so sure of that? To my mind, it is entirely possible that Enrico's murder and this letter of denunciation are related.'

'Then you are a poor investigator, Lord Somershill. Jumping to conclusions, when you should listen to the facts.' He hit the bed with a thump. 'Now, never mind all this nonsense about the letter. Tell me, what have you discovered so far?' He removed the spectacles from the bridge of his nose and regarded me closely. 'Do you have a name for me?'

'No. Not yet,' I said, a little defensively.

Bearpark pounced. 'So. What have you been doing then?'

'We visited the island of Burano,' I said.

'Burano? Is that where the fellow is hiding then?'

Giovanni caught my eye, urging me in some desperation not to say anything more. 'We were looking for Adolpho Bredani,' I said.

'Bredani? Why?'

'Because the man should have been at the water gate when I found Enrico's body.'

Giovanni cut in at this point, his voice nervous and soft. 'We thought it was wise to find Bredani, and then question him.'

Bearpark turned to his clerk sharply. 'And did you find him, on this escapade to Burano?' Even on his deathbed, Bearpark retained the capacity to intimidate his servants.

Giovanni was silenced, so I stepped in. 'No. We didn't. Bredani's family claim that they haven't seen him,' I said. 'But they were lying.'

Bearpark gave a sigh. 'You know that Adolpho Bredani is my wife's brother?'

'Yes,' I said, 'Giovanni told me.'

'So why are you suggesting that he's involved with this? He's a member of my own family.'

'I find his behaviour suspicious,' I said.

Bearpark repositioned the spectacles upon his nose, and then peered at me without blinking. 'Ridiculous. I've done nothing but help that man, so I can tell you this for nothing. He would never have been involved in such a crime.' Bearpark wagged a finger at me. 'He would not repay my kindness with such treachery.' He then began to slide down under the sheets, seemingly exhausted by this outburst. 'The man will be in a tavern somewhere, stewing in his own guilt.' He paused. 'Yes, yes. I know that he likes to drink a little too much, but he is no murderer. I expect he slipped away from his post to enjoy the carnival, and now he is too ashamed to face me.'

Giovanni sidled over to me cautiously, whilst not dropping his eyes from Bearpark. 'Oswald, please. My master is truly exhausted,' he whispered. 'I think you should refrain from asking any more questions.'

I bowed my head with some reluctance, because Giovanni was right. The old man had closed his eyes and was beginning to snore. 'Very well.'

I turned to leave the room, just as Mother burst through the door, followed by an entourage of servants and kitchen staff. At the head of this unexpected group was a boy who held a great tureen of soup aloft as if it were the Ark of the Covenant, whilst the cook brought up the rear, his arms folded and his face set into a scowl of disapproval. Hector scampered along in their wake in the hope that some of the broth might fall upon the floor.

'Come along now, Oswald,' Mother announced. 'You need to stop talking. The soup is ready.'

'We've finished anyway,' I said.

She didn't listen. 'Out you go. Master Bearpark needs his soup.' She gestured to the tureen with reverence. 'This broth was made to my own special formulation. An English soup to cure an Englishman.'

How I longed to tell the assembled company the truth. That Mother no more knew how to make a broth, than she knew how to sew a gown. Servants had cared for her since the day of her birth, and though she might sometimes loiter in the kitchen giving orders, they were usually ignored or immediately forgotten, once she had breezed out again. In light of this, I was finding it increasingly difficult to understand her sudden enthusiasm for domesticity.

I looked to Bearpark and saw a defeated man, lacking the willpower to resist the momentum of the soup and its many followers. I left him to Mother, but, as Giovanni and I reached the final few steps onto the *piano nobile,* we met Filomena climbing slowly towards us. She was holding a belly that threatened to destabilise her at any moment, so I stood aside to let her pass, and bowed my head. I will admit, I was sorely tempted to ask her some questions about her brother Adolpho, but she looked away upon seeing Giovanni's face, and only gave me the slightest nod in response to my acknowledgement.

When she was out of earshot, I said to Giovanni, 'Why is there such hostility between you and Monna Filomena?'

I thought he might answer with another of his infuriating shrugs, but instead he gave a short sigh. 'She's just an island nobody, Oswald. A peasant with the manners and morals of a fishwife. I don't know why my master married her.'

'I think you should show her more respect, Giovanni.'

He continued down the narrow steps, and didn't answer.

Chapter Fourteen

In those times I did not often seek solace in wine, as it had a disheartening effect upon my spirits, and my melancholia fed upon itself quite readily without the need for any further nourishment. After my interview with Bearpark however, I quickly found a servant and requested some sweet Malmsy, needing a tonic to soothe my growing unease. I couldn't find Bredani, I couldn't find Enrico's lover, and now there was a mysterious letter of denunciation to take into consideration. My investigation was stalling, and I had only five days to find a murderer.

I hid myself in a quiet corner of the *piano nobile* and nursed the large bowl of syrupy wine. I was feeling somewhat restored, until Bernard and his sister Margery decided to join me. Margery's bruised eye shone like a Sussex beacon, though she had tried to lessen its impact by draping her wimple across her face.

'Goodness me, my lord,' remarked Bernard. 'You are looking so pale. Do you need a tonic? I'm sure Margery could spare a drop of her St Thomas's water. It has done wonders for her recovery, you know.'

'No thank you,' I said swiftly. 'I'm just a little tired.' I then closed my eyes, in an attempt to discourage any further opportunity for conversation. My hint went unheeded however, for I sensed that the two pilgrims had drawn their stools close to mine.

'Have you noticed that the stars are brighter in the sky here, Margery?' said Bernard. 'I looked out of the window last night, and it was as if somebody had thrown tiny balls of fire into the sky.' I opened my left eye a crack, to see that Margery was nodding to this nonsense, whilst sorting through a purse of her pewter badges, holding each to the light for inspection. 'Have you observed the same phenomenon, my lord?' The man might have noticed a difference in the night sky, but didn't possess the wit to see that I was pretending to be asleep. I didn't answer, but this still didn't stop him from continuing. 'I wonder if we are closer to the sky here in Venice, than we were in England? I always felt that we were going down a hill as we travelled south. But maybe, it was just the opposite? Perhaps we were actually climbing a mountain?'

As Bernard continued in this vein, I genuinely fell asleep, only waking when somebody tugged at my sleeve with a vigorous shake. It was Giovanni. 'Oswald. Quickly. I have some news.'

I rubbed my eyes. 'What is it?'

He whispered into my ear, speaking to me in Venetian for once. 'Adolpho Bredani has been found.'

I sat up straight, suddenly revived. 'Good. Where is he?'

'At a tavern in *Dorsoduro* called the Bacaro da Mario. Do you know it?' I shook my head. Enrico had not dragged me to this particular inn on one of our many nights of 'entertainment', nor was it somewhere that I had played at dice. Giovanni was disappointed by my answer. 'I had hoped you might know the way there,' he said.

'No. Your man will have to lead us,' I said.

Giovanni frowned for some reason at this suggestion. 'Yes. Very well then.'

I stood up from my chair, to see that Bernard and Margery were still sitting nearby, with concerned looks upon their faces. Bernard might not speak Venetian, but he had clearly caught the tone of our conversation. 'Is there something wrong?' he asked. 'Has the murderer struck again?'

'There's nothing to be worried about,' I said.

I walked towards the door, but Bernard caught up with me. 'Do take care, my lord. I believe all this violence has been created by a celestial intervention. It would explain those small balls of fire that I saw in—'

I'm afraid that I closed the door, thus removing the need to answer him, then caught up with Giovanni at the bottom of the exterior staircase, where he was talking to the man who had located Adolpho. It was the fellow who held his head at an odd angle.

Giovanni nodded to me as I approached. 'This man tells me that Bredani is staying in a room above the Bacaro. With a woman.' Giovanni accompanied this disclosure with a short, disapproving puff of disgust. 'She is a whore, I believe.'

'Did this man actually see Adolpho?' I said.

'So he says.'

'And Adolpho didn't see him? They did work together here, after all.' I thought it unlikely that Adolpho would not have noticed this man, since his appearance was so singular. His jaw jutted out strongly to the left, whereas his prominent forehead leant to the right, as if the two features of his head were trying to balance on a set of scales.

Giovanni folded his arms. 'He promises that nobody saw him.'

'Then we need to get to this tavern quickly, in case Bredani moves on.' I pointed to the man. 'Can he show us the way there?'

Giovanni translated my question, and the man nodded his head enthusiastically on its strange diagonal axis.

'You need to gather at least two other men from the household to accompany us,' I told Giovanni. Then I placed my hand firmly upon the clerk's arm. 'This time they must be strong and young. Do you understand me? We might need to bring Bredani back by force.' He nodded without argument, for he was no keener than I was to wander into Dorsoduro with only this odd-looking servant as our guide and protector.

Now it was decided how we would proceed, I returned quickly to my room and picked out my oldest cloak and my sturdiest boots. I had advised Giovanni to do the same, though when he reappeared in the courtyard moments later, he had only tempered the elegance of his outfit with a grey woollen cape, and a pair of clean overshoes. It seemed he could not sacrifice his dedication to fashion, even though I had been at pains to warn him about our destination. I had visited many of the roughest, most dissolute of taverns of Venice with Enrico, but I had never even heard of Bacaro da Mario. If Enrico had avoided this place, then it promised to be truly appalling.

Our mistake, in retrospect, was to take Giovanni's advice and take the ferry across the Canal Grande, rather than use the Rialto Bridge. In theory, this should have been a quicker option, but the oarsmen who row their long *traghetti* boats from one bank to the other were involved in a heated argument on the opposite side of the canal, and we had to shout repeatedly to get their attention.

Once we had finally placed our feet onto the soil of Dorsoduro, our guide led us into the network of streets, his feet scurrying before us in short spurts of energy, like a mouse running from one hiding hole to the next. Our guards also seemed nervous, constantly looking over their shoulders and stabbing their pikes at shadows. We might only have been a few furlongs from their own *sestiere* of San Marco, but there was something about crossing the Canal Grande that had made them deeply uncomfortable.

Our guide eventually stopped outside an unpromising building at the end of a long alley, at a house that didn't advertise itself as a tavern, for there were no signs in the street, nor could we hear the noise of a crowd within. I will admit to feeling nervous myself at this point, but as we walked through a long and twisting hallway, we finally found a group of men and women sitting about a table and laughing. The men were poorly dressed, in rough leather tunics and dirty shirts, and the women were hardly dressed at all. As we entered the chamber, they stopped talking and turned in unison to look at our faces.

'Where is Adolpho Bredani?' I said quickly.

Nobody answered, apart from a man wiping out small bowls with a rag. He pointed to a narrow staircase in the corner, which we went up, before pushing our way into a dingy room. There was no sign of Adolpho, but the bed was occupied by a woman. She shouted something abusive at our entrance, before returning her head to the pillow. Giovanni shielded his eyes, as this woman was naked beneath the sheets.

'Where is Bredani?' I said, approaching the woman. She was thin, with pale skin and long red hair – so untypical of the usual Venetian – and I wondered if she had been captured by the Tartars and sold to this brothel.

She said something, but her accent was too strong, so I asked Giovanni to translate. His reaction to this request was to behave as if I had asked him to jump into a pool of freezing water, taking a few deep breaths before he then exchanged a series of quarrelsome words with the girl, whilst still holding his hand in front of his eyes, so as not to be offended again by her nudity.

'What's she saying?' I demanded to know.

Giovanni removed his hand briefly and turned to me. 'She says that Bredani left the room shortly before we arrived. A child knocked at the door with a message.'

'What message?'

'Somebody wanted to see him outside.' Giovanni replaced the hand in front of his eyes. 'She tells me that Bredani dressed quickly and left the room immediately. She thinks it was urgent.'

'Does she know where he went?'

'No. She says she has no idea.' Giovanni took another deep breath and coughed. 'She also says that Bredani can go to Hell.'

We clattered back down the stairs to the tavern, where the drinkers once again watched us with interested eyes, while the man in the corner continued to wipe out bowls with a rag. I could only assume he was the innkeeper, so I approached him first. 'Where's Bredani gone?'

He still didn't look up. 'He pays for a bed and a woman. I don't follow him around.'

I was feeling all the frustration of another wasted journey, when a woman tugged at my cloak. I had assumed she was young from behind, but now that I could see her face, her true age was revealed. She must have been in her fifth or even sixth decade. Her clothes had once been fine, but they were dusty and worn at the edges – the sagging neckline of her dress edged with patchy fur. She pointed to a broken door that appeared to lead into a courtyard. 'He went that way,' she told me.

'When?'

'Not long before you arrived.' She then held out her hand, expecting payment for this fragment of information. I indicated for Giovanni to retrieve one of his precious coins, when a girl burst in through this same broken door, and screamed that there was a dead man outside.

Giovanni and I pushed through to find ourselves in a small, enclosed courtyard that smelt as bad as a piss-alley. Before us, on the beaten earth next to a pile of broken bowls and plates, lay a dead man. His throat was freshly cut, and his blood was pooling across the ground. I rushed to his side and listened for breath, but could hear nothing, not even a shallow gasp for air.

As I shook the body to try to find any sign of life, Giovanni peered over my shoulder, crossed himself, and then whispered into my ear, 'It's Bredani.'

I looked at the dead man's face and a sinking feeling gripped my stomach. 'So it's him?' I sighed, realising that Bredani had been murdered only moments before we arrived, as his body was still warm to the touch.

I stood up and quickly looked over the wall of the courtyard into the alley beyond, in case our murderer was still lurking in the dark recesses of this covered passageway, but I saw exactly what I had expected. An empty corridor, with nothing but a solitary cat. Adolpho's murder had been performed with the precision and speed of an executioner, and such a man would not be hanging back, waiting to admire the repercussions of his crime.

I rubbed my face with frustration, and then turned back to Giovanni. 'Somebody knew we were coming. That's why Bredani is dead.'

Giovanni was now leaning against a wall and fanning himself. 'What do you mean, Oswald?'

'He was murdered so that he could not speak to us.'

Giovanni ceased the fanning and stood up straight. 'But how would anyone know that we wanted to talk to him? I didn't tell anybody.'

I felt a temper brewing. 'Where's our guide? The man with the strange head?' I found the fellow hiding in a corner of the courtyard, biting his nails. 'Did you tell somebody that we were coming here?' I said in my plainest Venetian. He shook his head vigorously, but was unable to speak. 'Were you followed?' I said, but still he could not answer.

Giovanni pulled me away with unexpected force. 'Please, Oswald. Leave this poor man alone. He's one of the most entrustful servants in the household.'

'The word is trusted!'

'There's no need to be angry,' said Giovanni. 'It won't help our investigation.'

'Of course I'm angry!' I said. 'Adolpho's murderer knew we were coming.'

Giovanni straightened his hair. 'I'm not so sure about that. It could be a . . .' He paused for a moment. 'I don't know the word in English. When two things happen together for no reason.'

'You mean a coincidence?'

His face brightened as he repeated the word. 'Yes. A coincidence. I did know it.'

'I don't believe in coincidences,' I told him. 'Especially not when I'm investigating a murder.'

'But sometimes such things happen, Oswald. A man such as Adolpho Bredani would have had many enemies. Anybody could have murdered him. Who is to say this crime has something to do with Enrico Bearpark?'

'I say it does.'

'But—'

At this moment, the red-haired girl appeared at the door to the inn. She had dressed herself in a loose chemise, but her pale, translucent skin was still conspicuous in the moonlight. Upon seeing Adolpho's body, she let out a short, frightened gasp, before trying to step back inside.

I acted quickly, grasping the back of her chemise and pushing her to the wall. 'Ask her who did this?' I said to Giovanni, as she spat at me and tried to get away.

I held her tightly, as Giovanni shielded his eyes once again and then translated my questions. Did Adolpho have any enemies? Who was the child who came to the door? What was the exact message the child conveyed? At each question she either spat at me or kept her mouth frozen in an unwavering scowl. Eventually we released her without having gained any useful information.

Then we climbed the stairs again to Adolpho's room and thoroughly searched through his belongings, finding only a rosary, a pair of clean hose, a hair comb, and a purse tied beneath the bedstead. When I opened this purse, I found three golden ducats, exactly like the ones I had taken from the house in Burano, and then, I'm ashamed to say that a madness came over me again, urging me to drop these coins into my own purse, just as I had done before – but this time my plan was foiled, for Giovanni was peering over my shoulder.

'Bredani had some money then,' he commented.

'Yes,' I said, trying to disguise my disappointment, before quickly closing my hands around the coins. 'Three golden ducats

is a large sum for a guard to have in a purse, don't you think?'
This was without mentioning the eight coins that were already
secreted away inside my chest.

Giovanni stood back. 'Bredani must have stolen this money,
Oswald. He was poor.'

'Or it was paid to him.'

'For doing what?' said Giovanni.

'It has something to do with the murder of Enrico Bearpark,'
I said quickly. 'I'm sure of it.' I paused. 'And whoever paid him
this money, then had him killed.'

'Why would they do that?'

'To stop him from talking to us, of course.'

Giovanni shook his head sceptically. 'No, no. I can't believe it,'
he said. 'Where is your proof of this, Oswald? Bredani was a
fool. The type of man who easily makes enemies.' Giovanni
threw up his hands. 'There's no proof that he had anything to do
with Enrico's murder. He could have stolen these three coins
from anybody.'

'It is more than just the coins,' I said calmly.

'Oh yes?'

I hesitated for a moment. 'Adolpho Bredani was the man I
chased from the water gate on the night of Enrico's murder.'

'But you said you didn't recognise the man you chased away,'
said Giovanni, now frowning.

'I didn't. Not before tonight,' I said. 'But now that I've seen
Bredani's face, I know it was him. There is no doubt.'

Chapter Fifteen

O ur two guards placed Adolpho Bredani's body onto a makeshift bier, but the innkeeper would not let us leave his tavern until we had settled all of Adolpho's supposed debts. When I refused to pay, a gang of men — occasional associates of the innkeeper, I presumed — appeared from nowhere and blocked our path. It was lucky that I had discovered Bredani's three golden ducats, as Giovanni would never have paid these debts from his master's purse. I made an effort to prize more information from the innkeeper in return for settling Bredani's debts, but, as might have been predicted, the man knew nothing and had seen nothing. He just wanted his money, and he wanted us to leave.

It was pitch black when we finally made our way back to Ca' Bearpark in San Marco, and by the poorest of luck Filomena was in the courtyard as we transported the body of her brother towards the lowest rooms of the house. I was unable to stop her from seeing Adolpho, and the cruel, bloodied wound that had opened his throat to the air. Adolpho's face did not bear the serenity and peace of death, instead it was set in a grimace of fear and pain.

Filomena screamed at the sight, then ran back to the external stairs, moving with surprising speed, given that she was so heavy with child. Her momentum petered out at the landing, where she fell against the corner spindle, and was caught by her lady's maid. I tried to give my assistance, but the maid practically barged me out of the way and then escorted Filomena towards her bedchamber, where the door was shut firmly in my face.

I dusted myself down, knowing that I must now inform John Bearpark of the murder, but just as I reached the door to the old man's staircase, Bernard dashed across the *piano nobile*, dressed only in his linen chemise. 'I understand there's been another killing, my lord?' he said breathlessly. 'And the victim is from this very household!'

I cleared my throat. 'Yes. It was Adolpho Bredani. A servant to Master Bearpark.'

Bernard put his hand to his mouth. 'You see. It's just as I said before. The murderer is picking us off, one by one.'

I put my hand on Bernard's sleeve, feeling a firm arm beneath the cloth. 'Calm yourself. There is nothing to be worried about.'

'But what should I tell Margery?'

'I suggest that you don't tell her anything,' I said, before releasing his arm and making my escape.

I knocked and then entered Bearpark's bedchamber, to find him seated in a chair by the window, having recovered sufficiently to be able to read a psalter by the flame of a single candle. For a moment his appearance shocked me, for the candlelight reflected so oddly from his spectacles that his eyes looked like two orbs of fire. As he turned to greet me, the angle of the light changed and the strange illusion dissolved.

'What's the matter Lord Somershill?' he asked me. 'Why all this noise and commotion?'

'Adolpho Bredani has been murdered.'

He peered at me for a moment, as if my words had not made sense. Then he lifted the spectacles from his nose and placed them into his lap. 'Murdered?' he said at length. 'Where?'

'We had news that Bredani was staying at an inn in Dorsoduro,' I told him. 'We went to find him, but . . . but we were too late. He had been killed only moments before we arrived.'

The old man suddenly looked as bloodless as a bowl of washed tripe. 'Are you sure?'

'His throat was cut, Bearpark.'

Bearpark slowly replaced the glasses on his nose and looked at me, dumbfounded. 'I don't understand.'

I was about to explain more when Mother made a sudden and unwelcome entrance. 'John. I have some news,' she said, as she rushed to Bearpark's side.

Mother's appearance squeezed the blood back into the old man's veins. 'I know about the murder,' he snapped at her. 'Your son has just informed me.'

Mother missed his tone, such was her agitation. 'No, no. It's nothing to do with the murder. It's your wife, John. The child is coming.'

'My son?' Bearpark's scowl dissolved into a broad grin. 'My son is coming.'

He went to stand up, but Mother almost pushed him back into the chair. 'You must stay here.'

'I will do no such thing!' he said.

She laid a firm hand upon his shoulder. 'Now, you must listen to me, John Bearpark. Your wife has had a terrible shock. She saw the face of her murdered brother, and it caused her waters to break.'

'She saw the body?' Bearpark turned to me. 'What fool allowed that? Was it you?'

What could I say? 'I tried to bring Bredani back quietly,' I protested. 'It was just unfortunate that Monna Filomena was in the courtyard as we returned.'

He gathered the energy to wave a fist in my direction. 'I tell you this, de Lacy. If your carelessness causes any problems to the birth of my son, then you will be very sorry. Very sorry!' There was suddenly a hard and cruel intensity in his eyes that did not wane.

'What would you have me do?' I protested. 'Leave the body of your wife's brother in a brothel? Would that not attract the attention of the Signori di Notte or the Consiglio dei Dieci? Or whoever else it is that you want to avoid?'

'Don't you dare to—'

'Do calm yourself, John,' said Mother. 'Your wife is perfectly well.' She pursed her lips and folded her arms. 'As you know yourself, Monna Filomena is a particularly young woman, so there is no need to fear that her child is in danger. And you really should not lay any blame at my son's feet. He was merely doing as you asked, and conducting his investigation.' She pointed to the pitcher of wine. 'Now stay here and take a drink. When the child is born, you shall be the first to know.'

Bearpark fell back against the spindles of the chair, no longer the angry husband, but once again a trembling and fragile old man. As a servant held a bowl of wine to his lips, Mother herded me out of the room. 'Really, Oswald. I do wonder at your behaviour.' As I tried to argue, she closed the door in my face.

That night I could not sleep, for the house was filled with the expectant, nervous energy of child labour. Filomena did not scream, instead she made a low, resonant growl that vibrated through the building as if a carpenter was using a pump drill somewhere in the lower parts of the house. There were footsteps as well. The hurried, determined footsteps of servants running between the kitchen and the bedchamber, and the slower, deliberate steps of a midwife, waiting for the next stage of labour. These sounds conjured unwelcome thoughts, evoking memories that I did not care to remember – so I closed my eyes, for I knew what was crouching in the corner of the room. It would not catch me out again.

At first light came the cry of a newborn child. I threw a cloak over my chemise and joined the rest of the household in the *piano nobile*, waiting outside the door to Filomena's bedchamber. Bernard wandered through the crowd in a daze, and though I tried to avoid him, he tapped me anxiously on the shoulder just as the child beyond the door let out a deafening wail.

'What's happening, my lord?' he asked. 'Has there been another murder?'

I was too tired to be polite. 'God's bones, Bernard! Monna Filomena has given birth. Can't you hear the infant screaming?' Bernard flinched slightly, as if Filomena's pregnancy was news to him. He was about to ask some other ridiculous question when John Bearpark pushed his way through us with all the vigour and determination of a young husband.

'Get out of my way,' he said. 'Get out of my way! I want to see my son.' The servants moved aside and cast their eyes to the floor, already knowing what Bearpark would discover when he looked upon his newborn child. There was no male heir swaddled in linen. Instead, Filomena had given birth to a daughter. By all accounts the child was a beautiful, healthy girl, and certainly she screamed well enough – but what are daughters in this world to some parents, other than a bitter disappointment?

Above the cries of the child, I could hear Bearpark's calls of anguish, and his condemnation of his wife's failure to provide him with a son. He even made the accusation that the child was not his. The servants heard every word of this onslaught against their mistress, and they looked to each other with nervous, fearful eyes. Bearpark's words did not frighten me, however. With each insult, a ball of rage swelled in my chest. When I heard Filomena crying, I could contain it no longer.

I charged into the room to find Bearpark looming over his wife, as she shielded the child from his eyes. For some reason my mother was also in attendance, pretending to do something useful with a bowl of water.

Bearpark looked up at my entrance, and squinted. 'What do you want, de Lacy?'

'Go back to your deathbed, Bearpark, and leave your wife alone.'

Mother interjected. 'Stay out of this, Oswald. It's between a man and his wife.'

'The whole house can hear this argument, Mother. Every servant, down to the lowest scullion. They are gathered outside the door.' I turned to Bearpark. 'You are shaming your wife, Bearpark. In front of your own household.'

The old man itched with fury. 'And what is it to you?'

Filomena looked to me with pleading eyes, and I could see immediately that she was not grateful for my intervention. Nevertheless I continued. 'You have a healthy child, Bearpark. Your wife has survived labour. For the sake of Christ, show her some respect and some kindness!'

Bearpark's fists balled, and the loose skin of his chin trembled with temper. He went to return fire, but he could barely form the words, and then, suddenly, he fell back against the bed post, clutching his chest as if he had just been struck by an arrow.

Within a flash, Mother was at his side. 'John? John? Are you unwell?' She helped him to a nearby chair, and then knelt at his side, holding his hand as tenderly as a child's. Bearpark was shocked, but not dead. As Mother fussed over the old fool, I looked once again to Filomena, but her face was resealed inside its mask, and she would not meet my gaze.

I stalked out of the room, ran down the external staircase, and let myself out through the gate into the long Calle Nuova, finding the narrow passageway swathed in a rising mist. My heart beat strongly and I punched the wall of the house, releasing all my frustration and anger at Bearpark against the coarse surface of the Istrian stone. I continued until I could stand the pain no longer, and then, as I nursed my grazed knuckles, I knew that I couldn't stay at Ca' Bearpark any longer. The old man disgusted me, my feelings for his wife troubled me, and my investigation was failing. It was time to get away. It was time to escape.

My decision to flee was made – though I cannot say where I was intending to go. Perhaps I might have found a place to gamble, or even have walked from the Molo and let the sea have my bones? But as I fled along the thin path of Calle Nuova, an arm crossed my path. Attached to the arm was a demon – its skin shining with menace and its nose as long and pointed as a shrew's.

I drew back until I registered that this was nothing worse than a mask. 'I don't have any money,' I said in Venetian, as a greasy rat scurried across my foot.

My assailant withdrew the mask from his face to reveal a pair of reddened cheeks, a pig-like nose, and tufts of blond hair. I should have realised before that it was Vittore. 'Are you going somewhere, de Lacy?' he asked me.

'What's it to you?'

He leant forward, and his breath assaulted me with the fumes of a night spent drinking. He prodded my cheek with his fingers as he spoke, tapping a rhythm that kept time with his words. 'I wanted to see you, de Lacy.' He laughed sarcastically. 'But when I get here, you've come out to meet me. Isn't that courteous?'

I pushed him away, but this only caused him to fall back with exaggerated mockery. I was no match for Vittore in a fight – we both knew that. 'You'll get your money,' I said. 'You don't need to keep reminding me.'

He bowed with more exaggeration. 'I'm sure you will keep your promise, my lord. I know how you English like to honour your debts, but I thought you might need reminding. Today is Monday. And I want my money by Saturday.'

'I know that!'

'Good. But just in case you should forget, I want you to think about your mother as well.'

I stiffened. 'Stay away from my mother,' I said. 'She's nothing to do with this.'

He grasped my tunic and pulled me to his face. Now I caught a sourness beneath the smell of stale wine. It was the stench of his teeth — two rows of stained, eroded stumps that were as rotten as his heart. 'Because I know how much you care about her,' he said.

'Are you threatening my mother?'

'Of course I am,' he laughed.

I pushed him away for a second time and bolted for the gate back into the courtyard to Ca' Bearpark. 'Keep away from her,' I shouted over my shoulder. 'You'll get your money.'

Vittore only laughed louder. 'I know I will.' He bowed with another of his exaggerated flourishes. 'Until Saturday then. Silent Englishman.'

I slammed the gate behind me, with his laughter still ringing in my ears. There was no escape from Vittore. There was no escape from this investigation.

Chapter Sixteen

Ifirst met Mary de Caburn in the summer of 1350, at Versey Castle, high up in the weald of Kent. In those days she was a scrawny, ragged little girl of ten, dressed in the clothes of a boy. A mother might have forbidden her daughter to wear the leather tunic of a lowly squire and to leave her hair uncombed, matted even – but Mary's mother had died many years before, leaving Mary and her sister Rebecca to flit about the Versey estate like a pair of feral pigeons. Their father, Walter de Caburn, cared as much for them as he cared for his dogs, and not nearly as much as he cared for his horses.

Mary might only have been a child at our first meeting, but there was something in her spirit that I had admired immediately. I was eighteen, and as green as the first leaves of spring, but even so, I had stepped in to prevent de Caburn from dangling the girl over the moat to the castle. His reason for doing this was to punish her, but it felt more as if it were for his own amusement. The man was certainly cruel enough to find this supposed lesson funny. In return for my small favour, Mary had saved my life, showing me a way to escape from her father's castle when the brute had imprisoned me later that same day, with the intention of putting me to death.

Not long after this incident, when Mary was eleven, she and her sister Rebecca came under my guardianship at Somershill.

My sister Clemence had married de Caburn – but the marriage had been short-lived. De Caburn had been murdered within days of their union, surviving only long enough to father a child – a boy named Henry, who was now seven years old and heir to the Verscy estate. Clemence curbed her tongue and tamed her temper over the years, but at first she was a poor mother to the girls, particularly after her beloved son was born. Equally, they were poor stepdaughters, always causing mischief and discord within Versey Castle. In the end, Mary and Becky came to live with me at Somershill, to alleviate the bad temper on all sides.

At first the girls were difficult. Wild, even. They refused to wear dresses, and they refused to attend their lessons. Once they even ran away to their aunt in London, in order to spite me, but this woman was no kinder to them than their own father or step-mother had been, and in time they came to trust me as the person who most cared for them in this world. I allowed them some freedom, as long as they behaved themselves within the house at Somershill, and didn't vex the servants or tease Mother's dog. As much as it might have amused me, and delighted them to grow up like a pair of savages, they had to comply with the rules of society. I had to think of their marriage prospects, which were already harmed, considering that they had lost their chances of inheriting Versey at the birth of Clemence's son. I found the wearing of dresses and the combing of hair was the minimum expected of a noblewoman in society. If I could foster this much adherence to manners, then I had been a successful influence in their lives.

It was Becky, the younger of the two sisters, who first caved in to vanity and staring at her reflection in the one polished metal plate that we kept for such purposes. She had always been the prettier of the sisters, with large blue eyes, and a short, turned-up nose that gave her the face of an angel. I remember watching Ada, the lady's maid, comb Becky's soft blonde hair and plait it into long braids that were then twisted under the knitted mesh of a crespine. The girl, at fourteen, loved the attention and fuss of such preening, while her sister Mary stood apart from them, with a scowl upon her face. Mary would allow her own hair to be combed, but it was coarser and wilder, and caused Ada to sigh at the knots and tangles in its tresses. Mary would only tolerate a single plait, and under no circumstances was Ada to use pins and jewels in her hair, not even for the feast of Corpus Christi, or the festival of Lammas.

There is something about the existence of two young and unmarried girls in a castle that sends up a flare. Or is it a perfume – like the bud of a rose, or the blossom of a May tree? Does their pollen float out across the estate and land in the lap of every man, whether he is old or young, married or not? However it can be explained, I soon found that we were often visited by knights and squires, even the sons of yeoman farmers. They made some excuse about wanting to discuss their rents, or the delights of a recent tournament with me, but truly they were hoping to catch a glimpse of the beautiful maidens that I had hidden in my castle.

How I then cursed the foolish troubadours and their passion for the poetry of love, prompting the men of Kent to leave many letters for the girls by the gatehouse. These letters were mainly left for Rebecca's attention, though not exclusively, and were sent by lovesick admirers, who could barely take their next breath, such was the pain of their ardour. Mary always threw her letters into the fire, but Becky kept hers in her mother's wedding casket – a treasured wooden box, covered in carved ivory, bone, and gilded metal. The only advantage of these letters was this – at least they encouraged Rebecca to learn to read, for little else induced her to attend her lessons.

I was asked, myself, often enough, by some leering knight or drunken nobleman, if I might take a fancy to one of the girls, seeing as they both lived under my own roof. As Becky skipped across the great hall at any given feast, and danced in front of the crowd, knowing that every man in the room was watching, they continued to make these vulgar suggestions until I was compelled to rebut their insinuations in the most abrupt terms. I admired Becky's beauty, who could not? But I was not in love with her. And I would certainly not 'take a fancy' to the girl, though Becky often flirted with me. I think my indifference amused her at first. Then it intrigued her, and finally it annoyed her.

It was a hot day at the end of July, and I had been over to Versey Castle to visit Clemence and her child Henry. Clemence had been in one of her acidic moods, chastising me for not managing the Somershill estate to the exacting standards of our father, and then criticising my scruffy clothes and worn boots. What else was I to wear about the Somershill estate? It was a farm, not the court of King Edward. Clemence's child, whom she would not release from her grip, had grizzled throughout our whole conversation like a cawing crow, until the boy's endless whine had given me a headache. On the way back to Somershill, I had stopped to supervise some of the hay harvest, but was then dragged into a discussion with the priest, who wanted me to fine certain villagers in the manorial court for letting their goats trespass on his glebe field. He had no idea of the identity of these villagers, and his only proof of trespass was the testament of his servant – a man who possessed the eyesight of a mole. I will admit to this, I was not in the best mood upon my return to Somershill.

The small tub was filled with warm water. The soap was sweet-smelling of musk and cloves. I intended to soak my feet and peruse the grubby manuscript that I kept under my mattress for such solitary moments. I had expressly forbidden anybody to enter the chamber, so when Becky flew in without knocking, I will admit to being particularly irritated. I told the girl to get out and leave me alone, but she begged to stay, swearing on her dead mother's grave that she needed to hide from her latest suitor – a boy who had been hanging about the house like the smell of boiling cabbage.

He was called Robert Wolfenden, and he was a particular pest – always finding some excuse to stay for supper, or join the family on a hunt. Sometimes his behaviour was merely comic, and Mary and I laughed secretly about his hopelessly lovesick antics, but on other occasions his obsession with Becky became so maddening that we were rude to his face, though he rarely took even our boldest of insults as a blow. In the previous weeks, Robert had become increasingly maudlin, bemoaning a marriage that was being forced upon him by his father, to a girl so unspeakably plain that he would rather throw himself from a cliff than join her in the marriage bed. These laments were repeated with such overplayed self-pity that I was tempted to ride with him to West Dean and show him the white cliffs myself.

The day was hot. My head was beginning to thump, and I lost the energy to ask Becky to leave. I was only soaking my feet, after all. And the manuscript under the mattress could wait until later. While I stared at the strange, quivering shape of my toes in the water, Becky sat on a stool beside me, and decried her own beauty in such florid terms that I was driven to smile for the first time that day. What a nuisance it was, to be so beautiful. How tiresome it was to have so many men in love with her. How she longed to be ignored by the world and given some peace. The girl had become ridiculously vain and self-centred in the preceding months, so my mocking suggestions that she could always lock herself in a tower, or volunteer to become a novice at the convent of St Margaret went completely unheeded.

Instead she looked up at me quizzically, before dropping her eyes and then regarding me through trembling lashes. It was a practised move that had no effect upon me – other than to provoke a certain sadness, a regret that Becky was no longer the dirty-faced child who kept pet rabbits in a box and liked to scamper through the fields, playing at sword fights with her sister. But this was wistful and sentimental. I put it from my mind, for we must all grow up. This world is not a courtyard of children's games.

I was surprised then, when the girl rose silently to her feet, stood behind me, and placed her hands upon my shoulders. 'Would you like me to rub your neck, Uncle Oswald?' I did not care for the use of this epithet. I was only her uncle in the loosest terms. The brother of her stepmother. There was no blood tie between us, so I had always requested that the sisters simply call me Oswald. But then I realised why I truly did not like the way she used the word. It reminded me of those used by the girls who stood outside the stews and brothels of Southwark, particularly the youngest ones, asking if the passing men wanted to be their 'daddies'.

I should have told her to go away, used my sharpest tones with the girl, for now she was rubbing her breasts against my back, and kissing my neck. Oh God. I will admit this, and only here. The feeling was sensual. It was more than that. It was arousing, and I had been starved of the female touch for a number of years, choosing not to visit the local inn where a gaggle of pockmarked girls plied their trade. I let Becky continue for longer than I should have done. It was a weakness. A mistake. For when I happened to look to the door, there was a face watching us. It was dark and thunderous. Steeped in condemnation and disgust.

It was the face of the girl whom I loved. It was Becky's sister, Mary.

Chapter Seventeen

After my encounter with Vittore in the alley, I lay on my bed for a while, deciding what to do next, and knowing that I needed to make more progress with the investigation – especially now threats had been made against my mother. Taking out my pamphlet from its hidey-hole, I read over my notes regarding the two main strands of my investigation and the extent of my discoveries this far. I had had no success in finding Enrico's lover, though I could not discount him as a suspect following Margery's garbled testament regarding the man's tendency towards violence. I had had more success with my investigation into Adolpho Bredani, if finding his dead body can be called an achievement. I could place Bredani near or at the scene of Enrico's murder, and he had been in possession of an unexpectedly large amount of money at his death – so he and his associates had to be my main line of investigation. The trouble was that I knew so little about Bredani. So far, my questioning had only elicited that he was a handsome and dissolute young man who couldn't really be trusted. Nobody could tell me where he went after hours, nor with whom he mixed. The man remained a mystery.

I turned my face to the bolster and gave a groan of frustration into the feathers, when an idea occurred to me. There was somebody within this very household who could tell me more about

Adolpho – his sister Filomena. This thought only provoked a second groan, since it was difficult enough to speak to Filomena under usual circumstances, let alone in the hours after she had given birth. I threw the bolster aside and got to my feet. I needed to try.

After breakfast, I sat in the *piano nobile*, on the chair nearest to Filomena's door, pretending to read a book whilst hoping to find an opportunity to creep inside her bedchamber when there was nobody else in attendance. This was a poor plan however, since there was a constant stream of visitors for the new mother, from the midwife to the scullion, and it seemed Filomena was never going to be left alone. Not even for a moment. In the meantime my insistence at staying in the *piano nobile* had not gone unnoticed, in fact I would say it had aroused suspicion. More than once Mother had tried to induce me to accompany her to the Rialto market, claiming that she needed to buy more Treacle of Venice. It was not until I had refused to join her for the fifth time that she finally left me alone.

No sooner had I lost Mother's company, than Giovanni appeared at my side, leaning over my shoulder to look at the book I was pretending to read. 'So, Oswald,' he said, when I deliberately turned a page that he appeared to be interested in, 'how are we to proceed with our investigation?'

'I just need to sit here quietly and think through the facts,' I said, hoping Giovanni would leave at this point, but instead he drew a chair up next to mine. 'There's no need for you to join me,' I said, turning another page. 'This might take a while.'

Giovanni smiled, bowed his head, but still did not take the hint. Thankfully he did not try to talk to me again, but instead he condemned me to a slower torment, by toying with the keys at his belt, running his fingers up and down their iron shanks before lifting them one by one and allowing them to fall back against the others with a sporadic clank. This was a deliberate test of my patience, but nevertheless it was a small battle that I was determined to win, and win it I did – for eventually Giovanni sauntered away, peeved by my fortitude at ignoring him.

I was feeling rather pleased with this small victory when Mother reappeared for her next offensive. 'Oswald,' she hissed in a loud whisper from the staircase that led to our bedchamber. 'Please. You must come and speak with me. There's something that I need to tell you.'

'You can come here and say it,' I said. She would not unseat me so easily.

Mother's whisper became hoarser and more urgent. 'Please. Oswald. I cannot say this in front of the others.' I looked about the *piano nobile* to see Bernard and Margery leaning against the open window at the other end of the room, and looking down nervously into the street. They seemed preoccupied by their own concerns, and had not even turned to take notice of Mother's performance. With some great reluctance, Mother then crossed the room and sat down upon the same chair that Giovanni had only just vacated.

She drew close and whispered into my ear. 'There's something I need to tell you, Oswald. It's about Monna Filomena.'

'Oh yes?' I said, turning a page and affecting disinterest.

She looked about the room nervously, waiting for a servant to pass, before she once again whispered into my ear. 'You know I've spent some time in the kitchen here?'

'Yes. You've taught them how to cook soup, I believe?'

She crossed her arms and sat back in her chair. 'Well. If you're going to take that tone, then I won't say another word.'

I turned a page. 'Please yourself.'

This answer caused her to wriggle with frustration, before she gave in and pinched my arm. 'Oh you will be very pleased to know this, Oswald. I can guarantee it.' She whispered into my ear. 'I would say it's vital to your investigation.'

She had intrigued me a little – but only a little. 'Very well then,' I said. 'What is it? This great revelation.'

She suppressed a small squeal of victory. 'The father of Monna Filomena's child is not John Bearpark.'

'Says who?'

'Everybody in the kitchen.'

I shook my head. 'Well, that's nonsense.'

'No, it's not,' said Mother, in a shrill protest. 'Everybody's saying it.'

I drew in my breath, and tried to remain unruffled. 'That means nothing. And anyway, how can you deduce what they're saying? You don't speak their language.'

She pursed her lips. 'I understand enough Venetian, thank you, Oswald.' She lifted her nose in the air. 'As it happens, I've spent rather a lot of time with the servants over the last few months, seeing as your company has been so poor.'

I ignored this gibe before asking the next, and inevitable question. 'So, who is the father of the child then, according to your new friends in the kitchen?' I attempted to pour a note of scorn upon my voice, to demonstrate how little weight I attached to this fanciful tale.

Mother either ignored my disdain or it simply didn't register, for her face beamed with delight at my question. 'That's what is so interesting about this story, Oswald. That's why I wanted you to know.' She looked around to ensure that Bernard and Margery were still at the other end of the room before she dropped her voice to the tiniest of whispers. 'The father is Enrico Bearpark. John's own grandson. Can you imagine the betrayal?'

I shut my book firmly and got to my feet. 'As I said before, Mother. The story is nonsense.'

'Oh yes. And how do you know?' she said, jumping up from her chair and following me across the room.

'I just do!'

I had reached the stairs, but she stood in my path. 'Apparently Enrico Bearpark used to spend a lot of time with Monna Filomena.'

I laughed. 'When? Nobody is allowed to spend time with her. Bearpark and his clerk make sure of that.'

I tried to push past, but Mother blocked my path with determination. 'I'm told that the girl sneaked into his bedchamber, especially when she was first married to his grandfather.' She drew breath. 'And Enrico was a very handsome young man, wasn't he? I'm sure he was a great success with the young women of Venice.' She pinched my arm. 'And just think, Oswald. At least any child that they conceived together would look like a Bearpark.'

This time I succeeded in passing her. 'I'm telling you again, Mother. It's not true.'

'But how do you know?' she called after me.

'I just do!'

As I slammed the door to my room, I wanted to laugh at Mother's story, but instead a low, churning disquiet was building in my stomach – for was this such a tall tale after all? Had I not wondered, even doubted, that Bearpark could still father a child at his great age – and yet a child would be expected from his marriage to Filomena, no matter at the disparity in their years. If none were conceived, then Filomena would bear the blame – for such failings are never the fault of a man. Under such circumstances, it was quite possible that she had taken a lover, though I could say, for certain, that it wasn't Enrico.

This succession of thoughts only made me feel uneasy. I felt pity for the young woman, but there was another emotion poking its unwelcome finger into my heart. Something that made me feel uncomfortable. Jealous even. I threw some water onto my face and then quickly returned to the *piano nobile*. More than ever, I needed to speak to Filomena.

Chapter Eighteen

Despite my vigil near to Filomena's door, it was the evening of that same day before she was finally left alone, and I was able to take my chance. I knocked and then entered the room to find Filomena sitting on a stool next to the fireplace. Her complexion was ashen and her eyes were tired, but even so her beauty managed to take me by surprise.

'May I speak with you for a moment, Monna Filomena?' I said quickly, embarrassed by my reaction, and hoping she could not see me flush.

'Does my husband know you are here?' she said, looking over my shoulder to check that nobody had followed me into the room.

I shook my head. 'No. I needed to speak to you alone, without his interference.' This statement only increased her apprehension, so I added, 'I promise there's nothing untoward, and I will be very quick.'

She hesitated for a moment, and then invited me to sit down on the stool beside her. 'Very well, Lord Somershill,' she said, allowing herself to relax a little. 'You may stay a while.'

It felt odd to be addressed by my title, especially as she had come to my salvation only two days earlier. 'Please,' I said, 'you must call me Oswald.'

She inclined her head. 'Then you must call me Filomena.'

I looked at her for a moment, feeling the heat of embarrassment crawl across my cheeks again. 'I haven't had the chance to thank you,' I said.

'For what?'

'For coming to my aid, of course.' I paused, knowing that this was hardly an accurate description of what had happened between us. 'I should say that I wish to thank you for saving my life.'

She smiled shyly. 'Are your spirits restored now, Oswald?' she asked, before a look of apprehension crossed her face. 'Or has your shadow returned? Is that why you wish to speak with me?'

'No, no,' I said quickly. 'I'm fully recovered, thank you.' I then cleared my throat confidently as if to demonstrate the thorough success of my recuperation. 'I just needed to ask you a couple of questions.'

She raised an eyebrow. 'Oh yes? About what?'

'The death of your brother,' I said, before regretting my bluntness, for my words caused her to recoil. 'I'm sorry that you witnessed the return of his body. I didn't mean for that to happen.'

She took a deep breath. 'Are you investigating Adolpho's murder now, as well as Enrico's?' she asked me.

'Yes, I am.'

'Why?'

'Well,' I paused, 'because I believe the two murders are connected.'

She sat up straight and turned to regard me dubiously. 'I don't understand.'

I drummed my fingers against my thighs, and tried to think my words through carefully before speaking. 'Well, firstly it was Adolpho whom I chased from the water gate on the night of Enrico's murder.' I hesitated. 'And then, when we found Adolpho's body, there were a number of gold coins in his possession. Nobody can explain where this money came from.'

'I see,' she said, with a long sigh. 'I didn't know that.' For a moment she appeared to be thinking, before she clasped her hands together and turned to face me, as if this were a manorial court and I were the judge. 'So, please, Oswald. Ask me your questions.'

I bowed my head in thanks. 'Do you know anything about the coins?'

She shook her head. 'My brother never had any money.'

'Could he have secretly saved them?'

She couldn't suppress a laugh at this question. 'Saved? Adolpho never saved a thing in his whole life. Every coin was spent before it dropped into his purse.' She turned her head and gazed into the fire. 'My brother was always asking me for money, but what could I give him? I'm not even allowed a few *soldini*.' Her tone became bitter. 'My husband and his clerk make sure of that,' she added, almost to herself.

I nodded in recognition of this unfairness, though not enthusiastically enough to provoke any further discussion on this topic. 'When was the last time that you saw Adolpho?' I asked instead.

Filomena paused to think. 'It was the morning of the *Giovedi Grasso*.'

'Do you know if he was intending to leave his post and go to the carnival?'

'I don't.' She fixed me with a stare. 'But if that was his intention, then he wouldn't have told me.' She suddenly looked away, rubbing her hands over her face and turning towards the fire. 'Adolpho was my brother, but we were not close. You must understand that.'

I paused, allowing her the time to relax her hands from her face. Instead of talking, we both watched the fire for a while as it hissed and crackled in the hearth – the flames dancing like a circle of charmed snakes.

'Is there anything you could tell me about your brother, Filomena?' I said eventually, though I was loathe to end this spell of silent companionship. 'Anything at all that could help me with my investigation?'

'I don't know what you mean?' said Filomena, not taking her eyes from the flames.

'Was there anything that made you suspicious about Adolpho's life, for example? Perhaps there was a secret that you both shared?'

She shook her head. 'I only knew that my brother was not a good man, Oswald. He was lazy and greedy, so I stayed away from him. Even when he came to this house.' Though her face was still turned towards the fire, I saw a solitary teardrop creeping down her cheek. Soon it was joined by others, and within moments her face was painted with tears. I placed my hand instinctively upon her shoulder in sympathy – but she tensed at my touch, so I withdrew it quickly.

'There is too much sadness in this world, Oswald. First my brother is murdered, and now I fear for myself and for my daughter.' She then rubbed her hands into eyes as if this would prevent the tears from flowing.

'You mustn't worry. Nothing bad will happen to you.'

She suppressed another sob. 'Can you be so sure of that?' Before I could answer, she turned to me sharply. 'I know what the servants are saying about me. Oh yes. They say that my husband is not the father of my child.' She managed to laugh, but it was an empty sound, quickly dying in the stuffy air. 'They say her father is Enrico Bearpark. A man who never took a woman to his bed in his whole life!'

I was a little taken aback by this. 'So you knew Enrico's secret then?'

She nodded, wiping her face with her sleeve. 'Yes, I did.'

'Was this common knowledge?'

'No, no. Not at all.' Her voice lost its momentum and returned to a whisper. 'I might not have known my brother's secrets, but I knew Enrico's well enough. You see, he was kind to me when I first came to Ca' Bearpark,' she said. 'We were both young, both trapped in this house with an old man, so sometimes I crept into his room at night to talk to him. Enrico confided in me.' She heaved a great sigh. 'We were friends, but never lovers. That story is a lie. I have never been unfaithful to my husband. Not with Enrico, and not with anybody else.' Then the tears returned with more force. 'But now I think my husband will use this foolish story as an excuse to rid himself of me. Just because our child is a daughter.'

I took her hand in mine, and this time she did not recoil. 'You will not come to any harm, Filomena. I will not allow it.'

'But what can you do?' she said. 'You'll be leaving Venice soon.'

'Not necessarily.'

She frowned. 'The galleys for Jerusalem will sail in a few weeks. We all know that. Now that there is peace in Hungary.'

'But—'

She withdrew her hand sharply. 'No. You must not make promises that you cannot keep, Oswald. It does not help me, and it does not help my daughter.'

'Then I will speak to Bearpark on your behalf,' I said, a little wounded by her words. 'I will warn him not to mistreat you.'

'No!' she said fiercely, throwing her hands up in alarm. 'You must not do that.'

'Why ever not?'

'Don't you understand?' she said, screwing up her face in anguish. 'If you speak to my husband, then it will only make matters worse for me.' She grasped my hands. 'Please. You must not speak to him. He will punish me for it.'

'Very well then,' I said reluctantly.

'Do you promise?' She glared at me. 'You must promise!'

'If that's what you want.'

She released my hands and turned back to the fire. 'My life isn't easy, Oswald,' she said grimly. 'So, please. Do not make it more difficult.'

An awkward silence followed this exchange, so I stood up to leave. 'I'm sorry, Filomena. I shouldn't have come here.'

She looked up at me with a start. 'Don't go, Oswald,' she said. 'Please. Stay for a while and talk to me. I never have any company.'

I hesitated. 'I don't know.'

'Please. At least pour me some water before you go.' She pointed to the earthenware pitcher on a nearby table. 'I'm so thirsty, but they only allow me to drink wine.'

I looked at this pitcher with suspicion. 'Are you sure it's safe?' I asked.

Filomena nodded. 'It's just rainwater from the well in the courtyard.' She let a small smile cross her lips. 'I wouldn't drink it in the summer. But it's sweet enough before Lent.'

I passed the bowl to Filomena, and after this I poured one for myself. I had not risked drinking plain water since we had passed through the Alps many months before, but this room was so warm and stuffy that I had also developed a raging thirst. Whilst this was not the fresh and icy water of a mountain spring, it did not assault my tongue with the taste of a ditch, as I had suspected it might.

I then found myself returning to the seat alongside Filomena, even though I had had every intention of leaving. The fire had died down a little, but the warm glow from the embers picked out the curl of her lip and the softness of her skin. 'So. What do you want to talk about?' I said quickly, making sure to turn my eyes back to the flames.

'Something that will make us merry,' she said. 'Tell me about London. The palaces and the great river. And your king.' Then she waved her hands in almost childlike excitement. 'No, no. Forget London,' she said. 'Tell me about your home. I want to hear about your castle and your lands.'

Since I had travelled to Venice, so few people had asked me about my life back in England. In fact, few people asked me anything at all – particularly in this household, where Bearpark liked to dominate every conversation with his own stories, always firmly extinguishing any attempts to change the subject.

And so, as Filomena closed her eyes, I told her about my house at Somershill. How it had once been a castle, complete with battlements, four towers, a moat, and a drawbridge. How my grandfather had demolished most of this building, claiming it was old-fashioned, and built a manor house in its place, with a great hall, a solar, and two retiring chambers where the men and the women of the de Lacy family could sleep, apart from their servants.

Then I told her about the village of Somershill, where my villeins and tenants lived in low cottages with roofs of thatch. When I described how these same villagers sometimes brought their cows and pigs into one end of the house in the coldest nights of winter, she began to laugh – for she had spent the whole of her life upon this lagoon, where the only farming to speak of was fishing. There were no flocks of sheep, or herds of cattle in Venice. The only livestock was the chickens and pigs that scratched about the streets and small patches of waste land between buildings, and these animals were certainly not given house room, at any time of year. The more I told her about my village, the more it seemed to amuse her.

The mood was light and cheerful, but just as I was about to laugh myself at the strange antics of the English, I sensed something in the darkest corner of the room, watching me intently from the shadows. Its cold, disheartening presence stopped me dead.

'Finish your story,' said Filomena, opening her eyes in displeasure. 'What's the matter?'

'It's nothing,' I lied, getting to my feet. 'But I think I should leave now. I've stayed too long.'

'No. Not before you tell me what's wrong.'

'I can't.'

She held her arm across my path. 'It's here again, isn't it?'

'I don't know what you mean,' I said, trying to push past gently.

'Yes you do, Oswald,' she said, standing up beside me and looking me straight in the eye. 'Your shadow. It *is* here, isn't it?'

I nodded.

'Where is it now?' she asked, casting her eyes nervously about the room.

'I don't know,' I said, looking to my hands.

She leant towards me and whispered softly, as if we were in church. 'What does it want?'

'What it always wants.'

'Which is what?'

I took a deep breath. 'It wants me to look into its face.'

Filomena took my hand. 'Then why don't you?'

'No,' I said firmly. 'I'll never do that.'

'But maybe you should, Oswald.'

'Why?'

She hesitated 'Because then it might go away.'

I was about to answer, when Mother threw the door open and strode into the chamber as if she were mistress of the house. 'Oswald?' she said, nearly dropping her small lantern upon seeing my face. 'What are you doing in here?'

Filomena and I jumped apart guiltily. 'I was just telling Monna Filomena about Somershill,' I said quickly, before adding, 'I was describing how our villagers don't build an upper floor to their cottages.'

Mother frowned, clearly not believing a word. 'This is a room of confinement, Oswald, and the girl has recently given birth. I doubt she cares a whit about cottages.'

'This *girl* asked your son for some company.' Filomena's words rang out across the room, both loud and confident, causing Mother to flinch as if they were the scorching fumes of a bread oven.

'You speak English?' Mother said, before turning to me. 'Monna Filomena speaks English, Oswald!'

'Yes. I know,' I said wearily.

Mother shook her head. 'I can hardly believe it. Goodness me.'

'What did you want?' I asked. 'We were having a private conversation.'

Mother ignored my question, before attempting to drive me towards the door, like a sheepdog rounding up a wilful ewe. 'Come along, Oswald. You need to leave. This is no place for a private conversation, even if it is in English.'

Filomena spoke again. 'No. It is *you* who must leave, Lady Somershill.'

Mother froze. 'I beg your pardon?'

Filomena continued. 'Please leave this room. I wish to finish my conversation with your son.'

'Then I must protest,' said Mother with a gasp of dismay. 'It is highly improper for Lord Somershill to be alone in a bedchamber with a married woman. Especially one who has just given birth. He should leave immediately, for both your sakes.'

'No. On the contrary,' said Filomena. 'It is very important that I speak to him.'

'And why is that?'

'Because I have some important information,' said Filomena. 'Concerning Lord Somershill's murder investigation.' Filomena did not break her gaze, despite Mother's best attempts to glare her into submission. 'But you may wait outside the door, if it pleases you,' added Filomena haughtily. 'It will not take long.'

Mother turned on her heel. 'I'm sure that won't be necessary,' she said, before stalking out of the room with her nose in the air. I might say, it was only moments before we heard her ear pressed against the wood of the door.

Filomena beckoned for me to sit down again. 'Please, Oswald. I do have something to tell you,' she whispered. 'That wasn't a lie.'

She sat and stared into space for a while, both twisting and then untwisting her hands until she drew the courage to speak.

'My husband wants you to find Enrico's lover, doesn't he? I've heard him speak to you about this.'

I nodded. 'Yes, he does. Do you know this man's name?'

She raised her dark eyes and looked at me suspiciously. 'Can I trust you, Oswald de Lacy? If I tell you this man's name, will I see him burning in the Piazzetta?'

I shook my head. 'No, no. Of course not.'

Filomena rolled her tongue around her teeth, still unsure whether to trust me fully, just as Mother tapped on the door. 'Do hurry up in there!'

'I'm telling you the truth, Filomena,' I said, ignoring the distraction. 'I promise. I will not hand this man over to the Signori di Notte. But I do need to speak to him.'

She took a deep breath. 'Very well then. Enrico had a lover named Marco. He lives with the sisters on the island of Santa Lucia.'

Chapter Nineteen

After the incident with Becky and the bathtub, I tried to speak to Mary alone – to assure her that nothing had happened. Mary was upset at first, but then she laughed the episode away, saying that men always found her sister irresistible, so it was hardly surprising that I had also fallen under Becky's spell. I made some great excuse about my role as their uncle, if only by marriage, and how it would be a dereliction of my duty to behave in such a way towards my own niece. This was a foolish argument however, because, how then could I justify my feelings for Mary? If such behaviour was inappropriate towards Becky, then it was no nobler when it came to her sister.

There had been a time in my life, when I was a boy, that the pretty and angelic face of Becky would have excited and enthralled me. Her hair was blonde, her eyes were large, her nose was up-turned and childish. But as I became a man, I learnt that there are other models of beauty. These faces might not attract the first attention, but they are, nonetheless, just as appealing to a man's eye. It could be the graceful gait of a woman's walk. The way she throws back her head to laugh. It could be the look of concentration upon her face as she reads her psalter. This is the subtle side of beauty, and is as rewarding as finding a shining pebble on a beach, hidden beneath the larger, more obvious stones. A man might think he is the only person to know of its existence.

And so it was for me and Mary. I found her to be a true beauty, though few felt she matched her sister. She refused to dress her hair. She would only wear the loosest of tunics, and her manners were sometimes as brisk and gruff as a huntsman. But she could ride horses like a knight, better than any man on the estate. She could shoot a rabbit with a longbow, and then she could skin and gut the creature. She kept deerhounds that were as fast and obedient as the king's.

But do not think her coarse and uneducated. For she would also sit with me at night and read. We could discuss the subjects that had interested me for so many years – subjects that nobody else cared to discuss, such as the trajectory of Venus, and the teachings of Aristotle. She even feigned, for my sake, an interest in the writings of Pope Pius. And Mary had extended my own interests into more popular books, such as the *Gesta Romanorum*, with its legends and classical histories, and tales of monsters and magicians. We laughed and argued over these stories. I liked them a good deal more than I let on.

By the time I was twenty-four and she was sixteen, I had asked Mary de Caburn to be my wife. I had expected my offer to be accepted immediately, and the marriage to proceed with all respectable haste. But my arrogance was soon punished. Mary was rarely disposed to make my life easy, and insisted upon time to consider the proposal, and to review this opportunity against her other options. What options were these, I argued with a gust of umbrage? She was the daughter of a dead knight, with a half-brother due to inherit her father's estate. She was neither rich, nor considered a beauty. I will admit that these last two points were made with some rancour, since she had hurt my feelings, and it will come as little surprise that these ill-advised comments prompted an immediate refusal.

I might have dismissed the idea at this point, but I loved Mary – and despite her obstinacy, I believed that Mary loved me. So, I tried again after the period of a month, this time using the tactics of flattery and humility. I even wrote Mary a poem, though it was so badly rhymed that it caused us both to cry with laughter. Comedy can be an aid to lovemaking, or so I'm told. There are plenty of wits who have won the heart of a lady – though I suppose they used clever observation and biting satire to impress their lover, rather than a foolish poem written quickly upon the back of a rarely used psalter. Nevertheless, this unintended approach assisted my cause, and did not elicit an instant refusal to my offer of marriage. Instead, Mary told me that she would consider my proposal again, now that it had been made with some modesty and lack of assumption. I will say this of Mary, she knew how to make me love her the more, for what satisfaction is there in catching the easiest prey? A man needs to feel that he has worked for his prize.

After another month, Mary de Caburn finally agreed to be my wife. It was then that I had to cross the next hurdle for the union. Or should I say hurdles, for both my mother and my sister were against the match from the start.

'You must have expected me to marry at some point?' I said to my sister Clemence, as she paced the room with her arms folded, while her faithful servant, Humbert, followed her with his eyes. The giant man was always at my sister's side. Silent, impassive, but ever watchful. No harm would come to Clemence while this man could protect her.

'No, I didn't expect you to marry,' she snapped. 'And certainly not to your own niece.'

'Mary is only my niece by marriage. We share no blood.'

Clemence stopped still and snorted. 'You *share* no blood with me, Oswald. Your own sister. So perhaps we should marry?'

The words were said, and could not be retracted. Yet none of us knew how to answer. Instead we let this most inflammable of family secrets blaze between us for a few moments, before it finally lost its heat. I looked to Humbert, but he would not meet my eye.

'I expected you to marry better than Mary de Caburn,' said Mother, as if Clemence had not made her last contribution. 'You are lord of the Somershill estate, after all. And who is this girl? A raggedy creature who used to wear braies and wield a sword.' Mother picked up Hector's paws and kissed his bristly muzzle. 'Mary de Caburn would do better to marry the blacksmith, wouldn't she, Hector? Then he could forge her a weapon. Or perhaps she could join those women who wander after armies and do all their cooking and washing. What are they called? Oh yes, camp followers.' Hector growled in agreement. He disliked Mary de Caburn and her pack of boisterous deerhounds.

I was astounded at these comments. 'Mary is the eldest daughter of a nobleman,' I said. 'Not only that, she is well educated.'

Mother shrugged. 'Yes. But what good has education done her? Only filled her head with inflated ideas of her own place.'

'She's a woman of standing, Mother. Lady Mary de Caburn. And soon she will be Lady Somershill.'

At these words, Clemence stalked across the room and grabbed Mother by the arm. 'Do you hear that, Mother? Mary de Caburn will become Lady Somershill. She will take your title. How will you like that then?'

Mother shook my sister away. There was nothing more guaranteed to change Mother's mind than hearing Clemence's opinion on a matter. 'Well. I'm not sure what I can do about it, Clemence. If your brother wants to marry the foolish girl, then that's his business.'

'But he's not my brother, is he?' Clemence lowered her voice. 'Not my true brother.'

Mother stroked Hector's head with increasing intensity, until her hand became claw-like and the stroke became a scratch. 'Well we all know that, Clemence. But nobody else does. So, I'll thank you to keep your voice down.' Mother looked to Humbert, but the man continued to stare into space, as if he had not heard a word of the conversation.

Clemence turned on her heel with frustration, marched towards the window, and let out a growl that rattled against the windowpanes and then reverberated across the solar.

When her rage had subsided, Clemence turned to speak again. 'So Oswald. What of your promise many years ago? That my son would inherit Somershill, as well as Versey Castle.'

'That wasn't my promise, and you know it. I only promised Versey to Henry.'

She curled her face into an ugly rosette. 'Yes. But I thought that you had decided not to marry.'

'No Clemence. I never said that either.'

Mother placed Hector upon the floor, and the dog began to snuffle about the reeds, looking for any stray food that might have been dropped by Clemence's young son, Henry. The child was a walking breadcrumb dispenser, leaving enough food in his wake to feed a flock of geese.

'You can't expect Oswald to become a monk, Clemence,' said Mother. 'You might have turned yourself into a drab donkey and decided not to marry for a second time. But there's no reason why Oswald should not take a bride.' Clemence let out a second roar, though its anger was diluted this time with frustration. I could hardly blame my sister for finding the term offensive. The roar did not dissuade Mother from continuing, however. In fact it seemed to induce further insults. 'And in a way, it is only natural justice that Oswald should marry Mary de Caburn.'

'Oh yes?' said Clemence, folding her arms. 'And why is that?'

'Well. Mary would have inherited Versey,' said Mother. 'Had you not married her father only days before his death.'

'My husband was murdered, Mother. You make it sound as if I lured an old man into a marriage contract upon his deathbed.'

Mother waved her hand. 'Doesn't matter how you die, does it? You're still dead.'

'Not quite,' I said, feeling the need to interject.

Mother groaned. 'Stop being so pedantic, Oswald. You've left this world, whether you die of your own accord, or somebody helps you along the way.' I tried to answer, but she spoke over me. 'The point is this. Clemence and her son Henry took Versey from Mary. So Mary will take Somershill from Clemence.' She stood up and clapped her hands. 'It seems entirely fair to me. So I think we should congratulate Oswald upon his choice of bride.' She turned to me. 'So, well done. I hope the girl will provide you with many children.'

At these words, Clemence picked up her skirts and sped out of the chamber, closely followed by her faithful servant Humbert, who had to duck to avoid hitting his head on the low lintel. Clemence then stamped her foot loudly onto each step of the staircase, before slamming the door at the bottom.

Mother sat down again upon her stool, and beckoned for Hector to return to her knee. The dog had found a knitted sock somewhere behind the stools and was now attempting to kill the thing by dashing it from side to side upon the floor, as if it were a rat. 'Clemence will come round, Oswald,' Mother said, as she patted her dog's head.

I couldn't help but laugh. 'Do you think so?'

Mother pursed her lips thoughtfully. 'Either that, or she'll plot against you.'

I gave another laugh. 'How reassuring.'

She looked up at me earnestly. 'There's no reason to laugh, Oswald. I'm being perfectly serious. Your sister can be a dangerous opponent. You know that.'

Chapter Twenty

I woke to remember that it was Tuesday, leaving me only four days to find the killer, or meet my fate at Vittore's hands, so I missed breakfast and went straight to see Giovanni, finding him in his office, kneeling in front of his small diptych. He didn't notice me at first, so I stood in the low doorway and watched him for a while. He held a new rosary tightly to his lips — a primitive-look-ing thing made from rough wooden beads, and I suddenly felt a small pang of guilt, for I had stuffed the rosary he had given me into a corner and then forgotten about it. When I coughed he quickly scrambled to his feet, darting in front of his desk, to obscure my view of some neatly stacked piles of coins. He put his hand behind his back and then dropped his rosary onto the table next to the coins. 'Oswald,' he said, with some breathlessness, 'I didn't see you there.' He smoothed down his hair. 'Were your hours of contemplation useful yesterday?' he asked.

I closed the door behind me. 'Yes. They were.'

Giovanni briefly checked his reflection in the small looking glass that hung opposite his table, before indicating for me to take a seat. 'This is welcome news.'

I remained standing. 'I have a name at last. For one of Enrico's lovers.'

He smiled cautiously. 'I see. How did you find his name?'

'That doesn't matter.'

Giovanni wiped a finger along the side of his mouth. 'So. Who is it?'

I hesitated. 'I'll tell you later.'

I could see that he wanted to press me for an answer, but decided against it. 'My master will be pleased. It has always been his desire that we find the friends of Enrico.'

'His lovers, you mean?'

'Yes, Oswald. His lovers.' Giovanni coughed, as if this word had stung his tongue. 'So, what will we do now?'

'I need to visit an island on the lagoon,' I said.

'Which island is that?' Giovanni backed against the desk, and let his fingers touch one of the piles of coins.

'It's a convent.'

His face suddenly darkened. 'Do you mean Santa Lucia? The convent of whores?'

'I do.'

'Women who claim to be the brides of Christ?' He clenched his fists. 'What is a man who loves other men doing there?'

'Offering an alternative service, I suppose?' Giovanni took a great inhalation of air, and was about to launch into a tirade, so I purposefully spoke over him. 'I don't care what you think about the place. I just want you to take me there.'

Giovanni hesitated. 'I can't,' he told me.

'Why not? I'm not asking you to get into bed with a nun.'

He crossed himself at my words. 'Mother Maria. Don't say such things, Oswald.' He then squeezed his hands together, as if in prayer. 'Please. I cannot set foot in such a place, as it would taint my soul and damn me for eternity.'

I have never understood why some believers have such little confidence in the strength of their own faith, that they fear even the slightest glance at evil will inevitably seduce them into Beelzebub's den. 'You have to accompany me,' I said. 'Sometimes people cannot understand my Venetian. Particularly on the islands.'

He trembled. 'I cannot go to Santa Lucia. You must believe me. Take the family's *sàndolo*. There's a man in the kitchen who can row you there.'

'I'd rather that you came with me.'

Giovanni shook his head and then fumbled about on his desk to retrieve his rosary, but only succeeded in knocking over one of the piles of coins. He turned and cursed his own stupidity, but when I went to assist him, he became aggressive. 'Please. Don't touch the coins!' he told me. So I deliberately knocked over a second pile, and then a third, just to annoy the fool.

He threw up his hands in a panic. 'What are you doing? I counted those out specially.'

As he attempted to round up the coins, I picked out a florin. He tried to grab it back from me, but I held the shiny circle aloft, and he could hardly assault me in order to retrieve it. He withdrew a little. 'Please give it back, Oswald. I've counted these out for my master.'

I turned the coin in my hand. 'Why do you have coins from Florence?' I asked. I then pushed my hand through another pile, spreading them across the table. 'And what are these?' I said, picking them up in turn. 'Coins from Genoa, Hungary, and France I think.'

'Master Bearpark is a merchant, Oswald. He deals with many nations. Of course he has such coins. You would find them in any merchant's strong box.'

'But what does he sell? There's nothing in his storerooms.'

Giovanni looked at me askance. 'Why are you looking in our storerooms? You have no business there.'

'It's hardly a secret, Giovanni. Anybody can see that the shelves of Ca' Bearpark are nearly bare.'

Giovanni turned his back on me, and nervously began to recreate the piles of coins. 'These times have been difficult for my master. The war with Hungary has ruined his trade.'

'But other merchants have stock.' I thought of the many small boats I had seen along the canal in the last few days, laden with furs, dyes, silks, and sacks of spices. These small vessels were transporting goods to the merchant galleys – ships that were now in a hurry to leave Venice. 'There's more to this than a problem caused by the war with Hungary, isn't there?'

Giovanni sighed. 'Yes. You're right, Oswald. My master has had problems since he sacrificed his cog ship for the dead of the Plague. He can hire other ships of course, but they are always small or slow. If only he could hire a galley from the Venetian fleet, but such privileges are preserved for the families of the Golden Book.'

I suddenly thought about the fee that Bearpark had promised to pay me for finding Enrico's murderer. 'Is Bearpark short of money then?' I asked, trying to smooth over the anxiety in my voice.

Giovanni shook his head. 'No, no. My master is a rich man. He has saved money all his life. There has been no need for him to trade for a number of years, but he will not give up. Even though he is so old and so ill.' He whipped around to face me. 'But you mustn't tell a soul about this. Do you promise? Master Bearpark likes the other merchants to think he is still prospering.' My nod must have seemed ambivalent, since his voice then rose to an urgent and shrill peak. 'You must promise, Oswald. Reputation is everything in this city.'

I sighed. The Venetian mask – so brazen and yet so brittle. 'I won't say a word.'

'Do you swear it?'

'Very well.' I walked to the door. 'And will you change your mind about accompanying me to the island?'

He hung his head. 'No, Oswald. I will never go to that place.'

Chapter Twenty-One

I departed immediately for the convent of Santa Lucia, as Mother watched me from her upstairs window. She shouted down to me as I boarded the *sàndolo* by the water gate, wanting to know where I was going, but I pulled the hood of my cape over my ears and pretended not to hear.

As the *sàndolo* swung out of our narrow canal and made its way into the Canal Grande, we passed so close to the buildings on one side of the water that I could almost reach out and pull limpets from the walls of the *palazzi*. My oarsman, a servant from the house, then rowed into the centre of the canal, where we were jostled by larger vessels making their way out to sea. On either side of us, women appeared at the heads of dark alleys, emptying buckets of shells into the water, whilst a dog barked at us from a wooden platform, the loose skin of its chin spilling out over a leash that was too tight about its neck.

As we rounded the end of the Canal Grande, we passed the tip of Dorsoduro and then headed out across the water towards the island of Giudecca. The convent of Santa Lucia was located to the south – at first nothing more than a thin line on the horizon – but then, as we sailed nearer, the island began to take on the form of a sea fortress, a square, flat-sided stronghold that seemed to float upon the lagoon.

During this journey I took the opportunity to make conversation with the oarsman as he followed the wooden poles that marked the safe routes across these shallow waters, avoiding the sandbanks that often lurked just beneath the surface. At first I had only wanted to practise my Venetian, as the man spoke with the same strong dialect that I had previously found so difficult to understand, but soon we were conversing on topics that went far beyond the weather and the names of birds upon the lagoon.

I told him of the Great Plague in England that had killed my older brothers and saved me from a life in the monastery. He had his own, sad memories of this contagion, as he had still been a child when it had swept through Venice in 1348, killing nearly every member of his family. It transpired that he had then been forced to seek sanctuary in the self-same convent to which we were headed. He spoke of the place fondly however, explaining to me that this convent was more than a haven for the unfortunate children of Venice. It was also often the place where rich families sent those daughters for whom they could not afford dowries. These young women often had little sense of religious vocation, and were frequently bored by the privations of the celibate life. As such, the abbess allowed them to receive male visitors, as long as a fee was paid to the convent – described, naturally, as a contribution to the work of their orphanage.

The story was scandalous of course, though I will admit that I was not scandalised. Nobody was being harmed by this activity, even if it was, in many respects, the business of a brothel. The sisters could choose their lovers, so the arrangement seemed to please one side as much as the other. And anyway, I had seen enough of the other style of brothel. The stews that clung to the riverbank at Southwark – full of thin, dead-eyed girls from the country, and frequented by toothless old men and foul-mouthed drunkards.

Once the *sàndolo* was tied to the moorings, I left the oarsman and followed the sandy path towards the convent. In the early spring light, the orange bricks of the walls blushed with the warm glow of embers upon a fire, and I thought that it was no wonder that the young men of Venice came here to escape the stifling air and the narrow alleys of the city, where eyes watched you at every turn. Out here on this lagoon island, the world seemed a happier, simpler place.

I knocked at the heavy gate to the convent and was greeted by a boy who opened the door to me and then quickly slammed it again in my face. I waited politely for a few minutes, but nothing happened. I tried to push at the door, but found it had been bolted, so I knocked again. An upstairs window finally opened, and an old nun with a white wimple and a black scapular leant out, and I recognised her immediately as the abbess I had met on the night of my visit to this place with Enrico, many months before. When she asked my business, I replied in my best Venetian, saying that I was looking for company.

She slammed the shutters and disappeared without saying a word, leaving me once again to wait by the door, hoping that somebody might admit me. After a few minutes, I banged again. Still nothing, and I was about to walk around the building in search of an alternative entrance, when the abbess appeared once again at the window.

'Are you English?' she asked me.

'Yes,' I shouted up to her.

'You were here once before, weren't you? With Enrico Bearpark and Vittore Grimani.'

'Yes.' I waited for her to ask about Enrico, but the question did not come.

'But you didn't stay, did you?' she said, with a sly smile.

I bowed to her. 'I was too drunk, my lady. I thought it would be an insult to the sisters.'

This comment caused her smile to wane, though it was impossible to tell if she had been flattered by the compliment, or simply amused by my obvious lie. 'Wait there,' she told me.

Once again she slammed the shutters and then made me wait for quite a while before she eventually appeared at the door. She looked me up and down with distaste, before finally admitting me into a large square courtyard that was bordered on all sides by the stone pillars and arches of a colonnade. Faces peeped at me from these pillars – they were mainly children, but there were older faces there as well. Some might even have been nearing their twentieth year.

'You're early,' she said, indicating for me to sit next to her on a bench. 'Most of our visitors come during the night hours.' She then shouted at the two small boys who were now climbing onto the wellhead in the centre of the courtyard before seeing how far they could jump. 'Is there a particular sister you wish to visit?' she asked me.

I cleared my throat, which felt dry and disobliging. 'It's not a sister that interests me,' I said.

She lifted her chin and scrutinised me with her beady eyes. 'Oh yes?'

'Enrico told me of a particular young man named Marco.' I coughed again. 'I wondered if he were free?' I felt myself colouring. Sweating even, and was pleased of the thin winter light, for it covered my ineptitude.

Once again the abbess made me wait for an answer. 'There is nobody here called Marco,' she said. 'You are mistaken.'

I reached into my purse and pulled out the florin that I had secretly taken from Giovanni's desk that morning. I didn't consider this as stealing – rather, as a justifiable expense. 'Are you sure that there's no Marco here?' She eyed the florin and then reached out to take it from me, but I quickly closed my hand about the coin. 'Let me see Marco. And then you may have this.'

She pursed her lips with irritation. 'He may not wish to see you. I cannot say.'

'I only want to speak with him. Nothing more.'

This comment was met with a shrug. 'I can ask,' she said, still staring at me. 'But I make no promises.'

Laughter, followed by playful screaming sounded in the distance. A bell rang, and the smell of garlic and fish drifted across the air. This place was like any other *campo* in the city – enclosed, noisy, and spilling over with life. I waited for the abbess to leave, or to call over one of the children to fetch Marco, but she continued to stare at me.

Then suddenly she smiled. 'Marco says he will see you.'

I looked about us. 'He does? How did you ask him?'

The abbess nodded her head towards a window above the furthest side of the cloister, where somebody was silhouetted against the light. 'You may go to him now.'

The abbess led me through the covered portico, up an elaborate marble staircase, and then along a dark passageway that ended in a great, carved door. I might almost have expected such a grand entrance to lead into the abbess's personal quarters, but she insisted that this was Marco's room. She knocked gently and then slipped away, leaving me to stand alone in the hall feeling as nervous as a novice waiting for a beating from the abbot.

The heavy door swung open and I entered the room to find a young man staring at me by the light of a small candle. The shutters were closed, and the room was dark, but even so, I recognised Marco immediately. He was the angelic-looking man who had stood beside the abbess on the jetty, on the night when I had refused to leave the boat. I cursed myself for not guessing that this man had been Enrico's lover, though he was hardly the embodiment of the violent murderer I had been told to expect. As my mother often likes to say however, a rosy apple may contain a wasp.

'Come in,' he said, looking me up and down. 'Close the door.'

I did as he requested, then trod cautiously across the highly polished floor of the large chamber. The walls about me were clad in embossed red leather and fine silks, and the room was bathed in the woody, pungent scent of myrrh. Marco dropped down upon a bed with carved posts and a studded headboard, then stroked at the pile of his velvet bedspread, in an act that seemed jaded. 'What can I do for you?' he asked, looking up from beneath his dark lashes. 'You asked for me by name?' He then let his hand slip beneath his chemise and rest upon the smooth skin of his chest.

'No, no. It's not that,' I said quickly, stifling a cough. How awkward I must have seemed.

He laughed, though once again it sounded hollow and weary. 'Don't be shy.' He patted the bedspread. 'Come and sit next to me. Tell me your name.' I removed my hat and sat down next to him on the bed, whereupon he ran his fingers though my hair. 'You're English, aren't you? I like English men.'

I stood up quickly. 'I'm not here for that reason.'

He raised an eyebrow and gave a short, scornful laugh. 'Of course not. You never are.'

'It's true. I came here to speak to you about Enrico Bearpark.'

He sat up abruptly, put his feet to the floor, and then walked to the other side of the room, where he collected a robe from a table draped with tasselled silk. He threw this robe over his shoulders, and held his arms across his chest, as if protecting himself from a cruel wind. 'You tricked your way in here. I can't tell you anything about Enrico.'

'I'm trying to find his killer.'

He looked over his shoulder at me suspiciously. 'You? Why should you care about finding his killer?'

'Because he was my friend.' I hesitated. 'And because his grandfather has asked me to investigate.'

'You've wasted your time coming here. You should leave,' he said.

He made for the door, but as he passed me I grasped his arm. 'Enrico was your lover, wasn't he, Marco?'

He tried to shrug me away, but I kept my grip firm. 'Why should I tell you anything? I don't even know who you are!'

'You do know who I am. You've met me before.'

He hesitated, before reluctantly peering into my face. 'I don't know you.'

'I came here, one night a few months ago, with Enrico and his friend Vittore? I wouldn't get out of the boat.' He still seemed puzzled. 'Do you remember? You watched us leave from the jetty.'

Marco gave a small and sudden smile of recognition. 'Yes. I do remember.' His smile turned to a scowl however, as he broke free of my grasp. 'You were the fool who robbed me of a night with Enrico.'

'So you *were* his lover?'

'What of it?' Marco dropped down once more onto the bed, stretching out his arms to display a sudden boredom with this conversation. When I didn't respond, he gave me a sideways glance, the candlelight now resting upon his halo of curls. 'Well, Englishman. What do you want to know?'

'Did you kill Enrico?'

He looked up at me for a second as if he could not believe that I had asked such a question, before throwing back his head in laughter. 'Me? Why would I kill that fool? Enrico Bearpark was nothing but a deceitful, corrupt liar, always meddling where he shouldn't. I wanted nothing to do with him.'

The words were bitter and practised. 'Why do you say that?' I asked.

Marco wrapped the robe about his shoulders again, as if he regretted this outburst. 'I have my reasons,' he said defensively.

'Is that why you attacked him on the night of *Giovedi Grasso*? Because he deceived you?'

He pulled the robe a little tighter. 'I don't know what you're talking about. I've never attacked anybody in my life.'

'That's not true, is it? I have a witness who saw you fighting with Enrico in the storeroom at Ca' Bearpark. It was on the feast of Saint Stephen last year.'

Marco laughed again. 'You've lost your mind, Englishman. I've never set foot in Ca' Bearpark,' he said, dropping his robe a little to expose a pale and slender body. 'Do I look like a violent killer to you?' he said triumphantly, before turning his face away from mine – his mood suddenly subdued. 'You're talking to the wrong man. If you want to find Enrico's murderer, then look for that brute he took up with.' He emitted a kind of snarl. 'The man he preferred to me.'

'Oh yes?' I said. 'Who's that?'

Marco tensed, a little cross with himself for being drawn. 'Oh, I don't know,' he said blithely. 'Some ruffian who builds ships at the Arsenale.'

'Why do you say this man is guilty of Enrico's murder?'

Marco hesitated before replying. 'I have my reasons.'

'Which are?'

He looked up at me cautiously, taking his time to answer. 'They were involved in something together,' he said quickly. 'It was dangerous. That's all I'm going to say.'

'Why was it dangerous?' I asked.

His answer was a growl. 'You're not listening to me, Englishman? I'm not saying anything else.'

'So, what's this man's name? At least tell me that.'

Marco shrugged.

This was achieving nothing, so I tried a new tactic. 'I think that you're lying to me, Marco,' I said. 'There's no man who works at the Arsenale, is there?'

Marco looked at me, his eyes flashing. 'He does exist! His name is Gianni,' he spat. 'Now leave me alone.'

'Gianni what?'

'I don't know.'

'So where does he live?' I asked.

Marco threw up his hands. 'In Castello.' He pursed his lips venomously. 'With all the other men who build ships for this city.'

'That's not enough, Marco. I need more information.'

'I don't know any more.'

'You must do.'

His voice became agitated. 'Why would I know where he lives? Go to Castello yourself,' he said. 'Ask around for Gianni. Somebody will tell you where to find him. Then you can ask him all these questions yourself.'

I bowed my head. 'Very well then, I will.'

'Is that all now?' he said impatiently.

'No. I need to ask another question,' I continued calmly. 'Do you know a man named Adolpho Bredani?'

Marco looked at me for a moment, and then let a puff of laughter escape from his lips. 'Who?'

'Adolpho Bredani.'

'No. I've never heard of him.'

'He was Monna Filomena's brother. He worked at Ca' Bearpark.'

Marco's face began to redden. 'You're not listening to me again, are you, Englishman? I don't know anybody with that name! Now I want you to leave.'

I refused to move, but at his third scream, the abbess burst through the great doors with two burly men, and for the first time in my life, I was thrown out of a brothel.

Chapter Twenty-Two

Upon my return to Ca' Bearpark I strode through the house with determination, avoiding all conversation and heading directly for Giovanni's bureau on the ground floor, where I found the man clicking beads across his abacus. He stood as I entered. His hair was glossy, smooth, and hung about his face like the curled fronds of a fern. Seeing his groomed perfection, I was suddenly reminded of my own scruffy appearance, so I quickly ran my fingers through the tangled brush that topped my own scalp, knowing that I would never pass as a Venetian.

Giovanni seemed pleased, and a little relieved to see me. 'I'm so sorry, Oswald,' he said. 'I should have come with you to the convent. I know that now.'

I nodded curtly to accept his apology. 'It's no matter,' I said.

'Did you discover anything?' he asked, holding out his hands to indicate that I should take a seat. 'Did you speak to Enrico's friend?'

'I'll tell you about it later,' I said, refusing to sit down. 'First I need you to take me somewhere.'

Giovanni frowned at this. 'But I promised to bring you to Master Bearpark. He wants to know your progress with the investigation.'

'So he's recovered from the shock of having a daughter then, has he?' I said wryly.

Giovanni began to touch his keys. 'No, Oswald. I'm afraid he's still in a terrible rage.' He paused for a moment. 'My master has heard an unpleasant story about Monna Filomena. Some say he is not the father of her child.'

'Oh yes? And how did he hear that foolish tale then?' I asked. 'He's an old man on his deathbed. Did you tell him?'

'No. Of course not! I do not indulge in—' he was struggling for the word, 'heresy.'

'You mean hearsay.' I said.

Giovanni shook his head adamantly. 'No. Heresy is correct.'

'Heresy means to speak against the church. Is that *really* what you wanted to say, Giovanni?' He was momentarily silenced. 'Come on. Get your cloak.'

'But won't you come and speak to my master first?'

'No. We need to leave now.'

He hesitated. 'But, but . . . where are we going?'

'I'll tell you later.'

A few more minutes elapsed before we were able to leave the damp, malodourous chamber, as Giovanni locked away piles of coins, and then turned the keys in numerous cabinets, before double-locking the door. He enquired if we should take the family *sàndolo*, in the hope that I might then reveal our destination – but I had determined to get well away from Ca' Bearpark before revealing our purpose, for I did not want any objections. Instead I told Giovanni that we would be walking this afternoon. The day was fine, and the winds of the Bora had dropped. The streets were bustling with many other people, so our progress would go unremarked.

We pushed our way along the canal-side paths and then cut through the alleys and *campos*, passing the everyday sights of Venice; a noblewoman being fussed over by her many lady's maids, a Moorish slave carrying a great sack of cloth upon his back, and a procession of Dominican monks, parting the crowds as they chanted their way to mass. The smaller canals thronged with the one- or two-man boats – the *piatte* carrying people, small sacks, earthenware bottles, and baskets of fish from one place to another. As we walked along these streets I often looked up to see a woman watching our progress from an upstairs window or balcony. These were not the maids or harried mothers of Venice, they were the richest women of the city, perched like exotic birds in the windows of their homes and displayed to the world. But these women were not the only eyes watching us, for I had also seen a familiar face again in the crowds. Always a few feet away from us, and always quick to disappear into the shadows when I turned around – it was the boy who had led me back to Ca' Bearpark for two *soldini* on the night of Enrico's murder. There could be no doubt that he was following me.

We had reached the borders of San Marco and Castello, when Giovanni put his hand upon my shoulder and forced me to stop. 'You must tell me where we're going, Oswald?' he said. 'Please. I need to know.'

I drew him to a low wall by a bridge, so that we might speak privately. 'We're going to the Arsenale,' I said.

Giovanni frowned and felt for his keys. 'What do you want to go there for?'

Behind us, two ragged men were arguing over a bottle of wine – a quarrel that had the potential to escalate into a fight. It was time to move on. 'I just want to see it,' I said. 'Come on.'

The Arsenale is in Castello, a few streets further into the *sestiere* than the decrepit tavern where we had previously met with Michele, and it seemed that Giovanni was no keener to visit this part of Venice than he had been on our last excursion. As we picked our way along the narrow streets, Giovanni informed me, again and again, that a person cannot simply visit the Arsenale itself, for it is the greatest shipyard in the whole of Europe – hidden behind the highest walls, and guarded by the most ferocious soldiers. In fact, Giovanni proved himself to be something of an authority on the whole subject of the Arsenale, and kept his narrative going for the whole of our journey. Soon I learnt, for example, that any house bordering the walls of the Arsenale cannot exceed two storeys in height, nor can it have any windows that face the shipyard. I even learnt that the priests of local churches are not allowed to hold the keys to their bell towers, in case they feel tempted to climb the stairs and take a look over the walls.

When I made the mistake of expressing some surprise at all this subterfuge, Giovanni puffed with indignation at my ignorance. Within the Arsenale, so he informed me, the Venetians make galleys that are unmatched upon the seas, using skills and methods that are known only to their shipwrights – so it is no wonder that the secrets of the Arsenale are so heavily guarded, and I was a fool to think otherwise.

Thankfully Giovanni's lecture had ended by the time we reached the Arsenale, but as we wandered about the periphery, I could sense the industry he had described. The biting stench of boiling pitch spread through the air, and, although I could see nothing but bricks, I knew we were only feet away from the workshop of many, many men. I could hear their shouts and whistles above the hammering and sawing and clanging of their frenetic production, as they toiled away building ships faster than any other yard in the whole of the world.

Giovanni stepped from foot to foot and seemed as nervous as a calf about to be slaughtered. On this side of the wall, we stood out as the only adult men in the street, and had already drawn the attention of the nearby women. These were not the wives and daughters who were framed in the balconies of San Marco or the Rialto, with their fur collars and braided hair, waiting for the world to pay attention to their prosperity and beauty. The women of Castello were feeding infants, scrubbing shellfish, or wringing out dirty clothes in the street. Nevertheless, they were every bit as interested in our progress as their wealthier counterparts had been, for almost to a woman they stopped what they were doing and turned to stare.

'Please. Why are we here, Oswald?' said Giovanni nervously. Then his voice fell to a whisper. 'We might be arrested.' He nodded into the distance, to where a guard stood at one of the smaller gates to the Arsenale, with his long pike resting at a slant. The man hadn't noticed us, and it looked as if he was attempting to sleep at his post.

'I met a young man yesterday at the convent. He was Enrico's lover,' I said.

'What is his name?'

'I told you before. That doesn't matter.'

Giovanni pursed his lips before speaking to me in a whisper. 'Very well then, Oswald. Perhaps you can tell me why we have come to the Arsenale?' He glared at me. 'Please, hurry up, and then we may leave.'

I took my time to answer. 'The man from the convent told me that Enrico had another lover.'

Giovanni crossed himself. 'Another one?'

I ignored this disapproval. 'Yes. A man who works here.' I hesitated. 'My contact is certain that this is the man who killed Enrico.'

'Oh yes? And why is that?'

I dithered again. 'He said that Enrico and this man were involved in something dangerous together.'

'What does that mean?'

'He wouldn't elaborate.'

Giovanni threw up his hands, to indicate his poor opinion of this whole story. 'Very well then, what is the name of the man who works here? Can you tell me that, at least?'

'It's Gianni.'

'Gianni who?'

'I don't know,' I said quickly. 'But I thought we might ask around here about him. Somebody must know a Gianni who works in the Arsenale.'

Giovanni gave an enormous guffaw at my last comment, a sound that was loud enough to draw more attention to us.

'What's so funny?' I asked.

'Do you know how many men work in the Arsenale?' he whispered.

'A few hundred,' I said boldly, attempting to disguise that this was a guess.

'No, Oswald. It is thousands of men. Thousands!' he said. 'How else can Venice rule the seas? Even our merchant galleys are built as warships.'

'Thousands of men. Are you sure?'

He nodded conceitedly. 'Of course I'm sure. And do you know the most common name in Venice?'

I shrugged, although I could already predict the answer.

'It's Gianni,' he said with another sneer, before smoothing down his hair. 'You've been tricked, Oswald,' he said. 'Your man at the convent has given you a very common name and sent you to a place where very many men work. He lied in order to get rid of you.'

'No,' I said stubbornly. 'I'm sure he was telling me the truth.'

Giovanni raised an eyebrow. 'Let's just get away from here, shall we? We can discuss this matter when we have returned to Ca' Bearpark.'

I was embarrassed, but too proud to admit defeat. 'There must be somebody around here who we can ask about Gianni,' I insisted. 'I know how much you Venetians like to spy upon one another.'

Giovanni stopped dead in his tracks. 'Venice has enemies everywhere, Oswald. That is why we watch each other.' I tried to move away, but he had cornered me against the wall, and I could not escape this next sermon. 'Oh yes. Our enemies send their agents to discover how we build our ships.' He waved his finger at me in the most irritating fashion. 'Or even how many ships we have in production. And this is not to mention the enemies we have amongst our own people,' he said. 'It is only three years since Falier tried to destroy our republic and seize power for himself.' He gripped my cloak and shook it for effect. 'And Falier was the cruellest of enemies, for he was our own doge!' He released his hands and dusted down my cloak. 'So you must understand then, why we watch each other.'

I straightened my cloak, but would not move. Giovanni had annoyed me with his lecture, so I will admit to taking an infantile pleasure in placing my ear against the wall of the Arsenale and then closing my eyes. I could tell that he was fretting at this, as he then tried to pull me away from the wall, but I would not be moved. Instead I let my mind wander for a while, as I imagined the secrets that were hidden beyond these bricks, and how much they might be worth to an enemy of Venice. As I did so, it was my own guilty secret that came to mind – the purse that I had hidden in my chest. The purse, filled with eight golden ducats that I hadn't quite got around to disclosing to Bearpark. But there was not just this money to consider. There had also been a second purse, the one containing the three ducats that we had found tied under the bed at the inn, on the night that Adolpho Bredani was killed.

I opened my eyes with a start and pulled Giovanni close. 'Something has just occurred to me,' I said.

Giovanni was now very agitated, with his eyes focussed on the guard at the gate to the Arsenale. This man was no longer sleeping, and appeared to be staring in our direction. 'Please, Oswald. We must leave immediately.'

I ignored Giovanni's plea. 'My contact at the convent spoke of Enrico's involvement in something dangerous,' I said. 'And now that I'm here at the Arsenale, I'm wondering if . . .'

'If what?'

'If Giovanni and his lover could have been engaged in . . .' I bit my lip, still unsure whether to share this theory.

'Engaged in what?' snapped my companion, now unable to hide his frustration.

I wasn't sure myself, and yet the feeling came over me again. The walls of the Arsenale were too imposing to ignore, and the secrets they hid were too valuable. 'It just seems strange that Enrico chose a lover who works here, of all places.' I said.

Giovanni shook his head. 'No, Oswald. I don't think it's strange at all. Enrico liked coarse men, and they come no coarser than shipbuilders.' Then he gave a short huff. 'That's if this Gianni even exists.'

'I didn't mean it that way,' I said.

'What do you mean then?'

I drew him closer. 'I'm wondering if Enrico and Gianni were involved in some sort of . . . spying?' Before he could object, I added. 'If they were selling secrets about the Arsenale, then it might explain the source of those golden ducats that we found under Bredani's bed at the inn.'

'I don't understand what you mean,' said Giovanni. 'Please. Let's go.'

'No. Wait a moment,' I said. 'Perhaps it was this Gianni who paid Bredani to kill Enrico.'

Giovanni shook his head in exasperation. 'But how would Bredani and this mysterious man even know one another?'

'They might have met at Ca' Bearpark.'

'You think a shipbuilder came to my master's house?' said Giovanni haughtily. 'I doubt it.'

'But Margery saw Enrico and his lover in the storeroom, we know that from her testament. Or are you doubting the word of a pilgrim?'

Giovanni flung up his hands. 'No, no. You're imagining stories that don't exist, Oswald. The murder has nothing to do with spying or hidden money. Enrico was killed by a man with tastes as evil as his own. He sought out wickedness and he got what he deserved.'

'You don't mean that,' I said.

'Yes, I do,' said Giovanni furiously. 'I never cared for Enrico Bearpark.'

The bitterness of his words shocked me. 'So, you're pleased he's dead?'

He drew in a great breath. 'He brought great shame to his grandfather, so yes. I'm not sorry. I'm not sorry at all.'

I threw a punch at Giovanni's head – the one I had been fantasising about for days. Sadly, the reality was not as satisfying as I had imagined, for Giovanni swerved nimbly, and I only succeeded in catching a lock of his glossy hair, nevertheless it felt good to have tried. I had not expected Giovanni to retaliate, as he had always seemed such a peaceable man, but he threw a punch of his own, and soon we fell into the filth of the street, brawling like a pair of urchins fighting over a crust of bread. A mob of women and children gathered about us almost immediately – shouting and jeering at our squabble, but unfortunately we also caught the further attention of the guard.

As the man strode purposefully towards us with his pike at the ready, Giovanni scrambled to his feet, before bolting into a side street. I tried to follow his heels, but my companion disappeared from sight, and soon I was lost in a labyrinth as complex as the maze within the palace of Minos. I ran up one dead end after another, and passed the same landmark repeatedly, until I turned a sharp corner to come face to face with three guards, one of whom I recognised from the Arsenale. The other two were dressed in the uniform of the doge's palace. I was cornered, and though I resisted, my capture was inevitable.

Chapter Twenty-Three

I had been imprisoned in a dungeon twice before in my life, and the experience does not improve with familiarity. I was shoved through a door that was only high enough to accommodate a child, and then I fell into a cell that felt as cold as a sarcophagus. The roof was so low that I was unable to stand upright, so I could do nothing but crawl onto one of the miserable benches that lined the chamber and curse the fact that my feet were already sloshing about the flooded floor. This was the Pozzi: 'The Wells'. Famed throughout the city as the doge's prison. The only light came from a small and perfectly circular hole that was quarried through the wall into the passageway and was located next to the door. I tried to speak to the guard through this opening, but the man steadfastly ignored me.

I knew there were other humans in my cell, as I had seen their shapes when the candle briefly illuminated my entrance, but they neither spoke to me, nor even moved to acknowledge my arrival. I only knew them still to be alive by the odorous stink of dirty, sweat-stained clothes that hung in the air like a miasma. These people were not dead yet, but they clung to existence by the frailest of yarns, only showing signs of life when the prison guard shoved a loaf of stale bread through the circular hole. When this happened, they jumped up and fought like dogs, pulling the loaf into a number of fragments and scattering the crumbs across the floor. A man who had been thrown aside in this fight now felt about in the water for a morsel of food, while the others returned to their benches, where they resumed their previous catatonia.

I cannot say how long I was imprisoned, for time does not exist in such places. The Pozzi were like caves – dark and unearthly. They had no conventional rhythm, other than the beat of water dripping from the ceiling. No light, other than the lanterns of the prison guards making their occasional survey inside the cells. No sounds, other than the snoring, groans, and occasional screams of the other inmates.

I felt as if I were trapped in Purgatory, with nobody willing to offer prayers for my salvation, but, after what seemed an age, a pair of guards eventually fished me out of the cell. I was then propelled along dark, thin corridors, through doors that were unlocked and then relocked, before being pushed up a narrow staircase to a room that was above ground. It was a relief to leave the damp murk of the lower floors, but our destination was no light and pleasant hall. In fact, it bore no resemblance to the room in which I had been interviewed on my last visit to this palace. Instead this was a chamber of medium proportions, without windows, somewhere at the centre of the palace, I guessed. In the faint orange glow of a lantern, I could see it was unfurnished, apart from a portable set of steps in the middle of the room. Above these steps, a heavy rope hung from the high ceiling – its pale, twisting yarns catching the light. Seeing this rope prompted a last and fruitless struggle against my guards, for I knew exactly where I was and what was going to happen.

I had been tortured once before, a number of years ago in Kent, and on that occasion my torturer had chosen one of those devices that are so popular in England – ostentatious implements, decorated with fiendish spikes and serrated blades. By comparison, these wooden steps and this simple rope seemed rather innocuous, as if it might be possible to withstand this variety of torment. The simplicity of this system was its very cunning however, for this torture would be every bit as painful as the suffering induced by the more obvious devices that were employed in my homeland.

At first my arms were tied behind my back, and then my bound wrists were attached to the rope. I was then forced to climb the three steps as my arms were pulled upwards behind my back. I was not yet dangling from my wrists, as I could rest my feet upon the top step, but if my answers did not please my interrogator, then the set of steps would be pushed away, leaving me to hang in mid-air until my arms were pulled out of their sockets and my ribcage splintered.

So, as you can imagine, I protested my innocence and then my outrage to the two guards, before pleading for mercy, but I was wasting my breath on this pair as they were merely the foot soldiers of this operation, and had no influence over my fate. I needed to convince their superior to release me – a man who eventually strolled into the room and began to pace around me slowly, like a wolf assessing its prey. I could not see his face clearly at first because the light was dim and my eyes were watering with pain, but from the fine cloth of his cloak and the soft, red leather of his boots, it was clear he enjoyed both authority and wealth. This was not a clerk with a self-important chain, who would transcribe our conversation onto a roll of parchment and then listen to instructions through a hole in the wall. This man bore all the condescending, self-satisfied, unhurried hallmarks of true nobility.

I tried repeatedly to plead my innocence until he demanded my silence. He then approached me, and now that his face was close to mine, I found myself noticing the small things about him. The insignificant details that had no bearing upon my fate. His skin was pitted with large pores – not large enough to render the man unattractive, but still visible at these close quarters. The edge of his fur collar was slightly wet and stained with red wine.

He spoke at last. 'Oswald de Lacy. Lord Somershill of England. Why were you at the Arsenale today?' He then walked behind me and placed his hands lightly upon the back of my leg, as if he might push me from the set of steps.

'Who are you?' I asked.

'My identity is not important. Answer my question.'

I dropped my chin to my chest, as it was becoming too painful to keep my neck raised. 'I was just interested in the place,' I said. 'Nothing more.'

'Oh yes? Why would you be interested in the shipyard of Venice?'

'I'm just a pilgrim,' I said weakly.

He gave a short laugh. 'I don't see other pilgrims visiting this place,' he said. 'So, did somebody ask you to go to the Arsenale?'

'No. It was my own idea.'

'Then what made you want to go there?'

'I'm investigating something,' I said.

'Investigating?' He put a little more pressure upon the back of my leg.

'The murder of Enrico Bearpark?' I admitted, as sweat beaded upon my brow and then dripped onto my feet.

'Why is Enrico Bearpark's death any business of yours?' he asked.

I tried to lift my head again. 'I was his friend.'

Suddenly, without forewarning, he pushed me forward so violently that I fell from the top step and dangled in space momentarily, before being able to just about touch my toes upon the step below. The pain in my shoulders was now searing into my arms and I felt as if I might pass out.

'What were you really doing at the Arsenale today?' he asked me, having walked around to face me again. 'Another lie, and I'll take the steps away.'

'I was investigating the murder of Enrico Bearpark. I told you that before,' I insisted. 'Enrico had a friend who works at the Arsenale. I just wanted to speak to him.'

'Why?'

'Because I'm told he was with Enrico, on the night he was murdered,' I lied.

'And what is this man's name?'

'Gianni.'

'His family name?'

'I don't know,' I admitted. 'I was hoping to find him, but then your guards arrested me.'

The man gave a short snort, stood back, and then clicked his fingers. At this small instruction, one of the guards appeared with a wooden chair that was placed near to the bottom of the steps. My interrogator took his time to lift his cloak and then settle himself upon this chair, whilst I tried to put as much weight as possible onto my toes, in order to relieve the relentless, agonising drag at my shoulders.

As he sat in front of me, he concentrated on his hands – running his nail from one thumb under the nail of the other, not bothering to look up as he addressed me. 'Let's say that I believe this story about your investigation into Bearpark's murder,' he said at length.

'You should do. Because it's true.'

'Then tell me what you know about Enrico Bearpark,' he said, leaning back in his chair and placing his red boot against the bottom step – causing the whole set of steps to shift a little across the floor.

'What do you want to know?' I said with a gulp.

'How did Enrico die?' he asked.

'He was killed during a fight at the carnival of *Giovedi Grasso*,' I said.

He pushed at the steps again. 'Who killed him?'

'I don't know.' My voice faltered, as I became seized with fear.

'Enrico Bearpark was denounced,' he said, staring up into my face. 'Did you discover that in your investigation?'

'Yes,' I said. 'But I don't know what the letter said.' A long spindle of dribble fell from my mouth, and only just avoided hitting his shoulder.

He jumped up at this, throwing me a look of disgust, before he clicked his fingers and summoned a guard to his side. A man appeared immediately, listened to a long and whispered command before leaving the chamber and returning with a roll of parchment. My interrogator then unravelled the document and read aloud. '*Beware Enrico Bearpark,*' he said. '*He is a deceitful, corrupt liar. Always meddling where he shouldn't.*' The man twisted his head to look up into my eyes. 'This was the denunciation. So what does it mean?'

I had heard these same words at the convent of Santa Lucia. They were Marco's. 'I don't know,' I said, as I choked, not knowing how long I could now maintain consciousness.

'Of course you do. You lived with Enrico. You're investigating his murder. Or so you say.' He looked up into my face. 'Are you going to tell me? Or would you like a little longer to think about it? Or perhaps I will assume that you are a spy. Loitering outside the Arsenale to discover our secrets.' He laughed. 'And you must know what happens to spies in Venice.' Once again he pressed his boot against the set of steps, causing them to move a little as I struggled, in desperation, to keep my footing.

'I'm not a spy,' I insisted. 'But I do know what the letter means.' The searing pain in my shoulders and neck was now so intense, that I feared I might vomit. 'But you have to loosen the rope first.'

'Why should I do that?'

'Because I can't speak if I'm being sick.'

My interrogator regarded me for a moment and then signalled to the guards that they might allow some slack in the rope. The relief was almost blissful, but now I had to tell them something, or they would pull up the rope again, no doubt harder and tighter this time. Fear will spark venal, unscrupulous thoughts, for we are driven to survive, above all other motivations. So, as the blood coursed back into my veins, a plan began to form. It was contemptible, and yet I knew it could save me. I could tell them that it was Marco who had written the letter of denunciation. He was the person who knew Enrico's secrets. If this was not enough to damn the man, then I could also reveal that Marco had taken other men as lovers. Surely these two disclosures would be enough to secure my release and send them after Marco instead?

This was the answer, and yet as Marco's name formed on my lips, I sensed that something was watching me from the darkest corner of the room. It could read my mind, and it could see my weakness.

'What's your answer?' demanded my interrogator.

I closed my eyes, trying to blot the creature from my mind, but as I did so, I felt its breath upon my cheek, and its fingers touching my skin, clawing at my conscience. 'I do know what the letter means,' I said at last, lifting my head as far as my neck would allow.

'Yes?'

'The denunciation is a slur against Enrico Bearpark.'

He grunted a laugh. 'Of course it's a slur! But what does it mean?'

I hesitated, taking a deep breath before I spoke. 'The letter accuses Enrico of taking men as lovers. That's why it says he was corrupt and meddling where he shouldn't.'

The man folded his arms and regarded me a little sceptically. 'Are you saying that Enrico Bearpark was a sodomite?'

I nodded in response. 'I am,' I said, knowing that they could not burn a dead man on one of their abhorrent pyres.

'You are certain about this?' he said.

'Yes,' I replied, as another trickle of my spit fell to the floor. 'I know it's true.'

'Were you Enrico's lover?'

'No,' I said calmly. 'I was not.'

'So who was?'

'His name is Gianni and he works at the Arsenale.' I managed
to raise my head again. 'That's why I was trying to find him.'

Ten times he circled me, slowly placing one foot before the
other on the dirty terrazzo, crossing the many stains of blood
that peppered the floor of this torture chamber. Then he stopped
with a sigh. 'Untie him,' he told the two guards. The men obeyed
and released my throbbing wrists from the rope, causing me to
fall forward in a mixture of relief and pain, unable to break my
fall, as my arms were too numb and useless.

As I lay upon the floor, the man leant over me to whisper into
my ear. 'My name is Ballio.' Then he kicked my stomach. 'What
is it?'

'Ballio.'

'When you find this Gianni, you tell me.' When my only
response was a groan, he kicked me again. 'Understand?'

'Yes,' I said weakly. 'I understand.'

Chapter Twenty-Four

If my mother and Clemence had not been overjoyed at my marriage proposal to Mary, their consternation was nothing compared to the misery it induced in Mary's younger sister, Rebecca.

I found the girl in the stables, crying into the mane of her handsome palfrey, though the horse remained unaffected by her anguish, and continued to chew at its hay with the rhythm of a swinging thurible. It confounds me why people seek solace in animals, for it seems to me that you might expect to receive as much sympathy from a velvet cushion or a length of polished wood.

'What's the matter with you, Becky?' I asked, though I already knew the answer. Ada, the lady's maid, had provided me with a long and tortuous account of the girl's woes.

Becky turned to look at me with a tear-soaked face. 'I thought you were in love with *me*, Uncle Oswald.' The awkwardness of this title still jarred, but it was untimely to reprimand her. The truth was, I was lost for words.

She buried her head once again into the mane of the palfrey. 'Because I love you,' she said. 'More than any girl has ever loved a man. And now,' she drew back her face and pulled the horse's hair from her mouth. 'Now I will never love another.'

I would tell you that I was flattered by this sudden outburst of devotion, but I knew Becky's nature of old – dramatic and inconstant. She had once threatened to jump from the north-west tower, when her ancient, flea-bitten cat had finally died. This had turned out to be an affectation only lasting as long as it took me to find a new kitten in the barn, so I had every expectation that Becky's supposed love for me would be equally short-lived. But, after the announcement of my engagement to Mary, Becky continued to cry for the best part of a week.

The next Sunday Mother took me to one side after mass in the family chapel. We walked back to the house, arm in arm, circling the great hall and then passing beneath the solar, as was our habit on a Sunday morning. Mary followed us, but she disliked talking to Mother, so she hung back and picked dandelion heads so that she could blow their seeds into the wind.

Mother looked back to ensure that Mary was out of earshot. 'Are you sure you are marrying the right sister, Oswald? The younger girl seems very devoted to you.' She gestured up towards the window of the ladies' bedchamber, where Becky's despond-ent face was watching us from behind the glass. Becky had refused to attend mass. Mother squeezed my arm. 'And I would say she is the prettier of the two sisters. She's the one I would have chosen, in your place.'

I smiled and waved at Becky, which only induced the girl to withdraw into the room and release a great wail that could be heard from our position below. 'I'm very fond of Becky, Mother. But it's Mary that I love.'

Once again, Mother turned her head to check Mary's loca-tion. Thankfully Mary had peeled off from this dull promenade to visit her horses in the nearby stables. 'But Mary is very mascu-line, don't you think? Always riding that burly horse of hers about the forest. With her legs straddling the beast.' Then she whispered, 'I cannot help but think this practice will cause you some disappointment on your wedding night.'

I tried to keep my voice equable. 'How else is a woman supposed to ride a horse, Mother? Particularly when she is hunting with a hawk.' I quickened my step, in the hope of losing her. 'Or perhaps you would prefer that Mary rode side-saddle and risked falling off?'

We reached the end of our promenade by the back porch, but Mother would not let go of my arm willingly. 'But Oswald. You must listen to me. Are you prepared to keep a firm hand on such a headstrong creature as Mary de Caburn? Especially as she bears a residual grain of her father's malignance. And we know what a murderous fiend he was.' I tried to break free. 'Mary's wildness concerns me, Oswald.'

I disentangled myself. 'It's her wildness that I love.'

Becky de Caburn was not to be my bride, but nevertheless, the girl managed to dominate my wedding day. The night before the ceremony was due to take place, she ran away from Somershill – though not without informing a selection of servants of her destination.

I wanted to find Becky that same night, knowing full-well that Mary would not agree to continue with the ceremony the next morning if her sister was lost, so I pulled on my boots with some irritation and rode out to retrieve the errant girl. I might add that I was not in the least bit flattered by this supposed devotion. Becky only wanted me because Mary had me.

I soon found Becky at the house of Robert Wolfenden – the boy who had previously followed her about the estate with the faithful eyes and flopping tongue of a puppy. I interrupted something of a feast in the Wolfenden household, as it transpired that Becky had married Robert that very day. At first, the family were concerned that I would be angered by their union, but Robert's father assured me that they were very much in love, and that his son would inherit both the Wolfenden family farm and another sixty-five acres from a childless uncle. I looked across the room at Becky's crowing face, and knew that this marriage had been prompted by spite. She no more loved Robert Wolfenden than she claimed to love me.

When the moment was appropriate, I took the girl to one side. She clasped me desperately and then flung her arms about my neck. 'I knew you'd come, Oswald,' she said in the breathy, exaggerated style that she had adopted of late, used exclusively for talking to men.

I gently freed myself from her. 'Of course I've come. You ran away!'

She spoke with the coquettish gasps that might work their wonders on other men, but had no effect upon me, other than to cause irritation. 'I knew that you'd come, if you thought that I'd married Robert.'

The girl had momentarily baffled me. 'What are you talking about? You *have* married Robert Wolfenden.'

She waved a dismissive hand. 'It can be undone. The marriage is not consummated, and it was just their village priest.' She grasped me once again about the waist. 'We can still marry.'

How could she not understand the situation? 'Listen to me, Becky. I'm marrying your sister. Tomorrow.' I looked into her eyes. They were glazed with the rosiness of wine and delusion. I needed to be firm and clear. 'I don't love you, Becky. I never will.' These words were harshly said, but with good reason. She needed to understand the truth.

Suddenly her eyes came into focus. 'No! That's not so.'

'It is, Becky.' I forced her to look into my face. 'I will never marry you. Do you understand me?'

Her face dissolved into rage. She was as furious as a small child who's been sent to bed early. 'No! You're lying. You do love me the best. It's me you want to marry.' She started to beat her fists against my chest, and drew the attention of some of the wedding guests who were sitting on benches nearby. They seemed alarmed, but looked away when I stared back at them, for every person in this room was a tenant of mine.

I grasped her fists and looked into her eyes. 'Listen to me, Becky. I can take you home. I can have your marriage annulled. But I will never marry you myself.'

Her face reddened. 'No! I'm not coming home.'

'Don't stay with Robert to spite me, Becky. It will not work.'

She wriggled free of my grip, and crumpled into a sob. Robert watched us nervously from the other side of the hall. He wore a concerned expression, as if he knew the nature of this conversation?

I put my hand upon her back, in an attempt to be sympathetic. 'Come home with me, Becky. I will sort this out later.'

She shook her head, though I sensed a weakening in her resolve.

'Come on. Come to my wedding feast tomorrow. Be pleased for me. Be pleased for your sister.'

I should not have mentioned my own wedding. 'No,' she said grimly. 'I will never watch you marry Mary.'

This was becoming tiresome. 'You needn't come to the ceremony. You may stay in your bedchamber, if that pleases you,' I whispered hoarsely. 'But you must come home with me tonight.'

Now she looked up at me. Her eyes were cold. The fury had dissipated and only a bold and calculated obstinacy remained. I might even say hatred. 'No,' she said. 'You and Mary will never see me again. That will serve you right.'

'It will not serve me right, Becky. You will only be harming yourself.'

Her eyes gave nothing away. 'One day you'll be sorry.'

How to convince such a stubborn creature that she was making a mistake. 'No. I won't. Now stop this nonsense and come back to Somershill.'

She growled at me. It was the low, feral snarl of the child she had once been — running about her father's castle, dressed in his old leather tunic, and wielding a rusty sword. 'Leave me here,' she said. 'I'll be Robert's wife. See how you like that!'

I heaved a sigh. 'Very well then. You have just married him, after all.' I waved at the fellow, who still watched us from the other corner of the hall. 'I shall leave you to it.'

She took my hand gently. I thought she had seen sense, but I was completely mistaken – for her words bore the cruel hiss of a serpent. 'I curse your marriage to Mary.'

I wanted to pull my hand away, but somehow it remained glued to her fingers. 'I don't believe in curses,' I said.

She smiled and dropped my hand. 'You'll see.'

Chapter Twenty-Five

I was released from the doge's palace to find that it was now Wednesday and nearly a day had passed since my arrest. As I hobbled across Venice, rubbing my shoulders at every third step in the hope that my arms still rested fully in their sockets, I could tell that my small spy was still following at a distance. When I went into Ca' Bearpark via the street entrance, I raised one of my battered hands to wave ironically at the young boy, and to my surprise, he waved back, so at least we both acknowledged how this arrangement worked.

It was late morning, and the house was quiet, so thankfully my return went unnoticed by Giovanni, and I was able to reach my room without a barrage of questions. My neck ached and my arms felt numbed and bruised, and after my incarceration in the Pozzi, I smelt as if I had been swimming in the filth of the River Fleet, just downstream from the slaughter houses at Smithfield.

I was attempting to remove my clothes when Mother blew in with her dog in her arms. Her face was animated and pink. 'Oswald! Thank goodness. It's true. You're still alive.' She dropped the dog and embraced me. 'John was especially worried about you.'

'I wouldn't want John to be upset,' I said, trying to untangle myself from her grip.

She drew back. 'Where have you been?' And then she held her nose. 'And what, in the name of the saints, is that smell?'

I held my arms in the air. 'Just help me out of this tunic, please.'

'But Oswald—'

'Please, Mother. Just do as I ask.'

She carefully pulled the garment over my head and then helped me to draw my battered arms through the sleeves. 'What happened, Oswald?' she said, as she looked at my blistered wrists and bruised arms.

'I was arrested.'

'Arrested?' Her face stiffened. 'What for?'

'Loitering outside the Arsenale.'

'Did they do this to you in the doge's palace?' I nodded. 'Well, what a disgraceful way to treat an Englishman.' She tried to take my arm. 'Come along. You must tell John about this outrage. He has many friends in the palace, you know. They must be informed of this—'

I slipped my arm carefully from hers. 'No, Mother. Please. Just let the matter lie.'

'But, Oswald. John is most anxious to speak with you.'

'I don't care.'

She gave a short snort of dissatisfaction, but had the sense to back down from any further argument. 'Very well. We'll speak later. Just stay here and rest.'

Rest? How was I supposed to rest? My whole body might have throbbed with pain, but I still had a murderer to find. I still had a debt to repay. 'Would you give me some money please, Mother,' I said.

'What for?'

'I just need it.'

I believe my approach was seen from the convent. In the pale light, I caught sight of figures at the windows, looking out across the silver waters of the lagoon and noting my progress. There were only a few boats out on the water that afternoon, as the leaden clouds of a storm were gathering overhead. The fishermen we had passed were rowing back towards the city and waiting for the rain to abate before they returned to the lagoon. My oarsman asked me to be quick when we reached the landing stage on the island, as he feared our return to Venice would be difficult if we delayed, but I had every intention of being brief. I needed only to speak with Marco and discover what he had truly meant by the words of his letter of denunciation. He would give me Gianni's full name, and then he would tell me the genuine nature of this 'dangerous' affair in which Enrico had involved himself. This time, I would not leave the convent until I was told the truth.

I thumped at the door, and was admitted immediately by an old man with a curved spine and a barnacled face. He didn't ask for my name, nor even appear surprised by my request to speak with the abbess. Instead he indicated that I should follow him through the convent, along corridors that were eerily silent – as if the whole place were deserted. It was so different to my last visit there, when children had run noisily about the courtyard.

The old man guided me along a portico, down three steps to a side door that appeared to lead into a storeroom, and I wondered if he had understood that I wanted to see the abbess? This was not the grand and opulently decorated door that I had expected to open into the private quarters of a mother superior. However, when he knocked at this simple, modest door, it was answered by the woman herself. She poked her head out to look me up and down, and then indicated that I may enter. The old man shuffled in after me, and then slammed the door behind him.

'What do you want?' she said. Her arms were folded and her face was cold.

'I need to speak to Marco,' I told her. The room was bare, apart from a wooden bedstead and a blackened crucifix upon the wall. It was a monastic cell, so different from the extravagant chamber in which I had met Marco on my previous visit.

She turned away from me and wandered to a low, barred window. 'Too late,' she said. 'He's gone.'

'Where?'

She cast me an accusing look over her shoulder, before turning away again. 'I don't know,' she said. As a momentary ray of sunlight caught her profile, I saw something in her face that I should have seen before.

'You *do* know where he is, don't you?' I said. 'Because Marco is your son.'

She turned back sharply. 'Who told you that?'

'So, it's true then?'

She pursed her lips, angry that I had drawn her.

'I need to speak to him,' I said.

'Why should I tell you anything? You! The man who sent the Signori di Notte here to take my son.'

'What?' I shook my head. 'Of course I didn't send them here.'

She drew her face into a scowl. 'You lie! We saw them coming across the lagoon, soon after your visit. They'd dressed themselves in the cloaks and mantles of ordinary men, but we're not stupid. Marco had time to escape.' Then she laughed at me. 'So, you see. You've failed. The Signori can burn somebody else on their pyre.'

'They must have followed me,' I told the woman. 'They've been spying on me, but I promise you that I did not give Marco's name to them. I would never do that.'

'Your lies mean nothing to me,' she told me. 'I know that you sent them.' Behind me, the elderly hunchback hissed a curse.

'No, that's not true,' I said, with all earnestness. 'I swear on it.'

She turned her face to mine, and looked down her nose at me. Her face shared the same structural perfection of her son's, but her skin had loosened from her skull, and deep vertical lines ran down her cheeks. 'It doesn't matter,' she told me with disdain. 'Because Marco has gone, for ever.'

'What do you mean?'

She looked to me with a superior smile, but would not answer.

This was a grave turn of events, for Marco was the only loose thread hanging from the tight ball of this mystery. If I could not speak to him, then I was not sure where I could turn.

I put my hand upon the abbess's arm, trying not to convey my despair. 'You must tell me where he is. Please. I—'

Before I had even finished the sentence, the crooked man was upon me, defending his mistress with the ferocity of a guard dog. With the momentum of his movement, and with the advantage of surprise, he was able to push me against the wall, but I soon stamped on his foot, causing him to fall onto the floor and shriek in pain. When I turned back to the abbess, she had shrunk away from me, like one of those pitiful women who are regularly beaten by their husbands, so I stepped away quickly, before asking her to sit. I did not want her to fear me, only to give me answers.

'Please, sister. Tell me where Marco is, and I can promise he will come to no harm.' As she turned her face from mine, my only option was to beg. 'Please. Just tell me where I can find him. I just need to ask him a few questions. Nothing else.'

She kept her face to the wall. 'No. I will never tell you, and you will never find him.'

'Please,' I said in desperation. 'Please. Think again.'

She let out a great, contemptuous laugh. 'Marco is gone, Englishman. Somewhere that you and your Signori will never dare to follow.'

Chapter Twenty-Six

There was no escaping John Bearpark on my return to the house, as Giovanni was guarding the water gate, ready to propel me to his master's bedchamber as soon as my feet crossed the threshold. I was exhausted, my arms throbbed with pain, and I was thoroughly dejected after learning that Marco had disappeared. As a result, I was not in the best of moods when Giovanni pushed me into Bearpark's bedchamber. In fact you might say I was spoiling for a fight.

The old man was sitting up in bed as I entered the long room, though his eyes were closed, his posture rigid, and I wondered at first if he were dead – placed like a stuffed bird in the centre of a feast table. The shutters at the window had been opened a little, and a thin stripe of light cast its smile across the floor, but other than this the place was still suffused with the melancholy of decrepitude and mortality.

Giovanni whispered into his ear and the old man woke with a start, feeling about the sheets until his spectacles were safely mounted upon his nose.

'De Lacy?' he said, peering at me from behind the bottle ends. 'Is that you?'

'It is.'

'So. Do you have a name for me? A name!' His words were croaked rather than spoken, and sounded like one of those oft-repeated sentences that are uttered by an old person whose mind has wandered.

'No,' I said firmly. 'I don't.'

At my response, the Bearpark's fragility suddenly disintegrated. 'Then what are you doing?' he shouted. 'If you don't find the murderer soon, then I'll be dead!'

'Look. I—'

He interrupted. 'Yet I hear that you were arrested outside the Arsenale? The Arsenale of Venice, of all places!'

'Yes,' I said rigidly. 'And then I was thrown into the Pozzi, before being tortured.' I lifted my sleeves to show him the raw, stinging wounds that marked my wrists.

Bearpark waved these injuries away dismissively. 'What did you tell them, eh?' he said. 'What did you tell them?'

'I told them the truth, Bearpark,' I said, replacing my sleeves over my wrists with some petulance. 'That I'm investigating Enrico's death.'

Bearpark banged his hand onto the bolster, releasing a bloom of tiny feathers into the air. 'By the bones of Saint Catherine, what did you do that for? Now I will have the bastards crawling all over the house.'

'I was being hung by my wrists from a rope, Bearpark,' I said. 'I had to tell them something. Or, would you prefer it if they had killed me?'

At this, the door opened and the room was suddenly invaded by a light that caused Bearpark to curse out loud. At first I thought our visitor was Mother, on one of her regular visits to Bearpark's bedside, but as the door slowly closed, I saw a different figure outlined against the light. It was Filomena, carrying a bowl of steaming broth with steadfast, unblinking concentration.

Bearpark squinted into the distance. 'Is there no peace? Who is it now? Not your damned mother, I hope.'

'It's your wife,' I told him. 'Bringing you some supper.'

The old man gave a grunt, and continued to watch Filomena as she cautiously made her way across the room, taking care not to spill a drop of the broth onto the floor. We had passed into Lent now, so this meal had been cooked with seashells and garlic, rather than meat. Perhaps Filomena had cooked it herself, which was why she was serving this dish to her ailing husband: another consequence of the ever-reducing household of Ca' Bearpark.

As she approached her husband's bed, the old man continued to grumble into his chin. 'What are you doing here?' he said in Venetian. 'I didn't ask for any food.'

Filomena lowered her head. 'You must eat, husband.'

'Must I?' he said with a grunt. 'What do you care?'

'I care that you're well.'

He let out a puff of anger. 'What nonsense you speak, woman. You'd sooner I died!'

Filomena froze for a moment and then carried on, as if Bearpark had never uttered such a cruel accusation. She then sat next to her husband with the intention of spooning the soup into his mouth. I think it was this final indignity that riled Bearpark to violence, for it was then that he deliberately struck out his arm and launched the bowl of soup against Filomena, causing her to scream as the steaming broth leached through her dress and scalded her skin.

I rushed to Filomena's side, pouring cold water from Bearpark's pitcher onto her skirts, before she pulled the sodden tunic away from her skin and ran from the room in tears.

'God's bones!' I shouted. 'What are you doing, Bearpark? How can you be so cruel?'

'What's it to you?' he said.

'She was only trying to feed you some soup!'

He wagged a finger at me. 'Who are you? Tell me that. To lecture me about my own wife?'

'You don't deserve Filomena,' I said.

'And I suppose you do?' A smile began to creep across his face. 'Oh yes, I've seen you watching Filomena. Wanting her for yourself.'

'I don't want her, Bearpark. I pity her. Who could not? With you as her husband.'

'Get out,' he rasped. 'Get out of my house. You and that old sow you call Mother. If I have to drink another spoonful of her soup, I might die. The stuff is poison!'

'Have no fears,' I said firmly. 'I have no desire to stay here.'

I turned to leave, but he shouted after me. 'You're no great investigator, Oswald de Lacy,' he shouted. 'You're just a cheat and a fraud.'

As I reached the door, Giovanni caught up with me and tried to block my exit. 'Don't worry, Oswald. My master's mood will soon improve. The birth of the girl has upset him. But if you go to your room, then he will soon forget about this.' He put an unwelcome hand upon my arm. 'I will speak to him on your behalf.'

'No,' I said, shaking Giovanni off. 'Nothing would induce me to stay in this house. Nothing!'

Bearpark croaked from his bed, having heard my words, proving that his hearing was better than he pretended. 'Good. Because you're banished, de Lacy. Banished! If I ever see you on these premises again, then I'll kill you myself.' His croak became a cough. The hacking, outraged cough of an old man whose last sands are tipping through the hourglass.

My heart thumped as I ran into Filomena's chamber to find her sitting on the edge of her bed with her skirts raised and a wet and folded sheet lying across her legs.

'Are you all right?' I asked. 'Did he burn you?'

'It's not as bad as I feared,' she said. 'The cloth of my gown is heavy, and only a little of the soup reached my skin.' She heaved a great sigh. 'It is my husband's behaviour that's caused me more pain.'

I sat down next to her on the bed and took her hand. 'I'm so sorry, Filomena.'

'It's not your fault,' she said wearily.

'It is. I'd angered Bearpark, just before you came in. It's why he behaved so cruelly.'

She regarded me for a moment. 'My husband is a cruel man, Oswald. You know that.'

'Yes, I do.' I hesitated. 'Listen, Filomena. I have something to tell you.' She gave me a suspicious, sideways look. 'I'm leaving Ca' Bearpark today.'

Her hand stiffened. 'Why?'

'Your husband has banished me from the house.'

'Why would he do that?' she said with a frown.

'Because I told him to stop treating you so poorly.'

She withdrew her hand sharply from mine. 'But I asked you not to defend me, Oswald. You promised!'

'But I had to say something to him, you must understand that. He threw hot soup over you.'

She put her head in her hands and groaned. 'I asked you not to interfere. Now my husband will punish me for your words.'

'No. I won't allow it,' I said.

She lowered her hands and looked at me with fierce, scathing eyes. 'But what can you do about it? You have no influence in this house. Especially now that you have been banished.'

I took her hand again, though she was reluctant to let me this time. 'Listen. I've had an idea,' I said, refusing to relax my grip. 'Leave with me, Filomena. Both you and your daughter. You don't need to stay here.'

Now her expression changed to a look of incredulity. 'What?' Suddenly she began to laugh, but it was not with joy. 'You want me to elope with you?' she said. 'Is that what you're suggesting?'

'I don't know,' I said honestly, as I hadn't given this proposal the slightest thought. In fact, it seemed to have fallen from my lips without passing through my brain.

'And where would we go?' she said, now succeeding in pulling her hand from mine. 'Jerusalem? England? Because we certainly couldn't stay in Venice.'

'I don't know,' I said again, my heart thumping.

'Exactly,' she said. 'You don't know!'

'I realise this idea comes as a surprise,' I said, trying not to be deterred by her reaction to my offer. 'But I can't leave you here with Bearpark. Not when he is so cruel to you.'

'Oh, don't worry about me,' she puffed. 'I have my own ideas for surviving this marriage.'

'Which are?'

She waved this question away and then turned her back to me, refusing to speak for a few moments. 'Do you pity me,' she said at length. 'Is that why you're making this extraordinary offer?'

'It started as pity,' I said frankly. 'But I have other feelings now, Filomena.' I paused. 'I've tried to suppress them, but they won't go away.'

She turned back to face me and raised an eyebrow. 'You've tried to suppress them?' she said disdainfully. 'How flattering.'

I rubbed my hand over my face. 'I'm sorry, Filomena. I didn't mean to be insulting.'

'Are you in love with me, Oswald?'

Suddenly I felt stupid and dumbstruck, and struggled to tell her that I wasn't sure.

'Perhaps you should be sure then,' she said. 'Before you make such offers.'

'I don't know how I feel exactly,' I said. 'Only I want to help you.'

She laughed again at this. 'Help me? How can you help me, when you cannot help yourself?'

'What do you mean?'

She hesitated for a moment. 'Listen to me, Oswald,' she said softly. 'I know what follows you, and I know why you won't face it.'

'No, you don't,' I said, taken by surprise. 'Nobody does.'

'Your mother cannot keep a secret,' she said. 'And I'm not the only subject of servants' gossip in this house. I have learnt enough of your history to guess the rest.' She paused. 'But you must listen to me, Oswald. Please, because it's important.' I tried to turn away, but she put her hand on my shoulder. 'You will never recover, unless you face it and stop running away.'

'I'm not running away,' I protested.

'Yes you are. You know it.' At this she released her grip, sat up straight, and bowed her head to me. 'So, I thank you for your kind offer, Oswald, but I choose my husband and I choose Venice.'

Her words landed like a punch, and left the throbbing blow of rejection. 'Please accept my apologies then, Monna Filomena. I spoke out of turn.' I cleared my throat of its sentimentality, stood up and then bowed my head. 'I wish you every happiness with John Bearpark, and I bid you farewell.'

She called to me as I reached the door. 'Don't be angry, Oswald. I'm only speaking the truth.'

I left the room and slammed the door in my wake.

As I walked into the empty and dark *piano nobile*, I kicked a stool and watched it hurtle across the polished terrazzo until it hit the wall on the other side of the room, and then came to rest accusingly on its side. None of the servants appeared to restore it to its rightful position, despite the resounding clatter that I had caused, so I did it myself, before sitting down upon it in dejection.

As I stared into the dimness of the long, unfriendly room, my anger turned to despair. My arms still throbbed, my debt still needed paying, and Filomena had refused me. It was then, in this darkness, that the glimmer of the eight golden coins crept into my mind. These coins were still secreted away inside a sock, within another sock, at the bottom of my oak chest. Since finding them on Burano, I had not even dared to look at them properly. I barely liked to think about them, since they induced a feeling of guilt, and yet I knew they were still there, hidden and gleaming with temptation.

They didn't belong to me, so it would be wrong to spend them, but then again, what else was I to do with them? I would not declare their existence to Bearpark – not when these coins could secure us a room in an inn for a few nights. Not when they could pay for my escape from this city and from my creditor. With these coins, we could afford a berth to Marseilles, where a family friend still lived – or, at least I thought he did. This man would probably forward me the funds for Mother to return to England at least.

The eight coins could pay for all this, so why not spend them? It was not as if I was planning to use them to play at dice. Then I took a deep breath. If I took the coins from the purse and used them to fund an escape, then what had I become? A person who does not pay his debts, and a person who steals evidence from an investigation. I would be a coward and a thief.

I let these thoughts trickle through my mind, and then I pushed them away, for it was better to be a thief with no honour, than a dead man.

When I told Mother that we were to leave Ca' Bearpark, she heaved the most wearied of sighs. 'First of all you forced me to leave England, Oswald, only to be driven across Europe like a prized heifer. Now comes the final insult. You want me to leave a gentleman's house to stay at an inn.'

I rolled my eyes. 'The pilgrimage was your idea, Mother.'

'It was nothing of the sort! You insisted I accompany you.' She picked up Hector and nuzzled his whiskery muzzle. As the dog tried to lick Mother's face, I caught a draught of his repulsive, fishy breath. 'Didn't he, Hector? We didn't want to come on this foolish journey, did we?'

I knew better than to argue further. 'Very well then, Mother,' I said. 'Have it your own way. This pilgrimage was my idea.'

She smiled. 'I'm glad you agree.'

'But if you agreed to be dragged to Venice by me, then you will agree to change our accommodation at my request.'

'I shall not! I've been nursing poor John through his sickness. And now I shall be needed at the side of his wife. I cannot possibly leave the care of that poor young girl to these Venetians. They will make her ill with all those shells they are forever boiling up.'

'You're not wanted here, Mother,' I said.

'Nonsense.'

'Very well. I didn't want to tell you this, but John Bearpark does not hold you in high regard.'

'More nonsense.' She dropped her chin and peered suspiciously into my eyes, as if trying to stare me into admitting that this was a lie.

'He called you an old sow,' I said.

She let out a great blustery laugh. 'A sow? John would never say such a thing about me. You're making this up, Oswald.'

'He told me so himself.' I paused. 'What's more. He also told me that he doesn't like your soup. He called it poisonous.' I paused again for a moment, allowing the insult to sink in. 'So, you see. The man is not your friend.'

'Poisonous?' she said with a frown. 'Are you sure, he used that word?'

'He said it to my face.'

Mother opened her mouth and then shut it immediately. 'Well. What an ungrateful ape.' She then clasped Hector to her cheek. 'Mind you, we never liked him, did we, Hector?' The dog gave a low growl, though this probably indicated that he was being squeezed too tightly, rather than being a sign of his aversion to Bearpark. 'The man has spent far too long on this lagoon. I've heard that the seawater creeps inside the brain, you know. And now I can believe it.'

And so, once our clothes and few belongings were packed into a chest, we set out for the inn. I had managed, at short notice, to secure a room in the Fondaco dei Tedeschi, near to the Rialto Bridge. As we departed through the courtyard, I felt Filomena's eyes bearing down upon me from the seat in her window. Her refusal still stung my heart, and her warning still rang in my ears.

Chapter Twenty-Seven

It was not only Filomena who watched our departure from Ca' Bearpark. My young spy was still on our trail as we left the house, his dirty head bobbing across every bridge and running along every canal-side pavement as we made our progress through the city. When we disembarked at our new lodgings, the boy appeared immediately from the crowd, before taking up his post on a nearby quay.

The Fondaco dei Tedeschi was a welcome change after the dark oppressiveness of Ca' Bearpark. Built at the foot of the Rialto Bridge, it was a complex of warehouses and living quarters usually reserved for the German merchants of Venice. Normally we would not have been welcome in this place, but they had spare rooms after the war with Hungary, and we were able to secure a single chamber that looked out onto the Canal Grande. The air was sweeter here and not trapped between the tall buildings of the side canal where Ca' Bearpark was located. Here, the water moved with energy and pace, along a course that was wide enough for the wind to lick at its surface and cause small waves and eddies – not stagnant with the effluent, kitchen waste, and scum that characterised the waters of the smaller canals.

Mother complained about my choice of inn, of course – I would not have expected any less – but this place was clean, the food was adequate, and open prostitution was discouraged, so what was there to moan about? Once I had offered the usual platitudes in response to each of her grumbles, I fell onto the bed and closed my eyes. This room was smaller and simpler than my bedchamber at Ca' Bearpark, lacking the nooks and crannies where my monkey liked to hide.

I must have drifted into sleep, for I dreamt that I was lying on the forest floor, deep within the Weald of Kent. As I looked up into the canopy, sunlight caught the leaves of a sweet chestnut tree, giving each saw-edged leaf the appearance of a delicate pane of stained glass. I was happier than I had felt for many months, finding a spot amongst the trees where the sun could warm my face, but then I became aware that somebody was nearby, watching me from the undergrowth. I looked up to see him in the glade ahead – the black cloth of his Benedictine habit outlined against the green of the forest. It was a face from my past. My old tutor from the monastery – Brother Peter. A man I had once loved. Very much. At first I turned away from him and tried to pretend that I couldn't hear his plaintive calls, but his voice was kind and soothing, as it had been in our early days together, so I could not ignore him. He knew what I had done, and he understood. He would not judge me.

We walked together through the forest, and as we stepped through the heather and bracken he encouraged me to drop each of the golden coins I had stolen from Burano into the grass, my conscience lifting with each disposal. Brother Peter smiled at me, but when I looked away from his face, I found that we were no longer in the forests above my estate. Instead, he had led me onto a lonely island in the middle of the Venetian lagoon. It was the Lazaretto with its bleak, marshy terrain, wind-blown banks of sand and lonely, crumbling church. I wanted to run, to get away from this place, for I knew what waited for me here amongst the lepers, wanting me to take its small skeletal hand and look into its face, but Brother Peter held me back. He wanted me to find the monkey. He wanted me to look at it, but I could not. I would not.

So I broke away from his grasp. I ran into the shallow sea, wading into the water and feeling its cold fingers at my skin. And now, though I tried to run, the mud held onto my feet, and soon Brother Peter caught up with me. He was no longer the reassuring, kind monk that I had known at the monastery. Now he was the angry, venal man of his later years, too ready to coerce and control me. He grasped my neck and held me under the surface of the sea, and in this water I saw a new world. The fishes that swam here were misshapen creatures, their backbones crooked, their eyes pitted, and their scales dull and flaking. I tried to close my eyes and pull away, but I could not escape. Though I thrashed my arms and tried to kick, Brother Peter held me there, as the fish bit at my face, until they had sucked the skin from my bones.

I woke with a jolt, feeling all the old melancholy return. The monkey might not be in this room, but I had not escaped it. Filomena was right. I turned over and tried to go back to sleep, when I heard a short sob from the bed next to my own.

I sat up and reached for Mother's shoulder. 'What's the matter?' She stiffened at my touch, so I removed my hand. 'Why are you crying?'

'Don't concern yourself on my behalf,' she said.

'Have I done something wrong?' I asked. I will admit to being mystified by women's moods. Too often I have caused offence without the slightest intention, or even knowledge of the event. My mistake has only come to my attention when I have been informed of it later.

Mother rolled over to look at me, her face tear-stained. 'It's not you, dear Oswald,' she said, 'it's me.' She emitted a long groan. 'I've been such a fool.'

'Why? What have you done?' I said.

She opened her hand to reveal a small square of wrinkled parchment. 'Oh Oswald,' she said, 'I'm so ashamed.'

I tried to take the parchment from her, but she snatched it back and screwed it up in her fist. She then launched the ball at the fire, taking perfect aim. The parchment caught alight in the embers.

'What was it?' I asked.

She waited until the fire had died back, and then she rubbed her eyes clear of their tears. 'It was a love letter. From John Bearpark.'

'What?' I said, unable to mask my shock, even disgust at this revelation.

She feigned a laugh. 'Oh don't worry. It was written nearly thirty years ago.' She began to shudder as the tears returned. 'When I wasn't such an old sow and my cooking was not poisonous.'

I now understood the reason for her tears – she had been wounded by Bearpark's cruel words. Words that I should have kept to myself. I put my hand upon her shoulder again, and this time she did not stiffen.

'Bearpark didn't mean those words,' I said. 'He was angry with me, and he's still very upset by the death of his grandson.' I was apologising for a foolish and cruel old man, and it did not feel comfortable. However, my words seemed to console her a little.

She sat up, and leant back against the wooden headboard of her bed. In the distance we could hear the banging and shouting of the kitchen servants as they put away their pans and kettles for the night. In the room next door, a German couple were arguing in the low, suppressed fashion of two people who really wanted to scream loudly at one another.

I got out of bed and poured Mother a bowl of wine. 'So, Bearpark was once your admirer?' I said.

She smiled at the memory. 'Oh yes, Oswald. But, he was also more than that. He was my lover.' She began to cry again. 'Father of poor little Katherine.'

'You had a child with him?' I said, nearly dropping the bowl to the floor.

'Yes. Every summer I would travel with your father to Southampton. It was my favourite trip of the year.' She gave a long sigh. 'Even though your father didn't want me to go.'

'I'm not surprised,' I said.

She waved this comment away. 'He should have paid more attention to me then, Oswald. Rather than spending all those hours in the taverns with the Venetian merchants.' She laughed at a distant memory. 'He always bought too much mace.'

I interrupted. 'How did you end up having a child with John Bearpark?'

'Because he was so gallant and handsome in those days, Oswald. Not like the crusted old prune you see now. We met each summer, for a number of years, until little Katherine was born. She was such a beautiful child. But taken from me by the pox. Probably my favourite child, as it happens.' She looked up mischievously to see if this comment had had its desired effect, but, when I didn't respond, she returned to her gloomy tone. 'Poor little Katherine.' She sighed. 'After she was born, I stopped going to Southampton.'

'Why?'

She held out her hands for the bowl of wine. 'Your father guessed, I suppose. He forbade me from making the trip anyway, and wouldn't give me a reason. John wrote me one last letter.' She puffed her lips. 'And that was the last that I heard of him.'

I walked to the window and opened the shutters, needing some fresh air after hearing this revelation. How could my mother have ever loved that repulsive man? How could she have dragged me all the way to Venice, on the pretence of a pilgrimage, when the real reason was her desire to rekindle an ancient love affair? And yet this was my mother. The most capricious, frustrating and headstrong of women. It was why I both loved and sometimes loathed her. I went to close the shutters, but, as I did so, I chanced to look down towards the decrepit wooden jetty that clung to the foundations of the Rialto Bridge like a cluster of limpets. There I saw the small boy who had been following me, sleeping like a she-cat among the crab cages.

'So, you hoped to rekindle your romance with Bearpark, did you?' I said as I turned back to the room. 'That's why you insisted we came to Venice?'

Mother wiped a tear from her eye. 'Yes, Oswald. And don't look at me in that way.' Her voice was no longer softened by tears. 'Just because a woman is sixty-eight, it does not mean she is dead from the waist downwards, you know! She still has desires.' Then the tears flowed again.

In that moment my anger turned to sympathy. I returned to Mother's side and let her weep onto my shoulder until her tears had lost their bite, and she could only lie in bed and close her eyes.

I woke the next morning with renewed purpose. It was now Thursday, and if we were to leave Venice quickly, then I needed to visit the Molo and find us a berth to Marseilles. I did not want anybody, especially Vittore or Signor Ballio from the doge's palace, to know our plans, so it was important that my little spy didn't follow me to the harbour. I pulled on my boots and my dullest clothes, and then looked from the window, to see if I could still spot the young boy asleep beneath the bridge. He was absent from his post when I looked at the rotting jetty however, so I knew that now was the right time to leave.

I was looking for a merchant galley once I reached the Molo – a ship with two masts and a castle at the bow and stern – for this was the style and size of ship that would be sailing to the west of Europe. Further along the quayside, there was a great deal of activity around the five Jaffa galleys, which were now preparing for their next departure for the Holy Land. As I had crossed the Piazza San Marco on my way here, I had seen their captains already waving their white banners bearing red crosses, to attract custom. Each man shouting the merits of his ship as opposed to the others, and offering his galley for inspection to any pilgrim who cared to look.

As I wandered through the crowds of the Molo, I made some tentative inquiries about the destination of various merchant galleys, until a man carrying a barrel of salted beef tongues pointed me in the direction of a smaller ship at the end of the row of masts. When I stood alongside this galley and called up to the deck to speak with the captain, a small, stout man appeared. As he looked down at me, I recognised him immediately. He was the droopy-eyed fellow that, months ago, I had pulled from the canal with Enrico's help.

A smile of remembrance crossed his face. 'Hello again, Englishman.' He looked over my shoulder. 'I hope you don't have that ruffian with you? The one who looks like a pig.'

'No, I'm alone,' I said.

'Come on board then.' I climbed a thin ladder to the deck of the ship and then the man led me into his quarters, which turned out to be little more than a low-roofed cubbyhole with a door. We sat together on a bench, and he offered me a mug of Paduan wine and a dried fig.

'So. What did you want to ask me?' he said.

'I need to leave Venice,' I said. 'As soon as possible.'

He looked at me strangely and stopped chewing. 'Oh yes?'

'It's my mother,' I said quickly. 'This city is harmful to her health.'

'Where do you want to go?'

'Marseilles.'

He wiped his lips clear of the wine. 'Aigues-Mortes is my next destination.'

Aigues-Mortes is a civilised-enough port, and under different circumstances it might have been acceptable, but I didn't know anybody there – certainly not anybody who would lend me money. 'Will you stop at Marseilles?' I asked.

The captain picked a piece of fig from his teeth and then laughed. 'Marseilles? That quiet little town. Not so kind to your mother's health either, I hear.'

I ignored his sarcasm. 'Look. Will you stop there? Yes or no?'

'I can do,' he said, after a frustrating pause. 'For a fee.'

'And when do you sail?'

'There's a high tide tomorrow night, so we'll sail with the retreating tide at dawn on Saturday.'

My debt was due on Saturday morning, so this departure would get us out of Venice with only hours to spare – but this should be sufficient. It might take Vittore a few hours to realise we had left on a ship. 'How much for a berth?'

He smiled and raised his bowl of wine to indicate that we were approaching the heart of the deal. 'Since you are my friend, Englishman, I can offer you a special price. Six ducats for you, and six for your mother.' He opened his hands and raised his palms, as if he were granting me a great gift of charity. 'It would be less of course, if we didn't have to stop at Marseilles.'

'That's far too much,' I said, ignoring his supposed warmheartedness. 'This is a merchant ship, not a pilgrim galley. And Marseilles is hardly out of your way, as I expect you will call in there anyway. If only to collect water.'

He cocked his head slightly. 'Maybe. But, don't forget that I have to accommodate two extra persons on board. And your mother will want some privacy. Think of the room that a woman takes up. Think of the disruption they cause on a ship.'

'Two ducats each.'

Now he threw up his hands in disgust. Bartering was such a tiresome activity. 'No, no. Four ducats each,' he said.

'I can pay no more than two,' I said. 'And I remind you of the service that I performed in pulling you from the canal that night.'

He sighed, and then smiled at me, before we eventually agreed on five ducats for the both of us, as long as I purchased a bed and a rope for Mother, a keg that we could fill with water at each port, and a food chest packed with twice-baked biscuits, ham, hard cheese, and almonds. The captain would supply us with some of his Paduan wine while we sailed, but what we ate was our concern. The crew would call us assumed names, and our embarkation onto the ship would be organised under the cover of night.

As I went to leave, he put his hand on my shoulder. 'So, are you going to tell me the real reason for leaving Venice? I don't believe your story about your mother.' He whispered into my ear. 'And I don't like lies.'

I regarded him for a moment, wondering if it was safe to tell him the truth, and then I thought back to our first meeting at the tavern. 'I have made an enemy of a man named Vittore Grimani.' For a moment the captain seemed confused. 'The man who threw you into the canal. The one who looks like a pig.'

'Ah, him.' He slapped my back. 'Then welcome on board.'

I left the ship feeling satisfied with this arrangement. Pulling my hood over my head, I walked back along the Riva degli Schiavoni making plans for our departure. The ship sailed the day after next, so I would not have long to organise my affairs. In addition, it was important that I did nothing to draw attention to our departure, so I decided to ask Mother to purchase the provisions for the journey, as she was not the one being followed about by a spy.

I was making such plans, when I passed two people that I had not ever expected to see again, particularly not outside in the streets of Venice. It was Bernard and Margery, huddled together with the captain of a cargo boat – a wide-bowed vessel with a single mast and a square red sail. The type of boat that usually carried goods across the lagoon into the river Po.

I hadn't wanted to speak to Bernard, but our eyes met and it was too late for either of us to pretend that this hadn't happened.

The captain of this cargo ship withdrew as soon as I approached, as if he was ashamed to be seen with the pair.

Bernard bowed deeply. 'Lord Somershill, What a pleasant surprise.' His face wore its usual, banal demeanour, as if he were smiling at an amusing, but undisclosed memory. 'We miss you terribly at Ca' Bearpark, but I hear you have found alternative accommodation?'

'I have,' and then quickly added, before he asked for our address. 'It's good to see that you and your sister are feeling well enough to venture out into the city again.' Margery stepped back and dropped her head in response to being mentioned.

'We needed to secure our passage to Jerusalem, my lord,' Bernard said. 'Otherwise we would never have dared to leave the house.' He dropped his voice to a whisper. 'The murderer has still not been uncovered, you know.'

'Shouldn't you be further along the Molo then?' I said, quickly changing the subject. 'The Jaffa galleys are over there.' I pointed into the distance, where the boats with the red crosses emblazoned across their sails were moored.

Bernard stared at me, as my observation seemed to trickle through his head. 'Ah yes,' he said at last. 'Thank you, Lord Somershill. How kind. But we've already spoken to our favoured *padrone* and booked our passage. I must say that his boat seems to be very seaworthy, and he has employed a good number of armed sailors for the journey, should we encounter any pirates. And Margery thought he was a lovely young man.' He suddenly laughed. 'Though the captains of these pilgrim ships do have to be at least thirty years old, you know. It's written in the ordinance.'

'How do you know that?' I asked.

'Because we visited the office of the *Cattaveri,* my lord. They explained all the laws concerning pilgrimages from Venice.' He smiled. 'Do you know, they will also deal with complaints against unscrupulous captains. Isn't that wonderful?'

'I meant how do you know that Margery liked this captain?' I said. 'Has she broken her vow of silence?'

Bernard gasped. 'Goodness me. My dear sister hasn't said a word since we sailed from Dover.' He then fixed me with an intense stare. 'Oh, we do miss your company at Ca' Bearpark, my lord,' he said again. 'I was so disappointed to hear that you and your dear mother moved out, but I do hope you're comfortable in your new accommodation.'

'Yes, thank you. Very comfortable,' I said, quickly stepping away with a wave. 'Farewell to you both.'

I strode back towards our lodgings, hoping not to meet any other unwelcome acquaintances, but as I left the Piazza and walked along a narrow passageway, I passed a tavern where I used to gamble. It might have been early in the morning, but men were already falling out of the door and twisting themselves into the street. Some were victorious, others defeated, but such is the nature of gambling – a volatile concoction of pleasure and pain. I should have walked straight past, but instead I stopped and felt at the single golden coin in my purse. I had retrieved it before leaving that morning, reaching inside the stolen purse without even opening my eyes, as if I had been putting my hand inside the mouth of a lion.

Now that the coin was in my hand, it felt solid and reassuringly sharp about the edges. What harm could there be in a quick game of dice? In fact, the more I thought about the idea, the more it made perfect sense. A win would increase our funds, and a good win would pay for Mother's passage back to England from Marseilles, without the need for me to borrow more from our family friend. An even better win would allow me to stay away from England for as long as I wanted.

I turned to enter the tavern, but in doing so I caught his eye. At first I thought it was the monkey, but as his face came into focus, I realised that it was the boy who had been paid to watch me. My small and dedicated follower. He was looking straight into my eyes, almost as if he had read my mind. This encounter caused me to turn on my heel and walk quickly away, almost falling into a group of pilgrims who were making their way to the hospice at Orseolo – their clothes bearing the unmistakable reek of three months on the road. Now, as I fought my way through the early morning crowds, I felt my panic rising. If the boy had seen me outside the tavern, then perhaps he had also seen me speaking to the captain at the Molo? In which case, my whole plan to leave Venice would be reported back to the doge's palace. I needed to corner the small irritant and discover what he had seen, but when I turned and looked for the boy, he had disappeared.

Chapter Twenty-Eight

I returned to the Fondaco dei Tedeschi to find Mother dressed and seated by the open window, clutching her dog in her arms and looking down upon the Canal Grande with her head covered by a woollen blanket. With the shutters pulled back, the room was as cold as a crypt.

'You're feeling better then?' I asked, laying my cloak upon the bed and pulling off my boots.

'Yes,' she snapped. 'Why do you ask?'

'You were upset last night.'

'I don't know what you're talking about, Oswald. There's nothing wrong with me.'

And so the subject of her romance with John Bearpark was closed, and I knew we would never speak of it again. There was, however, another matter that we needed to discuss, and this would be another awkward conversation. 'Mother. There's something I should tell you,' I said airily.

Usually such a sentence would immediately pique her interest, but she continued to look out of the window, her voice distracted. 'Yes, Oswald. What is it?'

'We're going to be leaving Venice. On Saturday morning.'

She shrugged, a little wearily. 'Very well then.'

'But we won't be travelling to Jerusalem.'

She merely shrugged at this as well. 'I didn't want to go

there anyway, Oswald. I've heard the place is crawling with flies.'

'So, you're not disappointed?'

'No, Oswald. I'm not,' she said with an unusual air of resignation. 'I just want to return to Somershill. To be in England again.'

I looked away and could not answer. I did not want to be in Venice, but equally, I did not want to be in England.

We sat in silence for a few moments. 'How will we return then?' she said suddenly. 'Have you found some other pilgrims for us to travel with? I hope they are a better quality of person than those fools we came here with. I know they were my own family, but what a miserable bunch!'

How was I to tell her that we only had money enough to reach Marseilles in the hull of a merchant ship, and thereafter we must rely upon borrowing some money from an old family friend? 'I'll tell you more later,' I said quickly. 'But first we need to pack our chest and buy a few provisions.' Before she was able to answer, I said, 'I have a list of foodstuffs. Perhaps you might go to the market and buy what's needed?'

'Or I can ask a servant to do it,' she said.

'No. I'd rather you went yourself, Mother. We don't want poor-quality provisions for our journey, do we?' I said, as she tried to object. 'You're so much more discerning than a servant.' I managed to deliver this piece of flattery with an encouraging smile. 'And perhaps it would be best if you did not mention it to anyone.'

'Mention what?'

'That we're leaving Venice.'

She looked at me suspiciously and might have asked more questions, when thankfully we were interrupted by a knock at the door. I asked Mother to answer, while I withdrew quickly into the corner behind the tall cupboard, telling her to say that I was out. So far, I had not received a visit from Vittore – but it could not be long before he sniffed out our new address and came to call.

The person at the door was only delivering a letter, however. From my position behind the cupboard, I could hear that Mother spoke to this man in Venetian, and I must say that I was surprised at her competency in this tongue.

She closed the door and then passed me the letter with some distaste, holding it between the ends of her fingers, as if it had been steeped in piss. 'It's from Bearpark,' she said. Her eye twitched at his name. 'His messenger is waiting outside. Apparently he will not leave until you answer this letter.'

I broke the seal and unrolled the parchment. The letter was indeed from Bearpark himself, though I could see it had been written by Giovanni, as the words bore the steady flow of a younger man's writing and not the spidery scrawl of an old man's hand. The message itself was short – containing a half-hearted apology for his behaviour towards Filomena, followed by a request, nay a demand, that I return to his service and resume my investigation into Enrico's murder.

'What does it say?' asked Mother, pouring herself a bowl of wine from the pitcher and trying not to sound particularly interested.

'It's an entreaty from Bearpark,' I said. 'He wants me to return to the investigation.'

She raised her eyebrows. 'And will you?'

'No.'

She allowed herself a satisfied huff. 'Good. Let the old toad look for the murderer himself.' Then she laughed. 'That's if he lives long enough.'

I opened the door to find that the messenger who had been waiting for my response was the servant with the lop-sided face. He was pleased to see me, but his oddly angled smile soon disappeared when I gave him his answer. 'Please tell John Bearpark that I will not return to the investigation,' I said. The man grimaced, for this was not the answer that he had been told to collect, and no doubt he feared the response he would receive when conveying it to his master. 'Tell Bearpark not to contact me again,' I said. 'Nothing will induce me to return to his house.' The man sighed, bowed to me, and then withdrew into the darkness of the passageway.

I was tempted to throw the letter into the meagre fire that was failing to warm the room, but the parchment was of good quality, and might be washed down for further use. With our funds so limited, I had no choice but to make such economies, but as I stored this roll of parchment in my chest, I found another letter hidden beneath the folded chemises and leather tunics. It was the letter that Enrico Bearpark had written to me, all those months before. His letter of friendship, warning me to take care with my disposition and inviting me to spend time with his friends in order to enjoy the delights of Venice. The letter looked back at me like an accusing child, so I stuffed it beneath my clothes and tried to forget about Enrico. My investigation into his murder had failed, and yet I knew that I could have found his killer – if only I had spoken to Marco one last time.

I closed my chest quickly as Mother addressed me, calling for me to join her on the balcony. 'Look,' she said, pointing towards the Rialto Bridge. 'That boy is out there again.'

'Which boy?'

'The one I gave some money to, on the night of Enrico's murder. He's been following you around Venice for days.' She turned to me with a look of amusement in her eyes. 'Don't say you haven't noticed him? Sometimes I do wonder why you call yourself a great investigator.'

'That was your name for me, Mother. I never gave myself such a ridiculous title.' I looked where Mother was pointing and could see the boy, leaning his head between the wooden struts of the bridge – a small, static soul in a sea of movement.

'What does he want?' Mother asked.

I went back inside the room and pulled on my boots again. 'That's what I'm going to find out.'

When I reached the bridge, the boy had predictably disappeared from sight, but this didn't mean he wasn't close at hand. The whole of Venice seemed to be at the market this afternoon, before the threatened storm unleashed its torrents of rain upon the city, so I wandered from stall to stall, pausing to buy some pressed dates and the small *zaletti* biscuits that fall apart so deliciously in the mouth. Now I sensed that the boy was only a few steps behind me, but also knew that I should not act in haste, for he would be as difficult to catch as an eel. When a man fishes, he needs bait – so I stopped a girl with a basket of freshly baked bread, pulled the small loaf in half, and held it behind me as I walked, knowing that the boy was now close enough to lick the crust.

After a while, I turned the corner into an alley, where the stallholders kept their baskets and wooden crates. The ground was littered with rotting fruit and leaves, so I picked my way carefully through the debris, making sure to hold out the bread so that the boy continued to follow. After turning another corner, I pressed myself against the wall, and as the boy crept forward, I grabbed him firmly, feeling his bones through his thin shirt.

'Who are you?' I demanded, when he had stopped squirming and kicking at me. 'Why are you spying on me?'

He squinted, pretending that he could not understand my Venetian.

I held onto his wrist with one hand and held the loaf above his nose with the other. 'Do you want to eat this?' He nodded, understanding that much. 'Then tell me who's paying you.' He tensed at this question, but didn't take his eyes from the bread. A line of spittle descended from one side of his mouth, as his stomach rumbled loudly. The boy was starving. As bony as a bat. But I could not let sympathy overrule sense, so I squeezed his tiny wrist a little harder. 'Tell me who's paying you, and then you get the bread.'

I held the bread a little higher above his nose, and he raised himself onto his tiptoes, as if he could eat its perfume.

'Is it the Consiglio dei Dieci?' He gave no reaction. 'Signor Ballio?'

The boy's eyes were fixed upon the bread, but at Ballio's name, he gave the slightest of nods.

'What do you tell them?' I said, holding the loaf nearer his mouth, but not so close that he could bite it.

The boy hesitated, but the lure of the freshly baked bread was too strong. 'I tell them where you go and what you do,' he said uneasily.

'Have you told them where I went this morning? To the Molo?'

He shook his head. 'No. Not yet. I see them at night.'

Now I grasped him by his collar, feeling the thin inadequacy of his tunic. In this weather a boy needed a thick cloak. 'Are you telling me the truth?'

He nodded desperately, then made a grab for the bread, so I gave him the whole loaf, keeping my hand on the back of his tunic as he tore away at the soft dough like a crow at a carcass.

'They don't pay you too well, do they?' I said in the end.

He nodded to this, but would not waste eating time by speaking to me. Looking down upon his small head, I could see that patches of his hair were as thin as an old woman's.

'What's your name?' I asked him, when he had finally stopped chewing.

'Sandro.'

'How old are you, Sandro?' I asked.

He shrugged.

'Would you like to earn some money?' I asked. The boy drew back at this suggestion. 'I just want you *not* to tell anybody at the doge's palace what I'm doing,' I said quickly. 'That's all I ask.' The boy still seemed suspicious. 'I'll pay you well, Sandro,' I said.

'Much better than they do. But you must stay with me at all times. Just so that I can trust you.'

Sandro thought about my offer for a while, studying my face for signs of treachery. In the end I seemed to pass the examination, especially when I gave him a *zaletti* biscuit, for then he smiled at me. A toothy, wide grin that thrust an unexpected spike of pain into my heart.

Sandro walked beside me as we neared the Fondaco, but we held back on the bridge when realising that there was a disturbance at the water gate of our inn. A group of soldiers in the uniform of the doge's palace had disembarked from a long *sàndolo*. Some were standing about on the jetty, whilst others were shouting up to a man who was leaning over a first-floor balcony. When I looked more closely, I realised that this was the balcony to my own bedchamber, and the man to whom they spoke was Ballio. I froze as another figure appeared alongside this man. It was my mother, and she was haranguing Ballio with waving arms and loud words. The tactic was working, since he began to hang back from her as if she were a rabid dog.

Sandro looked to me, then to the soldiers, and I wondered if he would give me away? I think the idea had occurred to him as well, but the loaf of bread and the *zaletti* biscuit had been enough to win his allegiance. For the time being anyway. We watched for a while, until the soldiers finally jumped into their boat and left the Fondaco, presumably since they could not find me – though I noted that Ballio made sure to leave a couple of guards at the water gate to wait for my return. I needed to get back to my room without passing these men, and Sandro seemed to read my mind, for he whispered to me that he knew another entrance to the inn, one that was only used by the servants.

Was it wise to trust the boy so quickly? I wasn't sure, but then again I was short of options, so I let him take me by his skinny hand and pull me into one of the very thinnest passageways I had ever walked along. No light pierced the warren of tunnels that we then followed through San Marco, though Sandro seemed to know his way intimately about this network of dark corridors, and soon we were at the back door to the kitchens of the Fondaco, where the scent of frying olive oil and fish filled the confined air with its strong perfume. The cook shouted at Sandro as the boy pushed the door to the kitchens open, but it was with a certain good humour, and the boy's retort was cheeky enough to make the woman smile. She even threw him a small piece of cheese rind, which he popped into his mouth, but did not chew upon.

Following the boy, I then ascended a narrow back staircase only used by the servants, until we emerged onto a passageway that led to my bedchamber. Sandro wouldn't leave the stairwell, knowing that his dirty face would not be welcome in the guests' quarters of this establishment, so in order to reward his loyalty and make sure that he didn't disappear, I pressed a *soldino* into his hand and told him to wait for me. If he did as I asked, then there would be another coin on my return.

Opening the door to my bedchamber with caution, I peeped into the room to check that it was indeed empty of soldiers. Mother was seated in a corner, with a bowl in her hands and the foam of ale across her top lip, whilst Hector slept at her feet. The dog did not even bother to raise an eyelid at my entrance.

Mother looked up despondently. 'Where have you been, Oswald?' she said plaintively. 'What an uproar I've suffered in your absence.'

She tried to stand up, but I raised my hand. 'Stay there, Mother.' I quickly walked to the balcony and looked down at the water gate, where the two soldiers from the doge's palace were still waiting for me.

'There were men here, looking for you,' she said.

I drew back from the window and closed the shutters. 'I know. I saw them.'

'What have you been doing? They were very insistent that they needed to speak to you. They've even left a couple of guards on the door.' She frowned. 'I'm surprised you didn't pass them as you came in, Oswald? They have very distinctive uniforms.'

I skipped over this question. 'What did they want?' I asked.

She gave a scowl. 'To speak to you, of course. They just kept repeating your name, over and over.'

'What did you say to them?'

'I told them to leave, because they were invading the bedchamber of an English lady, and I would not tolerate such disrespect.' She wiped the foam of ale away. 'I might have suffered a convulsion, had their leader not ordered me this mug of beer and spoken to me with some decorum.' She smiled. 'He was a gentleman at least. Not like those other brutes who pushed in at the door. His cloak was trimmed in the finest fur, Oswald. The very finest.'

'I don't care about his fur collar.'

She ignored me. 'And his shoes were made of the softest red leather I've ever seen.' Then she frowned. 'Though I must say that his complexion was a little oily for my tastes.'

'You didn't tell him anything, did you?' I said, feeling a panic rising.

'Signor Ballio only wanted to know why we had left the Bearpark household?'

'He told you his name?'

'Of course he did. In fact, he was the most charming man and invited me to visit him at any time in the doge's palace.'

'And what reason did you give for our departure?'

'I said that John Bearpark keeps a dirty house and that we were unsettled by the rancid food from his kitchen. That's why we left his filthy establishment.'

'Did he believe you?'

Mother gave me the oddest look. 'Of course he did, Oswald. Because it's the truth.' Then she frowned. 'Though, I must say that I don't know why the doge's palace would be quite so interested in our movements.' She raised her eyebrows and looked into space.

'Perhaps they have plans to invite us to a feast? Now that we are rid of Bearpark's low company, we have come to the attention of the doge.' She gave a short and haughty huff. 'No wonder that man was never invited to join their Golden Book. Who would have—'

'Mother, please. Did you say anything about our plans to leave Venice?'

She placed her hands back in her lap and spoke with calm consideration. 'No. Of course I didn't,' she said. 'Though I can't see why it should be such a secret.'

I hesitated, but it was time that she knew the truth – or at least the palatable version of it. 'I'm in dispute with certain people in this city,' I said. 'And I would rather that our departure went unnoticed.'

She scanned my face for more information. 'What people?' she asked. 'What dispute?'

'I'll tell you more once we've got away from here. But they are dangerous, Mother, so it's important that nobody knows our plan.'

She studied me again, discovering nothing more at this second pass. 'Very well then,' she said at length. 'But it won't be easy to depart from this inn without somebody remarking upon it.'

'That's why we will leave in the night,' I said, 'wearing our oldest and plainest clothes.'

'Are we to go in disguise then?' Her face lit up. 'How exciting. We will be like the Empress Matilda, fleeing from Oxford Castle in a white gown, so that she might not be seen against the frozen river.'

'A simple grey cloak will suffice, Mother. We just want to look like ordinary travellers.'

'And when will we leave?'

'Tomorrow night. In the meantime, you must buy those items I told you about before, whilst I stay hidden in this room. If anybody calls for me, then you must say that I've gone out and refused to disclose my destination.'

'I can't see why you wouldn't tell me where you were going,' she said. 'That's not a very believable story.'

I felt my chest tightening. 'Just say that you think I've gone out to gamble somewhere. That's why I was being so secretive.'

She arched an eyebrow. 'Gambling? That doesn't sound like you, Oswald.'

'Just say it, Mother.'

We might have continued our discussion, when there was a knock at the door. I panicked thinking that Ballio and his men had returned – though the knock was timidly made and was hardly that of a soldier's. 'By the breath of Christ,' said Mother. 'Who is this now? Anyone would think I was offering to hear confession in this room.'

The knock came again, and was a little more insistent at this strike.

Mother got slowly to her feet. 'Get under the bed, Oswald, and I'll get rid of them.' Now she shouted loudly. 'Don't come in. I'm not dressed.' Then she ambled to the door as I followed her instructions and rolled beneath the bedstead. Watching her feet from my hiding place on the shiny, ferrous-red of the terrazzo, I could see that she opened the door only the smallest crack. 'Yes. What do you want?' she said.

I heard a voice from the other side of the door, and when Mother finally allowed this visitor entry to the room, I knew their feet immediately. Their shoes were pointed and clean – immune to the filth of the streets, and their hose was knitted from the finest wool, that did not sag at the knees or ankles. It could be no other person than Giovanni. As I edged forward from my position beneath the bedstead to look at his face, I could see that he was unusually dishevelled. His hair was no longer curled, and he looked as if he had just risen from his bed. 'I'm sorry to bother you, my lady,' he stuttered, now bowing his head. 'I didn't wish to alarm you.'

Mother tilted her nose into the air, making the most of this apology. 'Well you did. Thumping on the door like Janus. What's the matter with you?'

He bowed again. 'Please. I need to speak to Oswald urgently.'

'He's not here. He's gone out gambling.'

Giovanni seemed uncomfortable. 'Gambling? But I must speak to him personally, my lady.' He poked a finger nervously into his ear. 'There's been a malamity at Ca' Bearpark.'

'Malamity? What are you talking about?'

'It is a tragic happening.'

Mother strode back towards the door. 'We have no interest in Ca' Bearpark, nor its malamities.' She put her hand to the door handle. 'Now please, go.'

Giovanni hesitated. 'Please could you ask Lord Somershill to return to Ca' Bearpark. As soon as he is able.'

'Why, in God's name, would he do that?' said Mother, now opening the door. 'Your master was very insulting to us.'

Giovanni's voice became desperate. 'Please, my lady. It's Monna Filomena.'

'What about her?'

'My master has locked her into a bedchamber and sent me to fetch the guards from the palace.'

Mother coughed. 'And why would that be?'

'My master believes she murdered Enrico. He wants to see her hang in the Piazzetta.'

I crawled out from beneath the bed, causing Giovanni to shriek. 'Oswald. You frightened me. Why were you hiding?'

'That doesn't matter. What are you saying about Filomena?'

Giovanni wiped the sweat from his brow. 'My master swears she is guilty of the murder.'

'That's ridiculous.'

The sweat now beaded upon Giovanni's top lip, like a raindrop on a pane of glass. 'I know. But my master says that her brother

Adolpho was the murderer. That it was a plan between the two of them to kill Bearpark's only male heir and keep his money.'

None of this made sense. 'But Adolpho was also murdered. Does Bearpark think his wife also killed her own brother?'

'He says that Monna Filomena was frightened that her brother would talk, so she paid somebody to kill him.'

This story was preposterous. 'What with? She never has any money!'

'My master has become wild with a madness, Oswald,' said Giovanni. 'I cannot reason with him. He swears his wife is guilty, and nothing will change his mind.'

He looked at me with red eyes. He was in earnest, and yet this sudden devotion to Filomena came as a surprise, for I had never seen him show anything but animosity towards the woman. 'Does Bearpark know that you've come here?' I said.

'No, no. He doesn't.' Giovanni wrung his hands through his hair, creating greasy lines through his uncombed locks. 'He thinks that I've gone to the palace. To inform the guards of Monna Filomena's guilt.' He started to shake. 'My master has lost his mind, Oswald, and you're the only person who can stop this. Please. I beg you. Tell him to release his wife. Tell him she's innocent!'

I reached for my cloak, when Mother pulled me to one side. 'What are you doing, Oswald?'

'I must speak to Bearpark, Mother. It won't take long.'

Mother pulled tighter. 'But what about these dangerous people who are looking for you?' she whispered. 'I thought you intended to remain hidden in this room.'

'I'll stay out of sight.'

Still she would not release her grasp. 'But what if the girl *is* guilty?'

'She's not.'

'You're so sure, are you?' She looked at me with a raised eyebrow. 'Her husband is very old. I can't imagine that she married Bearpark for any other reason than the size of his fortune and the promise of his quick death.' I tried to pull away, but she held onto me. 'Listen to me, Oswald. If Enrico Bearpark had lived, then he would have inherited Bearpark's fortune, wouldn't he?' She looked over her shoulder to make sure that Giovanni wasn't listening. 'Now that Enrico is dead, Monna Filomena will have it all.'

'Filomena didn't kill Enrico. And she didn't kill her own brother.'

Mother still refused to release me. In fact, she pushed me further into the corner. 'But it's not such an outlandish accusation, is it?' she said. 'And it was her brother who you chased away from the water gate, wasn't it?' She fixed me with one of her glares. 'That's what you wrote in your pamphlet.'

'You're not supposed to read my notes. They're private.'

She shook her head as if her snooping into my personal things were a mere triviality. 'I think you're being naïve, Oswald. You assume Monna Filomena is innocent, just because she has a pleasing face and a pair of bouncing breasts.'

'And you assume she's guilty because you're jealous of her.'

She reddened. 'What nonsense! I am a very fair-minded woman. Above such childish spite.' She folded her arms and fixed me with a stern glare. 'But I can't see that Bearpark would accuse his own wife without good reason. He might be a foolish old toad, but he must have some evidence against her.'

'Then he can tell me when I visit him,' I said, tying the cords of my cloak.

She gave a disgruntled shake of her head. 'So, you mean to go then?' she said. 'You will put your own safety at risk?' She rolled her eyes. 'No. You will put our safety at risk. For the sake of this girl?'

'I can't leave Venice without trying to save her, Mother. You must understand that.'

She sighed, before regarding me with a look of resignation. 'You're in love with the foolish creature, aren't you?'

I stood back. 'No. Of course I'm not.'

'There's no harm in it, Oswald.' She smiled. 'In fact I'm pleased that somebody has stirred your loins at long last. You've been miserable for too long.'

'I'm not in love with Filomena,' I said. 'You're totally wrong about that.'

'We'll see.'

I turned back to find that Giovanni was standing a good deal closer than I had expected. At first I thought he must have heard our conversation, but then I changed my mind – for his expression was hard to read. I only saw the slightest flicker of emotion behind his dark eyes, and, at the time I could not decipher its meaning.

Chapter Twenty-Nine

It wasn't long after our marriage that Mary told me she was expecting a child. This news should not have come as a surprise, since we had become enthusiastic lovers, after the fumblings and embarrassment of our wedding night. I was pleased to hear the news of the child, though not perhaps as pleased as Mary had hoped. For the truth was this: I knew the dangers of childbirth. Which man didn't? By conceiving a new life, we had put her own life at risk.

But Mary was excited at the news, and, over time, I became accustomed, even excited by the idea myself. Mary was young and strong. She would withstand labour and give birth to our child without any problems. Sometimes, however, when I held Mary in my arms and stroked her full belly, I could not help but dwell upon Becky's curse. How foolish I was to give any credence to such nonsense. I found it hard enough to believe in God, let alone curses, and yet her words did trouble me. More than I cared to admit.

Mary went into labour in the early hours of a Sunday morning. At first the pains were far apart in their frequency. The midwife was called, Mary was locked into the ladies' bedchamber, and I was locked out. I waited outside, but on the odd occasion that I was able to look inside the room, I could see nothing but the glow of a candle. The windows had been covered with thick tapestries, and the floor covered with rugs and furs. It seemed as if the chamber were a womb itself. Warm, dark, and red.

There was scurrying activity to begin with, but then the energy went out of Mary's labour, and it was replaced by long periods of silence. Mother urged me to go hunting or inspect the progress of the wheat harvest in the demesne fields. I couldn't leave the house however, I wanted to be with Mary – but every time I tried to enter the room, a dam of sturdy-looking women blocked my progress. Each had their sleeves rolled up. Each was sweating, since the heat in the room was intense and suffocating. They told me to leave immediately, in tones they would never normally use to their lord.

I began to sense that something was wrong on the second day of labour, though none of the women attending the birth would speak to me willingly. There were complications apparently. What complications were these, I demanded to know? Still, nobody would tell me. I was beginning to feel as important as the lowest kitchen scullion in this whole affair. Even though I had sired the child that was about to be born, and even though it was my own wife confined inside the wretched furnace-like room. In the end, I grabbed one of the younger women as she scurried through the door in search of fresh linen. Cornered by her lord, she had no choice but to tell me what was happening.

The child was in the breech position. Where the head should have been pressing against the neck of the womb, it was the child's bottom or its legs, she was not sure which. The women had tried to move the child back into the correct position, but it refused to budge. Inside the chamber I now heard Mary's calls. She sounded vigorous and affronted, and cursed me and her unborn baby to the high heavens. More than once, Mother rapped upon the door and told her that Somershill was inhabited by Christians who did not want to listen to such uncouth barbarity.

And so the labour dragged on into a third day. Mary's cries of indignation were gone, and in their place came only a soft groaning. I waited outside, still denied entry. But when I was told she was too tired to push, and that she ran a high fever, I forced my way into the dark and cloistered room and rushed to my wife's side.

She was laid in bed, in a loose chemise, with her long hair hanging stickily about her head. I lifted water to her lips, and then I held her poor and limp hand in my own and tried to whisper encouragement and soothing overtures of my love. But I'm not sure she even knew who I was. The vigour of life had left her, and she seemed dazed and disorientated. When she spoke, it was of the old days, when she had been a young girl. Of her pet cat and the great eagle that she had once nursed back to health. At that moment I felt both guilty and hateful. Our child was killing her, like a creeper vine strangling a precious tree. I wanted so much to bury my head into her breast and cry – but what purpose would such a display of hopelessness achieve?

I insisted upon examining Mary myself – much to the horror and violent protestation of the midwife. By this point I could no longer tolerate the woman's insubordination and constant warnings that this room was not a place for men. I had studied under a monastery infirmarer, so I knew enough about anatomy. I sent her from the room and then lifted Mary's chemise tentatively, before pushing her damp and lifeless legs apart. Looking at the opening to Mary's vagina, it seemed clear enough that the midwife's diagnosis was correct. There was nothing to see. The child was pressing only lightly upon the neck of the womb, and was not helping itself to be born. In fact, I doubted that the creature was still alive. There had been no discernible movement from beneath Mary's belly for many hours.

I was considering whether to push my hand into the birth canal and attempt to pull the child from the womb somehow, when Mary grabbed my hand. 'Oswald. Is that you?' She was lucid, though her voice was weak and thin.

I kissed her face. 'Yes, Mary. It's me.'

'I'm going to die soon,' she told me. It was her matter-of-fact voice, and I shouldn't have argued.

'No. Mary,' I said, trying to stifle my shock at this announcement. 'That's not true.'

'Yes it is,' she said, managing to conjure up some typical crossness from somewhere within her. 'Don't quarrel with me.' Then she whispered, 'I have something to ask of you. A promise you must make.'

'Of course, Mary. I promise to do anything you ask.'

'When I die, you must take the child from me.'

'What do you mean?'

Again the anger came. She squeezed my hand. 'Don't be foolish, Oswald! You know what I mean. Immediately after I've taken my last breath, you must cut the child from my womb.'

I dropped her hand. 'No. I can't do that. I won't do that.'

She rose from her bolster. 'You won't do it! You would let our child die, because you *won't* do it!' She fell back against the bed. Tears flowed from her eyes. 'I married a coward. Get away from me!'

I quickly grasped her hand again. 'I'm sorry, Mary. I . . .'

'Don't say you're sorry, Oswald. Words are nothing in this world.' She closed her eyes. The argument had exhausted her. 'I don't care what you *say*. I only care about what you *do*. Don't let my life mean nothing.'

'It doesn't mean nothing. I love you.'

'I want our child to live. Don't let them take him with me to the grave.'

'Then I'll do it,' I said, though the feeling was draining from my legs, and the sway of nausea was rising in my stomach.

She smiled. 'Don't take too long,' she whispered. 'The child is weakening. But he still lives.'

They say, in life, that there will come a time when you have to confront your worst fears. You will enter into the darkest, foulest cave, and in this place, the only enemy you meet will be yourself. As I held onto Mary's hand and watched the life retreat from her body, there could be no doubt that I was in that very cave. My life would never be at a lower ebb.

When she ceased to breathe, I wanted to run from the chamber and hide in the deep forest. Even throw myself from the tower, or tie a noose about a beam and let myself hang to death. Then we could all be buried together in the churchyard. Mother, father, and child. The end of our short-lived family.

Instead, I called the midwife into the room and asked her to pass me a knife. She knew what awaited. Perhaps she had done the same thing herself. I might even have asked her to undertake the task, but that was the coward's option. And, for all my faults, Mary had not married a coward.

I cut her belly from top to bottom, and though Mary's heart was no longer pumping, blood seemed to rush at speed from her body. Steadfastly I ignored the wanton flow of it, and I then reached my hands inside the cavity of her abdomen to pull a grey and slimy thing from her midst. It reminded me of the sea bass that I saw in baskets at Rye. I cared for it as much.

The midwife took the thing and rubbed the air into its lungs. And then it screamed for its mother. I screamed for its mother. I went to my chamber for many days and mourned.

Mother told me that I had a son, but I could not bear to look upon him.

Chapter Thirty

I sent Giovanni ahead to Ca' Bearpark and promised to follow. The man was reluctant to leave the Fondaco without me, but we could hardly both stroll out of the inn together, passing the two soldiers who were still guarding the main door. He had to trust me.

When I was certain that Giovanni had gone, I told Mother to stay in the room and keep the doors locked until my return. Whilst I was pleading for Filomena's release, she should pack as much as was sensible for the journey. I then went in search of Sandro, finding the boy where I had left him, at the top of the servants' stairwell. At first I couldn't see his face, as this shaft was devoid of natural light. But, as my eyes became accustomed to the dark, I found him slouched in a corner, gnawing at the cheese rind he had been given earlier by the cook.

He jumped to his feet. 'Yes, Master Oswald?'

His words caused me to smile. 'So. I'm your master now, am I?'

He gave a low and extravagant bow in response.

'I need you to lead me to Ca' Bearpark through the side alleys,' I said. 'Do you know the way from here?'

Now he laughed. 'Of course I do, master. I live in that street.'

*   *   *

When we reached Ca' Bearpark, I told Sandro to wait for me in the Calle Nuova, and to stay out of sight. The house was quieter than usual, lacking the thud of servants' footsteps, or even the scent of a cooking meal. Giovanni himself had opened the door to me. Bowing deeply, his face was anxious and sweating. His hair was still ruffled and sticking out untidily from his head. 'Oswald. Thank you. I didn't think you were coming.'

I removed my cloak. 'Is Monna Filomena still locked in her bedchamber?'

Giovanni shook his head glumly. 'No. They've taken her to one of the storerooms now.'

I thought of that network of damp and dark chambers that lay beneath the house. In this weather, they would be no better than drains. 'Just release her, Giovanni,' I said, pointing to the large ring of iron keys that he still kept hanging from his belt. 'You're able to open all of the other doors in this place.'

'The room is guarded,' he told me. 'They are . . .' He was struggling to find the right word, and then cursed himself when the vocabulary escaped him. 'The guards are tall men, Oswald. My master has employed them specially for the task.'

'Where did he find these men?'

He frowned and wiped a hand across his mouth. 'I don't know. I refused to help him, Oswald. The imprisonment is . . .' Once again he failed to find the word he was looking for. This was unlike him. 'It is not right,' he said in the end.

'Where is Monna Filomena's child?' I asked.

Giovanni frowned. 'She's been taken to Burano. To the house of her grandparents.'

This was sad news. 'So Bearpark has disowned the child?'

Giovanni nodded.

'Where is your master now?'

'In his bed.'

'And he still believes that you're fetching guards from the palace?'

Giovanni dropped his voice to a whisper. 'Yes. He does.' He took the cloak from me and clasped it to his chest. 'Please, Oswald. Go to him. Tell him that he's wrong.'

Bearpark's bedchamber reminded me of the crypt at the monastery, where I had laid out the dead for burial. This dark hall had been built without windows, so that the blowflies might not easily find their way through the cloisters and passageways of the monastery, and then lay their eggs upon the dead. As I prepared the bodies for burial, my work was always illuminated by the smoking flame of a tallow candle. It had an unpleasant smell, though nothing like the perfume of decay. Despite years of such work, I never became hardened to the fleshy, sour smell of death.

Bearpark's room was also lit by candles, though these were made of beeswax, rather than being sticks of rendered beef suet. The shutters were closed, and Bearpark's sheets were tucked under his chin, so that he looked like an infant who had been swaddled by his wet-nurse. As I entered, he looked up at me with a face so grim that I thought I might be staring at the Angel of Death himself. The only other soul in this airless prison was the old female servant who was pouring wine from a pitcher into a small bowl.

As I neared the bed, Bearpark focussed his eyes upon my face and grimaced. 'De Lacy? So, you've come back, have you?' He started to laugh, but the sound disintegrated into a hacking cough. 'My great investigator has returned.' Then he pulled an arm from beneath the sheet and waved it limply in my direction. 'We don't need you any more. We've found the murderer ourselves. Giovanni has gone to fetch the guards at the palace.'

'No he hasn't.'

The man fixed me with cold-blooded eyes. 'What do you mean?'

'Your wife is innocent, Bearpark. Giovanni knows this, as well as you do, so he came to find me instead.'

Bearpark attempted to sit up, assisted by the old servant, who hastily pushed another bolster behind his back, though she was roundly cursed for her efforts to help. 'Where is Giovanni!' he tried to shout, before his voice broke down into a cough. 'Get him in here, where I can see him. I know the wretch is hiding out there somewhere.' This shouting prompted another coughing fit.

Giovanni crept around the door and stepped into the room, hugging the wall with the stealth of a mouse trying to avoid the attentions of the kitchen cat. I was surprised to see his face at all in this room, as I had supposed he might hide somewhere in the recesses of the house and let me make all the speeches and entreaties on behalf of Filomena.

'Is that you, Judas!' boomed Bearpark.

Giovanni stepped forward into the candlelight. A little bolder now. 'I'm no Judas, master.' I had never heard Giovanni speak to Bearpark in such tones.

'I told you to fetch the guards, not this fool. Why have you disobeyed me?' Giovanni cowered at these words, losing his nerve almost as soon as he had found it.

'How could Giovanni report such a story?' I said. 'You have no evidence against your wife.'

'I have plenty of evidence,' said Bearpark. 'She's been a false wife to me. A betrayer. That child is not mine for a start,' he said. 'It looks nothing like me.'

'She's just a newborn infant, Bearpark. Babies rarely look human, let alone resemble their parents.'

He huffed at this. 'And it's a girl. I never sire girls. Every one of my previous children has been a son.'

'So you're accusing your wife of murder, because of the gender of your child?' I laughed. 'I doubt that the palace will be so impressed by that argument. Particularly as your wife is Venetian, and you are English.'

Bearpark pointed a finger at me. 'Stop twisting the argument,' he hissed. 'I know what you're up to. You want me to free Filomena so you can take her for yourself.'

I had the sudden urge to press my fingers around the old man's throat and then squeeze my hands together until he was dead, but I uncurled my fists and let the madness pass. 'Your wife is innocent, Bearpark. You know it.'

He shook his head, causing the jowls of his cheeks to flap like fishtails. 'No, no. It was her and her brother, Adolpho. And now she will hang for the crime.' The old man fell back against his pillow, then licked at his dry lips, indicating to the old maid that he wanted his bowl of wine. Then he let out a laugh. A dry cackle. 'Oswald de Lacy. The great investigator.'

I took a deep breath. 'Let Filomena go and I will bring you the true murderer.'

He cackled again. 'You promised me that last time. So why should I believe you now?'

'Because I know how to find him.'

He uttered a curse and tried to wave me away.

'Go ahead then, Bearpark,' I said. 'Send your innocent wife to the gallows. Think of that stain upon your soul. Think of the years you will spend in Purgatory, as you descend into Hell. Nobody on earth will pray for the remission of your sins.' Bearpark muttered an obscenity at this suggestion, but I could tell my words affected him. 'And then think of the shame to the name of Bearpark,' I said. 'Your wife will be hung in the Piazzetta, for all of Venice to see. And people will laugh at you for ever more. John Bearpark, the foolish old Englishman who married a murderer.'

Bearpark lifted his shaking hand to his cheek and began to scratch nervously.

'But think of the prestige,' I said, 'the honour to the Bearpark name, if you could present the true killer to the palace? Think how this could silence your rivals.'

He made a long and low rumble, as if we could hear the cogs and wheels of his mind turning slowly in their cavern. After a long pause he addressed me. 'You know where to find this killer then, do you?'

'I do.'

'Or so you say.' He sank back into the bolster. 'But you said that before, didn't you? And then you just kept me waiting.'

'This time I won't.'

He took a long gulp of wine, and then exhaled as if he were taking his last breath. 'You have one day, de Lacy.'

'And you will release Filomena immediately?' I said.

He slipped slowly beneath the sheets. 'No.'

'But—'

'Bring me this killer.' He coughed. 'Then you're welcome to her.'

I followed Giovanni down the stairs to the *piano nobile*. 'I want to see Filomena,' I said.

'You can't, Oswald,' said my glum companion. 'The two guards won't let anybody past the door.'

'Not even her lady's maid?'

'The maid has left, along with most of the servants.' He sighed. 'In fact, there are only a few men and that old woman left.'

'Is Monna Filomena allowed food and water?'

Giovanni nodded awkwardly. 'Only water.'

'Then I must be quick.' I tied my cloak. 'And you need to give me some money,' I said, pretending this was an afterthought.

Giovanni tensed at this request. 'Don't you have any of your own?'

'No. I left my purse at the Fondaco,' I lied.

'What do you need money for?'

'Legitimate expenses,' I said. 'You can write them down in your ledger, under my name.' The man still hesitated. 'Look! Do you want me to save Filomena's life, or not?'

He trembled a little. 'Of course I do,' he said, as he began to fumble around in his purse, before handing me the whole bag of coins with an air of finality. 'Here, have them all,' he said. 'Just save her life.'

I took the purse and then looked at his face – seeing a much-changed man. 'Why did you come to find me at the inn, Giovanni?' I asked.

'I'm concerned about justice for my mistress,' he told me.

'But I always thought that you didn't care for Filomena. Yet, now you are her champion?'

'I may not care for Monna Filomena,' he said. 'But I am a man of Christ, Oswald. I care about the truth.'

I tied the purse onto my belt and went to leave.

'Should I come with you?' asked Giovanni, as I reached the door.

'No,' I said. 'Stay here and make sure that Monna Filomena is cared for. I will return as soon as possible.'

I crept into the Calle Nuova, and looked up and down the alley for Sandro. The sky was overcast, and at first I could not see the boy. I will admit to panicking, when a small stone hit the back of my head and I turned around to find him leaping down from a high wall with the athleticism of a cat.

It was time to get away from this place, so I grasped his small hand and we made our way towards the Canal Grande. Here we would take the *traghetto* ferry to Dorsoduro, and while there was still light, we would hire a boat and seek out Marco.

I knew exactly where he was hiding. In truth, I always had.

Chapter Thirty-One

When I told Sandro where I was planning to go, he laughed in disbelief, calling me a madman. 'I'll hire a *sàndolo* and row there myself,' I told him. 'It can't be so difficult, can it? It's just a boat with an oar.'

This caused him to laugh even more. 'You won't be able to do it,' he told me. 'You're English.'

'You'll see,' I said.

As we reached the small quay at the tip of Dorsoduro, I told the boathand that I needed to rent a vessel in order to visit a lover on the island of Giudecca, no doubt paying twice the going rate for this small *sàndolo*, and more again for the privilege of a lantern. I was English, and this was Venice, so an inflated price for foreigners was entirely usual. And, as is also typical in Venice, the boathand protested that he had no interest in knowing my reason for wanting the boat, but then found a stool from which he might watch my progress across the lagoon. He would soon know that I was not heading for Giudecca.

Sandro stood on the wooden jetty and watched me attempt to manoeuvre the boat into the canal with a look of bemusement upon his face. I ignored his scorn, and tried to wield the long and awkward oar through the water whilst standing upright on the boards. The oar was much heavier than I had supposed, and I only succeeded in creating a great splash as the blade sped out of the sea, causing me to fall forward and nearly lose hold of the disobedient oar.

As Sandro had anticipated, I was not an able oarsman, so when the boy leapt into the boat and grabbed the end of the oar before it sank into the sea, I did not object. I had already told Sandro where we were going, so it was his choice to join me – and as long as he stayed in the boat when we reached our destination, he would be safe enough.

By now there was a mist descending in thin swathes across the lagoon, and there were only two hours of daylight left, at most. A light rain blew into our faces, and the occasional wave slapped against the side of our small boat, but otherwise we moved quickly enough through the water without meeting any other vessels. As he propelled the oar, Sandro sang a song that was both melancholic and dreary, as if we might be sailing towards a burial, but I knew that something worse than death waited for me.

As our destination loomed like a black ridge upon the horizon, I felt its eyes searching for me across the water. I caught a glimpse of its low form as it skulked along the shoreline with its hands to the ground, patrolling the narrow beach like a sentry guard. I could almost smell the reek of its matted, dirty fur. Oh yes, it was no wonder that I had kept away from this place.

'I will not look at you,' I hissed to the wind. 'Stay away from me.'

Sandro glanced up at my words – his face portraying surprise and then concern at my outburst.

I laughed, in an attempt to appease the boy. 'I was just cursing the rain,' I said. 'I hate this weather.'

Sandro frowned and then turned back towards the island, pushing the oar through the water with perfect grace until we hit the sandy shore. It took all of my determination to then swing a foot from the boat, and step out onto the land, chanting to myself that I must not be afraid. The creature was nothing but a figment of my imagination. An illusion. I needed only to ignore its presence and hold fast to my plan – because somewhere in the midst of this island, there was a man who knew the truth. A man who could help me save Filomena.

At first I struggled through the marshy reeds, not immediately able to find a path from this far side of the island to the buildings of the Lazaretto. Sandro had insisted that we sail around to this distant shore, to avoid our progress being spotted from the few boats that were passing along these same waters. Craft were not allowed to land on the Lazaretto, so we needed to keep our visit secret.

As I walked, the wind blew my hair wildly about my face and inflated my cloak until I looked as if I were myself a boat under sail. My approach to the simple square chapel would not easily be disguised, so I chose instead to walk with the steady intent of a man striding into battle. I kept my focus upon my destination, and if the monkey were trying to catch my eye, then I would not pay it an ounce of attention.

At this pace, I soon reached the outskirts of the small colony of lepers, where the reeds gave way to bare patches of earth, dotted with fig, and apple trees, and lines of mounded soil, waiting to be planted up in the Spring with beans and peas. A donkey leant over a broken fence and brayed aggressively at my passing, and some chickens ran in my path, clucking and flapping their wings with the usual, squawking terror at anything that wasn't another chicken.

This small patch of cultivated land seemed more organised than I had expected – in fact I would say it was as ordered and as well-kept as many of the virgates farmed by my own villeins back in Kent. This gave me some heart, until I caught sight of the lepers themselves, loitering in doorways or hiding behind trees. Some seemed human enough, with only the slightest disfigurements to their faces and limbs, but others had become as warped and decaying as a fallen tree – the swellings on their skin as clustered as the blisters of a jelly fungus.

The lepers watched me with cautious eyes, but they would not approach. Only an old and blinded man hobbled into my path, with his stunted, fingerless hand outstretched to me, and his voice still capable of begging for a *soldino*. As he neared me however, the others called out to him, warning him to keep his distance. They said that a shadow trailed me.

I kept my eyes facing forward, and tried to concentrate, as a man hobbled towards me from the direction of the chapel. He was a monk, a Benedictine, and though his black robes were dusty and torn, I could see immediately that he did not suffer with leprosy. 'What do you want?' he said, stopping only a few feet away from me, and waving his stick in my face. 'Are you a leper?' He spoke in Venetian, but his accent had the exactitude of German pronunciation – a style of speech I knew well from our stay at the Fondaco.

I bowed my head. 'I wish to speak with a young man named Marco. I believe he's recently arrived.'

The old priest attempted a shrug, but he was a poor liar. 'I don't know anybody with that name.'

I looked towards the chapel door, to see a figure quickly dart out of sight. 'So I wouldn't find him hiding over there then?' I said.

'Go back to your boat and get off this island,' he told me. 'You're not welcome here.'

'I mean Marco no harm,' I said, stepping towards the man. 'I just need to speak to him.'

The stick was raised again. 'There is no Marco here. This is the island of lepers. Leave now. This is no place for you.'

I reached to my belt and untied the purse that Giovanni had given me, then I made a point of jingling the coins within. 'Are you sure I can't speak to Marco?' I looked about the settlement, at the worn-out hovels, with rags at their windows and holes in their roofs. If ever there was a place in need of charity, then this was it – but the old priest turned his back on my coins and hobbled back towards his church. 'Take your money and leave!' he shouted over his shoulder. 'We don't yield to bribery here.'

I ran after him, but stopped short of touching the man. 'I must speak to Marco,' I said. 'I didn't send the Signori di Notte to find him. That story is wrong. They must have followed me to the convent.' I paused to catch my breath. 'I'm just an Englishman, investigating the murder of a friend.' He turned his head the smallest fraction at this remark. 'The dead man was also a friend of Marco's,' I said, as desperation crept into my voice. 'Marco can help me to find the killer. That's all I care about. No more, and no less.'

The priest paused for a moment, and I thought I had convinced him with my plea, but then he changed his mind. 'There's no Marco here,' he said, hobbling away again. 'I told you that before.'

I caught up with him and this time I stretched out a hand to clasp his arm. 'Please. Let me speak to Marco,' I said. 'A person's life depends upon it. I need only a few moments of his time.'

The old priest went to beat me away with his stick, when Marco ran out of the chapel and stood between us. He was also wearing the black habit of the Benedictines, and his head had been tonsured – his curls cut away to give him an older, less angelic appearance. 'Let me speak to him, father, and then he will leave us alone.'

'Do you know this man, Marco?' said the priest.

Marco nodded. 'I do, father. He's the Englishman I told you of before.'

'So he's not to be trusted?'

Marco hesitated at this question. 'No. But I will answer his questions, if he promises to leave.'

The priest regarded me suspiciously, slowly rolling his head from side to side, as if this might improve the quality of his assessment. 'Let's take him into the chapel then,' he said at length. 'A man will not bear false witness in the House of God.'

Marco bristled. 'No, no. Father. I would rather speak to him out here.'

'But—'

'I insist,' said Marco. 'This man comes from my old life. You must let me speak to him alone.'

The priest heaved a long sigh. 'Very well. But your visitor can pay for the interview, at least.'

'So you do yield to bribery then?' I remarked.

The priest only gave a grunt of indignation at this, before waving his staff at the lepers who had crept forward in order to enjoy a rare moment of drama. 'Look about you, Englishman,' he said. 'How do you think these people are fed? We grow a few vines in the courtyard, and there are a handful of goats on the grass, but do you think we go to the market when we don't have enough food?' I tried to answer, but he shouted over me. 'No! We do not. The market must come to us. And do you think we get the best food and the lowest prices for this privilege?' Once again I tried to answer without success. 'No!' he shouted. 'We do not. I call out my orders to their boats, and they tell me what money to leave on the jetty. Then they deliver the foulest cheese and the wettest grain. You might think there would be mercy for these poor, miserable people? But no, not at all. The merchants of Venice would profit from the misery of an island of lepers. Lepers! The most wretched creatures in the kingdom of God.' He held out a limp hand, exhausted after his tirade. 'So, I ask you to be very generous, my friend. Do not stint.'

How could I refuse such an oratory, so I gave the whole purse to the priest. I would tell you that the man appeared grateful for my donation, but he moved the coins about with his finger and then gave a derisory sniff. 'Go on then, you may speak to Marco.' He waved his stick at me. 'But be quick about it. Marco has his work and prayers to attend to.'

We sat on a bench beneath a tree that was growing through a crumbling wall, its roots clinging to the stone like leeches. The lepers kept their distance — only a solitary woman daring to creep nearer to spy at me from behind a makeshift fence. Her face was ruined by a great gaping hole where her nose had once lived, and suddenly I felt the full weight of despair bear down upon me. I knew exactly why the abbess had crowed that I would never dare to follow Marco here, for this was a hopeless, living Hell. It was death in the midst of life. Who would come to this place, unless afflicted with leprosy, or desperate to escape something worse? And yet, this misery and bleakness had not deterred my monkey from choosing this island as its home. In fact, it was this very wretchedness that had drawn it here.

'Why did you come to this place, Marco?' I asked.

'Better to die on the Lazaretto, than to be burnt on the pyre,' he said. 'The Signori will not seek me out here.'

'I didn't give them your name, you know.'

He rubbed his face with his hands. 'Just tell me what you want to know, Englishman, and then go away.'

'Very well,' I said. 'You wrote the letter denouncing Enrico, didn't you?' He stiffened. 'I know that it was you, Marco, so don't lie to me.'

'I only wanted to frighten Enrico,' he said. 'I didn't mean to cause any trouble.'

I stifled a laugh at this answer. 'Perhaps you should have thought about that before you posted the letter into the lion's mouth.'

He wrung his hands together nervously. 'I was angry with Enrico. I wanted to punish him for his betrayal.'

'But this was more than mischief, wasn't it, Marco? There was truth in your accusation.'

'What do you mean by that?' he said, looking up at me warily.

'When you said that Enrico was meddling where he shouldn't, you meant that he was spying on the work of the Arsenale, didn't you?'

Marco looked away nervously. 'I had nothing to do with it. I'm not a spy.'

'I know that.'

'It was Enrico, and that Gianni I told you about,' he said with a huff. 'Gianni told Enrico secrets about the Arsenale, and then Enrico sold them.'

'To whom?'

Marco paused. 'The Hungarians, I think. But Enrico wouldn't tell me for certain.'

'Why not?'

'I think he wanted to protect me.' Marco smiled momentarily at this memory before starting to pick nervously at his nails. 'The spying wasn't Enrico's idea. He was forced to take a lover at the Arsenale, or so he said.'

'Forced? Who forced him?'

The picking became more frenetic. 'I didn't ask, did I?'

'Why not?'

'Because I thought it was another lie.' He imitated Enrico's voice. '"*I only took Gianni as a lover because somebody made me do it, Marco. I don't love him really.*"'

'Do you still think that was a lie?'

Marco looked away. 'No. I don't.'

The light was fading quickly now, as a velvety darkness settled across the island. 'Did Gianni know that Enrico was using him to obtain secrets?'

Marco smiled spitefully at this question. 'He did. After I told him.'

'You told Gianni?' Marco nodded proudly. 'And this revelation drove him to murder Enrico in a rage?' I said. 'Is that what you're going to tell me?'

Marco turned his back on me. 'As I said before, I didn't mean to cause trouble.'

'And yet it seems that you did. Over and over again.'

Marco spun around and regarded me with accusing eyes. 'Have you ever been in love, Englishman? Do you know the pain of betrayal?' Now it was my turn to look away. 'Their affair might have started under false pretences, but then it changed. Suddenly

Enrico didn't want to see me any more. He told me that he loved Gianni. More than he could ever love me. Can you imagine how that felt? So I went to find this Gianni. I only wanted to see why Enrico thought he was so special. Is that such a crime?' He paused for a moment. 'But when I saw them together, I couldn't bear it.' Another pause. 'So I did something that I regret.'

'What did you do, Marco?'

'I waited until Gianni was alone, and then I approached him. I told him a lie.'

'What lie?'

Marco wiped a tear from his eye. 'I told him that Enrico still loved me, and that he still visited me at the convent. I told him that their love was a sham, because Enrico only wanted secrets about the Arsenale and nothing else.'

'Did he believe you?'

Marco's voice was faltering. 'Yes, he did. It made him angry.'

I raised an eyebrow. 'Angry enough to kill Enrico?'

'Yes! He flew into a violent rage at my words. He frightened me.' Marco turned his face away. 'I didn't know he would behave in such a way, did I? I only meant to cause Gianni the same pain that I felt. I wanted him to know what it was like to be deceived by Enrico. I didn't know he would commit murder.' Marco wiped his nose on the back of his hand. 'I didn't mean for it to happen.'

'And when did this conversation take place?'

Marco sighed. 'The morning of *Giovedi Grasso*.'

'And what was Adolpho Bredani's involvement in all this?' I said.

He frowned at this question. 'I told you this before, Englishman. I've never heard of anybody called Adolpho Bredani. I don't know why you keep asking me about him.' Tears now gathered in the corners of his eyes, and when he could no longer hide this from me, he covered his face with his hands.

To begin with I felt the impulse to comfort the man, but I resisted, for it was Marco's spite and jealousy that had caused both Enrico's murder and Filomena's imprisonment, even if these outcomes had never been his intention. 'I need to speak to Gianni,' I said. 'I want his full name and address.'

Marco slowly removed his hands and turned his head to look at me. 'Why are you doing this, Englishman? Do you understand the trouble you will bring upon yourself?'

'I'm trying to save John Bearpark's wife,' I said. 'Bearpark has accused her of Enrico's murder.'

Marco frowned. 'Monna Filomena? Why would she have anything to do with this? The old man is mad.'

'Bearpark might be mad, but he has imprisoned his wife in a cell, and wants to see her hanged for this crime. So, if you don't tell me where to find Gianni, then you will have another death on your conscience.'

He turned away and I could see that his hands were trembling. 'And if I tell you, will you leave me alone?'

I nodded. 'As long as you tell me the truth, Marco.' Then I pressed my hand into his arm. 'So don't lie to me.'

'His name is Gianni Ricci,' he told me with a sigh.

'Are you sure?

'Yes!' Then he gave a short and unexpected laugh. 'Do you know what his family name means in our language?' he asked. 'Curly hair. But the man has no hair at all. Just a bald, shiny skull with a birthmark across his scalp.' Marco wiped his hand contemptuously across his head as if to demonstrate the spread of this blemish. 'A great ugly purple stain.'

Across the courtyard, the old priest appeared at the chapel door with his hands folded, and I knew that my time was running out. 'And where does he live?' I asked.

'In Castello.'

'It is a big *sestiere*, Marco. Be more specific.'

'He lives in a small *campo*, next to the church of Sant'Antonio.'

I tramped back across the island, taking care to walk upon the spongy mounds of grass and avoiding the deeper channels and clumps of bulrushes. The rain was now falling in long rods from a darkening sky, but I was not disheartened – for I was close to catching my killer. His name was Gianni Ricci, and his motive had been jealous rage. I was not quite sure where Adolpho Bredani and the coins fitted into this – and perhaps they didn't fit in at all? Perhaps Bredani had just stumbled back to Ca' Bearpark on the night of *Giovedi Grasso* and discovered Enrico's body just moments before I did, then running away in guilt at having abandoned his post. After all, this had always been Bearpark and Giovanni's explanation for his disappearance.

I had assumed the coins were payment for his involvement in Enrico's murder, but I had no actual evidence of this – they could equally have come from a gambling win or even an unrelated theft. The case against Ricci was much stronger. I had a witness who had seen Gianni Ricci fighting with Enrico in the storeroom at Ca' Bearpark, and now I knew that he had been provoked into a furious rage on the morning of *Giovedi Grasso*. With this evidence, I could arrest the man. Filomena would be saved, and then I could make her mine.

I stopped for a moment and laughed at my own stupidity. Filomena was not a chattel to be handed between owners. Even if she would agree to leaving Venice with me, then what did I have to offer her and her newborn child? A hastily arranged escape in a dirty merchant ship. I could not even promise to take her to England, because I had no intention of ever returning there. But then again, we could hardly settle in Marseilles – a port that I had never visited, and where I had no way of earning any money, other than raising a loan from an old family friend – a man who might not even still be alive.

I was lost in these thoughts when I felt something brush against my fingers. Because my mind was elsewhere, I did not react at first – so when a small hand slipped into mine, I imagined it was Sandro's for some reason. Only when this hand squeezed my own with its long, claw-like fingers did I recoil, pulling away as if my skin had been burnt. And there it was, on the path before me, crouching on the ground and looking up into my face.

I wanted to run, and yet my feet were fixed like dowels into the mud. I tried to close my eyes, but the lids were sewn into their sockets. Its eyes peered into mine – just as they had when I had looked into its cage, all those years ago in Cheapside. On that day it had rejected my interest and turned its back to me, content to sit in its own wretched filth, but now it wanted my attention. It craved my love.

The clouds moved across the sun and the rain beat against my face with its icy fists. Now the monkey reached out again. Beseechingly. It tried to take my hand, but I could not touch its skin. It wanted something from me – something that I could not give. Despite everything, it still disgusted me.

For a fleeting moment, a ray of sun breached the clouds and warmed my face, and suddenly I felt ashamed of myself, of my cowardice and my intransigence. This creature had not chased me here without reason. It was lonely and wretched, and yet I ignored it with a wilful, determined resolve. Filomena had been right. I had been running away from it for too long.

And so, very slowly I held out my hand to touch its cold, hard-skinned fingers. My heart was in my mouth, and I felt my stomach twist, but as I held its hand, I did not feel the paw of a monkey. When I looked down, there was no leathery face, hunched back, nor fringe of dirty white fur. Instead, a small boy was looking back at me. He was my son – the boy I had pulled from Mary's womb.

When he smiled at me, a stab of love pierced my heart so deeply that I nearly called out in pain, but just as I went to grasp him in my arms, he faded. 'Hugh?' I said, as the sun disappeared below the horizon.

'Hugh! Come back,' I shouted. 'Hugh! I'm sorry. Come back.'

But he had gone, and though I hunted in desperation through the marsh I could not find him.

Chapter Thirty-Two

I sat on the bench of the *sàndolo* in silence until Sandro spoke. 'What's the matter with you?' he asked, as he manoeuvred the oar through the water. 'Have you seen a ghost?'

How could I tell him the truth? Instead I pretended that I had been disturbed by the lepers.

'So, did you get the name you wanted?' he asked, before smiling at me. His face reminded me instantly of Hugh's, and suddenly another stab of emotion cut into my chest. This time it was pity, not love. And this poor boy deserved my pity, for he had no mother or father, and lived by his wits in the filthy corners and alleys of Venice. This only evoked guiltier thoughts. My son Hugh had also lost his mother, but he might as well have lost his father at the same time, for I had done nothing but wallow in my own, selfish grief. I had run away from England and left him in the care of my sister – a woman who did not even recognise Hugh's claim to Somershill. I had even vowed never to return.

'Yes. I got the name I wanted,' I told the boy.

Sandro smiled again. 'So, what is it?'

'It's safer if I don't tell you,' I said.

He shrugged his shoulders. 'Don't you trust me?'

'It's not that I don't trust you,' I said. 'I just don't want to put you in danger.'

'But you want to talk to this man, yes?' I nodded. 'So some-body must lead you there?'

'I can find him on my own.'

He laughed this time. 'Just like you could row a boat on your own.'

I conceded. The boy was right, for I would need his help to find my way about the muddled confusion of Castello. 'Very well,' I said. 'His name is Gianni Ricci. He lives in the campo next to the church of Sant'Antonio.'

The boy laughed again. The food I'd given him had put some colour in his cheeks and some strength into his arms and legs, though he retained the disjointed, unstable gait of a walking carcass. 'Gianni Ricci,' he said, as if he was pondering the name. 'I wonder if he has curly hair?'

'No. He's bald,' I said. 'And apparently his head is covered in a great birthmark.' For some reason this caused Sandro to laugh so hard that he nearly dropped the oar, and I wondered, in retro-spect, if I had mistranslated the word.

The boy's laughter caused me to smile at first, but then another wave of pity engulfed me. Looking at the thinness of his arms and the ragged clothes on his back, I guessed that nobody cared about him in this city, since he slept in the street and he washed in the lagoon. Once I had departed from Venice with my mother, the doge's palace would discover his treachery, and then who would protect him?

I cleared my throat. 'So, Sandro,' I said, 'I have an offer for you.'

He stopped laughing. 'Oh yes?'

'I would like you to join my household. I will train you as my squire, and you can live with me and my mother, when we leave Venice.' I decided not to divulge that this departure would be happening in less than two days.

My gesture was not received with the gratitude I might have expected, however. In fact, Sandro's face fell so greatly that you might think I had offered to buy one of his legs.

'I just want to help you, Sandro. That's all. I can't leave you alone in Venice.'

'I was alone before you came here,' he said.

'Don't you want somebody to care for you?'

The boy tensed, and I knew that my words had struck a small blow. 'I don't know,' he said, after a long pause.

'Will you think about it, at least?'

He nodded solemnly and would not speak to me for the rest of the journey.

It was dark as I knocked at the door of Ca' Bearpark, to be admitted by Giovanni. Sandro stayed outside in the street and hid in a doorway. I noticed immediately that Giovanni had combed his hair and changed his filthy clothes for a clean tunic and hose, but he still possessed the pale, drawn face of a man who's just recovered from the sweating sickness.

'Have you found the murderer, Oswald?' he asked me by way of a greeting.

I nodded.

'Do you have him with you?' he said as he looked past my shoulder.

'Yes, I've asked him to wait outside.'

Giovanni gasped. 'Really?'

'Of course not, Giovanni! I need to speak to Bearpark straight away.'

The young Venetian frowned, a little offended at my joke. 'I think my master is sleeping.'

'I don't care,' I said, pushing past. 'I will see him now.'

Bearpark wasn't sleeping, though his eyes remained shut at my entrance. 'What do you want, de Lacy?' he mumbled as I approached the bed. 'Why are you disturbing me in the middle of the night?'

'I need you to provide me with a male servant,' I said. 'Somebody who's strong and able to make an arrest.'

The old man opened his eyes. 'So, you've found him then, have you?' he said. 'Who is it?'

'You were right, Bearpark. The murderer was Enrico's lover.'

He fell back against his bolster with a long groan. 'I told you to look for him, didn't I? You should have followed my instructions in the first place.' He struggled to sit up and Giovanni had to run to his aid. 'So, what's his name then?'

I hesitated. 'Just provide me with a man and let me bring the murderer to you.' I cleared my throat. 'When you've released Filomena to me, then you can have him.'

Bearpark huffed at this. 'Indeed?'

'Those are my terms,' I said.

'Oh very well, very well.' Bearpark waved his hand impatiently at Giovanni. 'Find de Lacy a man from the household.'

'There are no men left,' whispered Giovanni.

'What's that?' said Bearpark, holding a hand to his ear. 'Speak up. Speak up!'

'There are no men left in the household,' boomed Giovanni.

Bearpark frowned. 'What do you mean?' he snapped. 'What happened to them all?'

'They've all gone to other houses, master. There are no servants left here apart from myself and the old woman.'

Bearpark wiped his lips on the sheet, taking a moment to absorb this piece of information. 'I see,' he said, before clearing his throat with some determination. 'Then de Lacy may have one of the guards at my wife's cell.' He looked to Giovanni. 'They're still here, I take it?'

Giovanni nodded.

Bearpark then turned to me. 'I'll send the man to your inn at dawn.'

'No. I want to go now,' I told him.

Bearpark puffed his lips. 'Impossible. The man will want more money for wandering about Venice in the pitch black, and I'm already paying him and the other fellow enough, just to sit outside a woman's door.'

'The murderer might escape if we delay.'

'Then go and catch him yourself tonight,' said Bearpark. 'I'm not stopping you.'

'You know that I can't.'

'Then wait until dawn.' He closed his eyes again. 'Now leave an old man to sleep.'

When Sandro and I finally returned to the Fondaco, we both crept up the back stairs, even though the guards from the doge's palace were nowhere to be seen. I suggested that the boy join us in the bedchamber to sleep, but Sandro refused to step inside the room, and equally Mother refused to let such a dirty urchin past the threshold. In the end it was agreed that Sandro would sleep at the top of the servants' stairwell, so I gave him some of my supper and then retired to my own bed. The day had drained my spirit of any remaining energy, and I thought I might close my eyes and sleep for days. I fell into a contented slumber, and, for the first time in many months, I dreamt of Mary.

This contentment was false comfort, however. It was nothing more than a temporary truce before the true battle began.

Chapter Thirty-Three

After Mary's death, I took great trouble in commissioning her tomb. She would have a stone sarcophagus that would stand in its own alcove at one end of our family chapel. It would be raised upon a tall plinth decorated with acanthus and vine leaves, and accompanied by an array of carved mourners at her feet. Its lid would bear an effigy of Mary as she looked upon our wedding day. Beautiful and serene. In addition, I would also design a tomb for myself, and upon my own death we would lie, side by side, like the kings and queens of England.

Mother thought the whole exercise was a foolish waste of money, and didn't keep her feelings to herself. She joined me at the chapel the day that the tomb arrived. It had been hastily carved, and I was not satisfied with the standard of workmanship, so Mother did not catch me in the best of moods.

She walked about the chest, running her finger along the scrolled margin and then stopping to scrutinised the carved face that stared up at the vaulted wooden ceiling of the chapel with its painted eyes. Both Mother and I knew that this effigy looked nothing like Mary. We exchanged a glance, but she thought better of saying anything.

She tapped the chest and then stepped back. 'Very good, Oswald. Very good. A fine tomb for your wife.'

'Thank you, Mother. I'm certainly pleased with it,' I lied.

She cleared her throat. 'And when do you hope to move Mary's body here?'

'I don't know,' I said, feeling my heart begin to thump. 'I haven't decided yet.'

'Well, you should get on with it. Having gone to all this expense. There's no point leaving her in the graveyard.'

My chest tightened, as the sadness once again threatened to incapacitate me.

Mother must have sensed an imminent attack of grief, for she suddenly clapped loudly. 'Very good, Oswald. Will you bring Hugh to the ceremony?'

Once again I found it difficult to speak.

'The boy should see his own mother interred in this . . .' she waved her hand over the chest '. . . this sarcophagus.'

'I don't know. He's just a newly born infant. He wouldn't understand what's happening.'

'Even so. I think the boy should come,' she said. I went to argue, but she interrupted with a great sigh. 'You really should pay Hugh more attention, Oswald. He is your son, after all.'

'He's well enough, isn't he? You've employed a nursemaid for him.'

'Yes, but he still needs the attention of his father.'

I gazed back at Mary's tomb. How could I admit it? That I blamed this child for Mary's death. 'I've been too busy, Mother. This memorial has taken up all of my time.'

Something in this statement riled her. 'You know. I really don't believe that Mary would have wanted all this fuss, Oswald. I'm sure a brass plate upon the floor would have satisfied her tastes.'

'I don't think so,' I said, turning upon her sharply. 'It would not have sufficed at all.'

She frowned. 'Come along, Oswald. This great tomb is for your own benefit, not Mary's. She would have laughed at such nonsense.'

'That's not true.'

'Yes it is,' said Mother. 'The girl was never fond of artifice and display. I had a hard enough job getting her to brush her hair when she was a child, let alone adorn it with pins and ribbons. And do you remember how she refused to wear my turquoise necklace at your wedding?'

I leant against the stone of the chest and tried not to be provoked by these misjudged reminiscences. 'The necklace was too heavy for her.'

Mother made another of her small huffs, indicating that she found my last statement to be ridiculous. 'I find the necklace light enough, and I am a very delicate creature.'

She was provoking my anger. 'Why don't you go back to the house, Mother?'

'Not unless you come with me.' She gave an exaggerated shudder. 'It's too cold in this chapel. You will catch a chill in here. Or worse.'

'I don't care.'

She fixed me with a stare. 'Well, you should care. What is the point of inviting illness? Your wife is dead already, Oswald. For goodness sake, don't follow her into the grave.'

'Leave me alone, Mother.'

'I will not! You spend far too much time in here. Lamenting the dead.'

'It brings me comfort.'

'There are better memorials to your dead wife than this,' she said.

'Such as?'

She threw up her hands in despair. 'Your son, Oswald! Your living, breathing son.'

That night Mother brought the baby to me, wrapped tightly in his linen bands. The child's nursemaid trailed behind, keeping her eyes to the floor, shuffling like a penitent. I looked up to see that Hugh wore a bonnet edged with lace and embroidered with the letters H, D and C — *Henry de Caburn*. The bonnet had once belonged to Clemence's son, and must have been a passed-down gift from my sister. This pricked at my heart, for Hugh should have been wearing his own cap, embroidered with his own initials.

Mother held the small package towards me. 'Come on, Oswald. Hold Hugh. He's just been fed.' His nurse dithered by the door, unable to leave. Though she kept perfectly still, I could feel her anxiety radiating across the room.

I turned away. 'I'm tired. I'll do it tomorrow.'

Mother tried again, this time dropping the child into my lap, and then quickly stepping back before I had a chance to object. At this very moment, the nurse stepped forward, ready to leap to the child's aid, should I fail to hold him. Their movements were like the opposing steps of a dance.

I grasped the boy and rested his head into the crook of my arm. 'I can see you will give me no peace,' I said.

Mother smiled. 'There you are. See. You might enjoy spending a few moments with him.'

I looked up at their expectant faces, and my irritation melted a little. They were a meddlesome pair, but there was no malice in their actions. 'You can leave me now,' I said.

This caused both women to stiffen. 'Are you sure?' said Mother, exchanging a glance with the nursemaid. 'Hugh may start to cry again.'

'I thought he'd just been fed?'

She opened her mouth to say something, but the words faded to a short cough. 'Very well, Oswald. We will be in the solar. Call us immediately, if you need help. And keep the child's hat upon his head. And don't hold him too close to the fire.'

The nursemaid then tried to whisper something into Mother's ear, but she dismissed her with a wave, and when the woman appeared reluctant to leave the room, Mother gave her a forceful shove in the back.

I was left alone with my son. This tiny piece of creation that I had cut from Mary's womb. A fragment of sleeping humanity.

I wanted to care for him.

I wanted to love him.

But then I mustered the courage to look down upon his face. I pulled back the lace at the side of his bonnet, and I did not see the face of a sleeping baby. Instead two limpid eyes stared back at me from within their sockets of wrinkled skin. The nostrils were large and flat to the face, and the mouth was wide and lipless within a whiskered muzzle.

When I screamed, the thing screamed back at me, unsealing its jaws to reveal a vast array of teeth that were punctuated on either side by two fangs. I would have thrown it into the fire, but Mother raced in and grabbed the bundle from me.

'What are you doing, Oswald?' she yelled at me. 'Why are you screaming like that at your own child?'

'It's not a child. Can't you see it?' I said. 'It has the face of a monkey.'

Chapter Thirty-Four

Bearpark sent the guard to our inn at first light, as promised — a tall, strongly built man who appeared to bear me a grudge, though we had only just met. I ignored this mysterious hostility and told him to wait by the door as I raised Sandro from his improvised bed at the top of the servants' stairwell.

We then used the back staircase again to leave the Fondaco, before making our way across the city towards the *sestiere* of Castello. It was no longer raining at least, but a thick mist had descended on the city, bleaching the colour from the houses and obscuring our path. It was now that I was most grateful for Sandro's knowledge of Venice, though the boy was a little sullen and uncommunicative that morning. He led us quietly through the alleys and alongside the canals, and I felt completely lost until the great granite Columns of Justice rose up through the vapours like a forgotten temple.

After leaving the open space of the Piazzetta, we were soon in the warren of Castello, negotiating our way past mules, hand-carts, and women with baskets of fish. I did not look down to see what we were treading upon, though its rank perfume soon reached my nostrils. The guard followed us in silence, until we reached the church of Sant'Antonio, and I began to wonder how we might find one man in this morass of people, but once again Sandro came to my assistance. He asked me for a small coin and then waved it discreetly in the air, making a gesture that meant something to somebody, though I would hardly have noticed it. Soon another, equally thin and ragged boy appeared from a narrow gap between the tall buildings. He tried to grasp the coin from Sandro's hand, but my small friend was quicker and stronger, and held onto his prize with determination. This new boy would have to earn the money.

They held their heads together in conversation. A conversation that was punctuated with pointing and shoving, but which ended cordially enough with a handshake and the passing over of the precious coin.

Sandro then whispered to me. 'He's told me where to find Ricci. Come with me.' The guard and I then followed him along alleys so thin that the red dust from the brick rubbed off onto our cloaks, then through courtyards full of chickens and pigs, and small, shoeless children, and across bridges that were nothing more than lengths of decaying wood balanced over a ditch. Even my mute and hostile friend, the guard, decided to complain at this point, muttering that he would demand extra payment from Bearpark to compensate for the filthy nature of this assignment.

Just when I wondered if we could be pulled any further into this tangled muddle, Sandro tugged at my cloak, stood on his tiptoes, and then told me that we had reached our destination – Gianni Ricci lived with his mother in the first house to our right – a tall building, where a new floor had been built on top of an existing home, making the lower part of this house appear as if it were being pushed down into the mud of the lagoon.

I told the guard and Sandro to move out of sight, while I knocked at the low door, and waited for somebody to answer. The guard followed my order with a weariness, merely leaning against the wellhead at the centre of the *campo*, folding his arms and staring at the grey sky above us.

At my third knock, a woman opened a shutter at the window beside the door. Her hair was drawn back from her face with a white scarf, and her skin was as lined as a patch of clay soil after a long, hot summer. 'What do you want?' she said, looking at me with suspicion.

'I'm looking for Gianni Ricci.'

She slammed the shutter, so I knocked again, and this time she did not answer. Now I called the guard forward, and ordered him to kick the door open. He did so without the slightest hesitation or trouble, and then we ran inside the decrepit house to find Ricci. Ricci's mother followed us as we searched each room, screaming at us continually to get out – but in the whole house we found no sign of the man.

'Where is Gianni?' I asked his mother, when she had finally stopped screaming. The guard wanted to shake an answer from the woman, but I ordered him to step away. He obeyed this command with a foot-dragging reluctance, as if I had ruined a favourite game.

'Who are you?' she demanded to know. 'And what do you want with my son?'

'That doesn't matter. Where is he?'

'I don't know.'

The guard advanced again, so I held up my hand to signify that I did not yet require his services. 'Does your son live here with you?' I asked.

'Yes. But he didn't come home last night.'

'Why not?'

She regarded me for a moment with wary eyes. 'I didn't see what happened. I only heard the story from my neighbours.'

'What story is this?'

'They said he was taken by the Signori.'

I felt my stomach churn and my heart thump. 'The Signori di Notte? Are you sure?'

'Yes! That's what I said, didn't I?' She roared. 'People say that my son is a sodomite. That's why he was taken. But it's a wicked lie! Gianni is due to be married in a month.'

This was a bad turn of events. How had the Signori reached Gianni before I had? I hadn't told anybody his name, apart from Sandro. And then the painful realisation hit me, as I ran back along the low passageway of the house and looked with desperation into every room. I had put my trust in the boy, but Sandro was gone. He had betrayed me.

I strode with all haste through Castello towards Ca' Bearpark, with the guard at my heels, muttering that he still wanted to be paid, no matter that we hadn't made an arrest. I barely heard his words, for I could only think about Ricci and what he might confess to under torture – for I knew how quickly a simple length of rope and a set of steps could prise an answer from a man. If Ricci admitted to spying with Enrico, then Bearpark was doomed. I needed to warn the old man, but not because I cared for his fate, but because I needed to secure Filomena's release, before her husband was dragged to the doge's palace and then thrown into the *Pozzi*. Whether Filomena wanted to leave Venice with me, or whether she wanted to stay in this city, she would not remain imprisoned in Bearpark's storeroom.

We thumped at the door to Ca' Bearpark, but nobody answered at first, and I wondered if the Signori di Notte had already visited, but then the elderly maid opened the door a crack, and we were able to push past and run up to the door of Bearpark's bedchamber. In the whole of this twisting, meandering house, we didn't meet another soul.

I didn't bother knocking. In fact, I had half expected to fling open the doors to find another empty room – but I was wrong, for there was Bearpark, lying in his bed like a corpse.

He woke with a shock as I prodded him. 'De Lacy?' Then he smiled and clasped my hands in his own. For once his skin felt warm and supple. 'What are you doing here?'

'I have to warn you, Bearpark. The guards from the doge's palace may be here at any moment. You must release Monna Filomena straight away. And I think you should leave Venice.'

'I can't leave Venice!' he said, his voice trembling and weak. 'This is my home.' His eyes bore the bemused stare of a very old man.

Now that I was nearer, I could see a streak of blood upon his forehead. Not only this, his lip was swollen. 'What happened to you?' I asked.

He touched his face, and then looked at the blood on his fingers. 'I was attacked, de Lacy.'

'Who attacked you?' I asked.

He became agitated. Twisting his head from side to side, as if he had suddenly remembered the incident. 'Are they here?' He looked about the room with the eyes of a madman, until they landed upon the tall frame of the guard, and he let out the most terrifying shriek. 'Have they returned? Tell me you haven't brought them here with you!'

I laid my hand on his chest, in an attempt to quell his agitation. 'It's just the man you employed to guard Monna Filomena's door, Bearpark. Calm yourself.'

He relaxed immediately, and then squinted, in order to focus better on my face. When he still couldn't see me, he reached instinctively to the table beside the bed to find his spectacles, but his fingers alighted onto a broken frame and two circles of smashed glass.

'What happened here, Bearpark?' I said, taking the spectacles from his hand, in case he cut himself. 'Please. Tell me who attacked you.'

The old man only placed his hands against his bloodied cheeks and laughed like a lunatic until he started to heave, causing the guard to edge away towards the door in alarm. It was at this moment that the door opened, allowing the man to rush out as Bernard and his sister Margery ran in.

On seeing my face, Bernard stopped in front of me and performed one of his most expressive bows. 'Lord Somershill. Isn't this terrible?' He then waved towards his sister. 'Margery here has offered her services as a nurse to poor Master Bearpark, as he is covered in the most monstrous wounds.'

'Will somebody please tell me what has happened?' The pilgrim gave one of his awkward smiles, as if he didn't quite agree with something I'd just said, but didn't have the nerve to say so. 'Why is there blood on Master Bearpark's face?' I demanded. 'And who smashed his spectacles?'

Bernard gave his sister a sideways glance. 'You don't know, my lord?' I shook my head, causing Bernard to cough and exchange a look with Margery. 'Poor Master Bearpark was attacked by his wife.'

'What do you mean?' I said. 'Monna Filomena is locked in a storeroom.'

Bernard loudly sucked in air. 'I'm afraid to say that she's escaped, my lord.' He then looked to the ceiling, as if embarrassed to utter the next sentence. 'With the help of her lover.'

'What?' I shook my head, as if a rush of blood to my brain would help. 'I mean. Which lover? What are you talking about?'

'It is the clerk, Giovanni.' Bernard crossed himself. 'To think that the pair were the murderers, all along. Though Margery and I always maintained that the killer was connected to this household, didn't we, Margery?' He heaved a long sigh. 'Though we never guessed at such treachery.'

Now the floor felt as if it were undulating beneath my feet, and it was just as if I were back on that ship, crossing the sea from Felixstowe to Flanders. 'Giovanni?' I said in consternation. 'No, no. I don't believe it.'

Bernard crossed himself, and then swiftly offered me a chair. 'I'm afraid it's true, my lord. If Margery and I had not accosted them in this very bedchamber, then they would have killed poor Master Bearpark as well. They were upon him like a pair of dogs.' He waved to Margery, indicating that I was in need of some wine.

I fell onto the seat, but refused the sweet Malmsy wine that Margery offered me. 'I don't understand, Bernard,' I said. 'How did Filomena escape? There were guards on her door.'

'But there was only one guard this morning, my lord. Once the other man was sent to you at the Fondaco.'

I groaned. 'Don't tell me that Giovanni managed to overcome this man all alone?'

'No. I believe that Giovanni bribed him. He had the key to Master Bearpark's secret strongbox, you see.' Bernard dropped his voice to a whisper. 'I'm afraid he has also stolen a good deal of money.'

At these words, Bearpark coughed so violently that Margery ran to his aid and offered him a bowl in which to vomit. Thankfully he only produced a trail of bloodied dribble that caused Margery to flinch as she wiped his chin.

'I don't understand any of this,' I said, to nobody in particular. 'It doesn't make sense.'

'I know, my lord. It is a terrible shock,' said Bernard, patting me lightly upon the shoulder. 'An unfathomable sin. 'Tis a shame that Margery has no more of her miraculous St Thomas's water, as I'm sure it would revive your spirits.'

'But Filomena and Giovanni hated each other,' I said, still incredulous.

Bernard sighed, and then drew closer once more, to whisper into my ear. 'I won't speak too loudly, as I'm afraid this whole episode has caused Margery the most terrible upset. You see, it seems that Giovanni and Monna Filomena were sweethearts on the island of Burano.'

I thought back to my visit to Burano and remembered how Giovanni was known to the islanders. 'Oh God,' I held my head in my hands and groaned aloud.

Bernard continued. 'Giovanni brought the girl to Venice when they decided to marry. But then it seems that Master Bearpark saw the girl himself and fell in love with her, and instead of tell-ing him the truth, the two of them hatched a plan of betrayal.' Bernard sucked his teeth. 'No doubt they hoped Master Bearpark would die quickly, and then they could marry.' He clasped his hands together and then wrung them repeatedly in agitation. 'But, of course, Enrico Bearpark stood in their way.'

'Are you saying that they killed Enrico?'

'No, no. That was Monna Filomena's brother. They paid him to carry out the murder, I believe.' Bernard crossed himself again. 'What was that man's name, now? I always found him quite congenial, as it happens.'

'Adolpho Bredani.'

'Yes. That's the fellow.'

'But then he was murdered as well?' I said. 'Do you mean to tell me that Monna Filomena also killed her own brother?'

Bernard continued to wring his hands. 'I'm not fully in possession of the facts, my lord. But it seems that the evil pair must have paid somebody else to kill Bredani. Perhaps the man was threatening to reveal the truth? I don't know. But anyway, as I said before, Giovanni was in control of a lot of Master Bearpark's money, so he was not without the means to fund such a crime.'

'And Filomena's child? Is she Giovanni's?'

Bernard nodded, solemnly, and then crossed himself.

This whole sorry tale now fell into place, like quoits landing upon a wooden pin. The enmity between Filomena and Giovanni had been a sham all along, and I had been deceived as greatly as Bearpark. No wonder Filomena had refused my proposal that we leave Venice together. This had been her plan all along.

I lifted my head from my hands and looked about the room, trying to catch a skein of fresh air from within the stuffiness of the place. 'How do you know all this?' I asked Bernard, but the man was frowning at a distant thought and ignored me. Now I grasped him by the sleeve and shook him. 'Bernard! Answer my question. How do you know this?'

The man focussed his eyes upon me. 'I'm afraid that the pair told Bearpark the whole story, before they attacked him.' He crossed himself. 'I believe that they wanted to torment the poor man. I would say they were rather proud of themselves, you see.

It was their revenge.' Bernard looked to Bearpark's heaving frame with pity. 'Poor Master Bearpark. He was able to relate the whole story to us, but now it seems he is losing his mind.'

I needed to get out of this room and this house, for my shock was turning to rage. I was angry with both Filomena and Giovanni, but more than that, I was angry with myself – for I had wasted many months in Venice, imagining that I was falling in love with this woman.

As I reached the door, Bernard caught up with me and placed a hand upon my shoulder. 'I'm so sorry, my lord. Are you well enough to return to your inn alone?'

I declined his assistance, but as my foot crossed the threshold, I thought about Gianni Ricci's arrest by the Signori di Notte, and wondered if I should warn Bernard and Margery to expect a visit. Then I looked back to Bearpark as the old man stared blankly at the ceiling, and decided that there was no reason to make this disclosure. Not even the Signori could torture a man who had lost his mind.

I opened the door. 'Goodbye, Bernard.'

'Will we see you again, my lord?'

'No.'

'But surely we will be sailing in the same flotilla to the Holy Land?'

'I'm not going to Jerusalem,' I told him. 'I'm returning to England.'

'Indeed?'

'Yes. I have a son there. A young boy who is nearly two years old.' I felt my chest tighten. 'I've been away for too long.'

Chapter Thirty-Five

It had started to rain again, and a punishing wind chased me through the narrow alleys of San Marco and buffeted me beside the wider canals. I felt sick with anger, mostly at myself, for in this whole tale of deception and treachery, it was my own betrayal that stung with the most pain. I had abandoned a child. My own child – when I had promised my dying wife that I would love and cherish him. It was time to remedy my mistake. I would return to England with all haste, but there were no straight paths in this story. No easy progressions. As I turned a corner, I came face to face with my next obstacle. He put his arm across the alley and blocked my path.

'Going somewhere, de Lacy?' Vittore sneered.

'Just get out of my way,' I said, trying to push him aside.

Vittore took my arm, twisted it behind my back, and then threw me against a wall. 'Thought you'd escape from me, did you?' he said. 'Without paying your debts.'

The pain in my shoulder returned. 'No.'

'So, why didn't you tell me that you'd moved to the Fondaco dei Tedeschi?' He twisted my arm more vigorously. 'Did it slip your mind?'

I tried to kick him in the shin, but he was wearing thick leather boots, and I caused more pain to my own heels than I managed to inflict upon his leg. 'It's not Saturday yet,' I said, as he laughed at my attempts to escape. 'You'll get your money tomorrow, as promised. It doesn't matter where I'm staying.'

He drew close, and I felt the heat of his breath upon my ear. 'Tomorrow morning then, de Lacy. I'll be at the door to your inn at dawn.'

And I'll be sailing for Marseilles, I thought to myself. 'Very well, Vittore,' I said. 'Until tomorrow,' and then I shook myself free of him.

Upon reaching my chamber at the Fondaco, I tried to open the door, but found it locked. I knocked softly and waited, but nobody answered. Surely Mother was still in the room? I knocked again, and this time heard a shuffling from behind the door. A strange, quaking voice asked me to identify myself. It spoke in Venetian.

When the door finally opened a crack, I forced my way into the chamber to be confronted by a person dressed in the flowing gown and white turban of a Persian merchant.

'Where's my mother?' I demanded.

My question was met with a giggle. It was a familiar sound. 'Ha! See how I've duped you. My own son.'

I quickly shut the door behind me. 'God's bones, Mother! What are you doing?'

She spun around, so that I could admire her outfit to its full advantage. 'You told me to wear a disguise,' she said. 'Remember?'

I folded my arms. 'I haven't got time for such stupidity. We need to pack and leave.'

'Don't speak to me like that, Oswald. I've been ready to leave for hours. It's you that has caused the delay, with all your investigating.' She looked behind me. 'And where's that little urchin you adopted? I hope he's not trying to get into the room again.'

'I lost him,' I said.

'Oh. I see.' She looked at me quizzically. 'And do you hope to find him again?'

My answer was emphatic. 'No.'

She removed the turban from her head. 'Did you clear Monna Filomena's name?'

I turned my face from hers. 'No. I didn't.'

'So, she's guilty then. Just as I suspected.' She raised her eyebrows. 'She'll hang for this, you know. There's no sentimentality in Venice, Oswald. I've seen plenty of women dangling from the gallows. In fact, there was even a girl locked in that cage, the last time I was in the Piazzetta.'

I threw myself onto the bed and let my arms stretch out across the blanket. 'They can't hang Filomena, unless they can catch her,' I said.

Mother looked at me with puzzlement. 'Oh yes?'

'Because she escaped.'

'But I thought Bearpark had locked her in a guarded room.'

'She had some help.'

Mother sat down on the bed next to me. 'Was it you?'

I sat up and rested on my elbow. 'No, Mother. It was Giovanni.'

'I see,' she said. 'I think you'd better tell me the whole story, don't you?'

I lay back on the bed and stared at the wooden struts that ran across the ceiling, whilst a rain storm beat at the shutters. 'Monna Filomena and Giovanni were lovers.'

Mother gasped. 'Lovers? Are you sure about that. They never had a kind word for each other. And as for all those conversations that I overheard.'

'What conversations?'

She began to reel the cloth of her turban into a roll. 'They were always arguing, Oswald.' She wandered over to the pitcher and poured some water into a low basin. 'Of course, they pretended that they were discussing the weather, or the price of flour, but he was always calling her a whore, and she was always calling him a bastard.'

'Oh yes?' I said, lifting my head a little. 'And you could understand that, could you?'

'Yes,' she said, a little defensively.

'So, what are the Venetian words for whore and bastard then?'

Mother splashed some water onto her face. 'Are you testing me, Oswald?' She turned to look at me. 'Am I one of those witnesses you question at your manorial courts? Or perhaps you think me a foolish woman? An old crone who's lost her mind and pretends to have mastered a foreign tongue?'

'You can't have heard them correctly,' I said, falling back against the bed.

She wiped her eyes with the end of the turban. 'I'm neither deaf, nor stupid. I know what I heard, so you either believe me, or you don't.'

I turned onto my side, but her words would not leave my mind. Had Filomena and Giovanni truly called each other such insulting names? Mother's fluency in Venetian was much improved – but was it likely that she had understood such terms? And if she had heard them correctly, then these were not the names that lovers would utter to one another. The rain continued to lash against the shutters, and a cold breeze squeezed itself into the room and whistled under the door – loud enough to drown out even the deep, resounding voices of the German merchants in the next room. I knew enough of their tongue to know that they had been arguing about the bad weather, and whether it was safe to set sail for Candia the next day.

Mother presented me with a pair of muddy boots. 'You should put these in the bottom of your chest, Oswald. Or they'll cover your clean clothes in dirt.'

I grunted in response.

The wind blew the shutters open with a crash, and a bitterly cold wind invaded the room, so I had no choice but to raise myself from the bed and close them again. As I looked down onto the canal, I could see that the bottom steps of the water gate were now flooded. A few small boats bobbed about feverishly at their posts on the jetty, and the Rialto Bridge was barely a dark smudge.

Mother looked over my shoulder. 'It's a relief we're not sailing from Venice, isn't it, Oswald?' she said. 'This storm looks as if it will set in for days.' Then she rubbed her back and gave one of her groans. 'Not that I'm looking forward to sitting in the back of that cart again. Last time the juddering was enough to sieve the flesh from my bones.'

I looked away guiltily, wondering whether I should use this opportunity to admit the truth – that we were, indeed, leaving this city by sea? On the other hand, an early admission of this truth would give her too much notice to object. Then again, if I left the announcement to the last minute, Mother might be like one of those sheep that stubbornly refuses to board a river barge. I almost imagined her bolting through the Molo and drawing all kinds of unwanted attention – and we could hardly afford to be noticed, not when we were fleeing Venice with only hours to spare.

My mind was made up. I would tell her now, but as I turned back, I found she was leaning over my chest and lifting a pair of socks into the air, exclaiming at their dirtiness. As she did this, something fell to the floor with a thud. It was the purse I had stolen from Burano.

'What's this?' she said, picking up the small, leather pouch.

I rushed across the room and snatched the purse from her hand. 'It's nothing,' I said quickly.

'Really?' she said. 'You seem rather concerned about it, seeing as it's unimportant.'

'It's just some money that I've had hidden,' I said. 'For emergencies.'

She looked at me oddly. 'So how much do you have in there then?'

'I'm not sure,' I said with an unconvincing shrug.

'Then let's count it.'

I hesitated, for I had shied away, again and again, from looking at these coins, but why shouldn't I count them? What did it matter now that I had stolen them – for, how else would I pay for our passage to Marseilles? How else would I begin my journey back to England?

And so, for the first time, I shook the golden coins from the purse, let them fall onto the bed, and then took the time to study each one of them properly. They no longer prompted shame, only hope and joy. The joy of seeing Hugh's face again. I let Mother admire the golden coins, before I dropped them, one by one, back into the purse, but it was then that I saw it. Small, dull, and snagged onto the silk lining of the purse. I heaved a sigh as I examined it more closely, for I could not leave this city yet. Venice held one last claw in my heart.

Chapter Thirty-Six

I didn't knock at the door of Ca' Bearpark. Instead I climbed over the high wall from the street into the courtyard, and then dropped down onto the stones below. Thankfully my ascent went unnoticed, as nobody was venturing out of doors now that the storm was raging, and all the shutters of the neighbouring houses were firmly shut. Even the rats and stray dogs of Venice had forsaken the driving rain, finding some sheltered crevice in which to hide.

The courtyard was empty, so I quickly ascended the external staircase and then crept through the *piano nobile*. None of the doors was locked, and everywhere I met only darkness and silence – no sign even of the old maid who usually attended Bearpark. There were no lanterns or fires, and Ca' Bearpark felt as abandoned as a plague house after the Pestilence.

My thoughts turned immediately to John Bearpark, so I headed up his personal staircase, making sure to tread as softly as possible on each step, though when I reached his room I found it to be as deserted as the rest of the house. There was no sign of Bearpark at all, apart from his spectacles, which lay on the floor, next to his broken hourglass – the sands of time having spilled out into a small, conical heap.

I hesitated, deciding now to check upon Bernard and Margery's bedchamber. Once I had scurried back down the stairs to the *piano nobile*, I discerned a thin light from the crack beneath their closed door. I knocked gently, but heard nothing, so I pushed my way in to find another empty chamber. I noticed immediately that Bernard's cloak was hung upon a peg. Of more interest was the white habit of a Dominican priest, slung across the bed. As I lifted this garment for further inspection, a pilgrim's badge fell to the floor. It bore an image of the five geese of Saint Werburga and had once been sewn upon the sleeve of this same habit, alongside a whole collection of other badges.

I dropped the habit back onto the bed when I heard a low scream from somewhere below me in the bowels of Ca' Bearpark. I raced down the stairs to the courtyard, holding my cloak above my head to shield my face from the storm, for now the rain fell in angry batons, bouncing from the flooded courtyard in bursting crowns of water. Reaching the water gate, I could see the canal had risen so rapidly that the second step was already submerged, but then again we were only hours away from the high tide now, when this whole floor risked flooding. The gates were open, and outside in the canal, a wide cargo boat was moored against the side of the house – the type of boat that usually transported stones and timber about the lagoon or into the River Po. It caught my eye, not only because it was an unusual sight in this side canal, but also because I recognised the wide bow, and the red, square sail tied to its single mast. As the wind inflated and then deflated a heavy oiled sheet that covered the hull, I knew where I had seen this vessel before. It had been at the Molo, only the previous day.

The screaming came again – weaker this time, but not drowned out completely by the ferocity of the storm. The light was poor, and I didn't have a lantern, but I proceeded without much difficulty since I knew my way about this house without the need for a candle. Creeping along the passageway, I passed the servants' quarters, Giovanni's bureau, and the room where I had inspected Enrico's body, until I felt the cool, unpleasant sensation of water in my boots. I was heading for the passageway that was hidden behind the hanging carpet. Giovanni had told me that the small door at the end of this passageway only led to a cesspit. He had told me that it was a forgotten door, an unimportant, redundant access to the neighbouring house, but now I suspected it had found a different use completely.

I located the carpet quickly enough, lifted it from the wall, and then crept along this short passage to reach the door at the other end. This time it was not locked. Instead, it gave way at my push, opening far enough for me to look past into a dark chamber, across which I could see the shape of two people against the far wall. The air down here was poisonous and suffocating, caused by the waste matter that floated about in the water – Giovanni hadn't lied when he said it was a cesspit. I wanted to cough – but I held my breath, as the screaming came again, emanating from a second chamber that led from this first one. The door to this room was shut, but lines of light crept out between the gaps about the door-frame.

Holding my nose against the fumes, I waded across the room to reach the two people on the other side, pushing my way past a soup of floating filth. When I reached them, I found that their mouths were gagged with linen rags and their hands were tied with a rope that was then fastened to a metal ring on the wall. Now that I was closer I could see that it was Giovanni and Filomena. Giovanni was conscious, but Filomena seemed dazed, making only the lowest murmur when I shook her.

I had untied their gags, when the screaming came again from the next room. This time it sounded like the panicked, high-pitched squeal of an animal about to be slaughtered, and I could not ignore it. It was pity for this person that moved me to act without thinking of the consequences – but it was a mistake. Another blunder.

I forced the door open, and was met by a sight that I will never forget. This was not the person I had expected to see on the other side of this door. It was John Bearpark, no longer the weakened invalid lying upon his deathbed. Instead, his sleeves were rolled up and he was beating a man with a long ebony pole. His victim's face was bloodied and torn – just as Enrico's had been, but I could still make out a bald head, covered with a large purple birthmark. This was Gianni Ricci.

In those few moments, I imagined that this whole tableau was a horrific vision. The flooding chamber was another twisted creation of my ailing mind, and if I concentrated hard enough, then the whole illusion would dissolve. I even tried to pinch myself, but the sight before me was horribly real, and suddenly the whole sordid story of my investigation into Enrico's murder made perfect sense.

The old man stood back – shocked to see me. 'What are you doing here, de Lacy?' he said. 'This is none of your business.'

'Let this man go,' I told him.

Bearpark growled, as the weak glow of the candlelight illuminated his face and lent him the air of a madman. 'Keep out of this. It's between me and the man who killed my grandson.'

I waded through the water and tried to grab the pole, but Bearpark was surprisingly strong and resisted me. 'Didn't think I had it in me, did you? Well I'm still as strong as an ox,' he said. 'Once a soldier, always a soldier!' To prove this point, he then shoved me away, causing me to fall onto my knees. 'Did you think I was going to wait until dawn for you to bring him here?' He laughed. 'A Bearpark seeks his own revenge.'

I struggled back to my feet. 'But this man didn't kill Enrico, did he?' I said.

'Of course he did. You found him for me.'

'No, Bearpark. It was you. You are the murderer.'

Bearpark let Ricci go at my words, allowing the man to scamper away into a corner, where he crouched with his arms over his head. 'Have you lost your mind, de Lacy?' Bearpark managed to squeeze out another laugh. 'Again.'

'You don't fool me,' I said. 'I know what happened. It was you who forced Enrico to take a lover at the Arsenale, wasn't it?'

Bearpark's face darkened. 'You don't know what you're talking about.'

I pointed to Ricci's cringing form. 'You wanted Enrico to use this man to discover secrets about the shipyard. Secrets that you could then sell to the enemies of Venice.'

'I think you'd better shut your mouth,' he said.

'I thought it was just Bernard and Margery behind this. But now I see that it was you as well. All along. The three of you are spies.'

Bearpark let out a great laugh at this. 'Do you hear that, Bernard?' he shouted into the darkness. 'Lord Somershill thinks that we are spies.'

At these words, two men crept forward from the gloom. One was indeed Bernard, though he looked very different to his usual self. Gone was the foolish distant smile. Instead he looked at me with a sly malice. His companion's face was familiar, but this was not Margery.

Bernard raised his eyebrows in a pretence at being offended by my accusation. 'Spies, eh? And why would Lord Somershill think that? I'm just a pilgrim, waiting for a galley to the Holy Land.'

'A pilgrim remembers which English port he set sail from,' I said. 'Is it Felixstowe, or is it Dover?' My accusation only seemed to amuse Bernard. 'And a pilgrim doesn't pay a servant to dispose of a murder victim,' I added.

'Dear me,' said Bernard. 'What are you talking about?'

'I found a purse of golden coins hidden at Adolpho Bredani's house on Burano.'

'And what has this purse to do with me?' he asked.

'It belonged to you.'

'How could you tell?'

'One of your pilgrim's badges was snagged to the lining.'

Bernard shook his head dismissively at my words, his amusement now turned to annoyance. 'We haven't got time for all this
nonsense, Bearpark,' he said tersely. 'Our boat is waiting outside.'

'I haven't finished with Ricci yet,' said Bearpark in response to
this order. 'I need to know if he said anything to anybody else.'

'Oh, just kill the man,' said Bernard with a wave of his hand.
'It's too late for all this. We need to get back to Fusina while the
tide is with us.' When Bearpark did not react to this suggestion,
Bernard added, 'Hurry up, or I'll get Tamas here to do it for
you.' Bernard then turned back to me, presenting his companion
with a mocking bow of his head. 'You remember Tamas, my lord.
I'm afraid he's not really a pilgrim either.'

I looked again at the man who had appeared with Bernard
from the darkness, and suddenly realised how completely I had
been gulled by a long habit, a wimple, and a vow of silence. No
wonder Mother complained about Margery's heavy feet on the
staircase, or the way she liked to sit with her legs parted. For
Margery was a man. With his hood down, and his wimple
removed, I questioned how I could ever have thought this person
was female – for Tamas's hair receded to the crown of his head,
and his jaw was square and masculine.

'So, you *are* spies then,' I said.

'I prefer to think of us as merchants,' said Bernard rather
proudly, 'trading in information.'

'Who are you selling to? Hungary?'

'I have contacts in many courts across Europe,' he boasted.
'There is always a strong market for information. Especially if it
concerns the Venetian fleet. But, you're right. In this instance,
we found that Hungary paid the best prices.' He smiled. 'War
can be such a profitable business.' His smile then faded instantly.
'Unfortunately that unpleasant letter of denunciation ruined
trade. In fact, Tamas received quite a beating when the Hungarians
heard about it. But there you are,' he said with a small sigh, 'no
business is without its risks.' He turned back to Bearpark. 'Now

come along, John. Let's clear this all up quickly, shall we?' He pointed to me and then to Ricci, who remained slumped in the corner. 'Are you sure you don't need Tamas's help here? There are two of them. And you're not as strong as you used to be.'

'No, of course not,' said Bearpark with some umbrage. 'I'll deal with this myself.'

Bernard raised an eyebrow. 'Just as you dealt with Enrico, I suppose?' he said caustically.

'Enrico was my grandson,' said Bearpark. 'He was *my* problem to solve.'

'Indeed,' said Bernard, 'but you didn't do a very good job, did you? A very messy affair, if you ask me. We don't want a repeat of that disaster, do we?'

Bearpark now rose up like an angered bull. 'How dare you speak to me like that?' he roared.

'I'll speak to you however I like,' said Bernard, not in the least bit intimidated by Bearpark's ferocity. 'You work for me, remember.' When Bearpark continued to glower, he added, 'You are too proud, John, too proud. You should have asked for some assistance from Tamas, rather than engaging that useless servant to remove the body.' Then he gave a short laugh. 'And really, you might have used your own purse of coins to pay the fellow, rather than taking one of mine. Or at least you should have checked first that it was free of any clues which might give away our identity.' Bernard turned back to me. 'That was good work, Lord Somershill. I commend you on a rigorous piece of investigation. And I might say that you also did an excellent job in tracking down the Bredani fellow for us. We had had a hard time trying to find him after Bearpark's foolish mistake in engaging the man. But then you had the excellent idea of setting up a search party.'

I thought back to the evening when Giovanni had sought me out in the *piano nobile*, to inform me that Adolpho Bredani had been found in Dorsoduro. Bernard must have been listening to our conversation, and then passed this information onto Tamas. I felt enraged at this revelation and went to throw a punch at Bernard, but Tamas intervened, pushing my face so violently against the wall that my lips could taste the damp tang of the bricks. As Tamas held me there, Bearpark returned to his assault upon Gianni Ricci with greater savagery. Behind me, the poor man wailed – his thin calls of pain were only interrupted by the cold, smacking thud of Bearpark's fist against his face. When I could stand this no longer, I took a deep breath and then kicked the heel of my boot against Tamas's shin, causing the man to jump back and curse me loudly. He was not speaking Venetian or English. Instead, his words sounded Uralic, and I guessed at Hungarian. It was no wonder that he had sworn a vow of silence to hide his true identity.

Now free of Tamas's grip, I grasped the ebony pole that Bearpark had left leaning against the wall, thrusting it at my three opponents. 'Just go,' I said. 'Get out of Venice before you kill anybody else.'

Bernard folded his arms at my words, and John Bearpark gave a scornful puff of laughter. 'You've got yourself in a bit of a corner here, haven't you?' he said.

I thrust the pole into his face. 'Is this where you killed Enrico?' I asked. 'In this stinking, flooding chamber?' I looked about me, and thought of the wetness on Enrico's hose, and the way that Enrico's calls for help would have been muffled in this hidden place. Any screams that escaped would have been drowned out by the celebrations of *Giovedi Grasso*. 'You paid Bredani to get rid of his body, didn't you?' I said. 'A servant who you thought you could trust, because he was your wife's brother. The only problem was that I disturbed him in the act, and he had to flee.'

Bearpark clenched his hands into hard fists. 'The boy was a fool. He couldn't carry out the simplest of instructions.'

'But what about Enrico? Was he a fool as well?'

Bearpark's eyes flashed. 'How could I trust him? Blabbing our business about the city. Provoking letters of denunciation.

Sooner or later the Venetians would have worked it out. And do you know what they do to traitors in this city, de Lacy?'

'So you murdered him. Your own grandson.'

Bearpark suddenly lifted his hands to his face. 'I didn't mean to kill Enrico. It was a mistake. All he had to do was give me the name of his lover. That's all I wanted.' He gritted his teeth again, and there was anguish written across his face. 'Yet he kept it from me. Why?'

'Because he loved Gianni,' I said. 'He knew what you'd do to him.'

Bearpark then let out a great mocking guffaw at my words. 'Love?' He pointed at the pathetic man who lay crumpled against the wall. 'Look at this great object of desire.' He turned to kick Gianni in the stomach. 'Who could love that? Who could sacrifice themselves in order to save *that*?' Bearpark stopped and composed himself. 'I just asked Enrico to find a man at the Arsenale. I didn't tell him to fall in love with the fool.' Then he turned to me sharply, all the torment released from his face, and in its place a cruel smile. 'So, it was a blessing that you turned up from nowhere.'

'What do you mean?' I said nervously.

'Oh yes. It was a blessing indeed. I never would have found Ricci, if it hadn't been for you. I know you wandered off the path of the investigation a few times, but we were able to steer you back in the right direction, weren't we, Bernard?'

'What?' said Bernard, scratching his upper lip absentmindedly. 'Oh yes. Margery's testament was a fine piece of invention, wasn't it? Though I say so myself.' Bernard wagged his finger at me. 'You were getting a little too interested in Adolpho Bredani at that point, Lord Somershill, and we needed you to return to finding this man at the Arsenale.'

'So you see, de Lacy,' said Bearpark, before I could answer. 'Your mother turned out to be right. You were a great investigator, after all. You brought us the man we'd been looking for.'

'That's not true,' I said. 'I never told you Ricci's name.'

'You didn't,' said Bearpark, 'but your little friend did.' He paused. 'What is that small boy's name now? That's right. Sandro.' He gave a short snort. 'You thought he was working for the doge's palace, didn't you? So perhaps your skills of detection might need a little more honing, because the boy worked for me, all along.' He laughed. 'I might say that you both did.'

I felt nauseated, for Bearpark spoke the truth. Had I not tenaciously returned to this enquiry again and again, then Ricci would not be crouching in the corner of this cesspit, waiting to be beaten to death. I had been used unwittingly, but this was no time for remorse. I had to get out of here. I had to live.

Bernard grasped Bearpark's arm with impatience. 'Come along. Enough of this great finale. We need to get rid of these men and leave.'

I quickly scrambled to my feet, knowing that my only chance of escape was to keep Bearpark talking. 'And where do these two fit in?' I said quickly, pointing to Bernard and Tamas. 'Old friends from your days as a mercenary? Did they seek you out, when they knew you were in Venice?'

Bernard snorted. 'Let's go, Bearpark.'

I raised my voice. 'I assume it was this pair of pilgrims who rushed to the convent of Santa Lucia to find Marco? What was their plan? To torture a name from him?'

Bearpark smiled a little. 'Another investigative success, de Lacy. You did well, finding that boy at the convent, but it was a shame he escaped before we reached him.'

Bernard grabbed at Bearpark's sleeve again. This time he was aggressive. 'I'm warning you, Bearpark. Kill them both now, or I'll get Tamas to do it.'

My time was running out. 'Why do you hate Venice so much, Bearpark?' I shouted. 'You've been made a citizen, so why betray her to her enemies?'

Bearpark flung up his hands. 'Citizen!' He then spat into the water. 'What use is there in being a citizen in this city? I needed to be named in the Golden Book.'

'But you're still a respected man, Bearpark. You've prospered in Venice. Look at this grand house you live in.' I was becoming so desperate that I resorted to flattery. 'This is a beautiful *palazzo*. The best in the street.'

He laughed heartily, not taken in by these clumsy attempts to save my life. 'But you've also noticed that I have no stock in my storerooms. Haven't you, de Lacy?' he said. 'That I'm no longer trading.'

'You're not alone in that, Bearpark,' I said. 'The war with Hungary has caused problems for many merchants. But—'

He spoke over me. 'Do you think I wanted to donate my cog ship to the city, so that they could fill it with the dead of the Plague and sink it at sea? No. I did not!' He wiped the spittle from his mouth. 'I did it to win the favour of Venice. Their friendship even. So many of their number died during the Pestilence. Whole families of the nobility were wiped out completely, so there should have been an opportunity for me to join their ranks. To be treated as if I were named in the Golden Book. But, in spite of my sacrifice, they still hated me. They still conspired against me. They took everything that they could and gave nothing back. So I owe nothing to Venice!'

From the corner of my eye I could see that Bernard and Tamas were huddled together whispering while Bearpark gave this great oratory, and I knew that my only chance was to make a last, desperate appeal.

'Just let us go, Bearpark,' I pleaded. 'Make your escape. Nobody will tell your story. I promise it.'

Bearpark laughed. 'I'm not a fool, de Lacy. The moment we leave, you will run off to the doge's palace and tell of my deceit.'

My heart began to thump like a drum. 'Then just let Filomena go,' I begged. 'If nobody else.'

He laughed scornfully. 'Why on earth should she be spared? She's the very worst type of Venetian. A silent schemer. A betrayer. Another Venetian who will do anything for money.'

'But she's your wife, Bearpark. She gave birth to your child!'

He gave a long groan. 'That child is not mine, de Lacy! Whether it is my clerk's, or some other of my wife's many devotees, I cannot say.' Then he cocked his head and laughed. 'I might even have suspected you of being its father, de Lacy, had you been in Venice a little earlier. I know my wife stirs your loins. I only had to imprison the girl and accuse her of murder, to know that you'd come running to her aid like some lovesick troubadour. That you'd return to the investigation and bring me my man.' He jabbed his finger into my face. 'You're too obvious, de Lacy. Too easy to read.'

I went to protest, but what was the point? No words would save my life now, for the man was as cruel as a lion. As hardskinned and indestructible as a cockroach. In a different time, I might have admired his resilience, his desire to carry on living, even though he was so very old. Now I hated him with a violent passion. He would take the youth of others in order to save the remaining sands of his life. My last memory is swinging the pole at his head. After that, I remember nothing.

Chapter Thirty-Seven

There was a time when I desired death's dark veil. The silent oblivion of nonexistence. In those times, I would have remained in the shadows and not reached for the light, but Venice had changed me. Somewhere in the dark recesses of my soul, this city had rekindled my desire to live. The flint sparked, and I woke from my stupor to find myself alone. The filthy water was no longer lapping about my ankles – instead it covered my knees and was quickly rising with the tide, and it would not be long until this whole chamber became my watery grave.

I managed to stand. Thankfully my captors had left me untied, assuming that I had been beaten hard enough about the head to ensure my lasting concussion, but they had not anticipated my will to live; my will to return to Hugh. Now upright, I soon sensed that there was something floating near me. My first reaction was to recoil, but as my eyes adjusted to the dim light, I realised that it was a body, lying face down in the water – the corpse of Gianni Ricci. I reached out and pulled the sodden thing towards me, but as I lifted his head, I could see that Bearpark had finished the job. The man was heavy with death. His cheeks were swollen and bloody. No breath came from his chest, and he was difficult to hold.

I let him slide back into the water, then waded towards the door, heaved it ajar, and managed to squeeze myself into the first chamber, to find Filomena and Giovanni still tied to the wall. 'Where have you been, Oswald?' Giovanni said to me. 'You should have released us first.' I went to respond, but he didn't wait for an answer and soon he was shouting at me. 'Untie our hands quickly. Or we will be drowned.'

I leant down into the water and picked desperately at the knot that tied his hands to the ring on the wall. Once I had done the same for Filomena, she seemed revived, leaning her head against my chest and embracing me. As she broke away, I caught the expression upon Giovanni's face. It was an ugly grimace, and for a moment the intensity of his stare frightened me. Then he quickly shook his head, and the expression dissolved. 'We need to get out,' he said coldly, 'before we drown.'

We tried the door that led from the chamber back into the hall, but it seemed that Bearpark had had the foresight to lock this exit. I tried to kick it, and then pull at it, but we were trapped. The only other possible way out appeared to be a small grilled outlet high up on the wall. When I held Filomena up to put her hands through the bars of this grille, she said that she could feel cold, fresh air – so I knew that this flue must lead into the outside world. The hole was small however, and even if we could remove the grille, it was doubtful that any of us would be able to squeeze into this void. But what choice did we have? The water was now at thigh level. And then I had another idea.

'You still have your keys, don't you, Giovanni?' I said.

The man frowned. 'Yes. But I don't have the key for this door. I told you that before.'

I grabbed the ring from his belt. There must have been more than twenty keys hanging from the circle of black iron. Some were long and heavy, whilst others were delicate and short, decorated with filigreed bows and bands about the shaft. 'Just try each key in this lock. There can't be that many variations in lock design, can there?'

'Each lock is unique,' he told me. 'It will never work.'

I pushed Giovanni towards the door. 'Try it anyway!' I told him. 'What have we got to lose?'

Filomena and I then turned our attention back to the grille. She removed her tunic and crawled again onto my shoulders. Putting her hands onto the bars, she pulled with all the strength a person can call upon when facing death. The grille groaned and creaked until it came loose. In our excitement at this small success, we had forgotten about Giovanni, until we turned to see that he had managed to unlock the door.

'You did it! Giovanni!' I shouted. 'I told you that one of the keys might fit the lock.'

Filomena gave a squeal of delight, and I lifted her joyfully to the floor – but, as we waded across the room, Giovanni quickly slipped through the open door and then pulled it shut behind him. In a flash he had turned the key again, and we remained on the wrong side of a locked door.

I looked at Filomena, and she looked back at me in shock. What had happened? At first I thought Giovanni might be playing a trick, but this was no time for foolery, and anyway, Giovanni had no sense of humour. So we banged on the door, screaming for him to let us out. When we had finished screaming, we reverted to begging, and then Filomena began to wail. A wretched, heart-breaking sound that threatened to become a frenzied panic. I grasped her tightly to me, and, when her emotion had subsided a little, I suggested that we return to the grille, even though I knew this was an unlikely means of escape.

It was then that I sensed Giovanni's fearful, stifled breathing from the other side of the door. He was still in the passageway, so I knew that we still had a chance. I banged heavily on the wood and spoke in my clearest English, hoping that I could persuade him to let us out. 'Giovanni. Please let us out.' When this elicited no response, I made my tone softer. 'Giovanni. Please listen to me. We are going to die in here. Do you want our murders on your conscience? Because it would be a mortal sin to let us die in this room. There is no indulgence, relic, or rosary that would cleanse your soul after such a crime.'

A voice came from the other side of the door. It was angry and full of indignation. 'I don't care if you die,' he said. 'You are betrayalists! Both of you.'

'You do care,' I said, 'otherwise, why are you still here? You want to open the door, don't you?'

He said something in Venetian. I think it was a curse.

'Filomena has a daughter,' I said, hoping to appeal to his heart. 'Imagine the life of that poor child, growing up without her mother. And I have a son, Giovanni. I never told you about him before, but he waits for me back in England.' I paused. 'Yes, I have been a betrayalist, you're right. I have stayed away from my son for too long, so please, please don't let me die in here.'

'I don't care about your son,' he declared.

'Of course you do. You're a Christian.'

'No. And I don't care about Filomena and her bastard child either. I loved her once, but she chose to marry my master instead. Why do you think that I nearly killed myself, Oswald? I was not grieving because my family died in the Plague, as you thought. I grieved for Filomena.' His voice was becoming more shrill. 'Then I found my senses. For what is she? No better than those whores who wave their skirts to the sailors on the Mercaria. She threw away my love for the love of money. And now she has betrayed me again. With you. A rich Englishman. What a surprise! Do you think she loves you, because she doesn't. She only cares for your title and your money!'

His voice was beginning to fade, and I feared he had decided to abandon us. 'Please Giovanni! Just release Filomena. There is a chance for you both.'

He laughed. 'Don't you understand? I don't want her!'

'And I don't want you!' said Filomena. I tried to pull her away, fearing that her words would only make Giovanni more angry, but she shouldered past me, and put her lips to the door. 'Listen to me, Giovanni. You always pretend to be so pious. So devout. But you've locked me into a flooding room, because you want to punish me. That makes you a murderer, so how do you think I could ever love you?'

I pulled her away, but the damage was done.

'You are Satan's whore!' he shouted. 'Satan's whore! You want death, then you shall have it!'

I could hear him thrashing through the rising water as he made his way along the passageway. 'Come back, Giovanni,' I shouted. 'Don't do this! Please.' But my only answer was silence. A long, penetrating and terrifying silence, only punctuated by the sound of the water that was now lapping with determination at my waist. The air in the room was now thick with the corrupting fumes of the cesspit and I feared that soon we would both be as dead as Gianni Ricci. So I tried, once again, to barge at the door with my shoulder. I pushed and beat my hands at the wooden frame, but it would not give. The evil vapours were constricting my throat, and I coughed continually until I was almost unable to breathe, but if I gave up now, then I would die, and I would never see Hugh again.

It was then that Filomena tapped me on the shoulder, pointing to two hooks that had been driven into the ceiling near the door. Who knows what uses they had been put to in the past, but they had given her an idea that she whispered into my ear. I gripped a hook in each hand, and was then able to pull myself above the water level, so that I could now swing my feet at the door. Without the resistance of the water to impede my movement, the force of my kick was much harder against the wood.

At first I only made a small dent, and it was very difficult to hold my weight and also swing my feet at a door, but the threat of death is the greatest of motivators, and so I kicked again and again, until I had pushed the panelling from the frame, making an opening that was just large enough to allow a draught of fresh air to filter into the room.

Now that the air was sweeter, I tried again, and with Filomena's encouragement I was able to kick a larger hole in the door. At last there was a chance of freedom. Filomena climbed through the hole first, and then it was my turn to squeeze my way through. It was a good thing that I had lost my appetite in the last few months, for I might not have escaped if I had been any fatter.

Now free of the flooding cesspit, we struggled back towards the courtyard, where we fell onto the steps of the exterior staircase, as the rain beat down on our faces. We had escaped death, and now we felt the elation of being alive. Filomena took my head in her hands, and she kissed me. She kissed me as if she loved me.

I would tell you that this was the end of my story, but there is a little more to relate. For, just as we had gathered the strength to leave Ca' Bearpark, we heard voices. Someone was shouting my name, and before we had a chance to run up the stairs and hide, they had found us. It was a company of guards from the doge's palace, and at its head, holding a lantern aloft, was my mother.

'Oswald! Thanks be to God!' She ran over and clasped me to her chest. 'You're still alive. The boy told me you were here.'

'Which boy?'

'Sandro, of course.'

'He betrayed me, Mother.'

'Yes, yes I know all about that,' she said, as if this were a minor misdemeanour, 'but he heartily regrets it.' Mother moved aside, and in the gloom, I could see Sandro's dirty, trembling face. 'He came to see me, Oswald, and he told me the whole story.' She clasped me again. 'And now, you mustn't be angry, but there's somebody else who wants to speak to you.'

'Who?'

'I couldn't come here alone to save you, could I? So I went to the doge's palace and raised my old friend.'

I froze in alarm, as a pair of red boots and a fur-lined cape rounded the corner.

'You brought Ballio here, Mother?' I said.

'Oh, don't worry, Oswald,' she said, squeezing my arm tightly. 'Really. You have no reason to be afraid of the man. Not in the least.' She leant forward and whispered in my ear. 'I have explained everything.'

Epilogue

It was late April 1358, and the lagoon was a gentle, chalky blue as I stood beside Mother at the Molo, waiting to bid the pilgrims farewell. Today the Jaffa galleys were setting sail in their first flotilla towards the Holy Land since the war with Hungary had ended, and it seemed as if the whole of Venice had turned out to watch them leave. The doge himself had blessed their journey from the loggia of his palace, and the city could not have been a merrier place. Venice was open again. The pilgrims had returned to the city, they had spent a great deal of money here, and now they were departing on Venetian ships. It was a perfect piece of business.

When the blessing and the ceremonies were complete, the galleys set off from the quay to cheering crowds and the tumultuous cacophony of a band. There was a time when this music had tunnelled through my head and driven me half mad – but now I was pleased to hear these tunes, even the humming whines of the bladder pipes. In the last few weeks I had become reacquainted with joy. She had fluttered into my heart and reawakened my soul, and I had Venice to thank for this miracle.

Tomorrow we would set off on our own journey. A return to England. A return to my son. And I would leave this city as a citizen of Venice – a hero, no less. The Englishman who had unmasked a network of spies, saved a beautiful Venetian woman from certain death in a flooding cell, and then led the doge's guard in an intrepid chase across the lagoon in order to apprehend three traitors who were escaping in a cargo ship.

I was now famous, and I had even come to the attention of the doge himself, who had decided that I should be rewarded handsomely for my exploits. I did not receive any money from Venice herself, of course. Instead the doge demanded that Vittore cancel my debts, repay my forty ducats, and then double it. The porcine crook had refused this order at first, but when the Signori di Notte had threatened to investigate his gambling activities, the man had handed over the money quickly enough – though not without a show of bitter and vengeful umbrage. Vittore would always be my enemy, but he was a Venetian, and I was bound for home. I saw no reason for our paths to cross in the future.

Mother lifted her ancient dog into her arms, and we made our way into the crowds on the Riva degli Schiavoni, so that we might wave to the pilgrims as they sailed into the distance towards the Lido, and then out into the Adriatic sea. When Mother was finally tired of this sight, she passed her dog to Sandro. The boy was now my valet and most faithful servant, and I must say he looked rather smart, with his new cotehardie, woollen cloak and washed hair. You might ask how I could have forgiven Sandro – but I say this: he had been a starving, homeless orphan when I had first met him; he had deceived me for money, but he had redeemed himself by seeking out my mother and telling her the truth. In turn, she had understood enough of the boy's Venetian to rouse her 'great friend' Signor Ballio from the doge's palace. I would tell you that I had felt some obligation to give Sandro a second chance because of this, but I did so because it pleased me and because I cared about the boy.

Bernard and Tamas were never seen again after the guards boarded their cargo boat and found the pair hiding beneath the waxed tarpaulin. I heard that they named many other spies and clandestine associates under torture, admitting that they would sell information about the Venetian Arsenale to the highest bidder. I believe, once all their secrets had been squeezed, pulled and mangled from their mouths, they were then beheaded and thrown into the lagoon. Perhaps their headless, mutilated bodies will wash up one day in the Assassin's Canal, stranded by the high tide and left to rot in the mud of that particular dead end.

Bearpark suffered a different fate from his associates, however. He had been a citizen of Venice, and therefore he needed to be publicly tried and executed. Even though he was an old man, the Venetians had hung him *turpissime*, upside-down, between the two Columns of Justice in the Piazzetta. I watched him die myself. You might wonder that I could stand to witness such an execution, but this old man was responsible for the death of three young men, one of whom was his own grandson. He had disowned his infant daughter, and he had abandoned his wife to drown. I had no pity for him, and I could not forgive his wickedness. So yes, I stood in the front row, and I watched his execution, and when our eyes met, I did not look away.

I do not know the fate of Giovanni. After locking the door to the cesspit, he had disappeared from Venice. At first I hated him, but now I like to imagine that he has become a monk somewhere in a faraway abbey – a Benedictine brotherhood that is wealthy enough to afford his taste in clothes. I imagine him as a sacristan, in charge of the relics and treasures of the monastery, locking these riches away each night with a ring of heavy, clinking keys, before he retires to his room and spends his nights with a collection of rosaries and diptychs.

As the pilgrim galleys disappeared on the horizon, the music died away and the crowds began to disperse. It was then that I saw her, standing on the Riva degli Schiavoni with a child in her arms. She called out to me, though at first I could not hear her words – and suddenly I panicked, thinking that we might miss each other. But then she waved to me, before she blew me a kiss. It was the sweetest of kisses.

Filomena had survived the flooding chamber. She had survived the disgrace and execution of her husband, and now she would return to England with me. As my wife.

Acknowledgements

First and foremost, I would like to thank my brilliant editor, Nick Sayers. *City of Masks* took rather longer to write than I had anticipated, and for many months it was little more than a formless mass of words. It was only with Nick's calm and insightful editorial guidance that it finally became a novel. I would also like to heartily thank my agent Gordon Wise, whose encouragement and constant support has been invaluable. Gordon was voted Literary Agent of the Year in 2015, and it was very much deserved.

Writing can be a lonely business, so I want to thank these fellow writers for all of their invaluable friendship. Martine Bailey, Nick Brown, Antonia Hodgson, Rebecca Mascull, Laura Macdougall, Jake Woodhouse, all the fabulous writers from The Prime Writers and the Historical Writers Association, and my friends at Curtis Brown Creative. I also wish to thank my assistant editor Cicely Aspinall for all of her help and guidance, my copy-editor Charlotte Webb for a detailed and thorough copy-edit, and Kerry Hood and her wonderful team in the publicity department at Hodder & Stoughton. My thanks go as well to my American publishers, Pegasus, and especially Claiborne Hancock and Jessica Case for all of their enthusiasm and passion. It is fantastic to be supported by such a team.

Lastly I want to express my gratitude to my family for their endless encouragement and patience – my husband, Paul, and my twenty-something children Natalie and Adam. They are my first trusted readers, and I truly appreciate their feedback – both positive and negative! I would like to end by saying something about my father, who died suddenly just as I was finishing *City of Masks*. Unfortunately he never got to see that this book was dedicated to him, and I thoroughly regret now that I didn't think to tell him. Well Dad, I love you and this book is for you.

Author's Note

My first visit to Venice was in 1982, and I will admit that it was not necessarily love at first sight. My father had driven across Europe from our home in South London, and we were all in a fairly bad mood by the time we arrived in northern Italy after three days in a car. I vaguely remember that we parked somewhere near the long bridge that now links Venice to the mainland, and then made our way along narrow, crowded streets to the Piazza San Marco (St Mark's Square) until we sat down on the steps of the Basilica only for a pigeon to do something unpleasant on my head. I was a teenager so perhaps I can be forgiven for not seeing past these small annoyances, but I will admit to not thinking too much of Venice. It was only many years later that I discovered the true wonder of this city – I could even say that I fell in love with her. Yes, I was a lot older and wiser, but I also believe that Venice really impressed me this time because of our arrival by ship. It was then that she truly made sense to me – as a city of the sea. I should start by saying a little about the geography and history of this unique place. For those of you who are not familiar with Venice, she is an island-city located in the midst of a large lagoon on the north-east coast of Italy. The lagoon itself is a large and shallow expanse of water and marshy islets covering approximately 500 square kilometres, and is protected from the Adriatic Sea by the barrier islands of the Lido and Pellestrina. Within the lagoon there are something like fifty islands, most of which are uninhabited. Venice is the most populous of the inhabited island, but other islands, such as Murano, Burano and Sant' Erasmo also have communities that continue to make a living from the lagoon – not only from tourism, but also from other industries such as fishing, glass-making, boat-building and market gardening.

Venice is not a city of antiquity, as the lagoon was hardly inhabited at all until the fall of Rome in the fifth century. It was then that this backwater became a place of refuge for people escaping sporadic raids from the more northern tribes of the Huns, Goths and Visigoths tribes. Initially these refugees would return to their homes on the mainland as soon as danger had passed – after all, the Venetian lagoon was a malarial swamp – but over time they discovered that the lagoon had more to offer than just being a place of sanctuary.

The Venetians started by trading salt that was produced in the shallow waters, finding that sea trading was easier from their waterside homes; but soon they established trade routes that reached far into the East, purchasing spices, silks, furs, fabric dyes, precious stones, carpets and even slaves and then selling these goods to markets in the West. Thus the wealth of Venice was not built upon the old model of owning territory, instead it was built upon their unrivalled skills in sea navigation and trade.

Population growth followed this success, but the inhabitable land mass of the lagoon was soon too small to cope with the influx of peoples. The Venetians solved this problem by building their own land – sinking long timber piles into the bed of the lagoon, in order to create platform-like structures upon which they could then build their houses. The channels between these structures were dredged to form ditches that were deep enough to allow the fishermen and traders to berth their boats beside their homes, even at low tide. Over time these individual habitations grew closer and closer until they formed *sestieres* (or parishes). Eventually these *sestieres* joined together to form Venice, whilst the ditches between them became the famous canals of the city.

The mentality that drove the early Venetians to build a city in a marsh is the key to understanding the spirit of the place. In his book *Francesco's Venice*, Francesco da Mosto, a Venetian himself, tells us that Venice 'was created from nothing by free people, on islands in an empty wilderness. This is the essence of the city's unwillingness to be subject to anything or anybody.' Whilst the surrounding city states of Verona, Modena,

Padua and Milan were subject to the dictatorship of princes and lords, Venice held fast to her Republic, headed by an elected leader – the Doge – until she was defeated by Napoleon in 1797.

However, we should not run away with the idea that Venice was a paragon of democracy. Instead it is better to describe her as an oligarchy, controlled by a core of rich and powerful families, who were careful, nay paranoid, that one family might gain dominion over the others. These families had representatives on the Great Council of Venice, a body that met in the enormous and impressive assembly hall in the Doge's Palace – a chamber that you can still visit today. This Council elected the smaller Council of Forty, who in turn elected the Council of Ten on a yearly basis.

This smallest Council had two important purposes. The first was the gathering of intelligence via a prodigious network of spies and informers, and the second was to make quick decisions in conjunction with the Doge, especially if the Republic came under threat. These threats were two-fold – either from enemies within Venice herself, or from the many neighbouring states who were jealous of her wealth and position in the world. Venice did not want to be ruled by a foreign dynasty, nor would she tolerate any attempts by an ambitious Venetian to create his own dictatorship. In 1355, just three years before *City of Masks* is set, the city had suffered a coup, orchestrated by Doge Marin Falier. The plot failed and Falier was executed with the doors of the Doge's Palace open to the public, so that his death could be witnessed by all of Venice. Even now Falier's portrait can be seen in the assembly hall of the Great Council, covered with a black shroud and accompanied by the inscription, 'this is the space reserved for Marin Falier, beheaded for his crimes'.

There was no room for newcomers into the ranks of the Great Council, no matter how rich or successful you might become. In 1296 a law known as the *Serrata* was passed. Translated literally as 'the locking,' this law meant that only men from certain aristocratic families were eligible for membership to the Great Council. The names of these families were listed in a book that was known as the *Libro d'Oro*, or the 'Golden Book'. The historian John Julius Norwich tells us, in his book *A History of Venice*, that the *Serrata* 'created, at a stroke, a closed caste in the society of the Republic'. This barrier to political advancement for those not named in the Golden Book caused much resentment and dissention, but such was the power and control of Venice's Council of Ten, that the *Serrata* was never over-turned.

In *City of Masks* we meet a further arm of government – a group who were perhaps even more secretive and sinister than the Council of Ten. This group, the *Signori di Notte*, ('Lords of the Night') were noblemen who set themselves up as the supposed guardians of Venice's morality. When I first started researching for this novel I was under the mistaken impression that Venice had always been a permissive, decadent city, based largely on my knowledge of Venice in the 17th and 18th centuries. But things were different in the 14th century, when gambling, prostitution and especially homosexuality were often brutally suppressed. In his book *Homosexuality and Civilization*, the writer Louis Crompton tells us this: 'The medieval columns of Justice, dramatically visible from the lagoon, stand where they stood six hundred years ago, one surmounted by the winged lion of Saint Mark, and the other by Saint Theodore and his crocodile. In all likelihood more homosexuals died on this spot than anywhere else in Europe before Hitler.' So you can see that this is a different, darker, crueler, more oppressive city than we sometimes meet.

How then might we characterise the Venice of *City of Masks*? Whilst we tend to think of Venice as a romantic city, rich in art and history, she was actually considered to be a modern industrial power in this age. In the years before the Black Death of 1348, she was arguably at her commercial peak, and was one of the pre-eminent powers in Europe, controlling trade from Constantinople and selling her goods as far afield as Flanders and Southampton. In the next century, Venice was to lose this pre-eminence, following the fall of Constantinople to the Ottomans in 1453, and the discovery of the sea route to India by Vasco da Gama in 1497 – thus bypassing Venice in the East/West trade routes. These two events prompted Venice's slow decline into the city we often find depicted in art and literature – a city of decadence and pleasure-seeking. I'm thinking of Casanova, the flamboyant carnivals, courtesans, gambling and open prostitution, whereas the Venice I'm writing about was altogether a more serious place, concerned first and foremost with making money.

Not that she was completely solemn and lacking in diversion of course! In *City of Masks*, Oswald visits an island known as the convent of Santa Lucia – a convent that also doubles as a brothel. This might seem father rather far-fetched, but is based upon an actual Venetian convent of the early 1400s – the island convent of Sant' Angelo di Contorta. The Abbess of this convent, a woman named Clara Sanuto, notoriously ruled over a nunnery where the sisters had little regard for their vows, and were regularly visited by the men of Venice, some of whom were paying for sex. In those times, convents were often the repositories for young women of wealthier families, whose parents had, for some reason or other, been unable to arrange a suitable marriage for their daughters. The sisters of Sant' Angelo di Contorta did not necessarily have a religious vocation, nor did they have a taste for celibacy. In fact many of them ended up giving birth to children whom they then disguised as abandoned foundlings. The activities of Sant' Angelo did not go unnoticed by the authorities however, and, after sporadic raids, the convent was eventually closed on papal orders in 1474. Michael Prestwich, in his book *Medieval People*, tells us that there 'was no indication that the nuns of Sant' Angelo were forced to do what they did in order to make money; they were not running a commercial brothel. Rather, they appear to have provided a service of which the young men of Venice were only too eager to take advantage.'

I should also point out here that the island of the Lazzaretto is also partly my own invention, though it is based upon a real place – not the island of Lazaretto Vecchia or Lazzaretto Nuove, which were both used as quarantines during times of plague, but rather the island of San Lazzaro degli Armeni. Chosen as a suitable location for lepers because of its distance from Venice, it was established as a leper colony in 1182. This island is now a monastery run by Benedictine monks of the Armenian Catholic church, and can still be visited.

Venice was one of the first cities in Europe to suffer the devastation of the Black Death of 1348-50 – mainly due to her position as a hub for trade from the East, where the disease originated. The bacteria that causes the Bubonic Plague, *Yersinia Pestis*, originated in the Mongolian Steppe and travelled west in the digestive tracts of rat flees, forming an unwelcome and deadly stowaway amongst the many other goods being transported into Venice. Venice was badly affected by this epidemic, and by the time the Plague had abated, it is estimated that she had lost three-fifths of her population, with something like fifty noble families wiped out completely. But it was not just the devastation of so many deaths that caused such anguish in those years, it was also the very practical problem of how to deal with the dead – especially in a city where land was at a premium. At first barges were used to transport the corpses for burial on outlying islands of the lagoon, but very soon these mass graves were themselves overflowing.

In *City of Masks* I describe how John Bearpark donates his cog ship to the authorities of Venice, allowing the ship to be filled with the dead and then sunk out at sea. This is a story of my own imagination, as there are no recorded incidents of this happening – but the idea was inspired by a story that I came across when researching for the book. In the 1990s two ancient ships were discovered, buried in the lagoon beside the island of San Marco in Boccalama. This island is now submerged – such is the transitory nature of land in the lagoon – but San Marco in Boccalama was once a monastery, and in the years of the Black Death it was quickly designated as a site for burials. Faced with two mounting problems: the increasing number of dead, and the encroaching sea, it seems that the monks of San Marco then deliberately sank two galleys in the harbour in a vain attempt to bolster the sea defences of the island and save what was left of their burial site.

An aspect of Venetian life that features largely in the book is the industry surrounding pilgrimages. To undertake a pilgrimage was a common aspiration in the 14th century, and the average person hoped to visit a holy shrine at least once in their lives – though for most English people it was somewhere like Canterbury, Walsingham or Winchester. However, if you were wealthy or determined enough, then you might also hope to visit Jerusalem or one of the other shrines in Europe such as Santiago di Compostela or Aachen Cathedral – though such pilgrimages were rare, and if you managed to return home then you were viewed with awe, as these journeys were long and dangerous.

Many of the pilgrims making their way to Jerusalem chose to travel via Venice, mainly because the Venetians ran a very efficient and relatively safe operation to the Holy Land. The pilgrim galleys would sail from Venice in a flotilla known as a *Mude* to the port of Jaffa on the Mediterranean coast (near modern-day Tel Aviv) from whence they would travel overland to Jerusalem. These sailings were often delayed by their Venetian captains in order to encourage the pilgrims to spend more money and time in Venice itself – visiting the relics and shrines of the city. In this way, Venice herself became something of a destination on the pilgrim circuit.

I sometimes like to think of the Venetians as 14th century tour operators, selling their journeys to Jerusalem and hoping to sell return excursions via the Sinai or even Cairo. The Venetians certainly took this business seriously, even setting up a tourist office in Venice known as the *Tholomarii*, which could recommend accommodation and help a pilgrim to negotiate a berth with one of the galley captains. There was even an office set up to deal with complaints, known as the Office of the *Cattaveri*.

In *City of Masks*, Oswald finds himself in debt to Vittore, to the tune of forty ducats – so I wanted to give the reader an idea of the value of this sum in today's money. Information regarding historic exchange rates can be conflicting, so in the end I chose to use an amount that corresponded to the average cost of a return trip on a Venetian galley to Jaffa in the 14th century – which was forty ducats. Given that this was a long journey (taking five weeks in one direction) and given the risk to the boat and its passengers from pirates, inclement weather and potential hostility at any stopover ports, you can imagine that this was not a cheap undertaking. So, for the purposes of this book, I've estimated that the forty ducats that Oswald owes would be in the order of ten thousand British pounds in today's money.

Another point I should quickly raise regards the festival of *Giovedi Grasso*, which literally means 'Fat Thursday'. In Venice, this was a festival celebrated as part of the carnival season on the last Thursday before Lent, but you may also see this term used elsewhere for 'Maundy Thursday' – which, of course, is later in the church's calendar, being the last Thursday before Easter Sunday. Both are correct.

I hope this book has inspired you to visit Venice, especially if you have never been. Yes, it can be a crowded, noisy, confusing (and sometimes expensive!)

city, but you really only have to wander a few streets away from Piazza San Marco to find something of the city that Oswald visited six hundred and fifty years ago. Ignore the Palladian and classically-inspired buildings such as the churches of San Giorgio Maggiore and Il Redentore or the palaces of Ca'Rezzonico or Palazzo Grimani di San Luca. The Renaissance had not yet happened at the time I'm writing. Instead, look at the Basilica San Marco, the Doge's Palace, and the Piazza san Marco, then take some of the side alleys (you will almost certainly become lost!) and look upwards at the pointed, Moorish-style arches of the windows of the great gothic palaces, with their stone fretwork, trefoils, balconies and pilasters. Then look at well-heads at the centre of each small square (campo) and the thin, twisting streets that still follow their earliest routes, dating from the times when each *sestiere* was a separate island. And, if you have the time, take the vaporetto (water-bus) to the outlying islands of Torcello and Burano, and enjoy the city from the lagoon. She truly is a medieval masterpiece. I know of nowhere like her in the world.

I've spent the last two years writing and researching this book, but I could spend the rest of my life getting to know this city. For this reason, I cannot claim to be any sort of expert on Venice, and I must reiterate that this novel is a work of fiction. But, if you are inspired to learn more of Venice's history, then I can thoroughly recommend the following books.

Venice, Pure City, Peter Ackroyd
Pilgrims to Jerusalem in the Middle Ages, Nicole Chareyron
Homosexuality and Civilization, Louis Crompton
Elements of Venice, Giulia Foscari
Margery Kempe and Her World, Anthony Goodman
The Architectural History of Venice, Deborah Howard
The Art and Archaeology of Venetian Ships and Boats, Lillian Ray Martin
Francesco's Venice, Francesco da Mosto
Venice, The Hinge of Europe, 1087-1797, William H. McNeill
Venice, Jan Morris
A History of Venice, John Julius Norwich
Medieval People, Michael Prestwich